# LAND OF MOUNTAINS

**Other books by Elizabeth Maul Schwartz**

*The Texicans*  Maddog Press 2000 Historical Fiction: Texas and Mexico 1803–1836

*Troubled Sea*  Writer's Club Press 2001 Adventure in the Sea of Cortez

*Just Add Water*  Writer's Club Press 2002 Romantic comedy, boating adventure

# LAND OF MOUNTAINS

Elizabeth Maul Schwartz

*For Marcia Morse —*
*Thank you for being*
*my friend*

*love,*
*jim*

iUniverse, Inc.
New York  Lincoln  Shanghai

# Land Of Mountains

iUniverse, Inc.

For information address:
iUniverse, Inc.
2021 Pine Lake Road, Suite 100
Lincoln, NE 68512
www.iuniverse.com

ISBN: 0-595-29065-5

Printed in the United States of America

This book is dedicated to the loving memory of Lloyd Dooley.

# Acknowledgements

I guess there must be some writers out there who can get by without help from others, but I'm not one of them. For their contributions of both time and encouragement, I am grateful to all those who have aided and abetted this authoring habit of mine. If I were to name everyone who gives me moral support, this section would be a thousand pages long, so I'll just say thanks, and stick to listing the hands-on workers. One special person, however, deserves not only mention, but a medal: Robert, my husband and best friend, who is stuck on a forty-two foot boat with me when I am doing my most intensive scribbling.

And here's those helpful little worker-bees:

Monica Brooks: proofreader
Lurah Magee, SV *Orea*: proofreader
Rebecca Dahlke, SV *Paloma Blanca*: proofreader
Geary Ritchie, beach dweller extraordinaire: proofreader
Katherine Baccarro, nitpicker extaordinaire
Marilyn Olivera, SV *Tortuga*: proofreader
Jim and Gale Wilkins, SV *Priority*, proofreaders
Cynthia Smith, MV *Stormhaven*: proofreader
Members of the Mulege Literary Guild.
Members of the High Desert Working Writers Group

So with all that help, wouldn't you think **Land of Mountains** would be flawless? One could only hope, but any goof-ups that slipped through are purely mine.

# Preface

A work of "fictography"—autobiographical fiction—is often more fiction than autobiography. This is certainly the case with **Land of Mountains**, in which I have blended memories of my childhood in Haiti and some *very* creative license.

My parents, Johnnie Ruth Coffey and Fred Roy (Bud) Maul, descendants of pioneers who helped tame Texas, inherited what it took to brave new horizons. And believe me, Haiti was a very new horizon.

Life in the '50's on the island of Hispañola was no picnic. Living in a remote construction camp in a country thought by most to be uncivilized, we had about as normal a life as could be expected when plagued by hurricanes, floods, rabid dogs, mysterious tropical diseases and, of course, voodoo. Faced with life-threatening situations far more devastating than recounted in this tale, my parents somehow managed to keep some semblance of order in our lives while instilling in me and my sister, Arleigh, our own adventurous spirits. Thanks, guys.

Alas, even though my years in Haiti were, in many ways, the best days of my life, this yarn—with notable exceptions that shall remain unnamed—is one of almost pure fiction. My apologies to all zombies out there who feel that this is their story; any similarity to Black Frank is purely coincidental.

Sometimes when we reminisce, we like to think how things *should* have been. And if, when putting pen to paper, we gravitate towards fantasy, so what? Childhood is but once, and it ought to be magical.

# CHAPTER 1

▼

**Weclom to Port-au-Prince.**

Some welcome. They couldn't even spell it.

Gooey tarmac oozed around my brandy-new patent-leather shoes and damp heat wilted the Shirley Temple curls my mother had forced into my hair. I could practically feel the ringlets springing back to their natural orange frizz. I began to glow. Southern girls don't sweat, they glow. Rivers of glow ran through my hair, down my neck.

I looked back at the DC-3, hoping to see my mother and little sister. No luck. I should have waited inside with them where it was cooler, but as usual I was in a big old hurry. Grownups jostled by me, headed for the terminal building. I was of a mind to follow them, but I'd promised Mama I'd wait until she could get Sister awake enough to leave the plane.

I fanned myself with my hand and cocked my head. From somewhere beyond the air terminal the beat of a drum echoed, but not with the tinkling, cheerful sound of a Havana steel band. This was more of a tom-tom sound, with a steady, hollow THUMP-THUMP-THUMPing that reminded me of movies set in Africa.

My nose twitched. Something stunk up the thick air. Smelled to high heaven. Worse than my grandfather's one-holer in July. My nose followed the stink back toward the **WECLOM** sign, and I spotted something much more rotten than their spelling: stuck on posts next to the greeting was something really, really ugly. Several somethings.

Daddy says I have eyes like an eagle, but even so it took a second or two for what I was seeing to sink in. Or maybe I just didn't want it to. Matter of fact, if I hadn't spent so much time at all-day-for-a-dime matinees back in Texas, I probably wouldn't have even recognized a human head on a stake, but believe you me, that's what they were. Four of 'em. And even though I was upwind, my smeller told me they'd been there awhile.

I held my breath, waiting for Mama and Sister to finally get to the bottom of the clanky old ramp, but at about the same time they arrived, my brain and mouth went all cottony. I tugged at my mother's hand, thinking to tell her about those fly-covered, stinking heads, but could only manage, "Mama, I'm fixin' to throw up."

"Not now Lizbuthann. I see your father," Mother snapped. She was a mite miffed with me because I'd gulped down two frozen daiquiris on the plane—mine and my little sister's—and had asked for another before she looked across the aisle and realized what I'd done.

I wanted to protest that it wasn't *my* fault the stewardess was dumb enough to give a ten-year-old like me a loaded snow cone, but Mama made a beeline for the terminal building, yanking me along behind her. As I threw a last look at the scary heads, I decided it was a good thing Mama only had eyes for my daddy, because if she'd seen those heads, we'd surely have been marched right back onto that plane and the last thing I wanted right now was a bumpy return trip to Havana.

Daddy had a big smile on his face in spite of the fact that he was surrounded by gun-toting Negroes wearing wrinkled shorts. My father never wore shorts, nor did any other grown man I knew, but I'd seen those snooty-accented explorers wearing them in Tarzan movies and since they, like whoever was out there on the posts, occasionally lost their heads to savages, maybe my father was smart to stick with long pants, just in case there was a connection.

I longed to be in shorts myself; Mama had us gussied up, right down to white gloves, like we were going to church instead of taking a tummy-jolting ride just above the wave tops. It's a wonder they even *managed* to pass out daiquiris.

While Mama and Daddy hugged, Sister and I gawked at a huge black woman swathed in layers of multi-hued scarves who, like some exotic butterfly, floated towards us. She fluttered to the floor in front of us, lowered the basket she had balanced on her head and uncovered a collection of the most beautiful dolls I'd ever seen. Their heads, wrapped in brilliantly colored scarves, were topped with tiny baskets brimming with tropical fruit and flowers. Like the woman who sold them, the dolls were dressed in frilly blouses and brilliantly colored skirts. Sister and I were bewitched. We'd never seen a black-faced doll, much less any doll so spectacular.

I was reaching for one when Mother called out. "Girls, come over here and give your Daddy a hug," she said in a real happy voice, even though she had tears in her eyes. Tearing myself from the dolls, I pushed Sister in front of me. I hadn't seen Daddy in six months and before he left Texas he and I hadn't been on the best of terms. Even though mother read us his letters each week, my three-year-old sister barely remembered him. Sister whirled and buried her face in my waist, so it was left to me to break the ice.

"Hi, Daddy. Are there head hunters here?"

Mama shot me an exasperated look. "Don't pay any attention to her, Bud. Your daughter's drunk."

Daddy, who evidently hadn't seen those heads out on the fence, looked bewildered by my question, but he did that a lot with us kids. Especially me.

This little reunion wasn't going as planned and I could tell Mama was beginning to get upset because her eyebrows twitched. All she'd talked about since my father had left San Antonio was how, as soon as school was out, we'd be going to join him, and she was real happy about that. And even though I had serious doubts about this so-called great new life Mama was proposing, what with me having to give up my school and friends, I'd thrown up my hand during Show And Tell so I could share it with my classmates: "My Daddy's a damn builder and he's going to Hell and he's taking us with him," I'd begun, only to have my teacher, Mrs. Baldwin, grab my hand and march me straight to the principal's office.

The principal's job, as far as I could figure, was to spank kids who messed up, which I'd never done till now, so naturally I was real nervous. Mama says I have lots of nerve.

Principal Young didn't look young at all, but more like an old owl. Tufts of hair stuck out of and around his pointy ears. Coke-bottle-bottom glasses magnified his yellowish eyes. I expected him to hoot, but instead he asked me to explain myself, which I was much too scared to do—even if I knew what I'd done—so he sent me out into the hall while he and Mrs. Baldwin called my house.

When Mrs. Baldwin came out of Mr. Young's office she was smiling. She said they'd talked with Grandmother Hetta and that I should have a little talk with her and then, the next day, I could retell my story. And when we got back to the classroom she told the kids there had been a little misunderstanding and I wasn't in any trouble, but they crawdad-eyed me the rest of the day like I had cooties or something.

I was still worried about how I'd messed up when I got home from school, but nobody was mad at me. Mama smiled while Grandmother Hetta showed me this tiny dot on my little tin globe. Haiti, it was called, and we were going to live there because Daddy was going to build a dam. Boy, was I relieved to find out that I hadn't, with an angry, silent wish all those months ago, sent my daddy straight to Hades after that little set-to we had. Especially since I thought we had to go with him—pretty danged unfair, in my book.

That night in bed I eavesdropped on Mama and Grandmother Hetta's conversation in the living room. I'd never told anyone that, through some miracle of air vents, I could hear everything that happened in the living room clear as a bell. That's why I never protested when I was sent to bed even when there was a program on the radio I wanted to hear. That alone should have alerted the grownups that something was amiss, but they never figured it out.

I am an excellent dropper of eaves and find it pays off. For instance, one night I overheard my Aunt Marjorie, who doesn't have any kids and doesn't seem to like 'em much, telling another aunt that I was annoyingly precocious and even though she mispronounced it, I now knew, thanks to those air vents, how she *really* felt about me. I continued to be precious and she continued to pretend to be annoyed. I gotta say though, she's a pretty good pretender.

Anyhow, this night I was keeping my ears open for what my mother and grandmother had to say. Mama sighed and said, "I swear, sometimes I just don't know what to do with Lizbuthann."

Grandmother Hetta laughed softly. "Johnnie Ruth, I think you named Elizabeth for the wrong aunt. She's a sight more like your Aunts Arleigh and Ona than your Aunt Elizabeth. I should know, I was the oldest of all the sisters and practically raised them. And what Elizabeth Ann (Grandmother Hetta is the only person in all of Texas who pronounces my name so it doesn't sound like Lizbuthann) did today was pale compared to what you did to me when you were a girl."

My ears perked up.

"When you were little," my grandmother told Mama, "your wild aunts—you know what pistols they are—came for a visit to the farm and one of them told this joke: 'Two-piece bathing suits were all the rage and this woman, wearing hers for the first time, went down to Galveston for a vacation. She waded out into the surf and along came a wave and stripped off her top. She was left half-naked in waist-deep water so she knelt down and wrapped her arms around her breasts until she could figure out what to do. A little boy paddled up to her and said, "Lady, if you're gonna drown them puppies, I'll take the one with the pink nose."'"

Mama and Grandmama laughed and laughed, but I didn't get it.

Grandmother Hetta continued talking, saying, "You children were supposed to be asleep,"—I guess grownups never learn—"but evidently you heard your aunt's joke and told it the next day. In Vacation Bible School."

Mother gasped, but she was kind of giggling, too. "That must have set the gossips' tongues to wagging."

"Oh my, yes. I thought I'd never hear the end of it. The preacher almost had apoplexy and suggested that since your father had died recently maybe you'd fallen in with a bad lot. As if there was a bad lot to be found in Locker, Texas." They continued to talk and I drifted off, but not before I memorized the puppy joke for later, maybe for Show And Tell.

Anyway, thanks to grandmother's patient explanation, I knew I wasn't following Daddy into Hades when I stepped off the plane in Port-au-Prince, but it sure *felt* like it. I'd seen paintings in Art Appreciation of sinners burning in Hell, their mouths open in silent screams towards Heaven (like it wasn't too darned late!) and if I hadn't known better I'd have expected old Lucifer himself to suddenly appear in that sweltering terminal building.

Maybe it was the daiquiris, the heads, the heat, or all of those; the next thing I knew, I woke up with my head in the doll seller's lap and people fanning me while my mother hovered and Daddy paced and twirled a curl of hair near his temple that he worked on when he was upset. We call it his worry lock.

Mama elbowed aside a couple of Haitian kids who'd dashed in to snatch a few strands of red hair when I conked out. Sitting me up, she looked back over her shoulder at my father. "Lizbuthann's okay, Bud," Mama reassured him. "She does this a lot."

Daddy did not look reassured.

# CHAPTER 2

▼

All four of us crammed into the front seat of Daddy's spankin' new '53 Ford pickup for the trip from the airport to the hotel.

I wanted to ride in the truck bed, but after I'd fainted flat out at the airport my parents didn't think it was such a hot idea. Besides, Daddy had already hired some raggedy Haitian kid to ride back there so nobody would steal our luggage when we stopped for traffic or whatever. That ragamuffin had himself a full-time job, I'll tell you, even though Daddy hardly slowed down all the way through Port-au-Prince, especially when people looked like they were fixin' to throw themselves in front of us. Daddy said they were just looking to get hit because they figured we were rich and we'd give 'em money. Which I did.

Daddy'd given me a bag of centimes and candy when we left the airport, and it was my job, when we got completely bogged down, to toss a handful out the window to clear the crowd. So, while Daddy blasted the horn, cussed a blue streak and steamrolled our way along the jam-packed, narrow streets, I tossed the coins and mints to those we grazed.

Mama surely didn't approve of our methods, saying something about the dignity of the natives, but as far as I could tell the natives were enjoying themselves no end. Daddy said it was the custom, so Mama said, "Oh, well, then," and pulled Sister a little closer, like she thought I might get carried away and toss her tyke out with the money. 'Course, I wouldn't do that, since Sister was holding the two fantastic dolls Daddy bought from the riled up fat lady I'd scared half to death by collapsing in her lap, drawing the attention of two armed soldiers who thought she'd done something to me.

But Daddy had sorted out the mess at the airport and now he steered us through the shambles that was Port-au-Prince. Between cussing and honking he growled, "I need me a cold beer," and when I said, "Me, too," Mama gave me *the look* and said I was getting to be quite a handful.

I was about to say something that would land me in a heap of trouble, like, "Thank you," when Daddy took a sharp left turn through a gate that was thrown open in the nick of time by a grinning man in a white uniform. We screeched to a halt in the courtyard of Heaven.

Okay, so it wasn't really Heaven, but after the stinky hot airport and the filthy, crowded streets of Port-au-Prince, the Sans Souci Hotel and its park-like courtyard looked pretty heavenly to me.

Painted a dazzling white, the wooden building resembled a frosted ginger-bread house splashed with gumdrop colors that turned out to be flowering plants so brilliant and fragrant that they stung my eyes and tickled my nose. Lacy porches with curly eaves and banisters surrounded the whole hotel. I instantly fell in love, enchanted with the exotic charm of the San Souci's mystique. I'd learned those words, "exotic" and "mystique," in Vocabulary, and it's a good thing because otherwise I wouldn't have the words to describe such a place. Vocabulary, a special class at school, was where I showed my stuff and Mama said it was fine and dandy to learn new words so long as I didn't put on airs and sound too snooty around my cousins, who, to my mind, were dumb as dirt anyhow. Right now, though, even with my new fancy words, I was, well, speechless.

"Lizbuthann, you might want to shut your mouth before you catch a fly," Mama teased as we left the pickup and entered a reception area where black folks in white uniforms grabbed our bags and stared, wide-eyed, at my hair before backing out of the room. After being in the country for only a couple of hours I was wondering if I should borrow one of Mama's head scarves.

We passed through the hotel lobby and out to a garden/swimming pool/out-door bar area. Trees full of tropical fruits and bushes with six-inch flowers surrounded a grinning bartender. He turned up his radio. The music, as strange to me as everything else in Haiti, had an exotic clanking thump that didn't sound anything at all like Bob Wills and His Texas Playboys, but I liked it anyway. A body could hardly stand still. The rhythm moved you, made you want to shuffle your feet; sort of like a two-step, but faster.

Parking ourselves on cool, lacy ironwork chairs in the shade of a flame tree, which looked for all the world like an enormous poinsettia bush, Sister and I ordered limeade while our parents had a couple of beers. Just as my drink—a tall frosty affair decked out with a gigantic red flower, cherries, and lime slices—

arrived, a blue and yellow bird, danged near the size of a wild turkey, shook the air with raucous squawks while clumsily dive-bombing the table. After a few passes, the parrot crash-landed onto my shoulder, almost knocking me out of my chair. When we both caught our balance, he leaned down, his claws digging through my dress and into my arm, fished a cherry from my glass with his horny beak, and proceeded to demolish it.

Mama shrieked louder than the parrot and tried to shoo him away, but it was too late; cherry juice dripped a bright pink design on my new white dress.

Holding a seltzer bottle in one hand and a banana in the other, the bartender rushed over, wrestled what was left of the cherry from the bird's beak and sprayed my shoulder with ice-cold fizzy water. To stop the macaw's ear-splitting protest, he gave it a banana just in time to save my hearing. The parrot, whose name was Christopher Columbus, quieted down, held the banana in one crusty black claw and snapped it in half with that big black beak.

I was giggling so hard that Mama eyed my frilly drink with suspicion. She looked as if she were about to reach over to take a test sip, but then said something about losing a finger to that overgrown parakeet and stuck with her beer. I imagine I was grinning like a simpleton for I had fallen head over heels in love with the tropics, Port-au-Prince and my surprise-around-every-bend new country. I wanted to live in Haiti forever. Heads and all.

After another limeade, Mama said it was time to look at our rooms and made me return Christopher Columbus to his perch. He didn't like it much and began jabbering in what I figured was French.

Sister and I had our very own room with a porch that connected us to our parents' suite. With its dark, cool interior, smooth mahogany floors, ceiling fans and two big beds tented with mosquito netting, the room looked like the drawings of tents in a book called *The Arabian Nights* that an aunt owned, but which I really hadn't read, even though I gave it a try after my great-grandmother Stockman said it was a heathen work of evil. It was too hard to read, what with all those old fashioned words and such, so I soon gave up looking for the evil parts, but I did love those drawings.

Little chartreuse lizards hung all over the ceiling above our tent-beds, and although Mama wasn't crazy about them, they didn't bother Sister and me; we had a pet horny toad back in Texas and lizards and the like didn't bother us much, so long as they stayed on the ceiling and didn't drop on a kid's head when we least expected it.

Once in our room, we peeled off our sweaty dresses, put mine in the sink to soak, wiggled into bathing suits and streaked back to the bar area where the macaw still jabbered away.

Mama said we could go into the swimming pool only if Sister wore her Mae West—which Daddy blew up and put on her before we were allowed to leave our room—and we stayed in the shallow end and didn't swallow any water. The bartender, whose name seemed to be Robber, said he'd make sure we didn't drown and that he'd dumped chorine in the pool that very morning. I guess Mama and Daddy really wanted to be alone, because I know my mother saw the green stuff growing at the pool's waterline and normally wouldn't have let us in there for all the tea in China, chlorine or no. As it was, I knew we were still in for peroxided ears before the day was out.

Robber made us rum punches without the rum, adding extra grenadine syrup. He cut up pieces of mango and pineapple for Christopher Columbus, and taught us to say EYE-EEE-TEE: Haïti. He also told me his name was actually Robert, but was pronounced ROW-BEAR, and the name of the hotel, Sans Souci, meant carefree.

After sitting in the pool to cool down for awhile, we climbed onto barstools and ate as many olives as we wanted from a dish behind the bar. Robert said hardly anyone ever ordered a Martini anyhow. Robert was my kind of baby sitter, even if it did turn out that he was also a schoolteacher.

Teaching in Haiti, he told us, didn't pay hardly anything, so he worked part-time as a bartender to make ends meet. He spoke English, French and the language of Haiti, Creole, which is like French but sounds like you've got a mouthful of grits. We spent the afternoon sipping exotic fruit concoctions and learning some basic words and phrases. He wouldn't teach me any cuss words, just "*zut,*" which means "darn it."

"Monsieur Row-bear," I said, ready to try out my best new accent, "*ou et le…*movie theater?" I knew we wouldn't be in town long, but what the heck, maybe there was a movie playing that I could talk Daddy into.

"*Élisabet,*" he replied, shaking his head and making my name sound sooo sophisticated, "*en Port-au-Prince, il n'ya pas une cinéma.*" Port-au-Prince sounded like *Port-aww-Prance.*

"Well *zut, alors!*" says I. "If there's no, uh, *cinéma,* what do kids here do for fun?"

Robert grinned. "Well, few of them sit around the swimming pool drinking up my grenadine. We are a very poor country, so most Haitian children make their own games, swim in the rivers and in the sea, and many work."

I almost dropped my mango. "Work? Kids?"

"Oh, yes. They help in the fields, cutting sugar cane, as well as harvesting cotton, coffee beans and fruit. Some fish with their fathers or make baskets to sell to the tourists."

I had to think about that. It never occurred to me that kids might have to work, even though I remember my daddy telling me that when he was a boy he'd picked cotton and fed pigs. He'd made it sound like regular chores, like mowing the grass and washing the dishes.

It *was* something to ponder, but I figured I had plenty of time since I was gonna be here for practically my whole life. Mother had packed shoes for us for four years or so, guessing what size we'd be wearing year after year. Or rather, *I'd* be wearing, since Sister would probably get stuck with my hand-me-downs when she grew some. I was fixin' to ask another question about this labor thing when I heard voices in the lobby.

Two Negro men wearing dark glasses and Humphrey Bogart-style hats swaggered out to the bar. Their loud laughs and talk made me fidgety, even though I couldn't understand what they said. Maybe I just felt uncomfortable because I saw Robert sort of shrink, like he was trying to become invisible. I stared at them, even though I knew it was impolite; I had never seen a Negro in a suit and hat, much less sitting next to me. Back in Texas, Negroes mostly had their own bars, restaurants and even their own bathrooms. Once in awhile, when we were traveling, I was tempted to use their bathrooms when the Whites Only one was busy, but Mama wouldn't let me. She said it wasn't Christian to separate people like that, but if it was the law, I had to be respectful of the signs and besides, she doubted if the colored folks would want me in their bathroom anyhow.

The Haitian men gave Sister and me the once-over and asked Robert something that sounded suspiciously like, "Who are the brats?"

"*Touristes,*" Robert told them with a shrug, making us sound mighty unimportant. He was suddenly all humble, which, even though my Grandmother Mabel told me on more than one occasion that *I* could use a dose of, I didn't like Robert humble. It didn't fit his nature any more than it did mine and it made me wonder who these men were that they could cow a grown man so's you could almost hear him moo.

Robert wouldn't meet their eyes, keeping his on the already-polished bar he was polishing. He gave them their drinks and began re-shining the sparkling glassware. I couldn't understand the men—and therefore eavesdrop—and since Robert was acting like those Negro slaves in the movies who whiney-talked, and Sister had dozed off in a lounge chair, I wandered off to the lobby and picked brochures from a rack. I had just finished reading the last one when the men threw a few *gourdes* on the bar and left, and Robert came back to life.

"Who were those guys?" I asked. I wanted to add, *And why are you afraid of them?* but I didn't.

"No one important," he said, with a nervous shrug.

"Well, they look like gangsters."

Robert blinked, looked a little shocked, and then grinned. "You, my little American friend, are too smart for your own good."

"Smart alecky is what most grown-ups say."

Robert was much too polite to agree. He picked up one of the brochures. "So, what have you learned about Haiti?"

"Well," I sorted through the stack and pulled one out, "you have beautiful beaches, friendly people and," I read, "'Haiti's major exports are coffee…'"

Robert cut me off with a laugh. "These pieces of paper," he waved one in front of my nose, "are propaganda." He saw the question on my face and explained: "Propaganda is what you tell people who have no brains. No ears." Poking his finger between my eyes, he added, "You have to use your head to observe; think about what you see and hear for yourself. And most important, listen to the sounds of my country."

"I hear sounds, all right. Drums. Mama says they're going to drive her nuts."

"Your *mère* will get used to them. They never stop, except…." He stopped talking and got that nervous look again.

"Except when?" I prompted.

"Nothing for you to be concerned with. Just remember that here in Haiti, and especially in the mountains where you will live, nothing is as simple as it seems." He looked over at my sleeping sister, whose arms were wrapped around her new doll. "That doll, for instance. She looks like a toy, but is much more than that."

"I think she looks like Carmen Miranda, only darker. But she's just a doll."

"True, she is a doll, but she is made in the likeness of a very famous *voudou* priestess who lived here many years ago. A *maroon*."

Now this was getting interesting. While I'd seen plenty of voodoo stuff in movies, I never recalled seeing a purple person.

"My grandmamma says that movie hooey is mumbo jumbo and the work of Satan. She danged near had apoplexy when I told her about this one movie where voodoo folks were all dancing around, chewing on pieces of a roasted explorer. None of those dancers looked anything like Sister's doll, though, and I don't think they were purple, either."

Robert laughed his soft laugh. "*Maroon* is a word used to describe an escaped slave, not a color. And, like your *grand-mère*, many consider *voudou* the work of Satan, but it is much more complex than that. Here in Haiti, the slaves were not allowed to practice their own African religions, but were forced to convert to Catholicism. They did so, but incorporated their own gods and customs to form a religion of their own. But for your information, the followers of *vodun, voudou,* or as you call it, voodoo, do not eat people. That is only made up by your Hollywood."

"Hey, I thought you said there was no movie theater here, so how come you know about Hollywood?"

"Oh, we have films, just no real theaters. They are shown out of doors, and people sit on the ground. There is no schedule. Someone just tells someone, who tells someone else, that there will be a film on a certain night and where to go."

"Sounds like fun to me. By the way, Monsieur Robert you aren't one of those voodoo people, are you?"

"No, I am Baptist. I was raised in Cap Haitian by missionaries. They left a few years ago, when a new president of Haiti declared that our country have only two official religions: Catholicism and Voodou."

Oh boy, my Grandmamma Hetta, a hard-shell Baptist, surely was not going to like the sound of that one little bit. I decided not to mention it in my letters, in case she'd change her mind about coming to visit.

Robert was telling me as how *maroons* were escaped slaves who revolted against the French, and who used voodoo to get back at their owners, when he saw my parents coming and clammed up. Shoot, things were just getting interesting, but I followed his lead and began talking about the Citadel, a fortress in his home town of Cap Haitian. I didn't want Mama getting wind of this voodoo thing.

My mother had changed into a white linen sundress and let her shiny, coal black hair fall around her shoulders. Daddy's starched shirt and knife-pleated khakis sported a few dark drips from his still-shower-sparkled hair. The scent of her *l'huere bleu* cologne, which she'd bought in the Havana tax-free store and was just about the best thing I'd ever smelled, blended with Daddy's Aqua Velva aftershave. A couple of people peered out from the lobby, trying to decide if they were someone famous. They looked like movie stars. Everyone always said so. I figured I must be secretly adopted.

During my very first five-course dinner, I shared my fried plantains with Christopher Columbus while giving Daddy a running commentary of our trip from San Antonio to New Orleans to Miami to Havana, what my cousins were up to back home, and how many cows I now had in my herd at Aunt Anna's.

Mama eyed the macaw and said I'd probably catch some bird disease and Daddy said that that was the last thing I needed because he figured, what with the way I went on, I'd already been vaccinated with a phonograph needle. But he said it real nice, not like he was mad at me, and we laughed until tears ran down our cheeks. Sometimes we'd laugh so hard about something that I'd nearly wet my pants. Other people would look at us funny, but we didn't care. Those were the times I loved the most.

Sister—her real name is Arleigh, after my grandmother's sister, but I just called her Sister—was so worn out that she had to be carried back to our room. Our parents tucked us in under the mosquito netting, reminded us to only drink water from the jug on the bed stand, turned out the lights, left the porch doors wide open, and went to their own room.

Faint drumbeats floated in with a warm breeze as I cuddled my new voodoo priestess doll and slid into exhausted slumber.

I'd almost forgotten about the heads.

# CHAPTER 3

▼

I was the first one up the next morning, so I tippy-toed to the bathroom, struggled into my still-damp, slightly mildewy bathing suit and made a beeline for the pool where I shared *café au lait* and a *beignet* with Christopher Columbus. I was sipping my second cup and pumping Robert for information when Mama and Daddy showed up, told me to stop pestering the poor barman, and discovered I was drinking coffee, which was news to me. Ever since we'd left Texas, it seemed people kept giving me stuff to drink that got me in hot water. Back home I'd never had any choice; grownups just naturally knew what was bad for a kid.

Robert, while sprinkling powdered sugar on my fritter and mixing cane syrup into what I now knew was chicory coffee, taught me to read the breakfast menu, so after Mama snatched away my coffee, I translated the breakfast food choices for my family. Daddy, who hadn't learned much Creole because he had an interpreter working for him, was impressed and said I always was a quick learner and designated me as the family translator. I basked in the glow of his praise. Evidently he'd forgiven me for going against him back in San Antonio, painting the inside of his tow trailer Royal Blue—I had commandeered it for my clubhouse for a club of which I was, quite naturally, president—even though he'd told me not to. That was just before he'd left for Haiti, so I secretly figured I'd had a hand in running him out of town. Now it seemed all was forgiven, which made me real happy.

Before my parents showed up for breakfast, I had learned a lot from Robert. There was, he explained, a *petite guerre,* a little war, going on between the rich folks in the government, and the poor ones he called The People. That's the way he said it: "The People." I didn't exactly know who the People were, but I said I sure didn't want to be one of them if it would get my head plunked on a post.

Robert assured me that I was definitely *not* one of the People because I was white and not even Haitian and we didn't have anything to worry about, because whacking off foreigners' heads with a machete was real bad for tourism. Like setting *anybody's* head on a post in plain view of arriving tourists wasn't? Anyhow, that's when I definitely decided not to tell my family about the heads; Mama would get all fidgety and maybe not let me wander off like I'm prone to do. He also told me that Haiti means "Land of Mountains" in some ancient Indian language. *Indian?*

"Indian language, Robert? How'd Indians get clear over here? I thought they were all in Oklahoma."

Robert smiled. "Not the same Indians as in your cowboy movies. These Indians lived here many, many years ago, before Hispañola—that's the name of this island—was so-called discovered by the Spaniards.

"In fact, it was Christopher Columbus—the explorer, not this badly behaved bird—" Robert grinned and scratched the macaw's head, "who was responsible for killing all of the Indians. Now Haiti is inhabited by the descendants, not of Indians, but of slaves brought from Africa to work after the Indians were annihilated…murdered…by Mr. Columbus."

"Wow. You mean we get a school holiday for a murderer?"

"History books do not always tell the whole story, and I guess to most of the world a few less Indians here and there were not important in the larger scheme of life. Or so many still think. Someday I hope history will reflect the truth, but what does it really matter? Especially to *my* country. Haiti is so small, with so many problems, that it matters little to others what happened hundreds of years…"

A bell rang and Robert left for the front desk, so we didn't get to talk any more about this fascinating subject. I'd always had a sneaking suspicion that History was a waste of my valuable time since everyone seems to have their own version. Feeling that Robert had let me in on a big secret, I stored the information away for later use, like as an excuse not to do my History homework. I returned to slurping steaming *café au lait*, at least until Mama showed up and snatched it away.

After breakfast I reluctantly packed my bags, bid Robert and Christopher Columbus *adieu* and quickly found out why Haiti was called Land of Mountains; the first hour's worth of narrow, unpaved road leaving Port-au-Prince for what Daddy called Camp climbed upward through a series of dizzying switchbacks.

Daddy said it was only fifty miles or so to Camp as the crow flies, but this road looked to be laid out by goats, not crows. The company my father worked for planned to grade the washboards soon, but for now the trip took at least three bumpy hours.

My father blew his horn a lot and several times, even though he blew first and loudest, we had to back down to let brightly painted *camions*—open, top-heavy old trucks with bench seats in the bed and tin roofs for shade—get past. The camions overflowed with Haitians, goats, chickens, pigs, parrots, and baskets of fruit and vegetables. Some people rode the running boards, holding on for dear life and trying to suck themselves up small when we passed. Others rode on the roof. All, it seemed, were laughing, singing, squawking, squealing or bleating. I couldn't wait for a chance to ride on one of those exotic-looking buses, even if, like Daddy said, they had bad brakes. To make his point, he showed us what was left of a few camions at the bottoms of cliffs.

In addition to the camions, there were lots of people and animals walking, most of them right down the middle of the road. Little rickety-looking, over-loaded donkeys struggled with cargos of baskets, sugarcane and bananas.

"Hey Daddy, you'd better slow down before you hit someone's ass," I joked, earning me a severe scolding from Mama. When I lived dangerously, arguing that I hadn't said anything wrong because in the Bible they called a donkey an ass, Mama puckered up her lips and let out a sigh.

"See what I mean, Bud?" she said.

Daddy made an effort to screw the grin off his face. "Now, Ann," he said. My father calls me Ann, not Lizbuthann like everyone else, except when he's really mad, then he calls me "Jeezuzcrislizbuthann," which of course earns *him* one those Mama-looks. "Just because you think you know something, even if you might be right, doesn't make it okay to sass your mother."

When my father talks, even though he never raises his voice, it pays to listen. "Uh, sorry Mama," I said, trying to sound much sincerer than I felt. One of the things I hated about being a kid was always being wrong, even when I was right. I couldn't *wait* to grow up and be right all the time. But I evidently had a long way to go and if I didn't want to spend the next few years restricted to my room, I had to learn when to keep my big mouth shut. I turned my attention back to our fellow travelers.

Women with stacks of stuff balanced on their heads and wearing bright skirts and blouses, and men sporting loose white shirts, khaki pants and tall straw hats, led those poor little asse...donkeys, sway-backed-rib-poor horses, or the occasional scrawny cow, alongside the road. Everyone was barefoot, which I thought was a grand idea, but my mother said we'd get hookworms.

No one tried to jump in the truck bed because Daddy had covered it with a stretched tarp. Otherwise, he said, we'd have a bed-full by the time we got to the top of the mountain, and his pickup could barely make it as it was. We did get a few bumper riders, but we let them be. Almost everyone we passed waved and smiled; if they thought we were being snooty by covering up the pickup bed, they sure didn't show it.

At the top of the mountain Daddy pulled to a stop a little too close to the edge for my druthers. When he lifted the hood, steam poured out around the radiator cap and Haitians gathered to give Daddy advice he couldn't understand. Mama made us back off just in case it blew. She did let Sister and me buy some bananas and mangoes because they could be peeled, so while we ate them we looked down, way down, at Port-au-Prince and the winding road we'd climbed.

It was much cooler up this high and my backside got cold because my sweaty shorts and shirt had been stuck to the plastic truck seat. Mama said, as she shook out her damp skirt, that she'd like to make towel covers for the seat, but my father said she couldn't because of crabs.

"Crabs?" I said, "Up here?"

My mother shot my father an exasperated look that she usually reserved for me, crossed her arms in her no-nonsense stance and said, "You said it, Bud. Now you can explain it."

Daddy's ears turned red, a sure sign he'd messed up, but I have to admit I enjoyed his discomfort because for once I wasn't the one on the spot. What spot that was, I had no idea, and I probably could have let him off by saying it didn't matter, but curiosity got the better of my good judgment. I just stared at my dumbfounded father and waited.

"Lice," he finally said. "They're called crabs because they look like little tiny crabs under a magnifying glass."

"And they live on the seat?" I didn't like the sound of this one little bit.

"Well, no, they live on people. A lot of Haitians have them, especially some of the workers on the dam site. We wipe the seats down with disinfectant twice a day, so terry cloth covers just won't work out."

Well, heck, I knew about lice. Even back in school in San Antonio they checked us for head lice. What was the big deal? I shrugged, Daddy looked real satisfied with himself, and went back to venting the radiator.

I looked back at the turquoise of the Caribbean Sea far below, then walked to the other side of the road and gazed in the direction to where Daddy pointed and told us we were to live. The road snaked downward into a deep green sea of jungle, then rose again into even higher mountains. I could just make out the shine of a meandering river.

My ears picked up a steady, faraway drum beat and I was reminded of those Saturday afternoon Tarzan movies where the natives got restless and folks generally ended up tied to a stake while savage voodoo worshipers or fierce warriors danced around threatening them with spears. It suddenly occurred to me that since leaving Havana the day before I hadn't seen another white person outside my family.

"Daddy, is everyone here Colored?" I asked. That's not the way my cousins would have fashioned the question, but Mama had never allowed us to use the "n" word and always made us call Colored folks "Mister" and "Missus," except for a babysitter named Mary. She was just thirteen so we could call her Mary.

"Pretty much," he said, easing the cap off the radiator. "But I've noticed that all the money seems to belong to the light-skinned guys, who are still Negroes, but with white wives from France or high yeller Haitian gals who never come out of the house in the daytime, so as to keep their skin from getting dark. There's some real lookers out at night, I tell you."

Mama's eyebrows shot up, and he added, "Uh, or so your Uncle Lloyd tells me."

Daddy and Uncle Lloyd had arrived in Haiti first to build houses and get the construction camp ready for all the rest of the families who were coming to build the dam. Daddy said there'd be about fifty families, mostly Americans from Texas, and ten thousand Haitians living at the job site. They'd already cleared the jungle, run water pipes from a stream—we'd been sternly warned not to drink any water that wasn't boiled first—installed a generator and strung power lines to Camp. There was still a lot to do, he said, but shoot, by the time everyone else got there we'd have the place real modernized.

The best part of the trip to Camp was fording the rivers. Daddy stopped the truck, walked to the edge of the muddy, swift water and squinted at a pole, which he called a depth gauge, in the middle. White rings were painted on the gauge and he knew how many had to show above the water before we could cross. He got back behind the steering wheel, told us to open our door and put our feet on the dashboard, then he took off his shoes, rolled up his pant legs and left *his* door open. Sister and I squealed with delight and Mama giggled as we bounced across the rocky streambed, water running in one door and out the other. I wondered what the gas station guys back home, the ones who vacuumed our car floorboards every time we filled up, would think about this method of cleaning. Seemed real practical to me.

Also practical, if slightly embarrassing, were the little kids wearing shirts. Only shirts. They also had these little round bellies, which I thought were real cute until Mama told us they were malnourished, which means they didn't get enough to eat, or not enough of the right stuff. We knew about the right stuff, which in our case included Mama sprinkling wheat germ on just about everything we ate, and making us take daily doses of thick liquid vitamins that tasted okay, but went down like glue. Daddy warned my mother to leave that germ stuff out of *his* food, but I saw her sneaking a cupful into the meatloaf now and again.

Anyhow, most of the tiny villages we saw were near streams, and when one of these half-naked little kids needed cleaning up, mothers just dunked their babies' fannies right into the water and let them drip dry, so they didn't have to waste money on the likes of diapers. Now that's what I call practical, but I didn't think Sister would go for it.

We passed through a small village on the river, Mirebalais, where whitewashed houses—huts really—topped with a mishmash of palm-thatch and rusting tin roofs, leaned every which way in contrast to the straight walls of a tiny church that Daddy said was Catholic, so I knew we wouldn't be going *there* because my great-Aunt Elizabeth says the only thing worse than a Catholic is a Democrat.

Some homeowners had gotten artistic and painted flowers and animals on their huts and one house was bright purple with a beautiful lime green mermaid over the door. All the buildings were lined up around a dusty public square where a statue of some Haitian hero, his name long ago erased by tropical rain and heat, shared the space with a few sun-browned palm trees.

There was no one around, but when we got out to stretch, a few heads bobbed out of darkened doorways to get a better look at us. I was drawn towards the purple house, but when I wandered in that direction, Mama called me back. As I turned around, I caught a glimpse of a face in the window below the mermaid, but it was gone so fast I thought maybe I had imagined it. All the way back to the pickup, though, I had that feeling of being watched. Little hairs stood up on my neck and I walked a little faster than usual.

After that small town, we didn't see another house for twenty miles, until we reached a village which Daddy said was just on the outskirts of Camp. Daddy said that was because the company had recently built the road and the Haitians just hadn't had a chance to build near it yet and he must have been right because we did see scads more poor-looking folks walking on the road or clinging to bouncing camions. I figured they must be the People that Robert talked about because if, like Daddy said, only the light-skinned ones had money, these folks must be flat broke; some were so dark they looked almost purple. I considered warning these travelers headed towards Port-au-Prince that their heads might end up at the airport, but then I'd have to tell Mama about that gruesome scene, so I let well enough alone because, knowing my mother, she'd probably take us right back to Texas, which wasn't nearly as much fun as Haiti. Best I could tell, my new country was a child's paradise.

It didn't take Mama long to figure out it was a grown-up's nightmare.

# CHAPTER 4

▼

Camp, which was actually named Péligre after the small village nearby, sat on a plateau overlooking the Artibonite River Valley and the steep mountains beyond.

I knew all about plateaus because my Aunt Anna—who is actually my great aunt because she's my grandfather's half-sister—lives on one. Whenever we went to Grandmother Mabel and Paw Paw's ranch near Lake Travis in the Texas Hill Country, I'd stick around just long enough to be polite, then streak the half-mile up the hill to Aunt Annie's (that's what everyone called her) plateau.

I was named for this favored aunt. She had never married because she was rattlesnake bit when she was a little girl and couldn't have babies. She lived in a trolley car; the very one she'd ridden from her Hyde Park home to the governor's mansion in downtown Austin. She'd worked there as his seamstress, making all the gov's clothes, right down to his skivvies. On the side, she also fashioned fancy dresses for rich debutants, which was interesting since Aunt Annie wore only what Mama called shifts.

Anyhow, my great-aunt and the trolley system retired about the same time, so she bought the tram, had it hauled out to the ranch, and set it on her plateau. My daddy and his brothers added two flagstone outbuildings (a storage shed and a bathroom), built a cistern for storing rain water, connected all of it with a patio, then roofed over the whole danged shebang.

Aunt Annie placed her bed in what used to be the rear of the trolley, where scads of tiny windows gave you a view all the way to Lake Travis. Out what used to be the back exit was her bathroom, and the front door was, well, the front door. She had a wood stove for heat and cooking in the winter; in the summer she cooked outside on the patio. I loved staying with her because we ate fresh baked bread washed down with cistern water for breakfast and then bathed in the creek. Mama said if *she* tried feeding me bread and water and making me take cold baths, I'd have a conniption fit. She was probably right about that, but somehow Aunt Annie made it all seem like a grand adventure.

Hanging above Aunt Annie's upright piano, written in Arabic script and English, was a quote, **Women and men have been and will always be equal in the sight of God—Bahá'u'lláh,** which just about drove my grandpa nuts, because as much as he loved his half-sister, she was a Bahá'í and believed everyone in the whole world was equal. There were always lots of little dark people speaking strange languages camped out around her house which, of course, I loved, even though the members of the Bee Caves Baptist Church shot strange looks in my direction when Grandmother Mabel dragged me away from that "heathen on the hill" for Sunday services. When I grew up I wanted to be just like Aunt Annie: unmarried and a little loony. I'd as soon skip that snakebite, though.

So, like I said, I know about plateaus. The Haitian plateau at the Péligre dam site was pretty barren because Daddy and Uncle Lloyd—who wasn't really my uncle, but was taken in by Paw Paw when he and his twin brother were thirteen, but that's a whole 'nother story—had made it. Scraped the top right off a hill with a D-8 dozer. They'd also built fifty houses, a mess hall, and what they called a B.Q.—bachelor's quarters: a kind of hotel where single men like Uncle Lloyd lived. They ate in the mess hall, and so did we for the first few days, until Mama got the house squared away. From then on, we only had dinner at the mess hall on Friday nights. I always had fried chicken, which was actually Guinea hen, and ice cream. Until I got fat and Mama put me on a diet.

The first night in our new house was kind of spooky because we didn't have our own furniture. They'd stuck some bamboo stuff with hard cushions in the living room, and Daddy had scraped up four twin beds that were more like cots, a table and four chairs. Mama borrowed a few kitchen items from the mess hall so we could make breakfast, but that was it.

My room (okay, so Sister was in it, too, but she was too young to claim her half) was at the back of the house and behind it was a regular-sized yard, then a hundred-foot drop off straight down to the main road. Needless to say, Mama had quite a bit to say about that bluff practically on our back doorstep, for there was no fence or anything to keep a kid who wasn't paying attention from barreling right over the edge.

Way below, across the road, an aggregate plant ground away twenty-four hours a day, sorting rocks and sand into piles. After dark, the bright plant lights shone on the back of our house, streaming through the aluminum window louvers to make shadow-stripes on the wall across from my bed. In the silvery-blue spaces between horizontal bars, I made shadow animals with my hands like I'd done at my great-grandmother's house back in Austin. She lived right under one of those artificial moonlight towers that were scattered all over the city, put there by some folks who thought moonlight every night would be a neat thing. I agree.

But Austin was a long distance from Péligre, in more than miles.

That first night in Péligre, as I lay in bed listening to distant drums that by now I realized really never stopped, I couldn't fall asleep in spite of my long, dusty day on the rough road from Port-au-Prince. I was thankful for the light coming through the louvers because when night fell in the tropics, it dropped like a black velvet curtain. Walking back from the mess hall, even though the stars were really bright, we couldn't see our hands in front of our faces until Daddy turned on his flashlight. Outside the circle of light, my imagination—overactive, according to almost every adult I knew—conjured up all manner of scary, toothy critters.

Once in my bed, to take my mind from those imagined child-eating monsters, I used both hands to make a shadow-rooster strut across the wall just like Uncle Lloyd had taught me. Then I did a bear, but that was scary, so I was attempting a choo-choo train when my hands froze and I stopped breathing. Right in the middle of my shadow-show, blocking the light, loomed a human silhouette.

I gasped, staring at the wall, not daring to turn and look at whoever it was just inches from my head, outside the screen. A flimsy screen, I might add; we didn't have glass windows. The best I could tell, it was a man. A really huge bald man. I could hear him breathing until the blood pounding my ears drowned him out, but when I opened my mouth to yell for Mama I guess I must have fainted or something, because the next thing I knew it was morning and the bright sunlight streaming into my room made me think maybe I'd bad-dreamed the whole thing.

Until I went outside for a look.

"Lizbuthann, where are you going with your father's boots?" Mother asked as I was going out the back door for the second time that morning.

"Uh, well, I thought I'd shine 'em."

"Oh, that's so…sweet," she said, eyeing me with slight suspicion like she always did when I volunteered to do something against my nature. But she shrugged, unable to figure what evil motive I could possibly have. "When you've finished, come on in and I'll fix you some breakfast. Your Uncle Lloyd said he'd drop off fresh eggs and fruit this morning."

I stared at the mud-encrusted construction boots with dismay; a body could starve to death before getting *them* clean. Sometimes, like my Grandmother Hetta says, a little girl can be too smart for her britches.

I ran to the flowerbed behind my bedroom window, set one of Daddy's boots in the footprint I'd found on my first trip out, and pulled out the ruler I'd stuffed in my shorts. My father, I knew, wore a size eleven; the bare feet that left the prints under my window were at least four inches longer! I skedaddled to the front yard, away from those scary footprints, and plopped into a swing Daddy had hung from a tree branch. Sighing, I pondered my plight and began a half-hearted scrubbing of the grubby steel-toed boots.

Should I tell anyone my suspicions? And if so, would my story get my folks so upset that I'd become a prisoner? If my mother thought there was a giant peeping Tom about, I'd never be allowed to wander. 'Course, if I *did* tell, I'd get out of the nasty boot job.

I was saved from a decision when Uncle Lloyd drove up. Dropping the boots, I raced to meet him. He scooped me up under the arms and swung me around until we were both good and dizzy.

"Ann," (Uncle Lloyd calls me Ann, like Daddy does, because they're both partial to Aunt Annie) "you sure are gettin' big. Won't be long before you outgrow me being able to lift you."

"I grew a whole inch just lately," I bragged, throwing back my shoulders and locking my knees. It is my opinion that tall people get more respect, so I had been practicing walking with books on my head so I'd look taller. I suspected it wasn't working.

"Well now," Uncle Lloyd said, "I suppose someone as big as you are can handle this little problem I've got. I didn't quite know what to do with him, myself, so I thought of you." Uncle Lloyd reached in the back of his truck, handed me a covered cage and what I saw when I pulled the towel from the wire got an "Awww" from me. All thoughts of my shadowy night visitor vanished.

"Open the door and put your hand in. He's tame," my uncle prompted. So I did.

A tiny parrot, slightly larger than a parakeet, climbed onto my finger, ran up my arm and buried himself in my hair. I giggled, untangled him, held him in the palm of my hand and stroked his grass green feathers.

"Found him in the jungle," Uncle Lloyd told me. "His nest fell from a tree and one of my men hand-fed him until he could eat on his own."

I could tell the bird was still a baby by the downy little feathers sticking out at all angles around his head, giving him the comical look of an almost-bald old man with just fuzz left. The parrot was so sweet and cute and he loved being cuddled up against my chest like a human baby. Whenever I tried to put him down, he'd clamber back up my arm and crawl inside my shirt collar, where he'd chew on my hair and make little contented sounds. I suppose he missed his mother. Which made me glance towards the house where *my* mother, the one who disliked indoor pets, lurked. But I didn't have to worry for long; Pee Wee, as I named him, charmed Mama as fast as he had me.

Pee Wee and I had plenty of time to get acquainted because it took a few weeks for my Calvert Course home school stuff to arrive and I didn't even have many chores because we were still living out of suitcases. Anyhow, Mama hired a maid to do regular stuff around the house that I'd gotten stuck with back in San Antonio, like sweeping the floor and washing dishes and ironing Daddy's underwear.

This maid thing got off to a shaky start. The first one Mama hired, Tifi (pronounced Tee-fee, like teepee), drew all over the walls with the new set of Crayolas I'd thrown into my suitcase when we left Texas. She was especially fond of purple, which was also my favorite, and by the time I caught her, she'd used up half a stick. Goodness knew when I'd see another crayon store, so I took the set away for fear of spending years without purple. Even though I figured anything on those lime green walls was an improvement, and was tempted to do a little scribbling myself since I had someone to blame, I didn't want to use up all my crayons on that rough surface. Sister hit it a lick or two with her set, though.

Tifi quickly overcame her disappointment at having her budding art career cut short. She spent the rest of the morning switching the lights on and off and giggling. Said she'd never been in a grand mansion before, which bamboozled me until I realized she was saying she'd never been in *une grande maison*—a big house. I guess not, if she thought this was one.

Our *grande maison* was a three-bedroom cinderblock square with red cement floors, yucky lime green walls and a tin roof. Granted, unlike the Haitian huts I'd seen, we did have screens on the windows, but in our dining area the screens didn't even have louvers like the rest of the house. When it rained, which it did almost every afternoon, we had to roll down these woven sisal mats to keep the wind from blowing rain into our mashed potatoes. Our first day there, before we got the mats, it came a downpour and we learned the hard way that the red floor paint wasn't permanent. Except on our feet. Several weeks later our tootsies were still pale pink.

Anyhow, that first maid was more trouble than she was worth, so Mama demoted her to laundry girl and sent her off to the river to pound our clothes with rocks until our washing machine arrived from Texas. I dreaded to think what Tifi would do to an electric washer, but it didn't matter because one day she just walked off with the laundry and never came back. The next day another girl, older and also called Tifi, showed up and seemed to know what she was doing so we kept her for awhile. I found out her real name was Domenique, but everyone called maids *petite filles,* which actually meant granddaughter, and they shortened it to Tifi. Like Monsieur Robert had told me right off the bat, Haitians take a lot of shortcuts when talking.

Once Mama found out there were no poisonous reptiles in Haiti because of mongooses—little weasely critters that had killed off practically every snake on the whole island—I was turned loose. My bicycle was still on a ship, we had no television or radio, and here I was, for the first time in my life, free to do pretty much as I pleased, which would have been to ride my bicycle and watch television unless Eddie Fisher or Richard Nixon came on. Those two guys sent me scrambling for the OFF button.

Accustomed to accounting for my time to a whole passel of adults, from great-grandmothers to teachers, all this new-found freedom was a little overwhelming. I wasted a great deal of it trying to teach the yard boy, Guilliame, and Sister to read, both without much success. Sister was too young for what I was trying to teach, and Guilliame—William in English—although twelve years old, couldn't read in his own language, much less mine. Daddy said that nearly all Haitians were illiterate, but Uncle Lloyd said he was almost sure Guilliame's parents were married. They laughed, but I didn't get it.

I turned my teaching talents on Pee Wee and he was, by far, my star student. Okay, so he couldn't read either, but once he started talking, he never shut up. Except for what Mama called dramatic effect.

One of the things we enjoyed most was waiting for an unsuspecting visitor to spend five minutes saying dumb stuff like, "Polly want a cracker?" to Pee Wee. My little parrot would stare at them real dumb-like and then, when the sucker gave up and started to leave, Pee Wee would, with all the dramatic timing of Lucille Ball, deliver his line: "Birds can't talk." Of course, we eventually ran out of dupes, but for a while there, we were highly amused. Some might say we were too easily entertained, but I noticed more and more people dragged their own victims in for the bird treatment.

Within weeks Pee Wee could dance, play dead when I mock-shot him, sing "The Eyes of Texas," "Jesus Loves the Little Children" (a surprise for Grandmamma Hetta when she arrived), and "Put Your Little Foot." On that last one he'd do just fine until the very end, when he just couldn't get past ending in a wolf whistle. Then he began learning on his own, with mixed results. For instance, when someone, *anyone*, knocked on the door, he would call out, sounding just like Mama, "Come on in." We got a lot of strangers inside the house that way.

And then there were those choice words he picked up from Uncle Lloyd and Daddy, which he used to express his displeasure when we put him to bed for the night. Only covering his cage would stop the cussing, but even though Mother tried, with split second timing, to get him toweled down for the night before he could get wound up, Pee Wee's protests could be heard five houses away.

First thing in the morning, when Daddy got up to go to work, he'd open the cage and Pee Wee flew straight to my bedroom and under the covers with me. We spent all our time together, and it was nice to have such a grand pet, but I was starting to get a little lonely for other kids my age. Until the Boudreauxs hit Camp.

# CHAPTER 5

▼

Doux Doux Boudreaux was a year older than I was, a head taller, and already wore a training bra. She also had white-blonde hair cut in a Buster Brown do. Her real name was Dorcas, but we soon settled on the nickname Doux Doux— "sweetheart" in Creole, and pronounced Doo Doo. We enjoyed getting away with the slightly naughty play on words.

The Boudreaux bunch was from east Texas, but Uncle Lloyd said they were really coon asses from the bayous of Lousy-anner. Daddy explained that Papa Boudreaux was a Cajun and that's why he and all his kids talked funny. Doux Doux didn't speak Cajun or Creole like her father did, but she had his habit of starting sentences with "Mais, cheré," which was Cajun for "But, dear." She pronounced it "Maysha-ray," rhyming with "ray" instead of "ree." She also used a lot of dis's and dat's for this and that, and would say things backwards, like, "five or four miles down de road," instead of four or five. I thought she talked just fine, but when I tried it at home it went over like a poot in a pew.

Doux Doux had a bunch of brothers and wasn't one bit afraid of them. If they dared look at her funny she'd bop 'em a good one. On his days off her Pa—that's what she called her Daddy—would sit in the living room in his underwear and drink beer and pass wind. When he'd let go a big one, we'd fall to the floor gasping and clutching our throats until he threatened to throw an empty at us and we'd run off giggling to beat the band.

Doux Doux's mother, Clota Boudreaux—tall, elegant, unexcitable and very funny—seemed as though she belonged to an entirely different family. Always perfectly dressed in starched shirtdresses with the collar turned up so the points stood out on both sides of her neck, Clota seemed not to give a hoot about her family's rough and tumble nature. I noticed, however, that should things get a little too loud or rough, a slight lift of one perfectly plucked eyebrow brought all noise and fighting to a standstill. But it had to get pretty bad first.

I was fascinated with the Boudreauxs. They were as different from my family as if they were from another planet. They even *yelled* at each other, something totally forbidden in *my* father's house, but Daddy said that since they were typical Louisiana coon asses and didn't know any better, and so long as I didn't upset my mother by picking up any of their bad bayou behavior, I could be friends with them. Which was a good thing, because Doux Doux and I were going to be friends no matter what, and it's a whole bunch easier on a kid when she doesn't have to sneak around to do something she's bound to do anyhow.

Most mornings, Doux Doux and I were confined to our own homes, doomed to slaving over study guides administered by our mothers. The Calvert Course, designed for kids like us who were stuck in the middle of nowhere without schools, was a little harder than "real" school, because we had more essay-type exams. I liked it just fine, even though I couldn't simply memorize everything for a test, then forget it, like I'd done back in Texas.

Doux Doux's mama said she was hard to teach because she took after her father, but my mother enjoyed our lessons and said it was like going back to school herself. I was almost always a couple of days ahead because, even though we finished school early, Mama insisted I stick around until at least ten so I wouldn't get out of the habit of keeping regular hours. If it was up to me, I'd do a whole week in one day and have the rest of my time to myself.

Once freed for the day, we girls, me with Pee Wee on my shoulder or head, hiked miles along the jungle footpaths leading away from Camp in all directions. Finding perfect giant *mapon* (kapok) trees, we "borrowed" coils of rope from the jobsite when no one was paying attention, then strung Tarzan "vines" from the highest branches so we could swing from tree to tree, apeing the famous ape-man. Pee Wee was Cheetah and, with a little coaching, got to sounding just like that famous chimpanzee.

When not flying between treetops, we swam in a spring-fed pool until the adults found out we were skinny dipping in the camp's water supply. After that we paddled around in the shallows of the riverbank.

We stalked and captured huge tarantulas and four-foot iguanas for pets. 'Course Mama made me turn them loose when she heard that iguanas carried leprosy, and after my favorite dinner-plate-sized tarantula escaped his terrarium one night and climbed in bed with her. During frequent downpours, we gave up stalking unsuitable pets and read anything we could get our hands on.

I missed not getting the Sunday funnies, especially Brenda Starr, my very favorite, but I had some of her comic books—which I'd almost memorized word for word. When we got desperate, we'd make up stories and draw our own cartoons. We read our Nancy Drew and Hardy Boy mysteries until the pages were tattered. When we could get away with it, we'd sneak out one of the forbidden "True Confessions" magazines Clota Boudreaux kept in a trunk under her bed. Since the magazines were taboo, we read and re-read them—especially the smoochie parts—analyzing their content for hidden hints as to their disastrous endings.

The plots of these "confessions" were fairly predictable: the girl has a lot of yearnings and desires and the boy was always off-limits because he was from the wrong side of the tracks. Or vise versa. Anyhow, they would somehow end up alone at night—not very smart planning on the parents' part by my reckoning— they'd get to smooching, the boy would unbutton her blouse and the next thing you know she's in "circumstances" and being shipped off to a convent or a home for wayward girls. Of course, they always told everyone in town the girl had gone off to live with a grandmother or an aunt or someone out of state, but *we* knew where she was headed.

What we had more trouble with was what "circumstances" meant. The dictionary was no help at all on that word, but "wayward" worried me some, since I was considered by some to be just that: contrary, obstinate *and* resistant to guidance and discipline. Being already in the wayward category, I figured I'd have to watch my step, in case I ended up in circumstances. I wasn't all that worried though, because it always had to do with boys and I was safe because I planned to be like my Aunt Annie and stay away from 'em.

Anyhow, these magazines we sneaked away from Clota always featured some girl in circumstances writing her true confessions and warning others, like me and Doux Doux, against making her same mistakes. She didn't need to tell *me;* it didn't take a genius to figure out that kissing boys was a risky business. Doux Doux, on the other hand, dreamed of getting old enough to marry and have a big family. Why, I don't know, since it seemed to me her family was plenty big enough.

All these confessions of lust—another new word for me, which I figured out was one of the deadly sins, but I wasn't quite sure which one—set me to thinking about my own future. I knew exactly two adults who never got married and both of them seemed pretty darned happy about it: Uncle Lloyd and Aunt Annie. Daddy told me that Aunt Annie had once upon a time had a sweetheart, but he was killed in World War I. Uncle Lloyd was in the navy during World War II, so

I figured that *not* getting married had something to do with war. When I told Mama my conclusions, she just laughed and said I probably had it backwards.

Doux Doux and I got all excited when a new family arrived so we could move in on their books and comics. We scoured Camp for new reading material and I was thrilled to find a small book titled *Tell My Horse* on Mrs. Wilkin's bookshelf. I had already learned the hard way that you can't tell a book by its cover when the Thesaurus didn't have a danged thing to do with dinosaurs, but even so, when I got it home and *Tell My Horse* didn't turn out to be about horses at all, I was plenty let down, like at the movies when that roaring lion comes on at the beginning, and then the story doesn't have a single lion in it?

However, I got over my disappointment real fast when I read enough of *Tell My Horse* to see it was all about voodoo in Haiti. I quickly hid it from Mama's curious eyes so Doux Doux and I could pore over it again and again, studying voodoo gods and their ceremonies. When we were puzzled by something in the book, we'd sometimes get up the nerve to ask a maid or two about stuff we didn't understand, but we had to be very careful, because we just naturally knew our parents would have a cat if they thought we were fascinated by such a forbidden, and therefore exotic, religion. Not that we planned to join up, mind you, but heck, we were surrounded by it, so why not get educated?

Camp was shaping up. The mess hall served as a community center, post office, dancehall, church, and best of all, movie theatre. Once a week, unless the river flooded and the delivery truck couldn't get through, we got to watch a movie. 'Course we never knew what language it would be in and if it was some racy French thing we kids would be sent home right when they began taking off their clothes, but most times we got to stay. We also had a commissary where we could buy stuff with coupons from books bought from the camp manager. Then, to our dismay, they built a schoolhouse.

By now the family housing was full and there were all kinds of kids in Camp, but no girls the same age as Doux Doux and I, which was just as well because I find that when you put three gals together you almost always get trouble. There were two sixteen-year-olds in camp, a boy and a girl, who ignored us completely and were always kissing and making goo-goo eyes at each other. We kept a pretty good eye on them, waiting for them to do something for which they'd have to confess, but were disappointed when the girl was sent back to Texas to live with her granny and attend high school instead of going to a home for wayward girls. We were, quite naturally, doubtful at first, but she sent back pictures from school, so we knew she was in Marble Falls instead of circumstances. The boy, who moped around after she left, was finally sent home as well.

The departure of the last big kid left us at the top of the heap; queens of the mountain. Our adoring subjects, all the little kids in camp, were willing slaves who could be commanded to do things like put on war paint and let us shoot them. And just when we thought things couldn't get better, they did: Grandmother Hetta showed up, and then we got a neat new maid named Angela after yet another Tifi walked off with another load of laundry. Mama said at the rate we were running through maids we'd be out of underwear in no time and Daddy and Uncle Lloyd broke out laughing and told us that when they first got to Haiti, they had an old woman who did their laundry.

"She was about ninety," Daddy said.

Uncle Lloyd nodded. "If she was a day. We suspicioned that we were missing some underwear, but since we hadn't counted 'em, we couldn't be too sure."

"But then one day," Daddy said, taking up the story, "Lloyd and me was driving to the jobsite in a jeep and there she was, hobblin' along the side of the road. We felt sorry for her and offered a ride." He started laughing, then caught his breath. "That old gal hiked up her skirt to climb in the back and I said, 'Damn it all to hell, Lloyd, she's got on my damned red shorts.'"

"And I said," Uncle Lloyd said with a laugh, "'You want 'em?'"

They were both cracking up, so I asked, "So what'd you say, Daddy?"

"What do you think I said? I said, 'Not no, but hell no!'"

Mama was laughing as hard as the rest of us and said, "Well maybe we should try to find her. At least she already *has* underwear and maybe wouldn't walk off with the rest of ours."

So, even if we were in danger of having to go naked, Camp was turning out to be a really neat place and got even neater when Doux Doux and I got our horses. Wishes and Smokey Joe were not exactly prize horseflesh, mind you, but finding a nag in Haiti that wasn't swaybacked or hoof sore wasn't all that easy, and like Daddy said, don't be looking up a gift horse's rear. So we didn't.

I named my horse Wishes after a saying my Grandmother Hetta repeated to me whenever I tried to wish a problem away: *If wishes were horses, beggars would ride.*

And ride we did. Each day after our lessons, we'd hie off on our fiery mounts in search of slayable dragons and high adventure. We rode for miles along jungle paths crisscrossing the thick tropical forest, finding bananas, papayas, limes and avocados to bring home. Scouting for new sites for our ever-growing number of Tarzan ropes, we stumbled upon a deserted voodoo *hounfort* where we knew, thanks to *Tell my Horse*, mystical rituals were performed. We recognized it for what it was the minute we found it, because on one of our trips to

Port-au-Prince, Mama took us on a bus tour of the city and one of the tourist attractions was a *hounfort.*

The one we found in the jungle, unlike the *hounfort* made up for rubberneckers in Port-au-Prince, wasn't fancied up with colorful banners, doll-filled altars, hundreds of lit candles and the like, but the layout was the same. We found a few bleached bones tied with faded ribbons and, on a crude altar chiseled in a rock, melted wax. It was kind of spooky, what with us worrying that someone would show up and catch us snooping around, but, of course, that didn't stop us. We got in the habit of checking the *hounfort* out every once in a while, leaving a glass jar with dried fruit, candy, or marbles on the altar. The gifts were always gone when we returned, and in the jar we'd find a feather, a pretty rock, or a piece of ribbon. Unless Haiti had some super smart pack rats, someone was trading gifts with us. Doux Doux and I swore an oath of secrecy about our marvelous find, feeling it was wiser to let our parents think we were just out gathering fruit instead of swapping gifts with a voodooist.

Once in a while we'd take a new path, go over one too many a mountain, and get lost, but we almost always ran into someone walking along the trail and, since Daddy put out the word on the jobsite that there was a standing reward of a dollar to any Haitian who brought us home, we were pretty safe. A buck was a lot of money in a country where most folks only earned a hundred dollars a year. We were so darned popular we could hardly get anywhere for people trying to take us back. At first mother worried about us being out all alone like that, but my father assured her if anyone tried to keep *me* they'd probably pay *him* a dollar to take me back. Very funny.

Angela, the new maid, was from an island called Aruba, in the Dutch West Indies, and believe you me, *nobody* dared call *her* Tifi. She insisted on being called Angela, even by me, though she was a grownup. Mama didn't like it much, but Angela won in the end when she said, "Madam Calixte be *ma belle-mere*—my mother-in-law—and she be one mean ol' woman, so I want to be called Angela."

So Angela it was. She stood ramrod straight, had tawny brown hair, eyes and skin, and was very beautiful. She wore spectacular dresses printed with oversized flowers or fruit, and spoke her own brand of lilting, singsong English, as well as Papiamento, Creole and Dutch. Her husband, Jean-Paul, a large dark man with a wonderful smile and deep voice, was Haitian. He was also my daddy's foreman. What with Angela working for Mother, and with her husband's salary, Daddy said the Calixtes were doing pretty darned well for themselves and sure enough, they were soon able to build a house with a real tin roof instead of palm leaves.

Angela, who I would have hired for her dress alone—she arrived for her interview in a white frock printed with life-sized banana leaves and bananas—soon became my confidant and I could ask her stuff that I wouldn't dare ask my mother or grandmother. I could tell her almost anything. Or so I thought.

One day when it was pouring down rain and everyone was out doing something like working or playing bridge, I told her about finding footprints outside my window. I hadn't seen the man's shadow since that first night in Camp because no matter how hot it got, I shut those louvers tight every night. But just that morning, while planting poinsettias under my window, I saw those giant footprints again.

Angela shrugged it off and said, "You jus' imagine such 'ting."

"No, Angela, honest. I saw them. Twice. Come outside and…" I looked out into the downpour. "Oh, I suppose they're gone now. But they were there. Really." Then I told her about the silhouette my first night in Camp. Angela, usually an island of calm, looked pale and agitated as I told her my story. When I finished, she stared at me for a minute, then regained her composure and shrugged again.

"Peoples come," she said. "They go. We have many camp workers. It is not anyt'ing for little girls to worry wit'. Now, you help Angela wit' this sugar cane."

I peeled the sugar cane stalk and she cut it into small cubes for Sister and me to chew on when we wanted a sweet, then she made us both an Eagle Brand milk and 7-Up soda. Pee Wee was working his way through a second cane cube when I dared another subject.

"Angela, do you believe in voodoo?"

"Some do," she answered carefully.

"Do you?"

"Why do little white girl wan' to know such t'ing?"

My turn to shrug. "Just wondered. Grandmother Hetta says it's the devil's work."

"You *grand-mére* is very wise woman, but maybe she don' understand the ways of this country. Voodoo can be evil, that is sure, but not all the time. Sometimes, when someone don' understand something, they call it voodoo because they be scared or stupid. And some peoples, voodoo peoples or no, are evil clear through their mean old bones. And evil, be it in the name of one religion or another, has a way of using weak, scared and stupid peoples to work bad magic. I t'ink your *grand-mére* would be talking about those devil works, and she be right. But, like Angela say, there is good and bad in everyt'ing. You best not talk too much about what you don' understand, child."

"How about zombies?"

Angela whirled on me so fast I thought she was going to hit me. I ducked, but she grabbed my shoulders and gave me a little shake. "What I just say? I just tol' you to leave t'ings be. Now, shut up you mouth."

I must have looked funny, because she let me go like I was a hot potato. "Oh, child, Angela be so sorry. I don' mean to frighten you."

I was stunned. For one thing, no one, and I mean no one, was allowed to say "shut up" to anyone else in our house, much less yell it. Big tears ran down my cheeks, and I rubbed my arms where Angela had squeezed them. She didn't really hurt anything but my feelings, but I was upset that *she* was upset. Angela just stood there, wringing her hands and shaking. I threw my arms around her waist and buried myself in her arms.

"I didn't mean to make you mad, Angela. Really. I just wanted to know…oh, never mind."

She pulled my arms away and looked into my face, wiping my tears away with her hand. "I, too, am so sorry, child." She led me to a chair in the dining room and we both sat down. "Understand this," she said, "there be no walking dead. No such t'ing. And don' let nobody tell you such t'ing. And when they do, you come straight to Angela. I will tell you truth. *Bien?*"

"*Bien.*" And I did. Anytime something happened that required an explanation, I made a beeline for Angela. Like after the night when three perfect rings of fire burned high on the mountain slope across the river. Fires set by zombies, according to our yard boy, Guilliame.

I was waiting for Angela when she came to work the next day, eager to see what she thought, but she looked so tired and upset, I thought better of it. After my lessons that morning, I went out to saddle Wishes and was just cinching him up when Angela came out.

"You give that stubborn beast a good whack in his rib, child. He be blowin' up on you."

"I know. He always does. But he can't hold his breath forever, and when he exhales, I cinch in quick." As if on cue, Wishes let down his guard and I got two quick notches on him. "See?"

"I see one stubborn old horse and one even more stubborn little girl," Angela said with a weak smile.

"Are you all right, Angela? You look tired. You're not sick are you?"

"*Non bébé,* I just did not sleep well last night. And you? How you sleep?"

"Okay, I guess. Until the drums and the fires…."

"I t'ought so." She looked up at the mountain slope where three black rings still smoldered. "It is the first time I see this here. So many new peoples have moved up from the plains and Port-au-Prince because of the money and jobs...some peoples I did not wish to see. We were feeling so...safe here." She had a dreamy look, like she was a million miles away, then suddenly her face hardened. "You don' go too far from Camp today. You promise Angela, yes?"

Well, fooey. Doux Doux and I had planned to take a closer look at those fire rings. I even had on my bathing suit under my jeans so I wouldn't get my shorts and shirt wet when we swam the horses across the river. Now I knew Angela would be watching that mountain, and she had eyes like a hawk.

"Okay. Sure," I said, hiking myself into the saddle. As I rode away, I felt Angela's eyes boring into my back. Oh, great. Just what I needed, *another* adult telling me what not to do.

# CHAPTER 6

▼

"I hardly slept a wee-unk last night," Mama drawled the day after the *second* time the fire rings appeared across the river. "All those drums. What on *earth* are the natives up to?" She cut her eyes toward the kitchen where Angela stood sipping coffee. Angela'd taken to showing up every once in awhile on her day off, but stubbornly refused to join us at the table when she did. I think she just liked my grandmother and wanted to be there when there were extra mouths to feed. If she heard my mother's question, she chose to ignore it. Or maybe she simply didn't consider herself a native. Either way, the question hung in the air, unanswered.

I ventured a look in Angela's direction, and could tell from the straightening of the splash of sunflowers along her spine that she had not only heard my mother, but felt put upon by her question. Since I planned to pump Angela for information later and didn't want her miffed, I took it upon myself to fill the silence. And typical for me, I piped up without quite thinking the whole thing through.

"Some folks say it's a voodoo thing," I blurted, realizing immediately that I'd fouled up when all eyes turned from their chicken and dumplings to me. Foul. Chicken. Get it?

Trying to recover from my *faux pas*—that's French for messin' up—I added, "Of course, that's probably just a load of bull…loney." I grabbed my iced tea and downed a couple of gulps, wondering why I'd opened my big fat mouth instead of letting someone else come up with something. So, as I'm prone to do, I opened it again. "I think they build those fires when the moon is dark so they show up better. That way everyone knows where to find them."

"Everyone who? And why?" Daddy asked, but they were kind of casual questions, and he kept on eating.

With a very Haitian *nonchalant* shrug and wrist flip, I said, "Oh, you know, voodoo kind of people. Uh, pass the *poulet, s'il vous plaît*."

Daddy looked at the two untouched chicken legs on my plate, grinned, and handed me the platter anyway. I spent a long while searching for just the right piece, hoping someone would change the subject. Especially since Angela was giving me the evil eye from the kitchen and Mama was doing likewise from across the table.

"Black magic," Daddy scoffed, taking a big bite of one of Grandmother Hetta's famed and fluffy dumplings. Ever since she'd arrived, we'd been treated to her huge Sunday lunches, because she usually played hostess to whichever visiting preacher came to conduct services—except that one Sunday when she'd just grabbed a pot lid from the rack without checking it and steamed a bright green tree frog into our dumplings. That time we took the freeloaders to the mess hall for lunch. This Sunday, though, we were just family since it was the Methodists who showed up, and my grandmother couldn't abide Methodists. Or, evidently, her granddaughter bringing up witchcraft on the Lord's Day.

"Heathenism, pure and simple. Devil's work," she declared, spearing a green bean as if it were the Prince of Darkness himself. Bad enough for a Southern Baptist to be subjected to Methodists; all this talk of black magic had her dander in a dither.

I stuffed an overloaded fork into my mouth before I got myself in deeper by saying what I was thinking, which was that Doux Doux and I had warmed up to the idea that instead of praying for the strength to forgive our enemies, we could, with a little ingenuity, take a snip of hair, a bit of cloth, and some hay and, with a couple of well-placed needles, do 'em in. Someone deserving, of course, like that snooty new girl, Janet, who'd just moved into Camp. We hadn't actually tried the doll and needle thing yet, but Janet's day was a-coming if she didn't quit whining to her aunt—who whined to my mother—that we never played with her. She was such a sissy she wouldn't even ride horses with us, and forget the Tarzan ropes.

I decided a change of subject was in order. "Daddy, someone said that President Eisenhower is coming to Camp, 'zat true?"

Daddy laughed. "No, Ann. Wrong president. Paul Magloire, the president of Haiti, is coming here to dedicate the first official bucket of concrete poured on the dam."

"Oh," I said, disappointed. I'd already dug out my **I LIKE IKE** button, and didn't know where to find a **J'AIME MAGLOIRE** one. "Can Doux Doux and me come?"

Mother raised an eyebrow and tilted her head in my direction.

"May Dorcas and I come, please?" I corrected myself. Some of my family, namely my mother and grandmother, didn't approve of my nickname for my friend. Or my rotten English.

"Sure can," Daddy, who could talk anyway he wanted to, said. "Everyone can." Wouldn't catch him saying *you surely may*. "The cableway's up and operating now, we're just waiting for the batch plant to get finished. My first *un*official bucket gets dumped next week, but in about a month, when we're sure everything's running real smooth, the top man will give us his blessing. He's making a big deal out of how he's bringing electricity and flood control to his people, so his picture, taken with a bucket of grout will be plastered all over the country. He even gets to dump the bucket. With my help, of course."

Uncle Lloyd laughed and said, "Maybe we can make a big splash and dump Major with it."

I giggled. Against orders, Doux Doux and I had sneaked up to the dam site lots of times to commandeer more rope for our Tarzan swings, and to watch the cableway shack being built onto a foundation hanging right on the edge of a cliff. Daddy, from this high, glassed-in perch, could not only see the entire dam site, he probably also caught a glimpse of us kids on occasion, but he didn't let on.

Sitting in a throne-like chair, facing sets of levers, my father moved a bucket bigger than Doux Doux and I put together. Using brakes and clutches, he could maneuver it forward, backward, up and down. The bucket, at first filled with plain old dirt for practice runs, would soon carry eight cubic yards of concrete on each pour. On the other side of the river, the cables were attached to a tail tower on railroad tracks, and by moving the tail tower, the head tower, and the bucket, my father could put that bucket down to any spot in the gorge.

The temporary diversion dam that funneled the river away from where the real dam was going to go up was almost completed. Building a dam, as you can see, is a big job.

Doux Doux and I watched in fascination as the project plan unfolded, each new step bringing us closer to the day Lac Péligre would be formed. Then we built our own.

Uncle Lloyd was the one who walked up the dwindling stream to discover our own personal dam, our *piece de resistance*. Working over several weeks, Doux Doux and I had hauled rocks, some of which took both of us to carry, to build ourselves a little private swimming hole beneath a huge mapon tree. We didn't know that we were damming up the Camp water supply until we'd almost given poor Uncle Lloyd a heart attack.

He was concentrating on following the trickle of water in the streambed when, from on high, he heard a horrible yell, a terrifying ape-screech and almost got brained by his niece when Pee Wee and I swung just over his head and dropped, with a great splash, into our lovely kid-made Lac Lizbuthann. Ours certainly wasn't the largest buttress type dam in the western hemisphere, as Péligre Dam would be, but Uncle Lloyd, when he could laugh about it, said we'd done a right respectable job. But he cut down our rope and tore down our dam anyhow.

After that incident, Daddy decided that if I was so interested in dam building I should be allowed supervised visits to the jobsite, and that's where I saw Major getting to do what I longed to do: ride that bucket across the gorge.

Major Madden, his wife Monika, and their two kids lived next door to us. He wasn't really in the army, he just got that nickname when he was a kid because he was a major nuisance. I thought he looked like Perry Como and I guess I had a little crush on him. Anyhow, Major liked to stand on the tee bar holding the concrete bucket and ride that thing across the big, deep river gorge. Daddy and Uncle Lloyd both said he was nuts, but I thought it looked like fun. Fun I'd never get a chance to have, that was for certain; even if Daddy said it was okay, there was no way in heck Mama would allow it. I had to settle for riding horses and swinging on ropes for excitement.

Doux Doux and I were practically living on Wishes and Smokey by now. We had to study at home most mornings, but we'd get up real early so we could get the books out of the way and have time to ride before the afternoon rains. The minute we were turned loose, we stowed sack lunches in our saddlebags and were out of Camp a little after ten, scouting up adventure. We'd learned our immediate territory pretty well, marking paths we'd taken with bits of yarn, so the only time we got fouled up was when we wandered too far, but that dollar reward got us home every time. After a while we got tired of being led home and stuck to the trails we knew, which, by themselves, were getting more and more interesting. Especially in light of all those dead chickens.

You'd think, in a country where starving folks were always stumbling into Camp throwing up nothing but water, they'd eat chickens instead of hanging 'em up in trees to rot. But there they hung, and since our book, *Tell My Horse*, only mentioned chicken sacrifices and not hanging them around in trees, where they served no purpose to my thinking, it was time to very carefully pump Angela for information. I volunteered to dry the dishes after lunch, which naturally made her suspicious, so I had to be extra sneaky. I didn't want her mad at me again, but she *did* say I could ask her anything, didn't she?

As soon as I was sure everyone else was out of hearing range, I casually mentioned chickens hanging along the footpaths. After grumbling some cross-sounding words in her native Papiamento, she demanded, "Where you see these chicken?"

I wiped at a nonexistent spot on a plate, trying to figure a way to get around her question without actually lying. She always knew when I fibbed. "Oh, you know," I said, waving my hand vaguely toward the mountains, "on a footpath."

"Oh yes, I do know. On a footpath to no good, where little white girls got no busy-ness. No busy-ness at all. I have a mind to tell you *maman* to take that flea bite horse from you before you get in big trouble."

"But Angela, if Doux Doux and I didn't have our horses we'd just be stuck here with you." I gave her my most endearing look. "*All* day. *Every* day."

She laughed. "Oh, you gon' blackmail me, huh? I don' t'ink so. But, because I know you will leave me no peace, I will tell you about these chicken. *If* you promise not to mess wit' them. You promise Angela?"

I crossed my heart.

"*Bien.* These be chicken sign for special meetin' of *houngans* and *mambos;* voodoo priests and priestesses. They meet on *claire du lune*, the full of the moon. Before the meetin' the chicken be replaced with special *vèvès*, very beautiful flags made wit' silk and beads that shine in moonlight and lead way to the meetin'. There is for sure a *hounfort*, a voodoo meetin' place, somewhere up there." She studied my face for a trace of guilt, but I didn't even twitch. There was no way I was going to tell her we'd already found that *hounfort*. Or that Doux Doux and I had been exchanging little gifts with someone or something up there.

"What do they do at these meetings?"

"How would I know, child? I don' do voodoo."

"Angela, you're a poet," I teased.

"And you are a big pain in *la tête*. Now, you do what Angela say, and stay away from these chicken, or the loa will get you good."

"Which loa?" I asked foolishly. I immediately knew I'd messed up when Angela's eyes narrowed to slits.

"What you know about loa?" she hissed. "Where you learn this word?"

"Uh...didn't you just say it?"

"Don' you play wit' Angela, smarty girl. Now where you hear about loa?"

"I...uh...in a book?"

"What book?"

I shrugged. "Just a book I found. It's about Legba, Damballah, you know, those loa."

"Lord, child if you *grand-mère* hear you talk like this she be havin' fits. Get that book. Now."

I did. Everyone else had left the house, so we sat at the dining room table while Angela leafed through the pages of *Tell My Horse*. By the tongue clicking and disapproving grunts she was making, I knew she was not pleased with what she read.

I reached over her shoulder and pointed to a drawing. "I like this one," I said, hoping she could tell me something about it.

Angela studied the picture, then shrugged. "They have a god for everyt'ing under the sun. This be a mermaid. Not'ing evil about her, my guess. I remember my husband tell me she be carved onto fishing boats."

"But, why would—" I caught myself just in time. Had I finished my question, asked why this drawing would be on a rock in a *houngan* in the middle of the jungle, Angela would know where we'd been, she'd tell Mama for sure, and Wishes and I would be stuck at home until one of us reached twenty-one. And I don't mean in horse years.

"Why what?" Angela asked.

"Why do they have so many gods? Seems a lot easier to have just one."

"Who know, child? Not Angela, that be sure. One thing certain, though," she thumped the book, "the priests, they use signs, like chicken to lead you to ceremonies and if you follow those chicken, they lead straight to big troubles." She read another page or two, then her face softened, and she chuckled. "This woman who write this book be led up the garden path. She t'ink these priest let her in on big secrets when they only tell her what she want to hear. This lady better stick to her own Christian God back in New York."

Grandmother Hetta walked in about then, heard the word "God" and smiled approval at our topic of conversation. She'd' a had a stroke if she knew we were talking about following a trail of dead chickens to a heathen worship site. Angela slipped the book under a placemat, scooped it up and headed for the kitchen. I knew better than to try to get it back.

God talk was popping up around every corner, and no matter who was talking it looked for sure like I was on the fast track to a date with ole Beelzebub, even though my grandmother told me that children don't go to Hell. I tried to get her to zero in on an age limit, but she knew better than to give me too much rope.

Almost every weekend another religious group showed up and if they were anything near Baptists, Grandmother Hetta would feed them lunch. Uncle Lloyd said he figured the word must be out that a bunch of back-slidin', Saturday night dancin', bourbon drinkin' Texans had moved into the country, because missionaries practically swarmed out of the jungle to save our souls. I mean, here we were, in the middle of absolutely nowhere and who knocks on the door offering to lead us to their brand of God? Jehovah's Witnesses. Mormons. Seventh Day Adventists. Church of Christers. And, of course, Baptist missionaries with a hankering for souls and chicken and dumplings. It's no wonder the Haitians made up their own religion, because not one of those others had any decent drum beating or anything near the forbidden mystique of voodoo.

The *hounfort* Doux Doux and I had discovered was about five chickens from Camp. An hour after my talk with Angela we were headed that way, me feeling a little guilty until I remembered that I'd only promised Angela I wouldn't mess with the chickens. So I didn't.

Someone had been busy. The clearing at the *hounfort* was swept, a large pile of fresh logs were stacked in the fire pit and, surrounded by candles, a black Jesus hung on a six-foot cross. Red paint, at least I hoped it was red paint, dripped from His thorn and nail holes. Great Aunt Elizabeth would have said something about craven images, but Doux Doux and I thought it was pretty neat, if a bit gruesome. We'd never seen a black-faced Jesus, and I suspect this one didn't start out that way, because his hair was blonde.

The mermaid drawing on a flat rock was still there, and I was sorely tempted to swipe it because I liked it so much, but I knew better. Another rock had been added, this one with a palm frond painted on it in the same pukey lime green as the mermaid. A lime green, I might add, just like that on our walls at home. I knew the frond was a symbol of Haiti's independence, so it looked as though we had a patriotic paint thief at work.

"Too bad the *artiste* didn't get to that icky paint before they messed up our houses with it, huh, Doux Doux? You know, I think I've seen that mermaid before somewhere. And not just in that book, either."

"Where?"

"Can't remember. Oh, well. Would you look at all these candles?" I tried to picture how pretty they would look, all lit and sparkling under a full moon. So far I hadn't seen a darned thing that'd scare off a kid unless you counted those stinky chickens.

We checked out our jar and found the candy we'd left on our last visit had been replaced with several small seashells and smooth pieces of glass. I had seen this kind of glass before, on the beach. In fact, Daddy called it beach glass; pieces of bottle that were tumbled by the sea and sand until they had no sharp edges.

We left homemade fudge in the jar because our invisible friend seemed to have a sweet tooth.

I climbed on Wishes and took in the whole scene before we rode off. What with all the work being done, the meeting promised to be a humdinger and, if Angela was right about the full moon thing, Doux Doux and I had a whole month to do some pretty serious planning. I'm quite sure Brenda Starr would never pass up such an opportunity.

# CHAPTER 7

▼

"Lizbuthann," mother said, fixing me with a doubtful look, "why would you and Dorcas want to sleep out of doors? There are mosquitoes out there. Not to mention tarantulas and all sorts of other critters."

"Now Johnnie," Grandmother Hetta said, "don't you remember how you and your brothers and sisters liked to pitch a tent out back of the farmhouse when you were kids?" Grandmamma didn't interfere often, but once in awhile she came in downright handy. I felt slightly guilty though, using her good graces to pull a fast one.

Mama nodded. "Well, yes. I guess I do. But we lived on a ranch in Texas, not in the middle of a jungle." I could tell she was waffling, so I kept my mouth shut for once and let my grandmother handle her.

"And Texas doesn't have critters?" Grandmother Hetta said with a smile.

My mother frowned, but I'd won; Texas has bodacious critters.

Friday night, Doux Doux and I took our air mattresses, a loaf of bread, this neat new stuff they had in the commissary called SPAM—which Mama said had been around for awhile, but we never got to eat it back in Texas—lots of cookies and a couple of flashlights and set up our camp as far away from grownups as they'd allow. We'd told our parents we planned on a first-light ride, so Wishes and Smokey were tethered nearby. We even brought an alarm clock, but I was sure we wouldn't need it. Who could sleep with such an adventure in the making?

We settled onto our mattresses, munched SPAM sandwiches and watched a huge moon rise slowly over the mountains. 'You know Doux Doux, Velveeta cheese would make these sammiches just perfect."

"Yep," she said with a sigh. "I do miss it."

We ate in silence for a few minutes, exchanging Daddy's binoculars to gaze at the moon. "How come they say its made of green cheese?" I asked.

"Dunno. Looks more like Velveeta to me."

"You got Velveeta on the brain."

'Yeah? Well, you got Velveeta *for* a brain."

We giggled, then Doux Doux asked, "Mais cheré, you scared?"

"Nah. You?"

"Mais, no…uh…okay, a little."

I giggled again, this time a nervous giggle. "Maybe a lot. What do you think those voodoo guys'll do if they catch us spying on them?"

"Dunno, but our maid says witches turn folks into zombies if they don't like 'em, so that's probably what they'd do to us."

"Angela says there ain't no such thing as zombies, but she looked a little scared when she said it. Maybe she's afraid we'll turn that sissy Janet into a zombie and that's why she won't give us back the voodoo book."

Doux Doux sneered, "Hey, if zombies are dumb butts, Janet's already one."

We had a good laugh at poor Janet's expense. Mama had made me play with Janet the day before, but didn't push us to invite her to our campout, even if the scaredy cat would dare to sleep outside.

"You know," I said, "Guilliame says zombies are people who voodoo priests bring back to life and make them do their bidding. But that voodoo book says maybe the priests just use special poison to make 'em *seem* dead, then, after they're buried, they dig 'em up, wake 'em up and make zombies out of them. I ain't sure what they are, but I doubt Guilliame does either. Heck, he's never even been to school."

"Mais cheré, why were you talking to that yard boy about zombies?" Doux Doux asked with a yawn.

Oops. For some reason, probably because she'd think *I* was a big ole scaredy cat, I hadn't told Doux Doux about the footprints outside my window, or the fact that when Guilliame saw them he got all shaky and said, "Oooh-gah-oooh," sounding just like the horn on my Uncle Swid's old model T. It took me some thinking and figuring, but I decided he was probably using some form of *houngan*, which Angela had pronounced, "Ooohn-gahn." So now, finally, I knew the Haitian word for zombie: oooh-gah-oooh.

Once he'd seen those big prints, Guilliame flat refused to cut the weeds in that particular flowerbed. I'd catch him once in awhile, as he was sawing on the lawn with his machete, cutting his eyes toward the rising patch of weeds like they were gonna uproot, jump out of the ground and attack him. After some time, Mama noticed the ugly circle of long grass and weeds behind my room, the mess standing out like a sore toe next to the rest of Guilliame's velvety green manicured lawn. A lawn, I might add, that he kept that way using only his very sharp machete. Mama finally made me clear what she called "that briar patch" from our otherwise perfect lawn because she figured if the yard boy refused to do something about it, it was somehow my fault. It was, I guess, since I was the one who scared him.

And now that Doux Doux's mouthy maid had told her she could get turned into a zombie, I didn't think this the right time to mention that maybe I'd personally seen one. Well, the shadow of one. I mimicked her yawn and said, "Oh, I talk to Guilliame about all sorts of things." Doux Doux let that do for an answer.

We lay on our backs, watching hundreds of shooting stars streaking brilliant, even against the brightly moonlit sky. I could hear a faint hiss from my mattress and figured I'd have to re-pump soon, but I must have dozed off, because the next thing I knew, I was flat on the ground and the alarm was going off. I checked the time with a flashlight: eleven. Perfect. Except for that moon, which was so bright that I began to have second thoughts.

"Doux Doux, it's like broad daylight out here. What if someone sees us?"

"We'll just have to be real careful and, like we decided, not get too close—just get up that tree we staked out and watch. And we won't stay long. Who knows, maybe it'll all be over. I mean, you're the one who came up with midnight. We don't really know what time they start. Or even if they really do. Now, let's get moving."

"I guess you're right," I said, with more confidence than I felt. "Okay. Follow me and Indian-walk single file. And don't slice yourself up on the bob wire." I took Wishes' reins and, using a technique of silent walking I'd learned at Brownie Camp back in Texas, rolled my feet from toe to heel. The horse followed, his clomping silenced by two pairs of Daddy's Sears and Roebuck heavy-duty work socks slipped over his hooves and secured with rubber bands. Wishes wasn't real crazy about the idea and we had a little set-to when he tried to stomp my hand while I was putting on his socks, but he now seemed resigned to the new footwear.

Doux Doux and I had cut a hole in the barbed wire fence weeks before, because otherwise we'd have to enter and exit Camp at the guard shack on the entrance road and that seemed an invasion of our privacy, even if the guard was more often than not taking a snooze. Besides, there were lots of holes in the fence, made by Haitians who either worked in Camp or came around selling eggs, vegetables and stuff carved from mahogany. Of course, the hole we cut was a smidgen larger than average—big enough for a horse to clear the barbs—but we didn't worry much, because even if the grownups found our escape route, they'd just blame it on the Haitians, saying they were too lazy to come through the main gate.

Wishes shuffled along behind me, his sides just clearing the wire on either side of the cut. If I didn't quit feeding him extra hay and sugar cubes, we'd soon need an even bigger hole.

As soon as we felt safe, far enough down the path so as not to be seen from Camp, we mounted up and rode slowly along the footpath. We'd timed it the day before and figured thirty minutes would get us to the *hounfort,* but now that we were in the jungle at night, things looked different. Progress was slow. And scary.

In some places, huge mapon trees formed an overhead umbrella that blocked out the moon and cast us into tunnels of pitch black. The horses plodded on, following the trail. Occasionally something, Lord only knew what, rustled the thick growth by the side of the path. Once or twice Wishes flattened his ears and shied, but since I knew there were no poisonous snakes or tigers or the like, I just held onto his mane and whispered, mostly to comfort myself, "It's okay Wishes, it's okay."

We found the first *vèvè*, one of the shiny, colorful voodoo banners Angela had told me about, right where a chicken had hung a week before; a good sign that we were on the right track on the right night. We had added a few markers of our own along the path, like little strips of cloth where there were Y's, just in case we got turned around. After we'd been traveling for over a half hour, hoping we wouldn't meet up with anyone, we saw another banner swaying in the slight breeze. I smelled smoke and soon we saw the glow of a fire and heard drum-thrumming.

"We'd best leave the horses off the path," I whispered. "Back there, in that clearing, just in case someone comes along."

Doux Doux nodded and we led our mounts into the trees, tied them to a bush, and crept back onto the path. Wishes craned his neck to watch us leave and horse-snuffled his displeasure, but I knew he couldn't be heard above the singing and moaning that now accompanied the drumbeats.

The back of my neck tingled, always a bad sign.

Losing what little nerve I had, I stopped so abruptly that Doux Doux ran into me, spat out one of her Pa's favorite words, then gave me a hefty shove toward the observation tree we'd picked out on our earlier visit. Once I got going again I didn't stop until I was settled onto a branch about ten feet up.

Doux Doux had just climbed up next to me when the drums stopped beating, the singing broke off, and the jungle went silent. We froze in place, still unable to see the clearing, but afraid to make any more noise by moving further out onto the branch. There was nothing to do but wait. It was so still I could hear Doux Doux panting next to me. Worse, I could swear I heard Wishes horse-huffing. I seemed to be the only one holding their breath and I knew I needed to start breathing soon, because I was going all fuzzy.

I exhaled real slow and was feeling a little better when, from behind us, Wishes let out a big old horse fart that would put Doux Doux's Pa to shame. And from way down deep in my stomach, a giggle gurgled. I swallowed it back, but could feel Doux Doux's shoulders jiggling next to me and didn't dare look at her because I knew she was trying to stop a titter of her own. I was on the verge of losing it when an unearthly scream pierced the air, jarring birds from the treetops and killing all giggles.

The drums suddenly came to life again, their noise giving us a chance to scramble out onto a branch where we could see the *hounfort* clearly. I could now see the bonfire and some people, but hadn't had time to take it all in when, once again, someone or something screamed and the jungle went dead silent. The way Doux Doux was looking at me, eyes big as saucers, I thought for a minute maybe it was me who screamed.

For what seemed a jillion years, the jungle was quiet as a church. I considered trying a little prayer, but suspected it wouldn't do much good, what with me being somewhere doing something I wasn't supposed to.

Doux Doux's face went uncommonly white. I touched her arm and she practically jumped out of the tree, then slapped my hand away and made little mewing sounds while pointing towards something I couldn't see. I shifted my weight, slid into a tree crotch next to her and had just gotten settled when we heard that horrible scream again. It wasn't me for sure.

In the glow of a huge bonfire, about thirty Haitians I'd never seen before, all dressed in white, rocked silently side-to-side and then front to back, weaving in place to an unheard, inner beat. They ringed the fire, staring into it, spellbound. Without any drumbeats, singing, or moaning, the scene lit by the fire looked like those flickering old black and white movies made before someone figured out how to add sound and color. But the dancers had their own rhythm, and moved with it like kelp swayed by the sea.

Right next to the fire, in the middle of the clearing, a skinny woman with missing teeth and very dark, shiny skin, held a white chicken upside down by its feet. The woman took a deep drink from a bottle and spewed it on the chicken. The chicken screamed. I mean really let one go. Didn't sound like any chicken squawk I'd ever heard, I tell you.

The drums started up so fast and loud they almost scared the pee out of me, but I held on tight to the branch and watched, fascinated, as the woman raised her machete and lopped the chicken's head plumb off.

Now, I'd seen Grandmother Hetta wring many a chicken's neck, and while I didn't like it much, that's the way things are on a ranch: no dead chicken, no fried chicken. Grandmamma called it a practical fact of life. But this was different. As soon as the voodoo queen—which is who I decided she was—severed the unfortunate chicken's head, she drained the blood into a hollowed-out gourd, added clear liquid from the bottle, mixed it with her finger, raised the bowl to her lips, and drank deeply. Doux Doux gagged, but luckily the drums and chanting got real loud at the same time.

"Doux Doux Boudreaux, don't you dare puke," I hissed, even though I was real close to it myself. She nodded weakly and put her hand over her mouth, but I could see her shoulders jerk once in a while. "You wanna go?" I whispered, half hoping she did.

Doux Doux shook her head and said, "Mais, hell no to that." She tended to use profane language when she was scared. I could feel a cuss word or two forming in the back of my throat as well. Or maybe it was vomit.

My heart leaped as the voodoo queen took another deep drink from the bottle and then, as she lowered it, she looked straight at us. Her eyes were completely white.

Doux Doux gulped and whispered, "Oh hell, Lizbuthann, she sees us," but the woman just turned away, passed the gourd around to others, then the bottle.

Doux Doux and I breathed a sigh of relief as each person took a sip of the chicken blood mix, then washed it down with a big glug from the bottle. From my perch I thought I identified the bottle's contents: clarine. Daddy said Haitian clarine, or white lightnin', was ten times worse hooch than the stuff they made back during Prohibition in the States, and that any sane man wouldn't touch it for fear of going blind. Evidently the voodoo lady and her friends didn't know that, because they were drinking the stuff straight from the jug and dancin' and singin' and having a regular old party. I began to relax. Heck, other than a little chicken lopping, I didn't see much difference between this party and the Saturday night dances at the Camp mess hall.

In fact, nothing much happened for several minutes, and the night began catching up with me, I guess, because I was getting a little drowsy, until Doux Doux punched my arm and pointed. The dancers had formed two lines, facing each other, leaving a space in the middle like square dancers do. I guess they were flat out of chickens, because more bottles of clarine appeared and they were passing them down the line, everyone taking swigs while dancing in place.

The white-eyed queen moved to the head of the line, threw her arms up, said something I couldn't hear, and again the drums and dancing stopped. They all stood silently, still swaying a little, but staring into space, like they were waiting for something or someone. And they were.

Whatever was coming out of the underbrush sounded like a herd of thundering elephants. It was probably my imagination, but the tree we were in seemed to vibrate as the crashing noises got closer. Way too close. Doux Doux grabbed my hand so hard I thought it'd break, and pointed down. Leaning over, I saw a black shadow. The closer it got, the bigger it was.

Pulling my feet up onto the branch, I made myself as small as possible. I wanted to shut my eyes tight against the sight, to wish it away, but I couldn't. As if they had a mind of their own, my eyes were drawn to the shadow, then the shine of an enormous bald head as it neared our tree. I held my breath as the monster passed under us, barely three feet below my rear end. When it stepped into the circle of flickering firelight, we got our first good look: seven feet if he was an inch, and walking funny—real stiff and slow. A fluttering stirred in my chest.

Doux Doux was making pitiful little noises, like one of her kittens. For a girl who generally didn't seem to be afraid of anything, even boys, she was turning sissy on me real quick. Of course, I wasn't exactly a picture of bravery and calm myself. As a matter of fact, my ears rang and I was getting those nasty little flashes of light behind my eyes and that black-around-the-edges-feeling I sometimes got right before conking out. I swallowed hard, shook my head, managed to pull my hand from Doux Doux's death grip about the same time that the giant stopped dead in his tracks, turned, and looked straight up at us. His eyes glowed red.

"Zombie," I said, and that's the last thing I remember until I woke up on the ground with Doux Doux shaking me and yelling to beat the band. I managed to sit up, and as the blackness cleared from the edges of my vision, I saw that all the dancers had disappeared into the jungle, leaving me 'n' Doux Doux with a headless chicken, a bonfire, a few empty clarine bottles and, of course, a seven-foot oooh-gah-oooh.

# CHAPTER 8

▼

There's not much nice you can say about a zombie.

As I came to and gathered my wits, though, it occurred to me that on the plus side, even though this one was gigantic, he really wasn't seven feet tall; maybe just six-eight. Or nine. Or ten. And he didn't look all that unfriendly, either. Just kinda simple. Of course, I didn't know whether it was me falling out of the tree or this big guy crashing out of the woods that sent the Haitians packing, but if it *was* him who scattered the voodooists, I figured that Doux Doux and I really had something to worry about, because those folks were pie-eyed on clarine, and if my Uncle Herman is any example, strong drink generally makes a body courageous, if not too smart.

Doux Doux, who was leaning over me, fanning my face, looked up and let out a screech, ending my fuzzy remembrances of drunken relatives.

"What?" I said, trying to sit up, none too successfully. My arms felt like wet noodles and my head still spun.

"He moved," she whispered. "He took a step. This way."

*That* sat me up, but way too fast. Once again I saw sparkles.

"Mais cheré, don't you dare fade out on me again," Doux Doux wailed. She was as white as a sheet and I heard her teeth chattering. So were mine.

"I w-w-won't. Are you all r-r-right?" I managed.

"I t-think so. How about you? Think you can stand up?" She took my hand, never taking her eyes from the zombie.

I let Doux Doux pull me to my feet. As I rose, I gave myself a quick mental medical checkup. No apparent broken parts that I could feel, but I didn't bother looking for scrapes as I was keeping a wary, if somewhat blurry, eye on the hulk in front of us. I gave him a name: Black Frank, because he reminded me of Frankenstein's monster. Not that he had stitches in his head or anything, but he was big and scary. And very black. Black Frank seemed fitting. Besides, my Aunt Annie always says if you know a person by name they're less daunting, which is grown-up talk for not scaring the pee out of you. It wasn't working too well.

"*Z-z-zut,* Doux Doux," I said, my voice quaking, "what are we gonna do?"

"*Mais cheré,* I don't know, but we got to do something. We can't just all stand here looking stupid."

We all just stood there, looking stupid. For Black Frank it seemed natural.

I'd half-hoped one of the Haitians would come back, maybe planning to collect a couple of bucks for taking us to Camp, but no luck. I stared into Frank's eyes. The fire made them glow red. I hoped to heck it was the fire's light.

"Liz-buth-ann, *do* something."

I took a deep breath and pointed my finger at Frank. "*Parlez vous anglaise?*"

Doux Doux thumped me on the back in disgust. "Oh great, genius, you gonna *talk* him to death?"

Black Frank didn't move. Not a smidgen. He didn't even blink, or act like he heard me.

I tried again. "Uh, *creóle?*"

Nothing.

So, I sucked in a chest full of damp jungle air and, with knocking knees, took a step in his direction. I heard Doux Doux mewing behind me, but since Black Frank hadn't reacted to my bold move, I did it again. This time he rocked backwards slightly and his eyes widened, but his feet remained planted and his arms hung limply at his sides.

"Doux Doux, I think he might be a little afraid of us."

"Yeah? Well, I wouldn't stake our lives on it."

But I did, slowly moving to within six feet of him; close enough to where I expected to catch a whiff of decay, but he was surprisingly un-rotten and clean looking. His shirt was at least two sizes too small and his pants only reached half-way down his calves, but they looked like someone had pressed them. In fact, for a dead guy, he wasn't a bad dresser.

"What are you *doing?*" my fearless friend screeched as I inched closer and sized up the enemy and our situation. Unfortunately, when I fainted and fell out of the tree and then Doux Doux jumped down beside me, we had landed between Frank and the voodoo people, which left the big zombie between us and our horses. He stood right smack dab in the middle of the path, with dense bushes on both sides. I knew from experience that thick forest growth surrounded the *houn-*

*fort* in all directions, except for the one path which passed through the clearing. Maybe in the daytime I could have found another way out, but not at night, even in the moonlight.

We had two choices. We could take a chance and follow some chicken-blood-drinking voodooists into the jungle in one direction, or try to get around the zombie and back to our horses in the other. I decided we should take our chances on the lesser of the two evils—skirting a zombie instead of becoming one.

"I think we can get around him, Doux Doux."

"No way. I don't want to get any closer to that, that…monster, Lizbuthann," she growled.

She had a point. Just because Black Frank hadn't done anything bad yet didn't mean he wouldn't. "Okay, okay. Listen. Move up close behind me. I think I figured out something nice about zombies."

Doux Doux crept up and put her hand on my shoulder. "What?"

"They're real slow. And we're real fast. I have a plan. On the count of three, you run left and I'll go right. We can squeeze by him. Duck low, underneath his hands, and once past him head for the horses, but if he follows, forget the horses and hightail it for Camp. Okay?"

"Okay. Wait. What if he gets one of us?" Doux Doux asked.

"Then I'll run for help, because he sure as heck ain't gettin' me. ONE. TWO. THREE!"

We should have practiced. I'd forgotten old Doux Doux didn't know her right from her left. Sure enough, she ran bang into me, we danced a little, and then both took off on Frank's right side. If he hadn't been so slow, he could have easily reached out and snagged us both, but we whizzed by. When we were ten feet down the path, I glanced back. He was just turning around. In the moonlight his eyes no longer glowed red and, with those undersized clothes and that dumb look on his face, he looked more pitiful than scary. But that didn't keep us from beating it home.

Wishes ran like the wind, over streams, down hills and, giving me only seconds to yank my feet up on his neck to avoid snagging barbed wire, he shot through our hole in the fence as though he were threading a needle. I don't reckon I know how to tell when a horse is scared, but from the way Wishes bolted for home, I think he might have been. Anyhow, I let him have his head and hung on for all I was worth, forgiving him his stubborn, barn-runnin' tendencies for a change. Especially since, once we reached home I sort of dumped him and did the same—ran for my own barn.

Once in my backyard, I stripped Daddy's socks from Wishes hoofs, jerked off the saddle, removed the bridle, and put a rope halter on him, but I have to admit, I didn't rub him down like you're supposed to. I just threw a blanket over him and ran for the house. Leaving him "rode hard and put away wet" wasn't a good thing, because Uncle Lloyd said that's what happened to this lady down the street and she didn't look so hot. I made a promise to myself to give my horse a good warm bath in the morning, and left him slurping water.

I deposited my Buster Browns at the door and tiptoed in sock feet through the living room, hoping Pee Wee wouldn't hear me and start squawking. Once in the bathroom, I stripped off my clothes and stuffed them and Daddy's work-socks/horse-footwear, into the bottom of a hamper. I smelled of horse sweat and kid-stink, but didn't dare take a shower for fear of waking my parents. Once in my room, I slid open my bureau drawer, pulled on fresh underwear and dove into bed. I was still breathing hard when Mama came in to check on me.

"Lizbuthann, is everything all right?" she whispered so as not to wake up Sister.

"Yes, Mama. It just got too cold outside. Sorry I woke you up."

My mother looked at the thermometer on the wall, which read eighty degrees, shook her head and went back to bed.

I wasn't lying, I *was* cold. I huddled under the covers, shivering to beat the band and thinking about our disastrous night and wondering what the consequences would be. I never, ever, got away with anything, so doubted I'd start anytime soon.

I'd forgotten to shut the louvers, but didn't want to leave my warm bed to do so. I was feeling real funny, kind of giddy and silly. The light from the aggregate plant shone on the wall and, using my fingers and hands like Uncle Lloyd taught me, I made shadow animals on the wall, first a rabbit, then a barking dog. I finally began growing drowsy and was just slipping off to sleep when I was jolted awake by the sure knowledge that I had seen Black Frank before; at least his silhouette!

I must have yelled or something, because the next thing I knew the lights came on and both Mama and Grandmamma Hetta rushed into my room. I probably would have confessed everything right then and there if my teeth hadn't been chattering so hard, but I guess I got lucky, because instead of telling all and getting restricted to the house for the rest of my life, I just came down with malaria. At least that's what the doctor said.

I suspected I'd been cursed. In fact, later that morning I was sure of it when a witch doctor attacked me with needles. Through a haze of fever and delirium, I saw the boogie man evilly sharpening a two inch dagger on Daddy's whetstone.

"Mama!" I screamed, kicking out and catching my would-be attacker on the elbow. The needle he was sharpening went flying as the witch doctor fell on his behind. I was going after him when Mama grabbed me and held me down on the bed. Feeling her cool hands on my hot skin calmed me and I let her guide my throbbing head back onto the soft pillow.

"Honey, I'm right here," Mama cooed. "Just relax and don't be hitting out at Doctor Cordier. He just got here and he's going to make you well again. Now, just close your eyes because I know how you hate getting shots, but it has to be."

Hate doesn't begin to describe my feelings for needles and shots. I am terrified of them, even though, before we came to Haiti I'd been tortured by about a jillion: smallpox, typhus, tetanus, diphtheria and yellow fever, to name a few.

"I already had my shots," I protested, but my voice was weak and my throat hurt.

"Not for malaria, honey. I'm sorry, but you have to turn over now."

The Haitian doctor had a unique, and to my thinking, vicious, method for administering anti-malarial serum. For starters, he found the biggest, dullest needle in the entire universe, most likely a used one from a veterinarian. Okay, so he did try to sharpen it, but after this futile attempt to un-dull the tip, he drew serum into a syringe, removed the needle, held it, point down, between his first and second fingers and, with the flat of his palm, whacked the living daylights out of my rear in an attempt to deaden the skin. On about the third whack, he plunged the needle into my very tender and not-at-all-dead heinie.

By now, I was caterwauling and yelling things that normally get a body in trouble, but the worst wasn't over by a far cry. Doctor Death still had to clumsily screw the syringe full of very thick serum back onto a needle that was jiggling in my derriere, then pump in the stinging-est serum ever invented.

And he did this three days in a row.

It had to be a curse.

The second day it took both Mama and Grandmother Hetta to hold me down while old Doc Evil used me for a dartboard. The third day he gave me a pill, and took one himself, fifteen minutes before he even attempted the shot. I don't know what was in that pill, but Mama said after that, half the adults in Camp asked for a prescription because I didn't even fight back. It still hurt, but I flat didn't care.

And if those shots weren't bad enough, just when I was about to slip off and away into strange and wondrous fever land, they'd dump me into a bathtub filled with ice water. Malaria, as you can see, is not for the faint of heart.

Doux Doux came to see me on the sixth day, bringing Pee Wee in with her. I guess he'd been really ticked off, what with Mama not letting him into my sick room because I was thrashing around so much she was afraid I'd squash him. And him being so spoiled, Pee Wee began cussing a blue streak, screeching whole strings of words and phrases so vile she'd had to cover his cage most of the time lest Grandmother Hetta and the neighbors got their ears singed. Pee Wee was not a happy bird, and he let me know it by pulling out a whole chunk of my hair and trying to pierce my ear. Which would have been okay with me, because I'd wanted pierced ears for a dog's age, but Great Aunt Elizabeth said only Mexicans did that, so I couldn't.

"How are you feeling?" Doux Doux yelled.

"I ain't deaf, Doux Doux, I just have a fever."

She glanced back at the open door, and whispered, "I thought they'd turned you into a zombie. I swear, I did."

I laughed, and then groaned, because it still hurt to move anything. My skin and bones still felt as if I'd been worked over with a jackhammer. Even tiny little Pee Wee's weight on my head was painful, but I let him be, what with him being so mistreated as of late.

Doux Doux sat on the bed and leaned in close. "The grownups have been asking me about our campout, wondering why we came back home in the middle of the night. I told them you were feeling yucky, which you sure as heck backed up. When I first heard you were sick I thought maybe you were faking, but then I started getting scared when they wouldn't let me see you. What did you tell them?"

I thought about that. Lord only knows what I talked about during those high fevers. "Doesn't much matter what I said, I reckon, 'cause I was delirious and not responsible for my actions. That's what they say in Texas when someone gets drunked up and runs off the road. It should work here, I reckon. Except maybe with Grandmamma Hetta, who holds all drinkers responsible for their actions. She says some day it will actually be against the law to drink beer and drive in Texas, but Daddy says it's a man's right to drive down the road sipping a cool one after work."

Doux Doux looked at me funny. "What on earth are you talking about?"

"I have no idea. See, that's what I'll say. I'll just blame it on the fever."

"Mais cheré, if you say so. I want you to know that since you came down with malaria we all have to wear this stinky old mosquito repellant and take quinine pills every day. They taste bitter and give me a stomachache. Pa just puts quinine water in his gin and says if it worked for the limeys it'll work for him. He says those Brits conquered the whole world on gin and tonic, so those little rat bastard mosquitoes can just look somewhere else to stick their malaria."

Grandmother Hetta came in about that time with two dishes of ice cream. She gave me mine and handed Doux Doux the other. "Miss Dorcas," she said, "I think it might be prudent not to repeat everything your father says. Some folks might get the wrong idea and think you aren't a proper young lady."

"Yes ma'am," Doux Doux said. "I suppose you're right. Why just the other day I was telling someone about Pa's hellacious farts and—"

"Never mind," my grandmother said, rolling her eyes and scooting from the room. We did everything we could to stifle our giggles, but I know she heard us. And I also knew *I'd* hear about it later. But for now, we wolfed down cold, creamy homemade vanilla ice cream that soothed my burning throat. My fever was all the way down to about a hundred-fifty, so I felt a little better, but still woozy and hot. About ten seconds after Pee Wee and I finished my ice cream, I fell asleep and when I woke up, Angela, wearing a dress ablaze with bright pink bougainvillea blossoms, sat by my bed. Doux Doux was gone, as was the blinding headache I'd had for almost a week. Which was a good thing, considering that dress.

Angela felt my forehead. "Ah, better. Your fever has break."

"I feel like I'll break."

"Tomorrow you will be much better. Now, let me take you in for a bath. I will change you sheets while you soak those sore bones and then maybe everyone get a good night's sleep wit'out little white girls making all kind of noises, talkin' all the night."

"Uh, what did I say?"

"Not'ing makes any sense. Just hollerin' and talkin' 'bout someone call Black Frank, whoever that be."

I shrugged and winced. Angela clucked in sympathy at my pain, but gave me a look.

"So, you don' know not'ing about no Black Frank?"

I shook my head. Carefully.

"And," Angela said as she helped me from the bed, "I suppose you don' have no idea how *two* pair of your Papa's best work socks got so dirty it took Angela three days to bleach them out?"

I tried an innocent look, but Angela wasn't buying it. "I've a mind to slap you on the very place where that witch doctor stuck his needles."

"Witch doctor? I thought he was a real doctor."

"Some say so," she huffed, and pushed me towards the warm bath she'd drawn.

As I lay in the water, enjoying the lack of ice cubes and the weightlessness of the soft water against my sore skin, I heard the rest of my family talking quietly as they sat in chairs out on the lawn. Next door, Major Madden sang off key in the shower. Pee Wee sat on the edge of the bathtub, murmuring contented little parrot noises. I sighed with my own contentment, for it was a comfort to know I was safe and getting well and that everything was returning to normal.

Or as normal as life can be in a place where zombies lurk in the night, and a mosquito's bite can be deadly.

# CHAPTER 9

▼

"She is much improved," Doctor Devil told my family. "I do not think there is brain damage."

Daddy grinned. "How can we tell?" he said, and winked at me. Very funny.

Truth is, damaged or not, my brain ached and so did the rest of me. And even though I'd been pronounced "much improved," I was still pretty danged puny, which worked out okay since I had to stay home for the next two weeks to catch up on schoolwork anyhow. It didn't hardly seem fair that I lost ten days out of my life—not to mention that one of those days was my eleventh birthday—and then had to spend the next two weeks making up for it, to boot. Maybe Grandmother Hetta's old saying was right and I was reaping what I'd sown.

Finally the day arrived when I was allowed to take Wishes out for an hour, and he let me know, with a little nip at my shorts, that he was none too pleased that I'd left him alone for so long. Especially since, in his little horsey mind, he probably thought he'd saved me from death by oooh-gah-oooh. He was restless and wanted to gallop, but I reined him in and stayed close to home because, between falling out of trees and then getting drilled by Doctor Doom, my *derriere* was still a mite tender. We didn't even leave Camp, but Doux Doux still wouldn't ride with us. She'd let me know, in no uncertain terms, that it would be a cold day in you-know-where before she signed on for anything more adventuresome than a good comic book.

Since I was both house-bound and weakened, Grandmother Hetta took the opportunity to pressure me into playing with Janet, the big sissy who had come to Camp to live with her aunt. Doux Doux and I already knew, from previous tries when we were pushed to be sociable with her, that Janet wouldn't go near a horse, was scared to even try swinging on our Tarzan ropes, and *forget* swimming in the river. She wanted to have tea parties and play dolls, while Doux Doux and I were more interested in turning dolls into a means of revenge. But, in forced convalescence, and to keep the peace at home, I gave Janet a try and discovered she could at least play cards.

During rainy afternoons, Doux Doux would join us and the three of us played canasta using four decks so the game would last longer. We'd have card books spread all over the living room floor by the time Daddy came home from work. Grandmother and Mama seemed pleased that Doux Doux and I had admitted Janet into our little clique, even if for only a few hours a week. Janet, on the other hand, proved a reluctant friend. In fact, I got the idea she would rather be by herself, and that it was her aunt who had done all the whining about us being neighborly. Heck, Janet didn't even want to talk about Texas, or where she'd gone to school, or anything like that, but one day I overheard Daddy and Uncle Lloyd talking about her family.

"Guess what, Doux Doux?" I whispered the next day. "Wanna know why Janet's here in Haiti, living with her aunt, instead of back home in Texas?"

Wide-eyed, Doux Doux said, "Mais cheré, Janet's way too young to be in circumstances."

"Don't be silly. Of course she is."

"Then why is she here?"

"Because her mama's in jail."

Doux Doux's eyes bulged. "Mais no! What'd she do? Kill someone?"

"Best I can figure, from what Daddy and Uncle Lloyd said, she caught fish for her cats and they threw her in the hoosegow."

My friend gave me a scornful look. "You're makin' that up. They don't arrest folks for fishing."

"Travis County game warden did; caught my Uncle Hooks telephoning fish, and gave him a ticket."

"How can you telephone a fish?" Doux Doux scoffed.

"He took my grandmother's old crank phone, ran the wires into the water, cranked away, and fish came floating to the top. 'Lectrocuted 'em."

"Neat. Wonder where we could get us one of those phones?" Doux Doux got a dreamy look on her face, possibly thinking of unlimited fried fish. She shook her head and got back to the matter at hand.

"Lizbuthann, just what *exactly* did your pa and Uncle Lloyd say about Janet's mother?"

I shut my eyes, trying to recall the conversation. "Well," I opened my eyes, but looked at the ceiling, remembering the words, "Uncle Lloyd said, 'she's doin' time in the Austin jail for running a cat house and hooking.' That's exactly what he said."

Doux Doux burst out laughing.

"What's so darned funny?" I asked, puzzled.

But Doux Doux was laughing so hard she couldn't talk. She kept pointing at me, gasping for breath, until she finally managed, "What...a...dummy."

Her making fun of me was making me mad and Doux Doux must have realized it, because she got enough control of herself to talk, but little hiccup-ey giggles kept escaping. "Lizbuthann, for a smart girl, you can be soooo dumb. Janet's mom's a *hooker!*"

Now I was really bamboozled. Humiliated at being caught out ignorant, I nevertheless swallowed my pride and asked, "What's that?"

"A woman of ill repute. A fallen woman. A *whore*, you nincompoop." She pronounced it *hoor*, which could explain why, when I tried to look it up in the dictionary later that day, I couldn't find a thing.

My face must have told Doux Doux I was still mystified, so she set out to explain about women of the night. I mean, she probably didn't know all that much, but she *had* been to New Orleans, and she did have one full-grown brother who lived there. After her explanation, I still wasn't clear on what these women did to land them in jail, but I did understand enough to know that bringing up the subject with any adult was not a grand idea. I figured, like long division had, all these little mysteries would suddenly become crystal clear someday in the future.

Janet's status took a giant leap in our estimation. Anyone with such an exotic mother couldn't be all bad. In a fit of compassion for the unfortunate, temporarily-motherless child, we even rigged a double rope with a board and built her a sissy swing or two next to our Tarzan ropes so she could join us. So what did the little brat do? Fell out of a swing, ran home bawling, and ratted us out to her aunt. An army of machete-wielding grown-ups cut down a good many of our ropes, effectively severing our friendship with Janet, the snitch, for-*ever*. Lucky for us, she didn't know where all our swings were, and even more fortunate for her, we didn't have time to get a hank of her hair or a snip of a dress before we ended the relationship.

Not that we actually knew how to put together a voodoo doll. Yet. Our voodoo days had pretty much come to a halt the night of the zombie, because I secretly harbored a suspicion that it wasn't a mosquito bite which had made me sick. Doux Doux made no bones about her lack of interest in visiting another *hounfort* as long as she lived.

But all that didn't mean my curiosity was as dead as Black Frank. He was still out there, I knew, because the size gazillion footprints were back. I hadn't seen the big zombie, because I didn't have the nerve to leave the louvers on my bedroom window open at night. I did, however, check the flowerbed beneath my window daily and, once in awhile, there they were: Black Frank's oversized footmarks.

I decided it was time we met again.

Doux Doux wasn't exactly thrilled with the idea, but admitted the timing would be grand, because my mother, father and sister were going to Miami for a couple of weeks, leaving me with Grandmother Hetta. Angela would be around during the day, but at night my grandmother would be in charge; the very grandmother who could snooze through a Texas tornado. Doux Doux and I planned a sleepover, using our birthdays as an excuse.

Since malaria had plumb *rurnt* my eleventh birthday, we decided to have a dual celebration on the day of Doux Doux's twelfth. Grandmother Hetta made lemonade, Angela baked a cake, Clota Boudreaux grilled hotdogs and we invited all the kids in camp to our late afternoon birthday *fête*. By the time everyone left, my grandmother was worn to a frazzle, which was good, because we wanted her out like a light that night; the night we hoped to capture Black Frank.

For a corpse, Black Frank got around pretty good. Over several weeks I took pains to rake the flowerbed each afternoon and check for prints the next morning. A pattern emerged: my zombie almost always came on Saturday night. And that worked out just fine for us, because not only was Grandmother Hetta a heavy sleeper, but Angela, who had taken to staying at our house some nights while my parents were in Miami, had Saturdays off and was leaving for her own home soon after the birthday mess was cleaned up.

"So," Angela said as she gathered her sisal bags to leave the house on the eve of our birthday slumber party, "you girls goin' be good tonight?"

"Not really," I teased. Then I grinned and said, all innocence. "Doux Doux's just gonna sleep over. We'll probably play Monopoly and make fudge."

"I don't plan findin' chocolate mess all over my clean kitchen when I get back," she warned.

"We'll be careful, I promise. So, you're going to Port-au-Prince?"

"How you know I go to Port-au-Prince?"

Rats. "Oh, I don't know, maybe you told me?"

"I don' think I tell little white girls my personal busy-ness, but some of them have big ears and even bigger noses."

Someday, Lord knows when, I am going to have to learn to keep my big trap shut. Doux Doux and I had started hanging out down by the spring where the Haitian women did their laundry, and it was truly amazing what we learned down there. Unlike other adults we knew, Haitians would tell us all sorts of interesting gossip, like which bachelors were kissing the hired help, whose maid was going to have a baby, which household smuggled empty rum bottles down to the dump so no one could see there were so many, and that Angela and her husband were going to Port-au-Prince on Sunday.

"I guess I just heard it somewhere, then. What's the big deal?"

"Is no 'big deal,' smart girl. Just you stay out of Angela's busy-nesses if you know what's good for you. And stay out of trouble tonight. Your *grand-mère* don't need no more troubles right now."

My ears pricked. What did she mean by, "…more troubles right now?"

"What do you mean, 'more troubles right now'?"

Angela sighed. "You ask her. I will see you Monday. In my *clean* kitchen. Oh, and *bon anniversaire*." She reached into her big sisal bag and handed me a package, which I immediately unwrapped. To my delight, Angela had made me a dress to match her bougainvillea affair.

"Oh Angela, this is the most beautiful dress I've ever owned," I cried. "Thank you, *merci*." I gave her a big hug, then we did a two-cheek, French style air kiss before she sailed off to meet her husband. Angela didn't walk, she sailed. Swept. Glided, like a majestic galleon on the sea. As we watched her leave, several of the little kids in Camp ran out to greet her as she cruised along the road, and for each one she had a kind word and a hug. I figured I was the luckiest kid in Camp to have her in our household. I also wondered, for the first time, why she didn't have children of her own. It bore looking into, despite her warning to stay out of her busy-nesses.

Doux Doux and I played Monopoly until Grandmamma Hetta sacked out, then we made fudge, managing, despite good intentions, to spill cocoa all over the floor. We cleaned up as best we could, then went over our plan while impatiently waiting for the fudge to cool.

Just to be on the safe side, I waited to put Pee Wee away for the night until Grandmother was softly snoring, and then, as a test, tossed him into his uncovered cage. My grandmother didn't wake up, despite his ear-splitting squawks and screeches, but lights blinked on in several other households as Pee Wee tried to raise the roof off ours. I threw a towel over his cage and he settled into a little soft cursing, then went totally silent. I looked in on my grandmother. Sound asleep. Perfect. I eased the door to her room shut and went to my own.

"Where'd you put the net?" Doux Doux asked.

I led her into the bedroom closet where I had stashed the fishing net that some folks were probably looking for down by the river about then. I planned to return it the next day, so our weekly Camp fish fry would only be a few fish shy. Besides, we needed that net.

We hauled the heavy net outside and dumped it in the flowerbed. I then raided my father's tool shed, quickly spinning his secret numbers into the lock until I could pop it open and get inside. Don't even ask me how I knew the combination.

Manhandling a wooden ladder to my window, we climbed up onto the roof and spread the fishnet so it just reached the edge of the eave. Then, using a piece of wire I'd requisitioned from Uncle Lloyd's pickup, I rigged a trip wire, snaking it through the window screen, into the bedroom. That done, we put the ladder back in the shed, relocked the door, and went inside.

Once back in my room, I made a wrist loop on the end of the wire so that all I had to do was yank my arm, and *voilá!*: zombie fish. Then, unlike most nights, I cranked the louvers wide open so that when we darkened my room, the lights from the aggregate plant would shine on the wall. The trap was set, and we were the bait.

With all lights blazing in my room, we sat on the beds and ate fudge, read "True Confessions," and listened for any sound announcing Black Frank's arrival. I couldn't really concentrate on the story Doux Doux was reading out loud, even though it was an especially juicy one—the girl not only got mixed up with the wrong boy, he was a *Puerto Rican*! After the sixth or seventh piece, the fudge lost its appeal, but I don't think that's why my mouth was dry. My stomach wasn't so hot, either. I must have looked funny, because I caught Doux Doux studying me.

"What?" I asked.

"You feeling all right, Lizbuthann?"

"Sure I do. Why?"

"Mais cheré," she growled, "don't you dare faint on me tonight. I'm getting a little tired of you swooning every time things get rough."

"I won't. I promise. I think I've figured out why I—"

"Shhhh!" Doux Doux hissed. "I heard something."

My heart gave a little thump, but I willed away the sparkles and shades of gray trying to creep into my eyes. "Okay, this could be it. Act normal. Put away the magazine and get in bed. I'll take care of everything else." And although I was shaking like a cold puppy, I went through the motions of preparing for bedtime just as if everything were normal, just in case Black Frank was watching.

I took my time turning down the bedspread, fluffing my pillow, then hanging my shoes on a wall hook and stuffing them with washrags. I'd taken to this shoe-hanging habit after sliding my foot in with a big fuzzy tarantula one morning. Neither the spider, nor I, was very happy about it, either.

I went through my nightly bedtime routine, not that I thought the zombie was smart enough to notice anything out of the ordinary, but it doesn't hurt to play it safe. After fetching a glass of water for my bed stand, I turned off the lamp and jumped into bed fully dressed, socks and all. The minute I hit the mattress, I pulled a pillow over my head.

"What are you doing?" Doux Doux demanded.

"Whnsjdasnuff?"

"Lizbuthann" she hissed, "take off that pillow! How will you see him if you bury your head?"

I reluctantly removed the pillow and dared a peek at the wall; no shadows or silhouettes other than the lines of the louvers. I sighed with relief and slipped the wrist loop over my hand. "Maybe he won't come tonight," I said, hoping I didn't sound hopeful.

"You *said* he would."

"Well, maybe I was wrong. But just in case, one of us has to stay awake. I'll take the first watch if you want." I pushed myself up so I was sitting, and leaned against a pillow, but, realizing my head was actually resting on the screen, I scrunched down some. Who knew what a zombie was going to do? He could poke a machete right through the screen and pull my brains out and eat them. Or….

"Lizbuthann! He's here!" was the next thing I heard. My eyes flew open and I yanked hard on the trip wire around my wrist. I felt it give and heard the rocks we'd weighted the net with begin scraping down the tin roof, making enough noise to wake the dead. I feared that's just what we'd done. Doux Doux and I watched with frightened fascination as the net fell, with a SWISH, right over Black Frank's head. He never even batted an eyelash, if he had any; he just stood there.

"Mais cheré, now what?" Doux Doux asked.

"Huh?"

"What do we do, now that we have him?"

"Uh, well, I hadn't really thought about it."

"What?" Doux Doux screeched. I shushed her and pointed toward my grandmother's room. "What?" she said again, this time in a hissy whisper. "You said you had it all planned out."

"I did. I just didn't plan this far. What do you think we should do?"

"Well, we could just go back to bed and leave him standing there in the fishnet. Then when everyone wakes up in the morning and finds him in their stolen net, we'll be on restriction for the rest of our lives." Doux Doux has a sarcastic streak on occasion and I wasn't in the mood for it. In fact, her being a smarty pants gave me a dash of bravery. Or stupidity.

"I'm going out to talk to him."

"Are you nuts?"

"Look, Doux Doux, we already know he's slow. Look at him. He's had a net on his head for several minutes and he's just now trying to see what it is." We watched as Black Frank got his big hand tangled in the net. He moved as if he lived in molasses. "See. We can try to talk to him. Besides, if nothing else, we have to get the net back before he walks off with it."

Doux Doux hesitated, then said, "I guess you're right."

We put on our shoes and headed for the back door. On the way out, I peeked in on Grandmamma Hetta, who was snoozing nicely. When we tiptoed by Pee Wee's cage he made a little chirp, but when I lifted a corner of the cover, I could see he had his head buried under his wing. Satisfied that we were safe, we slipped out the back door and into the backyard where Black Frank stood, netted, not twenty feet away. He hadn't moved an inch.

"Frank," I whispered. He was still looking in the window, but on hearing me, slowly turned his head. I took a step toward him and pointed to myself. "*Bon nuit, monsieur, je m'appellel Elisabeth,*" I said politely, introducing myself with my French name. I pointed at Doux Doux and said her name. She gave me a disgusted shake of her head.

"Well," I said, "what do you *want* me to say?"

"Ask him if he's a zombie."

I gave her a look she deserved, then turned to Black Frank, who seemed to be grinning. Or snarling. It's hard to tell with him. Anyway, his big white teeth were showing. Nothing ventured, nothing gained, my Grandmamma Hetta always says. I pointed at him and asked, "*Comment t'appelles-tu?*"

His lips moved, like he was chewing something tough, which I really didn't want to think about. It was hard to see all that well through the fishnet, but it looked as if he were trying to talk. We waited. Watching him struggle to speak, I was reminded of one of my great-something-or-others who'd had a stroke and had to take time to form words she already had in her brain.

Doux Doux fidgeted and we were both having second thoughts about being caught out in the yard at night with a netted giant. After what seemed like an eternity, Black Frank mumbled, "François."

"Aha!" I said. "So his name *is* Frank. Instead of Black Frank, we'll call him François Noir."

Doux Doux rolled her eyes. "Mais, so what? What's important is that he talked! Come on, ask him if he's a zombie."

"I will not. It doesn't seem polite."

"Polite? Are you nuts? Okay, then, ask him where he lives. Is that *polite* enough for you?"

"Why don't you spend more time learning Creole and less time telling me what to say, Doux Doux?"

She glared at me and I thought we were about to have a fight, but this was definitely not the time, so I did like she said and asked François Noir where he lived. He slowly, and I do mean sloow-ly, turned and pointed down the road beyond the aggregate plant.

I was just getting ready to ask for a lit-tle more detail when the shift change whistle at the gravel plant blew, startling us all. François Noir, as if on cue from the signal, tried to take a step toward the bluff, then stopped in confusion. The net wouldn't allow him to move forward. His eyes grew wide, his bottom lip trembled, and he looked ready to cry.

"Doux Doux, we have to turn him loose. The night shift guys will be coming back to Camp, and Uncle Lloyd always drives by to check on the house when Daddy's not here. Help me get the net off."

"No how. No chance. I'm not gettin' that close."

"Okay then, I'll do it myself." I walked right up to François Noir and began tugging on the net, but he was too tall and too tangled. I cursed myself for putting the ladder away, because now there was no time to retrieve it before Uncle Lloyd came rolling in.

"Doux Doux, go get me a knife."

"Now, that's the best idea you've had all night, cheré." She ran into the kitchen and came back out wielding Guilliame's three-foot-long, razor sharp machete. François Noir took one look at it and began to whimper. Big tears ran down his cheeks.

"Oh, no. Poor thing, he thinks we're going to hurt him," Doux Doux said, forgetting she was afraid of him. She looked ready to cry herself. Just what I needed, two bawl babies on my hands and Uncle Lloyd heading up the hill any minute.

Doux Doux dropped the machete and ran over to help me untangle the huge man from our trap. Working together, we had some success, managing to drag the net from François Noir's head, but as soon as he could move, the big zombie began trudging toward the bluff. And although only one of his huge bare feet was still snarled in the fishnet, he was dragging Doux Doux, me, and the net along behind him. We had to get him free before he tried to go down the side of the bluff or he'd probably break his neck.

I let go of the net, ran back for the machete and, with a mighty swing, severed the fishnet behind his heel. Paying no mind to the piece of net still attached to his foot, he disappeared over the edge of the bluff just as the lights of Uncle Lloyd's pickup flashed on the front of the house.

Doux Doux and I dropped to the ground, shimmied through the back door and slid the inside bolt shut just before my uncle jiggled the door handle to make sure it was locked. We sprawled on the kitchen floor, not daring to breathe, until we heard him drive away. Evidently he hadn't spotted the machete and fishnet in the backyard.

Giggles bubbled up and we were rolling and wriggling on the kitchen floor, doing our best not to laugh out loud, when the lights suddenly blazed on and our laughter froze in our throats.

"What on earth are you girls doing down there? It's way past your bedtime," Grandmamma Hetta scolded, squinting at us. Without her glasses, I knew we were just a blur, so I grabbed a towel and started scrubbing the linoleum.

"Uh, we had to clean up some cocoa powder we spilled before Angela gets back."

"Well, you can do it in the morning. After church. Now get to bed so a body can sleep. Scoot."

Doux Doux and I peeled down to our underwear, dove into bed, and giggled for at least ten minutes more before falling asleep. But before I dozed off, I wondered where François Noir slept. And who took care of him. He surely didn't look underfed and his clothes, although they didn't fit so good, were clean. François Noir was important to someone, but who? The voodoo queen we'd seen at the *hounfort*? And if so, did that mean he really *was* a zombie? Brenda Starr would want to know and, as she would do, I intended to investigate.

# CHAPTER 10

▼

"Angela, do you think zombies have family?"

Today she wore poppies, great orange ones, printed on black cotton. Bright green stems and leaves formed stripes from the sweetheart neckline to a mid-knee hem.

Angela stiffened at my question, but kept her back to me and continued peeling potatoes. I half expected her to give me heck for bringing up the zombie subject, so I was surprised by her tone and answer. "I pray so, *bébé,*" she said softly.

In fact, I was so encouraged by her mild reaction that I dared another question where smart little angels would fear to tread. "And do you think they cry?" I asked, trying to sound matter-of-fact.

I'd pushed my luck. Angela turned and planted her hands on her hips, a sure-fire way to normally send me scurrying for cover, but I held my ground. Hinging from the waist, she leaned down with her nose about two inches from mine. Her breath smelled of peppermint and her skin gave off the tangy scent of the lime juice she used to lighten her skin. "Why you ask such question? What you been doin' behind Angela's back that she tol' you not to mess wit'?"

Her quick anger, all aimed in my direction, was pretty darned intimidating, but I stood firm when someone with more common sense would have fled. I swallowed my fear because I hoped that somehow Angela could help me figure out who, or what, François Noir really was. If she didn't kill me first.

Nose to nose, we had us a Haitian standoff going until I blinked, took a step back and shrugged. "I was just kinda wondering, that's all. I mean, if zombies are dead, and they had a funeral, what happens when, later on, some relative sees them up and wandering around? Would they still take care of them? Say, give them food and clean clothes and stuff?"

Tears sprang into Angela's eyes and nothing, not her fury or scorn, could have made me back off any faster. The last thing on earth I wanted to do was hurt her, but it looked as though I'd done just that. But why? Contrary to popular opinion, I do feel other folk's upsets, and hers made me ashamed of myself. Not knowing what else to do, I just stood there until Angela straightened up, wiped her eyes and sighed.

"Yes, child," she said. "I t'ink any family, and for sure any woman, would do anyt'ing to regain a child they t'ought lost. Getting it back would be a…God's…*miracle*. No matter," she got a faraway look in her eyes, "how…*dégâté*…that child be."

Angela gently pushed me from the kitchen, finishing her nudge with a love tap on my *derriere*. This conversation, it seemed, was over. I dove for the French-English dictionary. *Dégât* seemed to mean damaged, which pretty much would describe a guy who'd been dead for awhile.

"I think Angela may have had a kid that died," I told Doux Doux later that day.

"Mais cheré, how sad," she said. She had lost a little brother when she was just five, but her family still mourned his loss. Walter Boudreaux had lived only one short week, but still left a sad memory.

"If Walter came back as a zombie, do you think your mother would take him in?"

Doux Doux thought about this for a long minute and then asked, as serious as can be, "Would he be a pickaninny?"

Even though she'd used a word I wasn't allowed to use, her solemn question struck me as uncommonly funny, and I broke into giggles as I tried picturing the Boudreauxs with a little brown child.

Doux Doux's parents were not all that keen on Negroes. In fact, that was the only thing she and I ever really fought about. When we first became friends she used the "n" word a lot and said all Negroes were stupid and lazy, even though I don't think she really believed what she said herself. She loved Angela, and I know for sure she didn't think Angela was stupid or lazy. Doux Doux just had a bad habit of parroting her Daddy's dumb ideas, which I sure wouldn't have done when it made him sound so danged ignorant. In fact, he went nuts when my father even *suggested* we hire Robert, the part-time bartender from the Sans Souci hotel, to teach school in Péligre. Truth was, many of the grownups, even the ones who had practically turned the raising of their children over to their maids, couldn't imagine the little darlings being educated by a someone who wasn't lily-white.

Which became downright ironical when Miss Momo Iwakari showed up.

World War II had ended just a few years before and had left many folks in Camp with a serious dislike for the Japanese. Once, when we were at the beach, a man named Don had pointed out little round scars all over his chest and back where his Japanese captors had ground out their cigarettes. I had nightmares about this for a while and was grateful that neither my parents nor any other relative smoked, because with my penchant for trouble they might be tempted to flick an ash or two in my direction. And I was also thankful that my father, who had a bum leg from a horse accident when he was young, never went to war. Uncle Lloyd, who had been in the navy, thought the only good Jap was a dead Jap, which is why we were allowed to say "Jap" when we couldn't use the "n" word.

I didn't know anything about Japs except for what I'd read in a book I'd had back in Texas. It had drawings and woodcuts of people and typical scenery, along with descriptions of things like tea ceremonies. I was drawn to the prints of timid-looking women in kimonos pouring tea, or dancing with fans. They were called geishas, and I wasn't quite sure what they did besides look good for those fierce-looking samurais who, the book said, were prone to falling on their swords when they messed up. Seemed a mite severe to me.

Momo Iwakari looked nothing like anyone in that book. In her mid-twenties, she was short, but slightly stocky, and even though she had Japanese features, her clothes were western. Her shiny black hair was worn in a sort of Buster Brown "do" that looked like she'd put a bowl over her head and cut around it. She spoke English with a funny accent that someone said was typical Californian, but which I thought sounded Yankee-ish, having never known any Californians. My great aunt Elizabeth, I remember, said that we had a cousin with "tendencies" who had to go there to live with others of his sort, but I didn't have any idea what that meant, so I decided I'd wait until we were better acquainted before I asked if she knew him.

Miss Momo Iwakari was also our new schoolteacher and needless to say, as kids will do, we immediately nicknamed her Momo Harikari. From the day she first set foot in Camp, things just plumb went to heck in a hand basket.

Just for starters, we now had to attend school five days a week. At eight o'clock in the morning! After months of living on a loose schedule, we were totally unprepared for such a drastic and bothersome thing as regular hours and classes. And we certainly weren't ready for Miss Harikari.

"What, Elizabeth, is that in your mouth?" she demanded on that first day of school.

"Uh, bubble gum?"

"Is it, or isn't it?"

I felt my cheeks flame. "It is. Bubble gum."

"And why are you chewing it in my classroom?"

Her question stumped me. Instead of just telling me to spit it out, like any other teacher would do, she was giving me a way out. So, thinking quickly, I said, "I have to chew it to clear my ears. Otherwise they stop up." Boy, sometimes I'm so clever I scare myself.

"I see. Well, Elizabeth, if you must chew something for health reasons, I don't see why it needs to be full of sugar. Now, spit that out and try this. It's very good for you and won't rot your teeth." She handed me a tissue to spit my gum into—which I was very reluctant to do since I had been building it up, a piece at a time, over five days—as well as a square of something black. I eyed the stuff suspiciously.

"Put in on your tongue," she said.

I did. Salty. Not bad. Until it got wet and began to grow, and grow, and become very slimy. All I could think of was raw oysters, which I'd tried only once and ended up spitting back into my plate.

I gagged, spit the gob into my hand and croaked, "What *is* this stuff?"

"Seaweed. Very nutritional and the only thing I allow to be chewed in my classroom. I also allow cough drops, but not the cherry-flavored ones. I have my own special kind, so if you have a cough, just ask." No one, during the rest of the years we were together, dared cough.

Miss Iwakari was a stickler for rules, even calling role each morning, which we thought was hilarious since I was the only fifth grader, Doux Doux the only one in sixth, Janice represented the fourth, and the other six kids were in third, second and first grades. Since our home school lesson plans were dictated by Calvert Course, we devoted the first two hours each day to that curriculum, working separately, but all seated around a long, wide table in the center of the room. Miss Iwakari desk was at the end of the table, and a chalkboard covered the wall behind her.

Miss Iwakari's cruised around our table during Calvert Course time, spending a few minutes with each student and once in awhile helping those who held up a hand. Then, from ten until twelve, we had a class project in which we were all involved. One of the most memorable, and lengthiest, was a huge Mercator pro-jection (flat map) of the world on butcher paper, with each country painstakingly drawn and colored by hand. Once a country was on the map we had to do a report on its language, customs and dumb stuff like their major exports.

But all that came later. It was only Miss Iwakari's second day on the job when our worlds collided. And once again, I found myself at the center of the conflict. It was the "fixin'" thing that did it.

Miss Iwakari gave us homework on her very first day, probably just to let us know she wasn't someone to monkey with. We were to write a five-hun-dred-or-less-word essay describing our families and where we had lived in the United States. Since we all came from Texas, we thought the last part pretty silly; everyone in the whole wide world knows about Texas. But I dutifully wrote of the wonders of my home state and what I missed most, like Dr. Pepper, Brenda Starr and marshmallows. A grand report, if I do say so myself.

On day two, Doux Doux read her paper first, which I thought was pretty bor-ing because she left out a lot of really neat stuff, like how her dad could fart on command and her littlest brother was a bed-wetter. Miss Iwakari stopped Doux Doux several times to remind her that "that" is not pronounced "dat" even if her father said it that way. Then it was my turn.

"'My family and Texas,'" I began, then paused until Miss Iwakari gave me an encouraging nod. "'When we were fixin' to come here…'"

Miss Iwakari's shriek stopped me in mid-sentence. I looked at her, expecting to find a lizard on her head or something, but she just stared at me with an expression of pure horror, like maybe that lizard was on *my* head. No such luck.

"When you were *what?*" the teacher asked. I looked at my classmates, who were clearly as puzzled as I was.

"What, what?"

"Read it again."

"Okay. 'When we were fixin'…'"

"Stop!"

I stopped.

"What is that word? Write it on the board, please."

"Which word?" I asked, now completely bamboozled.

"The last one."

"Fixin'?"

"Yes. Write it on the board, please."

I moved to the board, picked up the chalk and printed, **FIXING**.

Miss Iwakari, while I was writing, had opened the huge dictionary on her desk. She'd brought it with her all the way from California and it was one of those big thick things that weighed a ton and you normally only found in libraries. She thumped the book. "Look it up, please."

"Look it up?" I asked. "Everyone knows what fixin' means." Except, it seemed, Californians, but of course I didn't say that.

She tapped the book again. "Look it up."

I dutifully turned the pages and came to **FIX.** There were several meanings. "Please read them to the class, Elizabeth."

"'Fasten firmly. To set firmly in the mind. To make rigid. To make permanent. To establish definitely. To set in order. To repair.'"

"Good, Elizabeth. Now, tell me what your opening sentence implies."

Now I was good and confused. "Implies?"

"What it means. What are you trying to say?"

"That we were fixin' to leave Texas and come here," I said, with a hint of impatience. What was wrong with this woman? Didn't she speak English?

Seeing I was genuinely flummoxed, Miss Iwakari turned to the class. "Can anyone here tell me what Elizabeth is trying to say?"

All hands flew into the air. "Dorcas?"

My best friend to the rescue. "Mais, she means that they were fixin' to come here. You know, get ready. 'Course, it has another meaning, but that's at Thanksgiving when we have turkey with all the fixin's."

Miss Iwakari sighed, walked to the chalkboard, erased my **FIXING** and wrote, **COLLOQUIALISM.** After only two days in this teacher's presence, everyone already knew to grab their personal dictionaries and look it up. I riffled through Miss Harikari's monster-sized book until I found it:

**Colloquialism: A colloquial expression; characteristic of spoken or written communication that seeks to imitate formal speech.**

"Fixing," Miss Iwakari said, "is obviously a colloquialism with which I am unfamiliar. In this classroom, all papers will be written in proper English and we will also speak it. I will not have my students sounding like...hillpersons."

She picked up my essay, fixed it with a critical eye, and added, "And penmanship must be legible. Because you did not know this, Elizabeth, you are allowed to *print* your paper for tomorrow's class. We will begin cursive classes immediately."

I told her that if she wanted a cursive teacher she couldn't do better than my Uncle Lloyd. Look what he's done for Pee Wee.

I ate dinner with Doux Doux that night and the Boudreaux kids gave me a hard time about my grueling day at the hands of the dreaded Harikari. Everyone was having a grand old giggle at my expense until a bellow from the head of the table cut us short.

"Hillbillies?" Mr. Boudreaux roared. "Mais, where does dat Jap get off calling us hillbillies?"

Doux Doux's mom shot him a dirty look. "Honey, you shouldn't be talking about the teacher like that. She's an American citizen, born in the United States, whose family was treated unfairly during the war. Growing up in a relocation camp couldn't have been easy."

"What's a relocation camp?" I asked, too fascinated with this piece of information to tell them that Miss Iwakari didn't exactly call us hillbillies, but "hillpersons."

"Prison," he barked, threw down his fork, and stomped off. As he left he added, "Where the little yellow bastards belong."

"Our teacher was in prison?" I asked.

"No, Lizbuthann. During the war Momo's family was moved, relocated they called it, to an inland camp, away from the California coastline, so they couldn't collaborate with the enemy."

"What's collaborate?" one of Doux Doux's brothers asked.

"Spy," I said. "Give information to the other side, especially Nazis." I didn't read Brenda Starr for nothing.

Clota Boudreaux gave me a squinty look, but then nodded. "Well, yes, that's what it means, but I'm quite sure Momo's family had no intention of doing so. Now I think it's time you went on home, Lizbuthann. Tomorrow is a school day."

Boy, did I know it. And I still had that essay to rewrite, which I did, burning the midnight oil like Abe Lincoln to get it right. After all my effort, you can imagine I was pretty disappointed when I got to the schoolhouse the next morning to find a note on the door saying that school was cancelled for the day. Walking to the rear of the building, I heard voices, When I peeked in a window, I saw Miss Iwakari and several parents having an argument. The teacher's cheeks were bright red and she had taken on a stubborn stance that I knew all too well, having used it myself a few times.

Straining to hear what was going on, I could only pick up the occasional word because the windows were shut tight. I knew from experience that I could crawl under the building and hear everything, but a past dust-up with a foot-long centipede that lived under there had a way of discouraging me from trying it again.

Just as my natural-born nosiness was about to overcome what little good sense I have, I caught the word "fixin'."

Minutes later the meeting broke up and Doux Doux's dad, along with two other parents, stormed from the building, leaving the door open. They looked as unhappy as I felt, because I just knew I had landed in deep you-know-what. Again. I joined the other kids who were milling around out front of the schoolhouse like cattle, took a deep breath, and stepped in through the front door to apologize for all the trouble I'd caused.

Miss Iwakari wasn't in the main part of the school room, but I heard soft sobs coming from the bathroom. What had I done? I crept out, softly shutting the door behind me, then broke into a run straight for home.

Mama, my grandmother and Angela were sitting at the dining room table having a cup of coffee and from their grim looks, I guessed the bad news had already beat me home. Or maybe not, because my mother asked, "Honey, why aren't you in school? Did y'all get a holiday that isn't on the schedule?"

"Uh, sort of," I mumbled.

"Is Momo sick?"

"Not exactly."

Mother huffed a big breath. "Lizbuthann, are you going to tell us what's wrong, or do I have to go find Momo?" When I said nothing, she narrowed her eyes. "Did you get kicked out of school *already*? It's only been three days!"

Her disapproving gaze sent me sidling towards the protection of Grandmamma Hetta, who put an arm around me and patted my hand. "Just tell us what's going on, Honey," she said, giving me a little squeeze of encouragement. So I did. When I finished, both Mama and my grandmother looked puzzled.

"I don't understand the problem. Did you rewrite the paper?" my mother asked.

I bobbed my head and pulled it from my notebook. "But I didn't get a chance to show it to Miss Hari...uh, Iwakari."

Mother raised an eyebrow at my near-slip, but she let it pass. "I guess we'd better go to the school house and straighten this out. Angela, will you keep an eye on the little one? She gets another pill in an hour if we're not back. Oh, and don't forget, no carbonated beverages, but she can have iced tea."

We walked up the dirt road that divided Camp down the middle, turned left in front of the mess hall, and arrived at the schoolhouse just as Miss Iwakari was leaving for her little cottage next door. Her eyes, which always looked puffy to me, were more so, and her cheeks were still red but she smiled a brave smile when she saw the three of us. I ran ahead.

"Miss Iwakari, I'm really sorry I caused so much trouble. I rewrote the essay, so maybe this will fix, uh, repair the problem." I offered the paper, which she took but didn't look at.

She gave us a little polite bow and said, "Please, won't you come in." For the first time, I detected a slight "r" sound to her "l's." Not only that, her entire manner had changed from bossy to, dare I say it? Shy! Like she had slipped into a movie role.

I had seen many a Southern woman go fey and timid in the presence of men, but it was one heck of a shock to watch my teacher change from Attila the Hun to geisha girl. My astonished stare must have brought her around, because she shook off the bowing, along with the accent, and said, "Elizabeth Ann, perhaps it is best if you stayed outside while I talk with your grandmother and mother."

Rats. Reluctantly, I backed out of the cottage, but as soon as the screen door slammed behind me, I about-faced and sat down, *very* close to the door.

"I have made a terrific mistake," Miss Iwakari said. We kids had already noticed that she got the words 'terrific' and 'terrible' mixed up sometimes. When she didn't get a response, she corrected herself. "I mean I have made a terrible mistake. I called your children a bad name."

"You did?" Mother asked.

"Yes. I said I would not allow your children to talk like hillpersons and that was an insult and not nice on my part. And now I feel I must take drastic action to atone."

Oh no! It was worse than I thought. I jerked open the screen door and ran inside. "You're not," I blurted, "going to fall on your sword are you?"

A horrified silence enveloped the room. Mother was so appalled that her mouth worked, but nothing came out. Grandmamma Hetta's cheeks turned a brighter shade of crimson than Miss Iwakari's. The four of us stood in various states of shock until, with a deep chortle that started with a very un-Japanese-lady-like guffaw, Momo Iwakari began to laugh and, unable to resist, we soon all had tears running down our cheeks. She finally caught her breath and managed to splutter, "Oh, my. That was so…bad…it's good."

I started to say something, but Grandmamma Hetta put her hand over my mouth. "I think, young lady, you'd best quit while you're ahead." And for once, I did.

But just because Miss Iwakari and I made our peace, didn't mean WWII was over in Camp. Uncle Lloyd said he didn't know what the hullabaloo was about; he figured calling the Boudreauxs hillbillies was a step up from what they really were: Louisiana bayou trash. Never mind that they had lived in Texas for years.

He also said that, as far as he was concerned, he liked to call a Jap a spade, but to keep the peace he'd make an effort to do better. Others agreed, but only after a couple of good old shouting matches between some parents, a letter of semi-apology from Miss Iwakari and a verbal treaty that colloquialisms, such as "fixing" and "y'all" would not be used in written reports. We would be allowed to speak Texan, but only if we could prove we knew the proper English words. "Ain't" was ruled out completely.

Any further differences would be sent to a committee consisting of Mother, Clota Boudreaux and Cynthia Smith, an uncommonly patient woman with excellent penmanship who was charged with straightening out mine.

Unsaid in any meeting, but understood all over camp, was that the word "Jap" was taboo.

Miss Iwakari ruled that henceforth her students would address her not as Miss Iwakari, which might *possibly* be mispronounced, but as Momo-san. Some of the men who had been in the war grumbled a little about that, but couldn't exactly find fault with it.

And just when our version of WWII ended, Haiti erupted in its own upheaval. It started right at our jobsite and this time, it wasn't my fault. Well, not entirely.

# C H A P T E R   11

▼

No sign of François Noir since the night, weeks before, when we'd netted him.

I left the louvers behind my bed open each night in hopes of seeing his silhouette, but finally, and a little sadly, I decided I'd scared him off for good.

I'd done a little investigating into how he'd disappeared over the bluff behind our house so handily and found, to my delight, that what looked for all the world like a straight drop-off really wasn't. A large boulder was lodged just under the end of the lawn and a deep cut—a path—circled it and lead into a shallow cave. From there an old goat trail zigzagged down through dense brush, ending up right next to the main road. Neither the path nor the cave were obvious from below.

I didn't tell Doux Doux of my discovery, but instead bided my time until I could put such a wonderful find to good use. The perfect opportunity came when, after waiting until I was sure no grownups were around, I set it up for Doux Doux to watch me tumble from Wishes, over the bluff's edge.

"Mais cheré!" she screamed. Crouching in the cave, I stifled my giggles as I heard her sandals flapping in her rush to where I'd vanished into thin air. When she knelt and peered over the bluff, expecting to see my broken body sprawled on the road below, I popped up right in her face and scared the you-know-what out of her.

Howling with laughter, I crawled back up the path, but Doux Doux was so furious she gave me a goodly whack on the shoulder that very nearly *really* pushed me over the edge. I tried to tease her out of her ill humor, but she stomped off and sulked a spell. Later that day, though, she had to admit that I'd pulled a good one on her, and said maybe we ought to play a prank on that dumb Janet. I agreed, but rethought it; what with Janet's big fat mouth, it was probably best to keep the path and cave our little secret, just in case François Noir ever returned.

We might have searched for him, but what with schoolwork, regular chores, Tarzan ropes and the like, we didn't get around to it. Well that, and the fact that Doux Doux swore an oath against having any more to do with voodoo or zombies. We were lucky, she said, we hadn't already ended up as oooh-gah-ooohs ourselves, or at the very least caught and punished for whacking a hole in the Camp fishnet. We were, she declared, just asking for it if we kept messing around with dead people. So we didn't.

The day after we'd borrowed that net for our little zombie-fishing expedition, we returned it to the river. Since we figured the men who checked their catch each morning would probably look downstream for the missing net, we rode along the riverbank a bit before snagging it on a log near shore. Sure enough, someone found it right away, and as luck would have it, Doux Doux and I were playing shuffleboard at the clubhouse when, thanks to us, a legend was born.

"Must'a been a monster," I overheard the safety engineer say. Andy Adams was an avid fisherman with a reputation for adding a foot or two to the ones that got away, and when I heard the word "monster" I figured we were in for one of his tall fish tales. I elbowed Doux Doux and winked. She put down her puck, we eased closer and climbed on barstools and ordered orange sodas.

"Yep," Andy said between gulps of beer, "damned fish tore a hole in that net you could drive a D-8 dozer through. Man, I'd sure like to of snagged that sumbitch."

Doux Doux jabbed me in the ribs and I felt her silently jiggling next to me. I didn't dare look at her. While the men speculated on what manner of demon fish could tear such a hole in that sturdy net, we wrapped our lips around the bottle necks to keep from giggling ourselves off those stools. I longed to brag about what *we'd* bagged in their dumb old fishnet.

We got ourselves under control enough to hang around and listen to the men who, after a few more beers, talked a fantasy fish into the real thing. A legend was born: Trashrack, the colossal cat.

Trashrack—so named because catfish are bottom-feeding scavengers—soon became the most sought-after creature in the Artibonite River Valley and his size grew with the number of times he got away. Folks—an acceptable colloquialism according to Momo-san *if* you knew the proper word was "people"—came from all over to try catching him. Rumors of sightings abounded. Mangled hooks were proudly displayed, proof that once again the wily cat had barely escaped. Harry Oxley, who by his own account was the best damned fisherman in the entire world, became obsessed and spent all his free time at the river until his wife threatened to let him sleep with that "damned overgrown anchovy." It wasn't long before Doux Doux and I plumb forgot we'd created the Trashrack myth ourselves, and spent hours manning our poles, trying to land him. Doux Doux began a serious search for a crank-type telephone to give him a little final call.

But even the quest for Trashrack took second fiddle as the Camp prepared for President Paul Magloire's visit. I never quite understood why, after Daddy had been dumping concrete into that dam for months, Magloire's was to be the first "official" bucket poured, but my father said it was all about politics and I guess that about said it all. He also said that Haiti was officially a democracy, which was a bucket of you-know-what.

For a month before the ceremony, people in uniform and dress suits began showing up to scout out suitable sites for tents, tables and the like. The mess hall cook was handed a presidential menu by one of the big man's aides and there was a brief scramble to locate *pâté de foie gras*, truffles and a recipe for *petit fours*— which is French for puny little cakes—until Cookie pitched a hissy and threatened to throw in the dish towel. The camp manager stepped in and suggested we throw a down-home Texas barbeque instead, and word came back via one of the suits that Magloire would be delighted. Turned out he was a Roy Rogers fan.

Daddy and Uncle Lloyd butchered a cow because they were raised on a ranch and knew how, and someone else built a huge pit for roasting it. Pounds of pinto beans simmered in cast iron wash pots, and sack after sack of potatoes got boiled, peeled and chopped for salad, but it was Grandmother Hetta's ingenuity that perfected the *piece de resistance.*

In my now-infamous "fixing" report, I'd mentioned that since leaving Texas I'd especially missed marshmallows and Dr. Pepper. My grandmother couldn't do much about the Dr. Pepper—although we tried a little prune juice and 7-Up concoction that tasted okay but gave us the runs—but she decided that marshmallows couldn't be all that hard to make. She and Momo-san turned it into a school chemistry experiment.

Using Momo-san's kitchen as a laboratory, we combined gelatin, sugar and egg whites with mixed results until perfecting a pretty good substitute. The gelatin mixture, once set, punched into rounds with a cookie cutter and rolled in powdered sugar, even resembled the store-bought ones back home. Better yet, they tasted and toasted like the real thing. For the big barbeque we made two hundred pink ones and the Camp manager got his hands on a bunch of Hershey bars that hadn't turned white yet and only had a few bugs in them. Grandmother already knew how to make graham crackers, so we were all set for a s'more fest. The dedication/barbeque/rodeo promised to be a grand event.

Rodeo? Well, sort of. When we found out that President Magloire was a western movie fan—and since we were bona fide Texans—Doux Doux and I put together a little riding and Wild West exhibition for his entertainment. We practiced daily, recruiting little kids as Indians and buffalo. I planned a perfect Grand Finale.

The officials scheduled a morning dedication so we could eat lunch before the daily rain, but it was still plenty hot. Tents and big containers of iced lemonade helped keep us cool as we anxiously awaited the President's *entourage*—that's French for a bunch of cars.

As part of the dedication ceremony, Momo-san's students, plus kids from the Haitian school, were taught Paul Magloire's political theme song by a very beautiful Haitian woman from Port-au-Prince. Some said she was the big man's fancy lady, and that she was: fancy. A vision of cool and chic in silk, Monique glided elegantly into our schoolhouse and our hearts. She was very pale, petite, soft spoken and made every woman in Camp, even my mother, who was well known for her beauty and fashionable clothes, look like a country bumpkin. I gawked at the woman's soft leather super-high high heels, then at my scuffed Buster Browns and felt like crawling under a rock. Even Momo-san, who was not easily impressed, was impressed.

Monique however, for all her mystique, turned out to be friendly, fun, and a little mischievous. Especially when, for the first time since the school house was built, there was a sudden and mysterious parade of male visitors. In fact, every man who lived in the bachelor's quarters turned up at one time or another, pretending a sudden, great interest in us kids. Uncle Lloyd showed up to check on the wiring, but Daddy said it was Monique's wiring he was interested in. Monique flirted with all of them, but each felt he was the only one. I had met my very first *femme fatale*.

What with learning new songs, making marshmallows and practicing for my rodeo, I was afraid I might not get into Port-au-Prince to buy my Grande Finale surprise, but Clota Boudreaux decided to go shopping, so Doux Doux and I tagged along and headed straight, as we always did, for the Iron Market.

The Iron Market was really a big old flea market under a metal roof. It was smelly, dirty and fascinating. You could buy all sorts of neat things there, like iguanas and boa constrictors, birds and cats, and plastic buckets and baskets, but I was after caps for my empty pistol. How could you have a cowboy and Indian show without cap guns? I was disappointed when they had no caps in town, but I did find a substitute. The show must go on, you know.

We were about to burst with lemonade while we waited for the fleet of shiny cars to arrive; limousines really, big and black with Haitian flags on their glossy fenders.

"Wow," I said. "What kind of cars are those?"

"Citroens," Monique told me.

"Lemons?" I said. "Daddy said he had one of those once, but it didn't look like that. It was a **Fix Or Repair Daily**. Get it? Ford."

Monique smiled. "*Non,* Elisabet, not *citron*: See-trow-en. Citroen. A French car."

"Well, those are about the finest cars I've ever laid eyes on," I said. "And some day I'm gonna have me one of those."

Doux Doux guffawed. "Not unless you marry a President. Or at least a doctor."

I shook my head. "Nope, I'm going to make my own money and buy it myself."

Monique patted my shoulder. "Good for you," she said, and she looked sad. Why, I couldn't figure out, what with her being so beautiful and all, but later on Mama said she thought maybe Monique wished she had a job instead of being subsidized. Whatever that meant.

Doux Doux barked another laugh at the idea that girls could buy their own cars and we were about to get into an argument when the President arrived and everyone started applauding. Why, I don't know. He didn't *do* anything. *Just wait*, I thought, *'til they see* my *show. Then they'll really have something to clap about.*

After a lot of glad handing, Magloire made a really long speech most of us couldn't understand, and then had his picture taken with the cement bucket, Daddy, the project manager and just about everyone else in Camp, including me. He patted me on the head and said I was a cute little girl, which for some reason teed me off. Or maybe it was the hot sun and the fact that we couldn't eat until he got through showing off for the cameras.

When we finally got around to lunch the Haitian bigwigs couldn't get enough brisket, beans, cornbread and potato salad. They laughed and pointed at each other as melted chocolate and marshmallow dripped from the s'mores onto their chins. Of course, not a dribble dared touch the elegant Monique, who wore, of all things, white silk to a barbeque.

After lunch, while the grownups sipped beer and French wine, we kids sang Paul Magloire's theme song for him (a little ditty about how he was everyone's best friend), then used one of the office trailers to suit up for the Rodeo and Wild West Show. Once in our costumes—she as Dale Evans and me as Roy Rogers—Doux Doux and I staged our little band of Indians and papier-mâché-horned buffalo.

Dale rode out first, at a full gallop, displaying the flags of Haiti, the United States and Texas on a broom handle. After a full circle of the "arena" she had Smokey give a bow, then signaled for the drum corps—toddlers with tom toms—to begin banging away.

The Boudreaux boys, whooping and howling, then chased buffalo into the barbeque area and began threatening volunteer pioneers with great bodily harm. The ferocious warriors danced, screamed and tied to the stake both the good natured Minister of Culture and President Magloire himself. Mr. Magloire, threatened with a rubber-hatchet scalping by a midget in war paint, mock-hollered for help and I, mounted on Wishes, streaked to the rescue. Barely two feet away from the wide-eyed President of the Republic of Haiti, I reined my horse to a dusty, dramatic slide, brandished my Texas Ranger cap pistol, and because I was out of caps, began hurling cherry bombs to the ground.

Wishes, it seems, had never been around fireworks.

My horse whinnied, bucked and sent me flying through the air. I landed with a thud, barely missing a tiny Indian, then everything went black. But before it did, I heard more fireworks. A lot more fireworks.

The official word from Port-au-Prince was that gorillas had attacked the President of Haiti.

What really happened? The limousine guards, who couldn't see the show, heard what they thought were shots and, thinking themselves under attack, panicked, and started shooting into the jungle. Then a couple of soldiers who had gone behind a bush to *fait pi pi*—Creole for taking a whiz—began shooting back, managing to pump several rounds into the presidential limousine before running out of ammo.

Daddy said he figured it was less embarrassing for the president's staff to blame the limousine's bullet holes on gorillas than on their own men.

"Gorillas, Daddy? I thought they lived in Africa?"

"Not gorillas, guerillas. Revolutionaries. I guess there's been some trouble with rebels in the mountains, the soldiers were jumpy about being away from the city, and when they heard the firecrackers…" He shrugged.

Uh oh. So it was all my fault. Just how much trouble was I in this time?

Uncle Lloyd must have read my mind. "Wasn't your fault, except that you shouldn't have been playing with fireworks. Magloire is asking for trouble, what with him refusing to hold a real election, and Lord help him if there's a revolution, because those soldiers are just about the sorriest bunch I've ever seen in uniform. It's a damned wonder no one was killed."

Whew! Oh, I knew I was going to pay for those firecrackers, because my parents never, ever let me play with them, but at least I hadn't started a danged revolution. The idea, however, was somehow appealing. I could almost picture myself astride my noble steed, Wishes, charging the presidential palace in Port-au-Prince, hollering, "Hold elections and remember the Alamo!"

"You mean there might be a war here?" I asked, somewhat hopefully.

"I'd hate to see it. We'd probably have to leave in a big hurry."

Leave? I hadn't thought of that. Leave Pee Wee? And Angela? Was this the People against the Government that Robert the bartender at the Sans Souci had warned me about when we arrived? And were they about to ruin my entire life?

Mother came into the room, heard what Daddy said and misread the stricken look on my face.

"Bud, you're scaring Lizbuthann." She sat down by me and took my hand. "Honey, don't you worry. If there is a problem we'll just go back to Texas where it's safe."

"But I don't want to go back to Texas! I want to stay here! I love it right here."

Mother sighed. "You know, sometimes things happen that we can't control and you're getting old enough to realize that."

I nodded and fought back tears, knowing she was right. But what I didn't understand then was that she wasn't talking about revolution, or leaving Haiti.

It was left to Grandmother Hetta to dole out my punishment, because Mama said she'd be the most fair. I thought that was a grand idea, counting on her soft spot for me, but I was dead wrong: "You could have blown off a finger, or put out someone's eye," she said, and then stripped me of my reins. Until further notice, Wishes was off limits.

So much for soft grannies; they really know how to hurt a kid.

# CHAPTER 12

▼

De-reined and put afoot; and by such a normally *sweet* old lady. No amount of whining or begging got me off the hook and out of detention, so I decided to make the best of it and be useful around the house. I figured if I made myself useful *enough*, maybe she'd give me back my horse to get rid of me, but she just ignored my scheming. Never mess with old people; they've been around too long to be fooled by the likes of kids.

Each day after school—I was not, Grandmother Hetta made it clear, to make any detours between the school and my house—I raked the flowerbed under my bedroom window smooth in hopes of finding a François Noir footprint. Still no luck. Rats, I needed a little excitement in my life.

One day, as I was putting the rake away, Guilliame, leading Sister aboard her donkey, Daisy, came around the corner of the house. Daisy sported a big straw hat, as did Sister. Sister's didn't have ear holes, but both *chapeaux* were decorated with freshly cut bougainvillea blossoms.

It was an uncommonly hot day in a place where heat is common, so she was only dressed in shorts. Sister, that is; Daisy wore fuzzy brown-gray, as always. Daisy and Sister made such a cute picture that I thought of running inside for my Kodak Brownie, but instead found myself standing dead still, staring at them. Or rather at Sister.

I lived in the same house with my little sister, ate meals with her, slept in the same room with her, for crying out loud. How could I *not* have noticed how *puny* she'd gotten. She was always on the skinny side, but now every rib showed and even through her tan, I saw little blue veins, like fish netting, just under her skin. Guilt hit me hard. Some folks say I tend to be a mite self-centered, but was I so occupied with my own stuff that I hadn't noticed what was happening to my precious little sister before my very eyes?

I dropped the rake and ran inside where I found my mother, grandmother and Angela (decked out in oversized pineapple slices) drinking coffee and looking grim. Now that I thought of it, I'd seen this scene often of late and should have known something was wrong. Then there was all that talk of medicines. Had I gone deaf *and* blind?

"What's wrong with Sister?" I demanded.

"Come here, sweetheart," Grandmother Hetta said, patting a chair between my mother and her. I took in Angela's long face, then my mother's damp cheeks and knew things were real bad. Mama dabbed her eyes with a hankie, then took my hand.

"Your sister," she said, fighting back tears, "has a problem with her kidneys."

I almost fainted. Not long before we moved to Haiti, my mother's sister had *died* of kidney disease. "Like Aunt Tody?" I managed to say, even though my mouth didn't want to work right.

"No, thank the Lord," Grandmother Hetta said. "Not like that. Your aunt's disease was incurable. With your little sister, we just have to wait and see if she grows out of it."

I almost fainted again, but this time with relief. "You mean she's not going to die?"

"We're all praying she'll get better soon," my mother said, avoiding my question. "And she's on a new medicine now. The doctor here is in contact with the specialist we took your sister to in Miami. We'll just have to wait and see. Meanwhile, all we can do is make sure she eats more, drinks lots of iced tea and water and takes her medications. And, as I said, pray."

I started to say they could count on me, but with my track record I was a little wary of making direct requests to God. What if Sister got sicker, no matter what we did? "What can I do?" I asked.

Angela smiled. "Elisabet, your sister, she look up to you and will do as you say. That I know. So, when you can, you should...I do not know the word...push?...her to eat more and drink much water. Yes?"

"Yes, I can do that. *Encourage* her."

Angela nodded and I saw her mentally file the word away in her head dictionary. "That's right. If you tell her to drink, she will. Then if...I mean *when* she gets better, you will have helped and if she...does not, it is God's will."

I didn't know about that last part. How on earth could God *will* a sweet little girl to get sicker? Not, by golly, if I had anything to do with it.

I started that day. The first thing I did was hit the commissary and spend all my coupons on Kool-Aid. Cherry; Sister's favorite. They only had five packages, so I went begging from house to house until I owned the entire Camp's supply. Sister also loved Ritz crackers, which were hard to come by, but the neighbors gave them up for the cause. I considered cadging a few candy bars for myself, but rethought it; I might need a favor from upstairs and using my sister's sickness to my own purpose wouldn't exactly earn me angel merit badges.

After meals, during which Sister moved food around on her plate with little interest, I played a game: I'd take a bite, then challenge her do the same. It worked. Within two weeks of starting my mission, Sister began filling out. The problem was, so did I. And after a couple of months of spending time with Sister instead of riding horses (even though Grandmother Hetta had lifted my punishment because I was being so sweet to Sister), swinging on Tarzan ropes (the ones the grownups hadn't found and cut down) and playing with Doux Doux, I began to resemble Porky Pig.

It was my mother who declared *c-c-c-c-c-'est tout*, folks, and put me on a diet.

Lucky for me, Sister's medicine kicked in about the same time as my rations were cut, so at least I wasn't tortured by having to coax my sister to eat food I couldn't have. And to Mama's credit, she decided that in support of my *regime*, the entire family, except for Sister, could use a few less calories and suddenly a lot of boiled eggs and salads were hitting the table instead of fried chicken and mashed potatoes.

Just as suddenly, Daddy took to meeting Uncle Lloyd at the mess hall for important business around breakfast and lunch time. About mid-morning each day, Grandmother Hetta had a pressing engagement with Cynthia Smith, who was known for her oatmeal cookies but who had been told not to give *me* any during my penmanship classes. Angela began bringing her own lunch. Only Mama and I were doomed to the calorie count. I saw my life ahead as one huge head of lettuce. I longed for ice cream, dreamed of swimming in chocolate syrup. Pee Wee looked tastier by the day—perhaps with a little cream gravy?

There seemed no salvation for me, but just when I was considering a tiny spoonful of white paste while straightening out the supply room at school, a wave of nausea washed over me and my teeth began to chatter. *Hooray*, I thought, *malaria*.

I'd lost *tons* of weight during that first bout with malaria, so I figured I'd gotten lucky. Not that I relished a date with Doctor Death and his nasty needles, of course, so to put that off as long as possible, I found a nice, warm, flat rock and stretched out under the blazing sun. The heat from above and below soothed my chills for awhile, but I was finally forced to head home when my head and neck began to thud with pain. Once in the house I sneaked a couple of Mama's aspirin, but they only made me sick. As I upchucked breakfast (all two hundred calories worth) I regretted not eating more. Heck, I could have had pancakes.

Crawling into my bed after several more bouts of vomiting I tried hard to concentrate on the bright side of malaria: I'd be back in my shorts in no time. And the longer I waited to tell anyone I was sick, the longer it would be until Doctor Dull Needles returned. I shut my bedroom door and I must have drifted off, because the next thing I knew, speak of the devil and up he'd popped. And he was using a blowtorch on my eyeballs.

Not really. The flashlight he shined into my eyes just felt like a blowtorch. Above the loud ringing inside my skull I heard muffled voices, but they seemed very far away. I fell back asleep, I guess, because lo and behold, when I next opened my eyes, who should I see but my Aunt Tody.

My aunt seemed lit from within, shimmering into focus just as I walked up to her. She wore a gauzy, gleaming dress and was lounging on what looked to be a fluffy cloud of cotton candy. I wondered if taking a wee bite would be impolite. I also wondered, since it seemed for all the world like I was in Heaven, how I'd managed to slip past the pearly gates guard, what with all the harm I'd done lately. Maybe Grandmother Hetta was right and all God's children do go to heaven and I'd squeaked in under the age limit.

"Oh my, Lizbuthann," Aunt Tody sang (she didn't talk, she sang), "look how big you've gotten since I died."

"I've been on a diet, honest."

"That's not what I meant, sweet girl. I meant you've grown so tall since I last saw you."

"They wouldn't let me come to the hospital, Aunt Tody. Or your funeral either. They said I was too young. I wanted to, though."

"Your parents were trying to protect you from sadness, Lizbuthann. It's okay, I got to see you when I could still enjoy your company."

I'd forgotten how much fun we'd had together before she got sick. All I had to remind me now were pictures of us together and a few letters. I suddenly became shy and couldn't think of much to say, since talking about her being dead and all didn't seem mannerly. "Uh, I like your dress, Aunt Tody."

"Thank you. It's a size eight."

"Dang, they have dress sizes in Heaven?" I said, and she sang a tinkling little laugh that sounded like church bells. "It's real pretty here, Aunt Tody. Nice and cool. Do they have ice cream?"

"All you want. But you can't stay."

"I can't?"

"No Lizbuthann, you have to go back. Your mother and grandmother have had enough grief for a while, so you have to stay with them for now."

"And Sister? She can stay with us too?"

My aunt nodded, a little sadly. "As much as I'd love to have you and your sister for company, it just isn't your time yet. Now, give me a hug and get on back. Your loved ones are very worried."

I ran to her and grabbed her around the waist, but as hard as I tried to hold on she just kept fading until I was grasping nothing but a blinding white light. I tried closing my eyes against the brilliance, but no luck; Dr. Blowtorch had hold of my eyelid. He let go and I saw my mother hovering right over his shoulder.

"Mama, Aunt Tody said I couldn't stay."

Which was kind of too bad, because the minute I returned, so did the pain. And this time it wasn't malaria; it was polio.

Unfortunately for me, the doctors in the States started experimenting with those sugar cubes soaked in magic polio vaccine after we left for Haiti. Just as well, 'cause Mama probably wouldn't let me have one anyway. Just kidding.

Sister had gotten a dose while she was in Miami, but the doctors in Haiti didn't have the medicine yet, *et voila*, look who comes down with polio. But once again, I got lucky. Oh sure I was really sick for a couple of weeks, but mostly with bad headaches and fever. I was left with slightly knocked knees, but was spared the horrors of those poor kids we'd seen in the movie news reels, the ones in iron lungs and wheelchairs. I think Aunt Tody had something to do with it, since she had connections.

I was, however, forced to wear some really ugly, braced high-topped shoes that made my Buster Browns look like Monique's high heels. I also had to do physical therapy; stuff like picking up marbles with my toes, but other than that, Daddy said I dodged the bullet. Well, he *actually* said there may have been a little brain damage. What a card.

The doctor, after two weeks of visiting my bedside three times a day, declared me ready to get up and go out. "Your daughter," he told my mother, "needs fresh air and exercise. In addition to marble therapy and wearing corrective shoes for a while, it is imperative she rides her horse at least three hours every single day. Oh, and she needs to gain some weight." The man is a medical genius! I mean, it made sense: cowboys are bowlegged and I was knock-kneed. And skinny.

And I didn't even have to hang around worrying about Sister, because I knew for a fact that she was going to be all right. Who was gonna argue with an angel?

Or my doctor? Ice cream was back and life was good again. I vowed to try to keep it that way for a change.

But someone had other ideas.

# CHAPTER 13

▼

Yep, that first year in Haiti was a ring-tailed tooter. I'd learned a new language, met a zombie, survived polio *and* malaria, and nearly started a revolution. I couldn't wait for 1954!

Christmas came and we decorated a banana tree with tinsel (which Pee Wee ate and Mama had to dose him with castor oil) and shiny glass balls we'd brought from the States. Frozen turkeys were flown in by the company Daddy worked for, Mama made her famous date nut rolls with cashews instead of pecans, Grandmother Hetta made peanut brittle, and we exchanged gifts.

Angela seemed pleased with the red lace slip I made her with my own two hands; it was somewhat lopsided, but she said she could roll it up at the waist. At the Iron Market I'd found Daddy and Uncle Lloyd some nifty cigarette lighters decorated with pictures of pretty girls on the beach. My uncle soon discovered that when he turned the lighter upside down, the girl lost her bathing suit. I'd forgotten neither of them smoked, but they liked the lighters just fine anyhow.

For Mama, I bought a beautiful purple silk scarf like I'd seen Monique wear except better because it had fringe with glittery glass beads. It came all the way from Paris and my mother must have really loved it because she put it somewhere safe and never wore it.

Also at the Iron Market, I spent a few more gourds than I'd planned to when I found a perfect Negro boy doll dressed in typical Haitian garb to go with Sister's voodoo queen. He must have been made in France too, because the first time Sister took off his clothes we discovered he had a little wienie. Mama put him somewhere safe as well.

I got Grandmother Hetta a set of mahogany salad bowls and a tube of Blue Star Ointment, just in case she got those crabs Daddy had told me about. She was speechless.

Uncle Lloyd gave me a whole stack of Brenda Starr comic books and the rest of the family gave me more Hardy Boys, Nancy Drews, and a huge watercolor set with special paper. Pee Wee tried to eat the paper pad, but soon settled on his own gift: a rare and shiny red apple.

The last night of 1953 started with *hors d'oeuvers*—French for puny sandwiches—and ended with a bang. A big party was in the works, but I had to work.

Camp was full of small kids whose parents liked to party past their children's bedtimes on Saturday night and since someone had to watch their kids, I figured it might as well be me and Doux Doux. For a price, of course. My allowance of a dollar a week was barely keeping Wishes in hay and forget saving up for my Citroen: I started a babysitting service.

Most parties, we kids were invited for the first couple of hours to eat and cut a rug or two before being sent home. After Daddy and I two-stepped, I'd waltzed with Uncle Lloyd, and then got in a lively polka standing on Mr. Blaha's feet, I'd round up all the little ones and take them to our house. Doux Doux and I covered the living room floor with quilt pallets and we were soon wall-to-wall in sleeping rug rats.

Doux Doux and I split the fifty-cents a head, plus a quarter more if someone wet his quilt. We gave discounts to families with more than three kids, and didn't charge extra for those times when Ma and Pa had a mite too much rum punch and didn't remember to pick up junior until the next morning. On those occasions however, the embarrassed parents usually gave us a big fat tip.

Once our charges were all dead to the world, Doux Doux and I played cards, read or sometimes just fell asleep in my room until the dance ended and parents came to collect their sleepy darlings.

The New Year's Eve dance promised to be much the same as any other, except we kids were allowed to stay until nine o'clock and the grownups had chilled several cases of French champagne to pop open at midnight. Doux Doux and I figured we were in for a lot of fat tips.

We had all the wee ones down for the night by ten, then played canasta and read "True Confessions." I set my Big Ben for 11:45 because Uncle Lloyd promised us a fireworks show at midnight and, after that other incident, I never planned to personally handle any for the rest of my life. Not even a sparkler. Everyone was really looking forward to the show; after all, Uncle Lloyd was a demolitions expert.

Around eleven, our eyelids began drooping, so we decided to turn out the lights and make shadow animals on the wall. I dozed off in the middle of Doux Doux's famous running coyote and the next thing I knew, the alarm went off. I shook her awake, we ran outside and clambered up the tree in the front yard for a better view. Pee Wee, pleased to be up so late, sat on my head and chewed my hair.

At midnight a rocket went straight up from behind the mess hall, followed by a barrage of starbursts and what looked like giant sparklers. Crates of fireworks made in China had been bought for the show, but we couldn't read the labels, so Uncle Lloyd kind of figured out from the pictures what each one would do. I didn't know what his grand finale was going to be, but Uncle Lloyd said his foreman had set up something spectacular. Boy, was he right.

After about five minutes of oohing and aahing, there was a long pause in the action and I had just about decided the spectacular finish had fizzled when a tremendous explosion threw Doux Doux and I clean out of the tree. Pee Wee took to the air with a loud screech. I guess. My ears were ringing.

All the kids began howling, but lucky for us our houses didn't have glass windows to shatter and slash tender skins. The company trucks parked out in front of the dance lost their windshields, but no one was in them to get diced up by flying glass. They never found even a splinter of the dynamite shack, or Uncle Lloyd's foreman. There was some speculation that he was blown to smithereens, but I bet he just took off rather than face my uncle. Five cases of French champagne bit the dust, along with all the bottles, glasses and plates at the mess hall.

But worst of all, I couldn't find Pee Wee.

Doux Doux and I spent the wee hours searching, wandering up and down the streets calling him. Mama finally made me go to bed, but only after she promised to leave the doors open in case he returned while I slept. He didn't. The next morning we expanded the search into the jungle, but still no Pee Wee.

I felt as though my heart would break. I cried until I got hiccups so bad that no amount of sugar would stop them. Mama, afraid I'd make myself sick, gave me half of one of those pills the doctor was so popular for and I settled down long enough to lose the hiccups. But not the tears.

Every adult in Camp took to the woods, calling for my parrot and the cats that had taken off following the blast. The stray dogs (we weren't allowed pet dogs in Camp) started coming back around that afternoon, the cats were generally located in treetops, but my parrot was nowhere to be found. After several days, I lost hope of ever seeing him again.

Daddy came home with another parrot, but I wasn't interested. He was big and dopey and had a mean streak (the bird, not Daddy) and couldn't even learn his own name, which was Dopey. Mother said I had doomed him with that name, but I didn't care. I wanted Pee Wee.

Months passed and still, every morning when I woke up, I had a moment of hope that Pee Wee would fly into my room and scoot under the covers. I said if I could get my hands on that foreman of Uncle Lloyd's I'd kill him deader than he already was. Grandmother Hetta said that wasn't Christian, but I didn't care. Besides, I'd already visited Heaven, slipped right in on the underage thing, so I figured I could have impure thoughts until I was at least thirteen. I regretted not asking Aunt Tody how long I actually had.

In an effort to take my mind from my grief, Daddy decided to teach me to drive.

A few months after we arrived in Haiti, Daddy had bought a 1948 Ford car from a German fellow who found out he could go back home without getting hung. I never found out what he did to get in hot water, but I do know it had something to do with the war because he told Daddy he'd seen Galveston through a periscope, which shook Daddy up a mite. Anyhow, Lutz returned to Germany and we got this *really* big black car.

Because the roads were so bad and the rivers so high, Daddy put truck tires on the Ford, lifting it an extra foot off the ground. It was quite a climb into that car, I tell you. I had to sit on two pillows to see through the steering wheel and even though Daddy built up the clutch, brake and gas pedals by tying on wooden blocks, my legs were barely long enough to reach them. It was, of course, a stick shift.

Sunday afternoons, Daddy drove us out of Camp so I wouldn't run over any of our little kids, down to the main road to where I could run over Haitian kids. Just joshing you. I only grazed a couple.

By the time we got back from my driving lessons, Daddy would mix himself a hefty rum drink and I needed a nap. Mother asked why we kept doing this to ourselves (and Daddy's clutch), but we insisted we were having fun. After some time, I could actually steer pretty straight, shift without grinding the gears, and stop *before* we ran into a ditch. Uncle Lloyd was so proud that I'd learned to drive that he let me drive his company truck. But only once.

No amount of driving, riding Wishes, or swinging on ropes lifted the lead in my heart. Not even the return of François Noir cheered me up; who needed that big old dumb zombie. I wanted my bird back.

The first night I saw François Noir's silhouette on my wall, I considered going out to talk to him, but didn't have the energy. The doctor said I was depressed and probably needed to take drugs, but mother refused him. I knew what was wrong with me; I was pining for Wee.

Anyhow, when I saw old François standing all dumb and dopey outside my window one night, I slammed the louvers shut. I heard him shuffle away after a while and muttered, "Good riddance to bad rubbish," and pulled a pillow over my head. But he returned the next night. And the next. I went back to closing the louvers, but I knew he was out there. I didn't care anymore.

One night, though, he actually knocked! I thought I'd have a heart seizure. What if Daddy heard him? François danged sure wasn't fast enough to get out of the way of a twelve-gauge shell. I flipped the louvers open and sure enough, there he stood.

"Git!" I whispered. "*Allez*!"

He reached out like he could grab my hand through the window and looked surprised when his knuckles struck the screen. He took a step back and turned to leave, but before he did he walked to Pee Wee's cage, which I'd put outside just in case my parrot returned in the middle of the night and needed a place to stay. He stopped at the cage, turned back to look at me, then reached out towards me again. I slammed the louvers.

"I swear he's trying to get me to follow him," I told Doux Doux the next day.

"Mais sure, that's what you should do, cheré. Follow a seven-foot dead man into the jungle at night. I do wonder, though, what he wants."

"Me too. Maybe we should find out."

"We? Mais cheré, you got a mouse in your pocket?"

"You know, Doux Doux, ever since you got titties you ain't no fun at all."

"You're just jealous."

"Am not."

"Yes, you are." She stormed off, but we made up soon afterwards. I figured she was suffering from hormones like I heard Mama's bridge club talking about. I didn't know what a hormone was, but evidently they made you real cranky.

Those bridge club ladies, by the way, were a fountain of information. All you had to do was keep your ears tuned to learn the most amazing things; they were better than the Haitian laundry hole when they didn't think you were listening. But I was. Right up until the day I decided to dazzle them with my French and announced that, since it was such a hot day, I thought I'd go into the bathroom for a nice cold *douche*. After that, Mama made sure I was elsewhere when they played cards at our house.

It was my own fault that Doux Doux and I had that spat over her boobies. What with me being in mourning, learning to drive, riding Wishes, going to school, babysitting, taking penmanship lessons, swinging on Tarzan ropes, and reading "True Confessions," I'd hardly had time to notice that Doux Doux was growing up. I mean fast. It seemed like one day she and I were swimming naked in the Camp water supply and the next she burst out of her training bra. And to make matters worse, she began making goo-goo eyes at this new boy in Camp and we know where that gets you; just read a couple of "True Confessions." Lucky for Doux Doux, the kid's dad got fired for messing with the payroll and they went back to Texas. In the nick of time, in my opinion.

That boyfriend thing seemed to be catching, because next thing we knew, Momo-san, who had us pretty well whipped into shape by now, got all moon-eyed. Okay, so her eyes were already slightly moon-shaped, but she now had them trained on someone besides her students.

We didn't get a school vacation, so we had classes year-round except for a few holidays such as Christmas, Easter and Momo-san's vacation. She was gone for a month, but it seemed like a year. Especially since she had become the latest subject for our Brenda Starr Information Club. Momo-san had a boyfriend.

We noticed Bob, one of the engineers, hanging around the schoolhouse now and again and figured he wasn't there to learn math. Mama said it wasn't any of our business, since he and Momo were both free, white and twenty-one. I reminded her that Momo-san was more yellowish in color, but my mother said I knew what she meant. I noticed, however, that neither my mother nor grandmother stopped me from talking about the lovebirds until I'd told all the latest. Like the fact that Momo-san and Bob were taking their vacations to the States at the same time. Coincidence? Brenda Starr wouldn't think so.

When the couple returned—on different days, but we weren't fooled in the least—they announced their engagement and we lost our after-school buddy. Up 'til then, Momo-san could always be counted on to play volleyball with us after supper, or maybe go for a short hike. No more, my friend. She was in love and walked around holding hands with Bob.

I was starting to get a lit-tle put out with all this love stuff. It was as confusing as religion.

By the end of summer, even Momo-san and Bob's big romance was old news and things in Camp were getting dull, so I turned my attention to François Noir again. Maybe it was time to find out what he wanted. Or at least where he lived.

Especially after the egg incident.

# CHAPTER 14

▼

I was the family egg floater.

All sorts of peddlers came through Camp each day in hopes of selling eggs, hand-carved mahogany *objects d'art*, fresh fruit and vegetables, as well as a mish-mash of livestock; dead and alive. I was a soft touch for the livestock; our chicken coop and animal pens out back housed a zoo of scraggly looking critters that looked in need of a meal instead of becoming one. I was, however, a hard sell when it came to eggs. My job was to make sure they weren't rotten, and my father said I was a natural because it takes one to know one. Daddy: what a joker.

If you take a fresh egg and plunk it into a bowl of water, it'll sink or stand on end if it's fresh, but once they start to rot, gas forms under the shell and they'll float like a balloon. Simple science. I performed another test, though: I also back-lit them with a flashlight or candle to make sure no baby chicken was incubating inside. Nothing worse than scrambled almost-baby chicken for breakfast. Yuk.

I got to know most of the peddlers pretty well, what with all the time we spent bargaining. They surely did love to barter, always starting way high so we could spend a while haggling to get the price right. If you paid the first asking price they got all huffy and wouldn't come back.

Anyhow, we were low on eggs one morning when this woman I'd never dealt with shows up. She had dark, skinny, stick arms and wore a huge straw hat pulled low on her forehead. I was a little doubtful of her claim that hers were freshly laid-that-day eggs, so we bargained awhile, she insisting her eggs were worth more than the going price since they were special. In fact, she said, why didn't I take one into the kitchen and crack it open; so I did. Or rather, I gave it to

Angela, who was dressed head to toe in mangos on brilliant green, for her to check out.

Sure enough, when Angela whacked that baby and slid it into a ceramic bowl, the yolk stood high and the white was perfect. Not a sign of chicken parts, either. 'Course, that didn't mean all the eggs were that way; I'd been snookered more than once with the old good-egg-on-top switch, so I floated each one while the egg lady fidgeted. It came as no surprise that she was a mite nervous around me; my mop of wild reddish-blond hair put the Haitians off until they got to know me better.

I ended up buying every egg, and the basket as well, because I have a fondness for baskets and hers was lined in my favorite colors: magenta and turquoise. Proud of my morning's work, I hoped, as a reward, Mama would whip up a batch of her famous deviled eggs, which she dosed with enough Tabasco sauce to water your eyes and leave a truly devilish tingle on your tongue.

But, when I paid the egg woman, I got a good look under her hat, and a devilish tingle of its own ran up my neck. There was something strangely familiar about her eyes; they were all cloudy looking and, from the way she acted, sensitive to the sun. I had a feeling I'd seen her somewhere before, but it wasn't until after she'd counted her money and left and I was loading eggs into Mama's wire kitchen basket that I remembered, with a heart leap, where and when. Almost like those flaming arrows in the only 3-D movie I'd ever seen, the egg lady's white eyeballs jumped out at me; she was the voodoo queen from the *hounfort* where we'd first met François Noir!

I sprang back from the eggs as if they'd sprouted fangs, but an unsuspecting Angela, her back to me, hummed a happy tune as she plated the test egg she'd whipped into a little mid-morning snack. I watched, temporarily frozen with fear, as Angela slid a fork through the *omelette* and prepared to take a bite.

Okay, so I probably overreacted, but I had to do something. Snatching up the wire egg basket, I gave it an underhanded softball windup and let it go in a high wide arc. THWACK! The basket connected with Angela's omelet plate, knocking it across the kitchen, and then following it up against the wall with a sickening scrunching sound as two dozen raw eggs splattered all over the freshly mopped floor. The crash and Angela's startled shout brought Mama and my grandmother on the run.

"What on earth? Oh, my!" Grandmother Hetta gasped, shaking her head at the goopy floor.

"Ooops. Talk about putting all your eggs in one basket," I said, hoping someone had a sense of humor.

They didn't. They all glared at me as if I were demented. I knew that word, because Momo-san had us learning a new word a day and this week we were studying words denoting states of mind. Demented just about summed up mine, I guess. And what was that other word? Paranoid. Maybe I was being paranoid, but there was no way I was going to let anyone in my family eat that voodoo witch's eggs. Lord only knew what she'd doctored them with. And now that I thought about it, I'd never seen her around camp before. Was her turning up on our doorstep a coincidence? Brenda Starr wouldn't think so.

Mama said the eggs were coming out of my allowance and worse than that, I figured I'd have to spend the rest of Saturday morning scrubbing guck from the floor, but Grandmother Hetta saved the day. She poured a goodly amount of salt over the whole mess, told me to wait a few minutes, *et voilà*; salt absorbed slime and I swept the whole mess up with a broom and a dust pan. You know, I feel sorry for kids who don't have grandmothers around to teach them stuff like that. I was sure gonna miss mine when she returned to Texas and, to my great sadness, she was already making plans to go home.

It didn't seem fair that Pee Wee was already lost and I would soon lose my grandmother, but when I said so, Grandmother Hetta told me to count my blessings instead of bellyaching. And Daddy said if they were going to hang me I'd want a new rope, so maybe I *was* being a little too selfish, but it's hard not to be when you're eleven. Taking Grandmama's advice, I added up my blessings and decided I was a pretty lucky kid; I had my own horse, a really good friend, a great family and Angela. What I needed was something to keep me from feeling sorry for myself.

The problem is, whenever I start looking for something to do, trouble has a way of finding me.

That witchy woman showing up at our house set me to thinking about old François Noir again. Maybe he lived with her? And if so, and if I followed him home, maybe I'd find out why he, and now she, seemed interested in me. Of course, they might ask the same question.

I secretly harbored a sneaking suspicion, one that I had not even confided to Doux Doux, that my illnesses, and maybe even Sister's, might have something to do with this white-eyed witch. After all, I did mess up her little soiree. Maybe she held a grudge, and a voodoo queen with a score to settle could be a bad thing, indeed.

Of course, I couldn't discuss this with any adult I knew without being subjected to some serious confessing, and I didn't even confide my fears to Doux

Doux because she might think I was hexed and not hang out with me anymore. With such a burden to bear, you can just imagine how my ears perked when the word "curse" came up at Mama's bridge club.

My mother, upon my heart-crossed promise not to say or do anything to embarrass her again, let me hang around the house during her bridge club meetings. If I kept quiet. So I did, and found that it is purely amazing what you can hear when grownups forget you're lurking. I was reading a comic book, half-listening to the women chat between bids, when I heard the word that snagged my full attention.

"...curse. I look forward to the day I don't have to worry about it anymore," Mrs. Brooks told the women at her table. "Two hearts."

"I know what you mean, Monica," another said, "they don't call it the curse for nothing. Three spades."

One of the women cleared her throat and nodded in my direction. "Uh, little pitchers." Four sets of eyes turned on me. I swerved my own eyes to my comic book, but I was still all ears. Were these women victims of a voodoo curse? And if so, how did it happen? Maybe I wasn't alone in this thing after all.

Even though Mama had never agreed with some of my greats and grands that children should be seen and not heard, I had, in this case, given my word to be quiet, so I waited until after bridge to bring up what I'd heard.

"Mama, uh, I was wonderin' about something."

"What, honey?" She was dusting yeast rolls before putting them in the oven for supper and a fine white cloud puffed from the pan. Wiping flour from her hands onto her apron—the cute one decorated with red chickens and rickrack— she slid the rolls into the hot oven. Still dressed and all made up for her bridge club, she looked like one of those women on TV advertising something by Kraft.

"Mrs. Brooks said she had a curse on her."

Mother lost her smile and looked flummoxed. "Well, I, uh...yes, I believe I did hear Monica mention something about that today."

"Well, I was wondering...what is she talking about?"

"Not anything for you to worry about yet, sweetheart. I'll let you know when I think you're ready. Now, go set the table like a good girl."

Well, so much for that. I figured the subject was as dead as François Noir, but a day later Mama came into my room while I was doing homework. Momo-san was in one of her Art History moods and I was matching up photographs of famous pictures—she said they were properly called pictures, not paintings— with the artist and title. I drew an arrow from Whistler to his mother, shaking my head at such a dumb test. What did they expect me to do? Match up Rembrandt's *Night Watch* with a little old lady in a chair? What a waste of my valuable time. I sighed and put down my pencil. "All done, Mama, can I go out and brush Wishes?"

"Actually," she said, "I wanted to talk to you." Her eyebrows twitched as she sat next to me, making me wonder what I'd gotten caught at now, but she held up a small book. "Lizbuthann, the other day? In the kitchen? You asked about the curse? Well, I was going to wait until you were twelve to give you this, but I decided if you were old enough to ask, you were old enough to have it now." She shoved the book in my hand and left.

*You're A Young Lady Now* was actually little more than a booklet. On the cover, a girl in blue jeans and pigtails leans on her mirrored vanity table and tells her reflection—a smooth-haired deb in a ruffled dress—"You're a young lady now." I read the book from cover to cover, looking at the drawings and trying to figure out what it had to do with curses. Mama had been so uncomfortable when she gave it to me, I didn't want to ask her what in holy heck a sanitary napkin had to do with voodoo. I shoved the stupid book into my desk drawer and, when my mother got around to asking if I'd read it, I told her I had and that it looked to me like becoming a young lady was too much trouble and I'd decided against it.

She smiled. "You won't have a choice, Lizbuthann, it just happens. Except to your great Aunt Annie because of that snake bite." I wondered where I could find me a rattlesnake.

Doux Doux must already have known about this "young lady" junk, because one day she started curling her hair and took to wearing dresses when she didn't have to. I even caught her flashing goo-goo eyes at Bob Smith, this new boy in Camp whose father was on temporary assignment at the jobsite. It wasn't long after he arrived that I realized I wasn't seeing much of my friend, and I was glad when that Bob Smith went back to the States, but Doux Doux went all mopey and moody. That girl's temperament was going downhill as her titties went up. It was becoming a test of patience, which I wasn't known for in the first place, to remain her friend.

Clota Boudreaux got in a shipment of magazines called "True Romance." Unlike "True Confessions," the new stories had happy endings; girl meets boy, falls in love, overcomes some hardship (another girl; parents), gets married and lives happily ever after. Not one of the gals got in circumstances or was shipped to a convent or home for wayward girls, but when I told Doux Doux that these stories were stupid and I was sure that the "True Confessions" magazines were probably right to warn us off boys, she pitched a hissy and told me I was such a child. This from a twelve-and-a-half year old.

Months passed without the return of Pee Wee, but I kept his cage clean and waiting out in the backyard. Still hopeful, I fastened bits of toast or fruit to the wire each day, but only managed to attract wild birds and the occasional mongoose. Not a peep from my parrot.

The reason I bring up the cage is that whenever François Noir showed up, which was at least once a week, he'd stare at it. Then at me. Then at it. I guess he wondered why I'd keep a birdcage with no bird in it. If his little zombie brain wondered about anything at all, that is.

I still wanted to know where that pesky zombie lived, so I decided to do some bodacious detecting. My plan was to meet the big guy out in the backyard one night, shoo him away and then follow. Simple, my dear Brenda. Doux Doux even gave up moping long enough to agree to come with me on my zombie hunt, figuring, I guess, that without little Bobby Dreamboat, her life was over anyway, so why not? The problem was finding a night when we wouldn't get caught stealing out of Camp on the trail of a seven-foot dead man.

The ideal time, of course, would be when we were babysitting and all the adults were at the mess hall dancing and drinking, but then we'd have to abandon our kids, so that was out. The second best time was when the adults went home *after* all that dancing and drinking. We picked a Saturday night in October, hoping François Noir would show.

But we hadn't counted on Hazel.

Mother Nature has a way of messing with your plans. About noon on the day of our planned oooh-gah-oooh safari, the weather turned uncommonly still and balmy. Mama said it was going to storm; she could tell by the way her hair frizzed. Mine was always frizzy, so I couldn't tell the difference, but by mid-afternoon I longed for a nice cool breeze to lift the awful heat. Watch out for what you wish for, they say.

Round about four o'clock, huge black clouds moved in, followed by a wind like we'd never seen up in the mountains. Things took to the air all over Camp; the Madden's chicken coup (complete with squawking chickens), Mrs. Magee's brand new bed sheets which she'd just gotten via mail order from Florida and hung out to air, and anything else that wasn't nailed down. I barely had time to catch Pee Wee's cage before it, too, sailed over the bluff.

Then came the rain. We were used to rain, like almost every day, but this downpour was what Uncle Lloyd called a frog strangler. An Arkansas dew. And that cool breeze I wanted? There was a scramble all over camp for anything at all with long sleeves.

I thought for sure that the planned party at the mess hall would be cancelled, but since they had to shut down the jobsite due to the high winds and rain, they decided they might as well dance. Not that it mattered to me one way or the other, because even though I'd planned on making this the night we'd track François Noir, there was no way, with this weather, that we'd follow that zombie *anywhere*. If he had a lick of sense he wouldn't even show up, which, of course, meant he probably would.

After their parents dumped them off, we bedded down the little ones early, digging out every sheet and blanket we could find to keep them warm. It was still pouring *chats et chiens*, so before he and Mama left for the dance, Daddy'd covered the dining room windows with heavy plastic sheeting to keep the driving rain from, well, driving past the sisal rollups and right on through the house. At least we were dry, if chilly.

Our house didn't have heat, unless you counted the gas kitchen range, but we'd been warned not to use it for warming the house; something about it sucking all the oxygen out of the air. Which didn't make much sense since, with a high whine, plenty of air was whizzing around the edges of my father's makeshift rain stopper. What with all that flapping plastic, rain walloping our tin roof and thunder booming almost constantly, we had to practically yell to hear each other. They probably just turned up the music at the mess hall; a good blow never stopped a good dance.

To warm the kitchen, Doux Doux and I made cookies, figuring we weren't using the range for only heat, so it would be alright. We were on our fourth batch when a gust blasted the back door open and I saw, silhouetted in the aggregate plant lights, that dimwitted zombie, François Noir. He was standing where Pee Wee's cage had *been*, for crying out loud.

"Mais cheré, what a pea brain," Doux Doux said, clucking and shaking her head.

"He looks so cold and pitiful."

"You gonna ask him in for hot chocolate and cookies?" Doux Doux drawled.

I gave her the look her sarcastic remark deserved. "Hey, what a good idea."

"What? Are you nuts, Lizbuthann? He might eat one of the kids and their parents would never pay us."

"Well, not invite him in, exactly. Maybe just take him some cookies."

"Lizbuthann, we are talking about the walking dead here."

"Yeah, well, nobody's perfect," I threw back. Sometimes I crack myself up.

I grabbed my rain slicker and galoshes from the closet; Mama had fashioned my rain gear from a man-sized company-issue mackintosh, cutting it down as best she could to fit me, but it was still pretty clunky. I stuffed the pockets full of cookies and went outside onto the small covered porch. Leaning into the heavy wind, I looked back at Doux Doux, who was watching nervously from the door-way, then I took a deep breath and stepped into six inches of mud and a wall of water. My yellow sou'wester went sailing into the treetops like a wind-swept canary, forcing me to turn my back to the blinding rain. Pulling the attached hood over my head, I yanked the drawstring so tight my eyebrows pushed my eyes partially shut. I was beginning to think this might not have been one of my better ideas, but poor François Noir looked so *pathetic*.

I slogged backwards to reach the big guy, who was still rooted in place and staring, thick as a brick, at the space left by Pee Wee's old cage.

"François," I yelled over the storm. "Want a cookie?" I held out a handful of soggy macaroons.

He turned and looked at me. In the ghostly glow of the plant lights through the rain, I saw the dullness leave his eyes, replaced by...what? Recognition? He smiled. Or grimaced. Whatever, white teeth glowed in his dark face. He looked like a big old dumb boy and I wondered if he was; a boy, I mean. I'd always assumed, because of his size, that he was a man. Now I wasn't so sure.

"*Biscuit?*" I repeated, offering once again a damp clump of coconut and almonds.

He just stood there so I gave up and had about decided to get out of the weather when he reached out, ever so slowly, and took one. Well, he took them all, but who's counting. His huge hand moved up and stuffed the whole gooey mess into his mouth. Actually, most of it went on his face, but he must have got-ten some past his lips, because he stood there chewing like a cow on cud. Now that I'd given him a treat, I was trying to figure out how to get rid of him. It was really cold, it was getting late, and who knew when some parents would show up to claim their little carpet crawlers? Finding a zombie in my backyard would be bad for business.

"Now, François, it's time for you to go. Go on home, now," I said, making lit-tle shooing moves with my hands. He didn't budge, so I raised my voice. "Git."

I might as well have been talking to a fence post. I gave up and had turned away from him to go back into the house when his huge hand clamped down on my shoulder.

My heart went as dead as old François Noir himself. Unwelcome, but very familiar little flashes pinwheeled around my eyes. My chest went as cold as the wind swirling around me, giving my heart an ice ache like I got in my temples when I gulped slushy lemonade too fast. Right then, though, I was gulping for air.

When the zombie's monstrous mitt clamped onto me, Doux Doux let out a loud gasp that I heard above the storm. She stood, fixed in place by fright, in the door opening.

"D-D-Doux Doux," I squeaked, once I got my mouth to work again, "get the machete and stand by." She didn't move for a second and I thought my words had been carried away on the wind, but then her colorless face disappeared from the doorway, and I was left in the lurch with a dead brain. And this time it was mine.

I couldn't think. Now what? I tried taking a step, but François Noir had a death grip on me and with a zombie that's serious business. I knew he could break not only my shoulder, but the rest of me, like a matchstick. With dread surging through my body, I slowly swiveled my feet in the mud to face my captor. Well, I actually would have been looking him in the belt buckle if he had one. As it was, all I could see was an intricately woven sisal sash decorated with sea shells; pretty fancy duds for a corpse.

When my brain clicked back to life, I came up with two choices: I could try punching him in the gut and probably break my fist in the process, or I could try to fool him into letting me go so I could run like the devil. I reached into my pocket and took out more cookies, hoping he'd reach for them with the hand vise-gripping my shoulder.

"S-s-so, François *mon amie*, you want a cookie? François want a *biscuit*?"

"Birds can't talk," he said.

I couldn't believe my ears. Really, I couldn't believe my ears. I figured the wind was playing tricks with sound, or that I hadn't heard it at all, but he said it again: "Birds can't talk." In English! And not only did he repeat himself, he said it in *my* voice. Or rather like Pee Wee mimicking my voice.

About that time Doux Doux flew from the kitchen waving a machete in one hand and a black iron skillet in the other. François Noir whimpered, let go of my shoulder and headed for the bluff.

"Doux Doux!" I yelled, "Stop!"

She did, but I could tell she was set to do battle. Or maybe cook breakfast. I grabbed the machete from her and took off after François Noir, whose head was just disappearing over the edge of the bluff.

"Where are you going?" Doux Doux yelled, an edge of hysteria in her voice. "You come back here, you hear me, Lizbuthann?"

"I'll explain later," I hollered. "Stay with the kids."

"You get back here, you moron! What will I tell your mother?"

"Tell her I've gone after Pee Wee," I threw back over my shoulder, and then took a giant step into space.

# CHAPTER 15

▼

We later learned that Hurricane Hazel packed winds of one-hundred and fifty miles an hour and the eye passed right over Haiti. 'Course, I didn't know any of this when I tracked a dead man over the edge of a bluff, but it wouldn't have mattered: I wanted my parrot back, and François Noir seemed to know where to find him.

The big zombie made the mistake of stopping, maybe to wait for me, right under the cave's overhang. In my rush to follow, I overshot the edge of the bluff, went airborne, and my galoshes connected solidly with his back. He made a little OOOMPH-ing sound as I jackknifed and my middle whomped against his head, knocking the wind from me, and François Noir from his feet. He took a header onto the slimy mud path and we tobagganed for the next hundred feet, he on his stomach, me on his back. He slid with increasing speed headfirst, feet-first, and everything-else-first, before we landed in a heap against a boulder within ten feet of the road. I do not recommend zombie sledding.

Out of breath and dazed—although in a zombie's case that's pretty much a natural state—we nonetheless managed to scramble behind a bush when headlights flashed by. As soon as the truck raced past, throwing mud three feet in the air and all over us, we slogged our way down the road. And I do mean slogged.

A foot of water ran over the gravel road and, from the sound of the river's roar, I guessed it wasn't just rain runoff. I was right. We hadn't walked more than a quarter mile when a river of people, dogs, horses, donkeys, goats and the occasional cart came rushing at us, then past. Whatever they were fleeing was so threatening that in their haste to get away they gave little notice to a seven-foot oooh-gah-oooh and a four-foot redheaded white kid.

I gotta hand it to ole François Noir; when he *had* to move, he could cover some territory. His stride, slow as it seemed, was actually three times as fast as my little legs could churn, but we were making okay progress in spite of the water and wind. I had no idea where we were going and began to question just how bright it was to follow a zombie into a raging storm. I kept looking over my shoulder, worried that Doux Doux had tattled to my parents and, like a scene from a horror movie, villagers with torches and pitchforks were hot on our tail.

The water level on the road continued to rise, but Noir didn't seem to notice. He took a sharp turn off the main road, toward the river; not a great idea, judging from the frantic refugees fleeing from that direction. Just in case one of them took the time to get a look at me and maybe try to collect a buck by dragging me home to Daddy, I put my hood back on to hide my hair. There was no disguising François Noir.

When the water started slopping over my boot tops, I tugged on the zombie's arm, which is much like yanking on a fire log, and got about the same response. Pushing in front of him—no easy task in flooded galoshes—I sloshed backwards, facing him to snag his attention. A bad idea, as it turned out; evidently stopping required a little planning ahead on his part.

I was flat on my back and in danger of being stomped by a number twenty sandal before whatever brainwork it took to halt his forward motion kicked in. He teetered dangerously, spun off balance in an effort to keep from squashing me like a cockroach, and went down hard, butt-first, into the swirling muck. I was so tired I considered taking a breather, but changed my mind when a little snake tried using me for a life raft. Screaming, I jumped up and flung the snake away, right into François Noir's lap. He and the snake both looked a little stunned, and then, ever so gently, François Noir picked up the reptile, stood, and placed the little creature in a tree crotch. I felt a little guilty because, left to me, that snake would have been a goner, what with my opinion that the only good snake is a dead snake.

Witnessing his act of kindness, I realized that François—deader than dirt as he was—cared for life, and that I had nothing to fear from him. But that certainly didn't mean I trusted his judgment, if he had any.

"François, where are we going? And how far is it?" I shouted above the storm, not particularly expecting an answer.

He pointed toward the river.

"Uh, you know, that might not be a real good idea," I yelled in the understatement of the year.

He continued to point and, in a glare of a lightning flash that was instantly followed by a deafening clap of thunder—no *one*-one-thousand, *two*-one-thousand stuff; it was right *here,* right *now*—I spotted a lone shanty near the river bank. Or rather, where I figured the bank *used* to be. The shack, which seemed to be our destination, listed badly and looked as though it would soon be headed downstream. I just hoped we wouldn't end up going with it.

François splashed on toward the hut, seemingly unfazed by the scary weather. Heck, he probably drank lightning for breakfast! I stopped, too tired to go on, and when he discovered I wasn't on his heels, he turned and wolf-whistled.

Zombies can whistle?

Just to prove they can, he did it again.

Above the rumbling thunder, the roaring river and my thumping heart, there was an answering whistle. One I knew so well: Pee Wee!

Overjoyed, a new spurt of strength surged through me and I splashed ahead, even though the water was now knee-high and had picked up speed. The current threatened to sweep me off my feet and my galoshes, filled with water and heaven knows what else, were holding me back, but if I pulled them off I'd be left barefoot. That, in light of the little snake incident, was out of the question. Nothing to do but push on. It was only when I stepped into a deep hole that I remembered I was a lousy swimmer. Oh, and also afraid of the water. Sure, I swam in the shallows often, but I could touch and see bottom there. Now I could do neither. I was, as my Uncle Lloyd would say, in a heap of harm.

As I went under, my slicker filled with silt-laden water and I was sinking fast when François' huge black hand snatched me up and threw me, like a tow sack of potatoes, over his shoulder. Together we trudged on toward the shack.

Lightning flashed almost constantly now, rolling from cloud to cloud. As we neared the thatched hut, I saw it begin to move, shifting position as water undermined its supports. By now I had clambered up onto François' shoulders and, after almost swiping me off with a tree branch, he adjusted his course to avoid low-hangers. From my perch I watched as the hut's door was ripped from its hinges by a blast of wind, and went floating down the river. Next stop, the Caribbean Sea, a hundred miles downstream.

And I knew exactly where, too. Daddy and I had gone down to the mouth of the river during a flood and saw all sorts of debris riding the muddy water into the sea. Dead horses, pigs and cows shared the rampaging water with huge trees and every sort of slimy critter. Patrolling for an easy meal, their dark gray fins slicing the water, sharks waited. I tried to not think about becoming shark bait in the near future.

I heard screeches rising above the storm and scrambled off François' shoulders just before he took my head off on the doorframe of the hut. He didn't fare as well himself; he banged his noggin several times and ended up wedged in the door opening. While he was trying to squeeze through, I waded—actually, I practically dog paddled—to a line of covered cages against the wall. A wall, by the way, that was starting to buckle. Snatching away the soggy rags, I discovered dozens of frantic parrots and macaws shrieking and beating their wings against the wire and each other. And in the last cage, along with ten other wet, frightened birds, was my Pee Wee.

"Come on in," he said, mimicking my mother's voice so well that for a heart-stopping moment I thought Mama had somehow found us.

I opened the cage door and snagged my parrot, suffering several of his roommate's bites as a reward. Cuddling Pee Wee, I gave him a big kiss, wrapped him in a piece of the cage cover, stuck him inside my hood and pulled the strings tight; I wasn't taking any chances on losing that little guy again. He kept up a muffled string of bird conversation going, first telling me how pretty he was and then that birds can't talk. I had never heard such a sweet sound.

I wanted to take my bird and bolt for home, but we had to save the others; it was only a matter of minutes before the entire shack floated off down river, carrying the trapped birds to a watery grave.

François wasn't what you'd call handy with his hands, so it was up to me to open the cages after he lugged them to higher ground a few feet from the shack. Some birds, reluctant to leave the cage and terrified to the point of looking like zombies themselves, had to be pulled out. Others fought back, biting and squawking all the way. One big macaw, capable of taking off a finger, gave François a particularly hard time, but the zombie never flinched as he gently freed the bird.

To make a bad situation worse, most of the birds had had their wings clipped and couldn't fly. Once freed, those that could took off into the storm-tossed sky and found refuge in treetops, but those that couldn't climbed on François, who soon looked like an aviary perch at the San Antonio zoo. Lucky for me my slicker was too, well, slick for them; the last thing I needed was a bunch of birds weighing me down as I was barely staying above water as it was.

We had just released all the birds when, with a crash, the little hut broke loose and tumbled end over end downriver. I shuddered to think what had almost happened to those birds, especially my Pee Wee. It was definitely time to make tracks.

Actually, what we needed was a boat.

Since my perch on François' shoulders was now *very* occupied, he tucked me under his arm and trudged toward home. We made it back to the road, which was more like a swift stream, but still easier going then where we'd been. There was no way on earth I could climb that slimy bluff back up to my house, so we joined the pack of refugees headed for high ground via the main road. Soon I was able to walk on my own and, in my slicker, with mud smeared all over my face, I didn't stand out in the crowd. I was, however, a mite concerned about sneaking François past the guard shack. Even though the old guard was half-blind, I suspected he just might notice a seven-foot oooh-gah-oooh covered in screeching birds.

I needn't have worried. I turned to say something to François, and he was gone.

"Jeezuz*cris*lizbuthann," Daddy roared. "Where have you been?"

It was time for some very quick thinking. "Uh, didn't Doux Doux tell you?"

"She said you went to get Pee Wee."

"That's right. And I did." Gee, I can be sooo clever.

Silence followed. Well, silence in the form of talk; the downpour on our tin roof sounded like we were inside a train engine. Uncle Lloyd, Mama, Daddy and Grandmother Hetta all stared at me, waiting to see what I would come up with next, so I threw off my hood and slicker, unwrapped Pee Wee and produced him with all flourish of a magician.

"Tah-dah," I said, and took a bow. Pee Wee shook himself and said something really rude.

Uncle Lloyd grinned, but Mother screamed and pointed in horror. I didn't think Pee Wee had been *that* rude.

"Oh, hell," Daddy said.

My grandmother went all pale and whispered, "Oh, dear God."

I wondered if I'd sprouted horns, but it was worse than that. I was covered, head to toe, with leeches. It was my turn to scream.

There's not much nice I can say about leeches. They are slimy and, when removed, leave an itchy red spot, as well as all manner of nightmare material. Uncle Lloyd did a real good job of getting them off me, though; didn't singe me even once with his cigarette. My mother, who had gone greenish, fled the room, but Grandmother Hetta stayed, holding and patting my hand while Uncle Lloyd barbequed bloodsuckers. Daddy paced, twirled his hair and cussed. Pee Wee paid special attention to Daddy, no doubt hoping to pick up a few new words. I remained uncommonly calm, not even fainting once.

After the leech ordeal was over and I'd bottled them in alcohol so I could show them to Doux Doux, I had a big breakfast and went to bed. It was still stormy and dark, but the rain had let up a little. What we didn't know was that the worst part wasn't over. We were marooned.

Péligre was cut off from the rest of the world by Hurricane Hazel's fury and, in no time at all, our supplies dwindled. Daddy and Uncle Lloyd estimated it would be a week before the floodwaters went down to a point where they could rebuild the roads, and who knew how long before trucks with provisions could get in. Our water supply was fouled as well, so all water had to be boiled and strained and doctored with iodine. To make matters worse, five thousand Haitians were stranded with us, so what stocks the commissary had didn't last long. We ate all the frozen stuff first, because if the diesel fuel ran out, we would lose electricity. All things considered, Camp was better off than most of Haiti, for at least we had food, shelter and no one was injured, unless you count leech attacks. I was, however, in dire need of bird food.

"Lizbuthann, did you bring all those parrots home with you?" Mama asked, peering out back where about fifty brightly feathered birds roosted on top of our chicken coop.

"Uh, well, I guess they sort of followed Pee Wee," I said, wondering where François lurked, since he had obviously dropped off his flock. Bless Doux Doux's little heart, she had not told anyone about him, only that I had heard Pee Wee squawking and went out looking for him.

"Well, then, daughter dear, you can sort of feed them."

Doux Doux and I saddled Wishes and Smokey and went out into the jungle in search of food each day. It wasn't hard, since the storm had knocked papayas, avocados, cashews and the like out of their trees and all we had to do was pick them up before they rotted. We gave the good stuff to our parents to share with everyone else and fed the overripe stuff to our birds. Or rather, *my* birds; Doux Doux, my mother, and Guilliame made that very clear as the backyard bird poop piled up. Guilliame threatened to quit if I didn't do something about the pesky birds over-fertilizing his garden, so I was kept hopping; first finding food for, then cleaning up after, my new flock.

Doux Doux suggested that I'd have less to clean up if I stopped feeding them, and I saw the wisdom of her words, but didn't have the heart to cut their rations. Lucky for me, many people in Camp started adopting them, so little by little I won what Uncle Lloyd called the Bird Turd War. Very funny.

With all this stuff going on—us being on the brink of disaster and starvation and all—wouldn't you think they'd cancel school? Not on your life. Which isn't always fair, I've found. And just when things started getting back to normal, we ended up smack dab in the middle of a real revolution.

This time I didn't even start it.

# CHAPTER 16

▼

François took a powder after the Pee Wee adventure. I began to worry about him a little, but Doux Doux said that he probably decided that hanging out with me was just too much trouble. Such a smarty pants, my friend.

Doux Doux and I, having had just about all the excitement we needed for a while, got back to the regular business of being kids. Or what passed as regular for us: school, riding horses, swinging from Tarzan ropes and running the snoopery end of our Brenda Starr Club. We even somehow managed to stay out of hot water for a spell. I was trying to be especially well-behaved because Grandmother Hetta was leaving for Texas soon and I didn't want her to worry about me, as she was prone to do. When she did leave, though, I was really sad and moped around so much that Daddy took pity on me and began hauling me off to work with him for a couple of hours now and again.

My father had this really neat job. As a cableway operator, he got to build the dam. Oh sure, others helped, but in my mind the fact that he actually poured the concrete made him the most important.

Some genius engineer figured out that concrete sets up better when poured at fifty-five degrees Fahrenheit, which Momo-san made us convert to twelve Celsius since we were studying the metric system. I actually preferred the metric system because everything is in tens and a lot easier to remember than feet, inches and all that stuff. Anyhow, I don't think, with the exception of when Hurricane Hazel roared through, it had *ever* been fifty-five in Haiti, so they built an ice plant for cooling what my daddy called the "grout."

"Once the grout mix is just right—cement, sand and ten pounds of chipped ice—I dump all eight cubic yards right where they need it," he said, pointing to the scaffolding and forms far below, in the dry river gorge.

"It's like a recipe," I said, and Daddy grinned.

"That's right, Ann, and we're building one mighty big cake."

Using levers, Daddy maneuvered the bucket full of concrete to where a ground crew, using an air ram, would release the gooey mixture into a waiting wooden form. Sometimes, when there was no wind whistling down the valley, no big bosses about, and it was not a tricky dump, he let me do it. I couldn't tell anyone, not even Doux Doux, that he let me work the levers (he kept his hands over mine, just in case) because he'd get fired and we'd have to leave Haiti and I sure as heck didn't want that to happen. Uncle Lloyd, who was the only one who was allowed to see me pour a batch, said I was Daddy's only son. That Uncle Lloyd: such a clown.

Without Grandmother to go to bat for me, I took extra care to keep my nose clean, even though it isn't my true nature. But I had a past, and just about the time I was congratulating myself for staying out of trouble, Angela decided to clean up my raingear, which had been just *fine* hanging in a closet, thank you very much. She was laying for me when I walked through the kitchen door one afternoon. I'd never seen her so angry.

"Child!" Angela hissed, keeping her voice low so Mama, who was sewing in the bedroom, wouldn't hear. When Angela called me "child" in that tone of voice, I was usually in for it. I tried backing out the door, but she caught my arm.

"What?" I said, trying to think what had made her so mad. Other than the chocolate milk mess I'd left on the counter that morning when I was running late for school, I couldn't think of a thing.

She reached in the pocket of her hibiscus-splashed frock and pulled out a *vevé,* a voodoo banner. "Where did you get this...this...t'ing?"

I was genuinely bamboozled. "Me?" I said.

"Yes, little smart girl. Who else be wearing you raincoat?"

"Uh, well, nobody, I guess?" I said. I must have looked truly puzzled because she let go of my arm and stepped back. "Uh, where did you find it, Angela?"

She pushed me outside and pointed to my mackintosh hanging on the clothesline and a memory flashed: I had grabbed a colorful cloth covering Pee Wee's cage on the night we rescued him. Oh, boy. I tried thinking fast, but couldn't come up with anything clever; I'd flat forgotten all about that cloth, and I certainly hadn't known it was a voodoo flag. Stalling, I opened my mouth to deny everything, but Angela put a shaky finger on my nose.

"Do not. Do not even *t'ink* about lying to Angela. If you do, I will make you life a misery. Now, where you get this?" She shook the banner in my face and I could see it matched those on the dead-chicken trail, as well as the cloth lining the basket I'd purchased from the white-eyed egg witch.

Dead chickens, *vevés*, *hounforts*, oooh-gah-ooohs, the witchy woman, and then Pee Wee held prisoner added up to no good, and they were all linked by one thing: the zombie. I had a sudden and dreadful thought: could François be in trouble? Had that old egg-hag-witch-woman taken revenge on him for guiding me to my bird?

I must have turned pale, because suddenly Angela looked concerned instead of mad. "Are you all right, child?"

"Y-yes. I think so, Angela, but I have something to tell you."

I left out nothing: silhouette, voodoo meeting, zombie, fishnet, witch/egg woman, Pee Wee. All of it.

Angela let me talk, never once interrupting as I spun out my ill-fated tale, mess-up by mess-up. Hearing my own yarn unfold—at times as dramatic as any in "True Confessions" stories—I began to feel more and more wicked. Not only had I been disobedient, thoughtless, reckless and stupid, my actions had put others in harm's way. I mean, who in their right mind would go out *looking* for witch doctors and zombies? Brenda Starr hunted down Nazis, but at least she had backup: Basil St. John, mystery man. Doux Doux and I only had each other.

Angela remained stone-faced throughout my story, except for a twitch or two when I told the juicy parts, like when I fell out of the tree into the voodoo meeting, and the zombie-netting. When I finished she sat in silence for a full minute before bursting into laughter.

"Oh, child," she said in her soft lilt between guffaws, "you be something. That be for sure." Then she caught her breath and became serious again. "But, if what you just tell me be true, and I t'ink it is because no one, not even you, could make it up, I should probably tell you *maman* and get you fanny pinked up with that little switch of hers she never uses. I sure should." I must have looked worried, because she added, "But I will not."

I heaved a sigh. Not that my mother would actually use a switch on me, but she could do much worse, like maybe take Wishes away for life this time. I must have looked a bit too relieved, because Angela wagged her finger before my nose.

"Don' get happy yet, you wicked girl," she growled. "I am not so finish wit' you. "Angela must t'ink about all this, and what we should do."

"Do?"

"Oh, yes. Do. You and this family be in danger."

"Oh, that oooh-gah-oooh wouldn't hurt a fly, Angela. Honest."

"Maybe, maybe not."

"I just know he wouldn't, Angela. He looks scary, but he acts like a little kid. He even gives me small gifts once in awhile. Not much, maybe just a pretty rock, but always something. Wait here, I'll show you what he gave me."

I raced to my room, dug into the bottom of my book locker and found the belt François Noir gave me to hold my rain gear closed on the night of the Pee Wee rescue. The delicate shells woven into the intricate sisal pattern rattled as I stuffed it into my pocket and headed back outside. As I passed her room, Mama, never turning from her sewing machine, said, "No running in the house, Lizbuthann. And I hope you didn't wake your sister from her nap."

"No ma'am, she's out like a light." I slowed my pace and joined Angela at the clothesline where she was unpinning laundry, stuffing wooden clothes pins into her pockets as she went. The smell of freshly washed clothes wafted on a breeze, bringing unexpected tears to my eyes: Grandmother Hetta always had that fresh-soap smell.

"I miss her, too," Angela said. "Your *grand-mère* be one fine woman."

"How did you know I was thinking of her?"

"I be witchy woman, child, and don' you forget it." She giggled and I began to laugh with her, until she stopped suddenly. "Oh, child!" she said, putting her hand to her cheek. "That fish! Trashrack! My husband, he spend so much time tryin' to catch him."

I shook my head slowly and we roared with laughter again. Angela had a way of making me feel better and I vowed to do anything *not* to upset her ever again. That lasted about one minute, until I pulled the belt from my pocket to show her. She took one look at it, dropped the laundry basket, screamed and fainted. So much for not upsetting her.

I was on my knees, fanning Angela's pale face with a pair of Daddy's under shorts when Mama came on the run. Kneeling down next to me, my mother grabbed a washcloth from the laundry basket and sent me to wet it with a nearby garden hose. By the time I returned, Angela was sitting, but her eyes remained closed and she was white as death. I dabbed cool water on her forehead and she opened unfocused eyes, but some pink flooded her cheeks.

"Oh, Angela, I'm so sorry," I said, forgetting that my mother was right there next to us.

"Lizbuthann, what did you do to our poor Angela?" Mama demanded. She looked around for any snake, lizard or spider that I might have inflicted on the unfortunate woman.

"Uh, well, I—"

Angela interrupted me. "The child don' do not'ing. Not'ing at all."

Mama didn't look convinced, but sighed and helped Angela to her feet. We guided her inside on the couch, where my mother insisted Angela rest for a bit and Angela, for once, didn't protest. I made her a cup of tea and within a half-hour she was back to her old self: grouchy.

My mother checked on us often, but was soon convinced Angela would live. "Do y'all think you'll be all right here if I leave? My bridge club meets in a few minutes, but I can cancel."

"You go on, Mama, I'll stay with Angela. We'll be just fine, won't we?" I looked at Angela, who bobbed her head.

"Well, I guess, if you say so. If anything happens, you run over to Clota Boudreaux's and get me, you hear, Lizbuthann?"

"Yes, ma'am. I will."

As soon as my mother left, Angela sat up, took a deep breath and said, "Tell me 'bout this oooh-gah-oooh of yours."

"Well, he's big. And bald. And why'd you go and faint on me?"

"Jus' the surprise. This, uh, zombie? He be old?"

"No, just bald. I think he's young. Well, not young, young. Maybe twenty? Yeah, I'd say François is about that, but it's hard to tell what with him being so dim and all."

Angela whispered, "François," caught her breath and I thought I was going to lose her again.

"Put your head between your knees," I yelled. I didn't know if it worked or not, but I'd seen it in a movie. She didn't conk out, so I guess it did. She sat back up, became very calm and demanded I tell her everything I knew about François.

I recalled every detail about the big guy that I could remember and then added, "The only thing I can't figure out is why, from day one, he seems to have been following me. I mean, he showed up at my bedroom window our very first night in Camp."

"Red hair," Angela said.

"Huh?"

"You hair. He be drawn to that nest of red on you head."

I thought about getting indignant over her calling my hair a nest, but while in my fantasies I saw myself as Brenda Starr, in truth I more resembled Little Orphan Annie.

"How do you know that?" I asked.

"Because, child, I might know this François. I t'ink I know who he be."

# CHAPTER 17

▼

"Who be he?" I asked, truly puzzled by Angela's statement.

"A very long story, child."

"I got time."

Angela sighed and took a sip of tea.

"It may be I made that belt for him. I t'ink he be my baby brother, for sure. My papa, he die when I was young girl, just a few years older than you. My *maman*, she lonely and poor, so she marry to this Haitian man who bring us here. I did not like him. He be mean. And big. Ugly, like big monkey."

"Gorilla?"

"No, this man not brave enough to be rebel. He only beat on little kids."

I let it go. "Like you?"

She shook her head. "I old enough to stay out his way, but after my brother, François, born, he just barely walk when this man start hittin' him. Poor child, he could not do not'ing right. *Maman* and me, we try to safe him, but we be two small women and one day when I come back from the market, I find François all bloody in the head, and the man, he gone for good. But it be too late for that boy. He never get right in the head again. And so sweet, that boy. Never hurt nobody. But he suffer. Bad *mal de tête*."

"Headaches?"

Angela nodded, her eyes misting up. "I would hold the boy, sing songs and tell stories I make up just for him. One story, about little white angel girl wit' red hair like fire. I have this doll, I t'ink you call Rag Ann?"

"Raggedy Ann. I used to have one."

"That be it, child. Somebody at mission give her to me when I was *petite fille*. I tell François, when he hurt too bad, that this angel doll, she can stop head pain. He believe so much her magic, his head sometime stop paining."

"So that's why he follows me? He thinks I'm an angel?"

"Well," she smiled, "he don' know you."

"Very funny. But wait a minute," I said, "if the bad man was gone, why didn't François stay with you and your mama?"

"He did, for a time. But then he gots very sick wit' fever. Bad fever."

"Like I had?"

"Worse. Much worse. This boy, he go to sleep and not wake, the fever so bad."

"Poor François," I said. "No wonder he looks so sad. He's had such a hard life."

Angela shook her head and began to cry, burying her face into her hands. I just waited, not knowing what to do. Finally, she patted her eyes dry with the edge of her skirt.

"No, child."

"No, what?"

"No child, François he not have hard life. He have no life. He *mort*."

"*Mort?*"

"Yes, dead. He never wake from that fever. He is gone for ten years past."

My heart gave a little thump and my mouth went dry. "Angela, if François died ten years ago, and now he's out walking around, that would for sure make him a—" I stopped, not wanting to be the one to say the obvious. I mean, calling someone's little brother a zombie is just not polite.

Angela made little shrugs with her shoulders and wrung her hands, as though trying to choke her dress, on her hibiscus print hem. "Then I must t'ink…well, I just don' want to."

I didn't blame her. What if my little sister, God forbid, should die and then ten years later I found her out walking around? How would I feel? Angela looked so miserable I had to say something.

"Look, Angela, we don't know for sure it's him."

"Child, I t'ink so. He was stole."

"Stole?"

"Yes, and it be my fault. All my fault." She collapsed in sobs again.

"How could it be your fault, Angela? You were only a kid, and he died of fever."

"Yes, so they say. But it was me s'pose to sit up all night, keep watch on his grave. *Ma mère* and me, we was too poor to pay for cemetery guard."

"A cemetery guard? What's that?"

"When peoples die in Haiti, is custom to hire man to sit by grave for three day. Three day be enough time so body no good to voodoo peoples."

I was trying not to picture what a body would look like after three days underground, or even in one of those little cement houses I'd seen in the cemeteries. "Oh, yeah, now I remember reading about that in the book you took away from me. So what happened?"

"Well, first we have visit. All neighbors and relatives, they bring food and drink and then when it get dark, I go to sit wit' grave until midnight. But I t'ink someone give me somet'ing bad in my food, because I fall dead asleep. And when *ma mère*, she shake me awake, François, he gone. And child, when we bury him, he be wearing the belt I made."

Yikes! I couldn't dig that belt out of my pocket and throw it down fast enough. I was more frightened by the idea of falling asleep in a cemetery than anything else Angela told me, but the whole thing was plenty spooky. No wonder she'd gotten so angry with me that day when I asked if she believed in zombies; she secretly suspected she might be related to one, and she felt guilty that she had, through negligence, caused him to be raised from the dead.

"Well, then," I said with great authority, "we'll just get him back from those grave-thieving villains." I hoped I sounded as confident as Brenda Starr would have. I pictured her with that little balloon over her head, saying the same thing.

Angela cocked her head and gave me a doubting look. "How we do that?"

"Uh, well, we'll think of something."

Angela nodded. "I hope so, child."

*Me, too*, I was thinking, but I said: "Count on it."

So, typical for me, I had taken on a big load this time. It was up to us—well, me—to come up with a way to save François from the witchy egg woman. Or so I guessed. I wasn't even sure he needed saving, but if he did need help, what could I do? And how? And then what? Research was definitely in order.

"Angela, I need that book, "Tell My Horse," back.

Angela stood and walked to the kitchen, climbed on a stool and dug it from behind several bags of flour. Dang, that was the only place I hadn't looked.

She caught my look and gave me a smarty-pants grin.

Miffed that I had been outwitted, I snatched the book and stuck out my tongue. Angela laughed as I sat down and began to read, searching for clues and making notes. Brenda Starr in action. I was determined to learn everything I could about zombies, or more importantly, how to get one from the clutches of a witch doctor.

For several days Angela and I pored over that book whenever no other adults lurked in the house. I couldn't even tell Doux Doux what I was up to since Angela and I swore a bond of secrecy, deciding that the fewer who knew, the safer we, and they, would be.

Angela began making discreet inquiries about the witch woman, even though we were not absolutely certain she had anything at all to do with François. She carefully questioned the other maids in Camp, as well as residents of her village.

I checked the backyard each night, hoping for François' return and trying to figure out how we could arrange for Angela to get a look at him if he did. There was, after all, the off-chance that he was just a plain old zombie and not her brother-the-zombie at all. I also made a few inquiries of my own.

"Mama," I said one day as we walked home from the commissary, "did you know that fever can kill you?"

"Well, yes. I guess so, if it goes high enough. But don't worry, honey, these days we have medicine to take care of such things, if that's why you asked."

"Not me. I mean, did you ever know anyone who died of fever?"

"I guess not. Not from fever alone, anyway. A lot of people died from flu years ago and there was a girl who went to school with me who didn't die of fever, but hers went so high that when she got well all her hair fell out." She ruffled my mop and added, "Obviously, you didn't even get close."

I smiled, but was thinking about what she said. "This friend of yours, did her hair grow back?"

"Nope. When we got older and she started taking an interest in boys, she told me she almost wished she had died from the fever, because in those days wigs were hard to come by and boys just made fun of her bald head. Funny thing is, once she got a wig and learned to paint on her eyebrows, as was all the rage any-how, she turned out to be a beautiful woman. Works out that way sometimes. Why do you ask?"

"Oh, just something I read about."

The clues were adding up. We dumped the groceries in the kitchen and I lingered to help Angela put them away. As soon as Mama was out of earshot, I whispered, "Guess what, Angela? Very high fever can make your hair fall out. And François is bald." Lizbuthann Starr: girl sleuth.

Angela nodded and we talked quietly, two conspirators on a mission.

Mama came back into the kitchen and smiled. "What do you two always have your heads together about? I swear, if I didn't know better I'd think you were cooking something up."

"Us? Nope, nothing important," I said.

Mama didn't look convinced, but I was being so good these days she probably didn't want to rock the boat. Daddy even kidded her at supper one night, asking what she'd done with his daughter, Ann, and who was this kid at the table? Ha-ha.

Truth is, I didn't have time to get into hot water. Right after school each day I went on the hunt for François, and since Doux Doux was all in love again with a new boy in Camp named Roger Wales, she didn't even ask to tag along. If I hadn't been so engrossed in the hunt for François, I probably would' a had my feelings hurt.

I rode back to the *hounfort* and left fudge in a Ball jar, but when I returned the candy had turned into a moldy mess. I rode mountain paths to the more remote Haitian villages, just in case I caught a peek of François, but no luck. I even left cookies outside my window, but a stray dog found 'em. Poor thing was so skinny I didn't have the heart to run him off like I was supposed to. I even started secretly sneaking food out for the poor mutt after dinner, which was completely against the house rules.

There were lots of stray dogs in Haiti, but we kids were told in no uncertain terms to have nothing to do with them. Daddy said they were a nuisance and got into the garbage and stuff. The soldiers shot them on sight. I knew the grown-ups were only trying to protect us kids, but there was no way I was going to let an animal go hungry.

Ti-chien—little dog, as I called him—was scrawny, scruffy and flea-bitten, but he had these big sad eyes and he wagged his tail as he slunk forward for his nightly handout. He was smart enough not to brave Angela's broom of doom during daylight hours, but when lights went out in the house, he was patiently waiting for his evening meal. Sometimes I could only manage bread, but he was just as grateful for that as he was leftover steak.

I knew better than to ask Daddy if I could make a pet out of the dog. My father didn't like dogs, because when he was a kid his father had kept more than thirty redbone tracking hounds that had to be fed and cared for, so to my Daddy dogs were just a big pain in the you-know-what. Besides, I had Pee Wee.

Once, when I took off up a trail on the lookout for François, I heard a noise behind me and found Ti-chien trotting down the path behind us. Wishes gave him a dirty look and one swift kick when he got too close, but after that they seemed to make their peace. It was kind of nice having a dog along for company, but as soon as we neared Camp, Ti-chien dropped back and I wouldn't see him again until after lights-out.

That little dog didn't stay little. After a few weeks of regular meals, Ti-chien filled out and grew. And grew. I began to suspect there was a fence-jumpin' German shepherd somewhere in those Haitian hills.

Doux Doux began sneaking leftovers to my house after dinner as Ti-chien's appetite became more demanding, and picky. Bread scraps no longer did the trick. He'd just snuffle them a little and turn up his nose. Unfortunately, as he grew more confident about his next meal, he also began losing his fear of humans and I knew this to be very bad for a dog in a country like Haiti. Dogs that did not cower and run away from people found themselves targets of very practiced rock throwers. Doux Doux and I had quickly learned that even bending towards the ground, pretending to pick up an imaginary rock, sent threatening Haitian dogs skittering for cover.

Now I worried that, by making Ti-chien healthy and well-fed, I had put him in danger. As Grandmother Hetta always said, "No good deed goes unpunished."

Daddy was probably right when he told me to leave well enough alone where dogs were concerned, but, of course, my father knew nothing of Ti-chien and I intended to keep it that way. Angela, however, was harder to keep in the dark.

"Child, you see that big ole shaggy *chien* be hanging 'round the back door last evenin'?" she asked. Angela usually left before dinner, but had stayed on to use Mother's sewing machine to whip up yet another flower-festooned creation.

"Uh, nope." I crossed my fingers behind my back.

"You would not be feedin' any ugly old *chien*, would you? You know you papa tol' you about these thing. These dog be dangerous. They have sickness and they mean. You better not let Angela catch you feedin' one."

"Yes, ma'am."

She glared at me for a moment, then dropped her eyes and her voice. "I ask all 'round. No body be seein' this François."

I giggled. "And he ain't someone you'd readily forget, I reckon. Same here. No footprints last night, or any night. Nothing. You know, it's been over three months now since I've seen him. Maybe he left for good."

"I pray not. Oh, what I would give to see that boy again."

I couldn't stand the pain in her eyes, so I fibbed. "We will. I just know it, Angela," I said, although I doubted it.

"I hope so, child."

And we did. Or *I* did.

But boy, oh boy, did I land us *all* in deep you-know-what this time.

# CHAPTER 18

▼

The hunt for François stalled as the months went by without a trace.

I gave up on ever seeing him again, deciding that he really was gone for good. I didn't tell Angela what I thought, though, because she still held out hope she'd see him and that when she did, he'd prove to be her long lost brother.

Truth be told, I was a little relieved by the zombie's disappearance, since his presence had almost always caused me problems, and right then I had a far bigger problem: Ti-chien.

Not only had the stray dog grown huge, he was also becoming way too bold about his appearances around Camp. And on top of that, he was fiercely protective of me and, oddly enough, Wishes, who had finally quit trying to kick his brains out. Even worse, when Ti-chien followed us up into the mountains, he growled, bared his teeth and made threatening moves towards Haitians walking along the trail. Lucky for him they were bad shots and he was only grazed a few times by their rocks. More dangerous to his well-being than his bad behavior towards strangers, though, was letting Angela spot him hanging out behind the chicken coop in broad daylight. She launched a couple of rocks of her own and Ti-chien wisely retreated, but he just wasn't humble enough about it to keep out of trouble. Doux Doux said he just took after me.

"I run off that flea bite *chien* again today," I heard Angela tell Mama.

"Poor thing's probably just hungry," my mother said.

"He don' look hungry," Angela grumbled. She eyed me with a mean squint and planted her hands on her daisy-covered hips. "He look like *somebody* be feedin' him good and I better not catch that somebody. If I see him near this house again, I whack off his tail."

Mama just smiled, but I took the threat seriously: Angela wielded a mean machete. Doux Doux and I had to do something about our dog.

"*Our* dog?" Doux Doux scoffed. "Mais cheré, when did he get to be *our* dog?"

"Well, you feed him, too."

"I bring food for you to give him. There is a difference. And I'm not the one he follows around, the one who started feeding him in the first place. Anyhow, just what are you gonna do? Cut off his rations before Angela lops off his tail?"

"It's an idea, but I was thinking maybe we could find him a home. I mean, he's a good looking dog now and maybe some Haitian would like him for a pet."

"These Haitians out in the mountains can barely feed themselves, much less a huge dog. Besides, what're you going to do? Put up a sign, 'Free Dog to Good Home. Contact Lizbuthann'?"

She had a point. As bad as I hated to, I stopped feeding him, and after a few nights he quit hanging around. I felt awful, knowing he was out there, probably hungry, but it was for his own good. Then, late one night, I woke to his pitiful whines and knew I could not let him starve. I rummaged around in the icebox and came up with some cheese slices before going outside. Ti-chien looked sickly-thin and I felt even worse that I'd let him down, but he didn't seem all that hungry. He took the cheese from my hand, ate with little gusto, and then slinked off.

I didn't see the dog again for a few more nights, but when I did hear him whine and went out to check on him, I was horrified to find a bag of bones that could barely stand on his wobbly legs. Upset to the point of tears, I rushed back to the kitchen for a bowl of milk, but he wouldn't touch it. Trying to encourage him, I reached out to scratch his ears and was dumbfounded when he growled, bared his teeth and, when I jerked my hand away, he snapped so close to my fingers that his hot breath felt like a steam burn. Scared witless, I jumped back out of his range just as he struck out again. Clumsily regaining my balance and, using every bit of calm I could possibly gather, I tried sweet talk, but it came out in a warble.

"Gooood d-d-awg. Ni-ccce dawgggie," I stuttered while taking baby steps backward, toward the safety of the house. Ti-chien wasn't buying it and, in a move faster than I would have believed possible, he practically jumped straight up and landed between me and the back door. With unbelievable strength and fury for a dog that had looked to be on his last legs only minutes before, he attacked the air around him as if at flies, and began an eerie moan-y, growl-y whine that made stood my neck hairs on end. He was one mad dog.

Mad dog! My brain raced. What did I know about mad dogs? Rabid dogs? What I did know was that I was in deep trouble.

"T-ti-chien," I stuttered, "it's me. Lizbuthann. Good boy, Ti-chien."

He stopped growling and cocked his head, looking confused. I swear he was squinting, as if trying to remember me. Encouraged I took a little step towards him, hoping to circle around and make a break for the door. This was a mistake.

Ti-chien charged, snarling and gnashing the air and filling the night with very scary howls. As he moved in on me, I saw white foam boiling from his mouth and red hatred burning in his eyes. There was no doubt that the little dog I had saved from starvation now wanted to kill me, and there was only one thing for me to do: I screamed bloody murder.

The neighbors' lights began to come on, but my own home remained dark. Where was everyone? Then I remembered; Mama had that big electric fan on in their room. The one with the motor that drowned out the growling aggregate plant so they could sleep. It also seemed to work well on growling, howling dog noises, as well. Maybe Sister would wake up and go get them? I could only hope.

Ti-chien made another lunge at me, but I leaped back just in time. He was working himself into a real frenzy now, running around me in circles and charging in if I moved. I didn't dare look away from him, so I spun round and round, trying to keep an eye on him and getting pretty dizzy in the process. At least I *hoped* I was just getting dizzy; the last thing I needed to do right now was to faint, even though it was mighty tempting.

I was only ten feet from the open back door of my house; ten feet from safety. It might as well have been a mile. Even if I somehow managed to fake him out and run like the devil, I doubted I could make it before he jumped me from behind. I could hear Wishes in his corral starting to whinny and stomp the ground and was glad he couldn't get out, because I know for sure he'd go after Ti-chien and maybe get hurt. Ditto with Pee Wee; he was squawking, but safely caged. That was *some* fan Mama and Daddy had in their room.

I desperately tried to think up an escape plan. Maybe, if I timed it just so when Ti-chien went by in one direction, I could make a break for the door in the other? Once again Ti-chien circled, but this time I was ready. With a thundering heart, I counted to one, sucked in a deep breath and willed my weak legs to run two whole strides before tripping on an untied shoelace.

I went down like a sack of potatoes and watched in frozen horror as Ti-chien dashed in for the kill. Wouldn't you know it? Just when I needed a good fainting spell, danged if I could muster one. Resolved to meet my fate, I closed my eyes and steeled myself for hot breath and drippy fangs, but was surprised to find myself, instead of being ripped to shreds, sailing through the air.

I was flying, just like Peter Pan; rising up and away from danger. It was a wonderful feeling. Peaceful. I must, I thought, be on my way to Aunt Tody, assuming the age limit thing hadn't kicked in. If it had, then what the heck, anything was better than becoming dog meat. But then, with a bone-jarring WHOMP, I landed. Opening my eyes, I found myself not in Heaven, but, even better, on the kitchen floor.

Scrambling to slam the door shut, I heard blood-curdling yelps and looked out to see Ti-chien flying through the air himself, landing with a rib-cracking thud, and then making a frenzied run at none other than my favorite zombie, François.

Big, old, slow François was no match for the dog's speed, but he made up for it in sheer bulk. Even when Ti-chien dashed in and clamped down on the big man's ankle, the bite sending a spray of zombie blood into the air, François simply kicked him away. Ti-chien sailed straight up once more, but this time, when he crashed to earth with a groan, he collapsed in a still heap. The dog didn't move again, and when I looked back to check on François, he was gone; a good thing, because just then Daddy came running into the kitchen, gun in hand. About time, I'd say.

"What in the hell?" Daddy yelled and started out the back door.

"No, Daddy! There's a mad dog out there. He tried to bite me," I said.

"You stay here, Ann," he said, shaking off my hand. "I'll be careful. Can't no dog stand up to a sawed-off."

Mama and Sister, who had come into the kitchen by now, watched with me as my father stepped outside and waved off those neighbors who had *finally* started showing up. "Keep back," Daddy warned, "Ann says we got us a mad dog here." He walked cautiously towards the unmoving form of Ti-chien, circled once and poked the dog with his gun. Ti-chien made one feeble nip in his direction, but it was his last: Daddy stepped back and calmly let go with both barrels.

"We will," Doctor Hypodermic said, "have to start inoculations immediately."

I didn't like the sound of that.

"But for the first one, we must go to Port-au-Prince. The rest we can do here, after I get the serum."

*The rest?*

"Then," Doc Disaster continued, "if tests prove the dog not to be rabid, we can discontinue treatment."

"How long will it take to find out if that dog was mad?" Mother asked.

"I will take the dog, or what's left of him after that gun blast, with us to Port-au-Prince. Most of his head and the brain seem to be undamaged, so we should have the results within ten days."

*Ten days?* I *really* wasn't liking the sound of this, not at all.

"Wait a minute," I said, "what inoculations? And if we can stop them in ten days, how long does this so-called treatment last?"

The doctor gave me a wary look. He knew how hard to handle I could be when he had a needle in his paw.

"Fifteen days. Once a day. Starting as soon as we get to the hospital in Port-au-Prince."

"What if I don't want any old shots? Can't we just wait and see if Ti…uh…that dog was sick? I mean, I might have to get all those shots for nothing."

The quack shook his head. "We cannot take that chance. If we do not start the treatment, and it proves to be hydrophobia, you will die a horrible death. Now, who else may have had contact with this dog?"

What could I say? Well, I could say: *There's this guy named François, but he's already dead so I guess rabies wouldn't be any big deal.*

"Lizbuthann," Mama said, mistaking my silence for a stall. "Tell us anyone who had anything to do with this damned dog."

Yikes, when Mama cusses, it's serious. So I blurted, "Doux Doux."

"Lizbuthann, our friendship is definitely *o*-ver. Finished. Done," Doux Doux growled on our way back from Port-au-Prince. "If I had the strength, and my stomach didn't hurt so much, I would kill you right here in the ambulance."

"I'm sorry, Doux Doux, really I am. Mama made me tell. And the truth is, what if Ti-chien did have rabies? I mean, you petted him, too."

"Oh, shut up."

So I did. But all the way back home, I worried about François, and whether I should tell Doux Doux about him. Or the doctor, for that matter. If I told Doctor Dumb, though, he was sure to blab to Mama, and I'd be in trouble again. Danged if you do, danged if you don't.

I had just about gotten up the courage to tell the doc that he had another customer out there somewhere when we pulled up in front of what used to be our velvety green lawn. Guilliame, the yard boy, stood in the road, pacing and throwing his hands around. Angela, Sister, Mama and Daddy watched as Uncle Lloyd, driving a D-8 dozer, scraped what was left of our grass into a huge pile of dirt. Another man transferred the pile into a dump truck with a front end loader.

"Mais Lizbuthann, what are they doing?" Doux Doux said, forgetting she wasn't speaking to me.

"Beats me," I said, jumping from the ambulance. "Ouch," I added when I tried standing straight and my sore stomach pulled me over in a crouch. Doux Doux had the same problem. That shot in the stomach not only hurt going in, it made the muscles cramp, and thanks to all those hours swinging on Tarzan ropes, we both had stomach muscles of iron. Well, Doux Doux did, mine were somewhat damaged by that little bout with polio, but I still had tough enough gut muscles that even Doctor Whacker had trouble pounding in his needle of torture. It looked like Doux Doux and I were doomed to walk hunched over like little old ladies for at least ten days, maybe fifteen.

Angela saw me and came on the run. "Oh, *bébé*, you be all right?"

"Yeah, I'm okay, thanks. What are they doing to our yard?"

Mama, hot on Angela's heels, rushed up and gave me a hug. "Oh, honey. I'm so glad you're home safe and sound. I told Bud I should go with you, but he thought I'd better stick around here and he was right. I had to keep everyone away from the yard. All the places where that dog might have dripped saliva or blood must be removed. Poor Guilliame is beside himself. He'll have to start all over on our lawn. I don't know why that mongrel had to pick *our* yard to die in."

Angela gave me the eye, but I just shrugged. "Yes, child," she said, "and how it be that you be outside jus' when dis flea bite *chien* show up? Just bad luck, I s'ppose?" She put a great deal of sarcasm in that, "I s'ppose?"

I wisely kept my big trap shut, but saw Doux Doux start to open hers so I poked my finger into her stomach. She let out a blood-curdling yell and doubled over even farther. Lucky for me, no one saw me do it. Several people rushed over to see what was wrong and by that time I had her in a headlock that resembled a hug.

"Oh, poor Doux Doux," I said sweetly, "does your stomach hurt as much as mine? Here, let me help you into the house and into a nice comfy chair." I grabbed her shoulder a little harder than necessary and shoved her through the front door. Once inside she turned on me, fists balled up and ready to do battle.

I put up my hands in surrender. "I'm sorry, Doux Doux, really I am. But there's something you don't know and if we tell them about Ti-chien who knows what else they'll find out. We have to get our stories straight before we say anything to anyone."

"What stories? You fed the damned dog and now we are doomed to two weeks of shots in the gut. End of story, just like our friendship."

"Oh, don't be so testy. How was I to know Ti-chien would go nuts? Besides, there's something you don't know yet."

"Mais, what?"

"Well, I—"

Daddy stomped into the living room, strewing fresh dirt from his shoes onto Angela's clean floor. He sat heavily into a chair and wiped sweat from his forehead, then twirled his worry lock. "Dammit all to hell, ever since we got here it's been one thing after another. I'm thinkin' I just might send y'all home to your Grandmother Hetta."

My stomach, the part that wasn't throbbing in pain, dropped.

"But Daddy, none of this is your fault. Besides, we like it here. I *love* it here."

"Ann, you've had malaria, polio and now maybe rabies, for crissake," he said as he rose, paced and twirled his hair.

"Well heck, Daddy, nobody's perfect."

Daddy stopped in mid-stride and burst out laughing. He left shaking his head and I heard him, over the grinding and screeching of the D-8, tell Mama and the others what I'd just said. There was a roar of laughter and I figured Daddy would enjoy telling that one on me for years. Well, if we all lived that long.

# CHAPTER 19

▼

Lucky for me, my father wasn't all that serious about sending us back to Texas.

Mama said he was just upset because men think it's their job to keep their families from harm, and Daddy was disappointed that he wasn't doing such a hot job of it in this godforsaken snake pit of a country. I reminded her that there weren't hardly any snakes in Haiti, much less a pit of them, but she just gave me a look and said, "It's an *expression*, Lizbuthann."

"Yes, ma'am."

She plopped down on the couch and fanned herself. "I wish my mama was here."

I was surprised, not that she missed Grandmother Hetta as much as I did, but that she thought of her as her mama. It had never occurred to me that when I got *that* old I'd still need my mother to soothe away my troubles. I tried doing some quick math in my head, but it just gave me a headache, so I asked, "Mama, just how old is Grandmother Hetta?"

"Well, let's see now. She'll be…sixty-one this year, because she had me when she was twenty-six."

Sixty-one minus twenty-six would make my mother…"You're thirty-five?" I blurted.

"For crying out loud, Lizbuthann, don't make it sound so *ancient*."

"I didn't mean it that way, it's just hard for me to think of you ever being, well, really old."

She chuckled. "Well, I hope to shout I make it that far. I guess when you're almost thirteen, anyone over fourteen seems like an antique. I can remember when my father passed on, I was ten and I thought of him as old, but now I realize he was a young man, just a year older than I am now."

I couldn't even *think* about having my daddy "pass on." In the South, nobody just upped and died, they passed. Actually, I had a hard time thinking of anyone being dead, even though I knew they were, because the two deadest people I knew kept coming back on me; Aunt Tody in dreams, and François in the flesh. Okay, so maybe dead flesh, but still flesh.

"What happened to him?" I asked.

"Hmmm? Who?" Mama asked. She looked sad and deep in thought.

"Your father. Why'd he d...uh...pass?"

"Oh. Well, I guess he had what they'd call a stroke these days, but I think it was disappointment that killed him."

"You can die of disappointment?" I asked, alarmed. Hadn't she just told me that Daddy was disappointed because he couldn't protect us from harm?

Mama must have made the connection and sensed my concern, because she was quick to say, "Oh, not like your daddy. He only worries about the big stuff and he handles that real well. My father, he was a rich man at one time, but in nineteen-twenty nine the stock market crashed and he had all his money in cotton futures. He lost almost everything except what we then called the country house in Locker; the one your Grandmother Hetta lives in now. Truth is, we were probably better off than most. He even managed to open a small store, but he never was the same. Died of a broken heart soon after the crash."

"But Mama, didn't you get mad at him? I mean, he upped and died and left Grandmother Hetta with no money and all you kids? Seems to me he took the easy way out."

Mother gave me a strange look. "I guess I never thought of it that way, but if your daddy did that to me I'd kill him all over again."

We both laughed, but it pained my stomach so that I doubled over. I was to get my third shot that day, but already had two large knots on my gut, both of which hurt like heck. And if that wasn't enough, I was worrying myself sick over François. I'd heard the doctor say that anyone bitten by a rabid dog had to begin treatment within five days, which gave me two days to find him and rat him out so he could get inoculated. And, even if I did find him, how does one go about holding down a seven-foot zombie and sticking a needle in his middle? Fourteen times?

Daddy was already asking questions about that night, suspicious that something was squirrelly with the entire Ti-chien story. Our mouthy pill-pusher told him the veterinarian in Port-au-Prince said the dog's neck was broken, and there was evidence of a violent struggle that obviously wasn't with me; I wasn't missing any skin.

Mother's voice brought me back from my depressing thoughts. "Lizbuthann, I know you were feeding that dog." She didn't say it as a scold, but I was shocked anyway.

No use denying it. "I'm sorry, Mama. He was hungry."

"And we don't like to see animals suffer, do we?" She sighed. "It was the wrong thing to do, but your heart was in the right place. I don't think we need discuss it further, if you know what I mean."

I did. It meant that Daddy didn't need to know.

"Besides," Mother continued, "you've surely learned your lesson when it comes to strays. And, even though I know that Dorcas is angry with you, you were also right to tell us she'd been around the dog. That makes me proud. Never, ever, honey, be afraid to tell us the truth." She got up and left the room, patting me on the head on the way out.

I felt lower than a snake's belly. She was proud of me? If she only knew. I decided it was time someone besides me did know the truth.

Angela hadn't been in the kitchen two minutes that morning before I motioned her back outside. She put down her sisal carryall, took off her big straw hat and followed me out the door.

"What it be, child?" she asked.

"François."

"You find him?"

"Uh, no, he sort of found me."

Angela gave me an impatient snort. "Sort of? What you mean, 'sort of'?"

"Ti…uh, that mad dog? When he had me cornered in the backyard the other night? Well, I fell and he was moving in to get me when all of a sudden I was lifted into the air and thrown into the kitchen. By François, Angela. He saved me from that dog. He saved my life."

Her eyes brightened and she smiled. "He be such a good boy."

"Yes ma'am, I believe he is."

"And he be back since that night?"

"Not that I can tell. And believe me, I've looked and watched. Angela, we have to find him."

Angela shrugged. "He be back. We find him."

"No, Angela, we have to find him right now. *Tout de suite.*"

"*Tout de suite?* Why?"

"Because, Angela, that dog bite...bit...François."

Angela crossed herself and said something in Papiamento. "Why you wait so long to tell Angela, Elisabet?"

"I'm sorry, really I am. I sort of thought...uh, uh..."

"Uh, uh, what?" she almost yelled, then looked back at the house and lowered her voice. "What?"

"Well, since François was, like, already dead and all that maybe it didn't much matter?"

Angela seemed to think about that, then shook her head. "Have you t'ought about this? What if François not be François, *my* François. What if he be a witch-woman slave zombie."

"You mean, what if he is a real zombie?"

"Yes. One that do evil, and then he go mad?" Her eyes were wide and I suddenly understood.

"Oh, dear," was all I could say. My mind reeled at the picture of a seven-foot rabid zombie rampaging through Camp. Look what had happened with a mid-sized dog. We had to do something, for sure.

"Angela, we have to do something, for sure."

"Yes, child. And I know what that be. Put on you shoes, Angela will walk you to that doctor for you shot."

I groaned. "Why don't you just shoot me?"

"Don' you go temptin' Angela."

Doux Doux waited by herself on the clinic's front porch when we arrived. She was going through this phase where she despised everyone, including her mother, which was probably why she was by herself. When the doctor arrived, I let Disagreeable Doux Doux go first, and immediately after her injection she stomped out without speaking to me. Fine: I had important business with the doc anyhow, business that my former friend couldn't be trusted to hear.

The shots were becoming less painful, or maybe it was just that I was resigned to them. Or perhaps it was Angela, wearing a bright red number dotted with lime slices, holding my hand and singing a lilting Caribbean ballad for me while the doc rammed a million-inch needle into my gut. I decided to make sure she came with me every day from now on, even though Mama had seemed a little hurt when I told her I wanted Angela to go with me this time.

After my injection, I waited for Angela to say something to the doctor about our problem, but she just stood there. I tried giving her the go-ahead with a tilt of my head, but she ignored me and watched as the doctor—Jean-Claude Cordier, according to the certificates on his wall—put the needles in alcohol and begin to tidy his little office. Which, by the way, was already very tidy. And white. Everything that was paintable had a fresh coat of shiny white enamel, even the floor. A gas refrigeration unit stood in the middle of one wall flanked by glass-fronted cabinets holding carefully labeled bottles and boxes.

It occurred to me that, when I wasn't sick, the doctor really didn't have much to do. So far there had been only a couple of serious accidents on the jobsite and those guys were already dead on arrival at his office, so other than an occasional broken arm or case of malaria, he probably sat around studying those medical manuals lining his bookshelves. No dust on those books, or anything else. And after that one trip to a Haitian hospital in Port-au-Prince for my first shot, I was mighty glad he insisted on giving the rest of them himself, because I'd seen outhouses cleaner than that city hospital.

I was studying certificates issued by the University of Bruxelles and a medical school in Guadalajara, Mexico, when Doctor Cordier turned around and looked startled to find us still there. Especially me, since I generally made tracks away from him as soon as possible. For the first time I noticed how young he was, and that he had big, soft brown eyes behind those bottle-bottom glasses.

"Is there something else I can do for you, Mademoiselle Elisabet?"

Mademoiselle Elisabet? I felt like a real heel after all the names I had privately called *him.*

Angela spoke up, in English. "We wonder. If a people don' get this inject, what happen?"

The doctor sighed deeply. "Madame Calixte, Mademoiselle Elisabet must have these injections. I have already made that clear. Without them, if the dog proves rabid, as I am certain he will, she will die a horrible death."

"It's not me we're asking about," I blurted, "but someone the dog actually bit."

"Someone else?" He looked puzzled. "I thought you and your friend, Mademoiselle Boudreaux, were the only ones to have contact with the dog."

"Uh, well, not exactly."

"You are saying someone else may have been infected?"

"Maybe it be," Angela said. She was wringing her hands by now and her eyes were moist.

Guiding Angela by the arm, he led her to a chair, and then sat across from her. I pulled up a stool and joined them.

"I think you should just tell me the whole story," he said, reaching for a jar of candy and offering us one. We took our time unwrapping the waxed paper. The doc leaned back in his chair and quietly waited.

Finally, unable to stall any longer, Angela looked at me, but I nodded for her to go ahead. I figured I'd get all tongue-tied.

"There be this boy, or maybe he be a man…"

Angela began telling Dr. Cordier our story, but right off the bat, when she reached the part about François lurking around my house, the doctor held his hand up for her to halt. He rapidly shut the clinic door so no casual passersby could overhear. When he sat down and nodded for her to continue, he had a worried frown on his face. I had heard that the doctor was very concerned with the *image* of Haiti and her people. I suppose going to school in other countries had made him aware of the poor opinion most folks had of Haiti and Haitians. It didn't sit well that one of his fellow citizens might be terrorizing a little white girl. I thought I'd better set the story straight.

"Oh, Doctor Cordier," I said, "Angela didn't mean that this man is bad or anything. He's just a little…" I touched my head, "slow."

The good doctor looked relieved and nodded for Angela to continue.

"The child be right," she said. "She say he don' come all the time. Sometime he be gone for long spell. And that be the way it was when the uh, *chien féroce* try hurtin' this girl. She," Angela nodded toward me, "have not see this boy for months. Then, *voila*! He t'row her." As she said this, she threw her arms wildly into the air, causing the doctor to scoot his chair back. He looked downright alarmed.

"Who throw…uh…threw her in the air?" he asked. "The dog?"

"No, that boy. He throw that girl," she pointed at me, "Elisabet, in the air."

The doctor's mouth fell open. "To save me," I explained quickly. "He threw me away from the dog. But the *chien*, he bite…uh, bit, the boy. François." I had to stop hanging out so much with Angela.

The doctor rubbed his chin in a doctorly way and asked, "This François, what does he look like?"

Angela shrugged a "who knows" shrug, so I said, "Really big, bald, and very dark. And real slow."

"Ah," said the doctor.

"Ah, what?" Angela demanded.

"Ah, *that* François," he said with a smile.

You could have knocked Angela and me over with a feather.

"*That* François?" I managed to say.

"Yes," the doctor said, "I know him and I know where to find him."

When what the doctor just said finally sunk in, I felt a wonderful calm settle over me, and a great weight—a great *dead* weight—lift from my shoulders. The secret of François' existence had been a heavy one. Doux Doux and Angela also knew of him, but were in no more of a position to help him than I was. Now an adult, one with a great deal of authority, was in our inner circle, and as I let out a sigh of relief, I realized what Momo-san was talking about when she quoted Shakespeare about tangled webs and deceit.

I vowed to stop deceiving.

Which lasted about two minutes.

# CHAPTER 20

▼

"I am afraid, ladies, that we may have to resort to some measure of deceit," Doctor Cordier told us.

Oh, well, so much for my good intentions.

Angela squinted at him. "What you mean?"

"There is the matter of François' *tante*."

"What aunt?" I asked.

"The bird lady of Mirebalais," the doctor said, which had Angela and me exchanging confused looks.

Angela frowned and blurted, "He don' got no aunt. I know, because I be his sister."

Now it was the doctor's turn to be confounded. Confusion seemed to be in the air. "You're François' sister?" he asked.

"Yes. Well, I was," Angela said, "until he die."

"He die?" The doctor and I were both starting to sound like Angela.

Angela gave a snap of her head. "*Fevre.* Ten years past."

The doctor turned to me. "Perhaps you would like to explain?"

"Well, we figure François is a zombie," I said, thinking I sounded quite reasonable.

The doctor, on the other hand, looked at Angela and me as if we were loony, so I thought I'd best clear things up for him.

"It's like this, doctor: François, he died of fever, then they buried him. He disappeared from his grave because Angela fell asleep, and now he's back. At least Angela *thinks* it's him. She hasn't actually seen him yet, since he, uh, *un-*died."

Sounded perfectly clear to me, but evidently Doctor Cordier wasn't as bright as I thought. He sat back down, fixed me with a look and let out a long breath. "Let us see if I grasp this correctly. You and Angela think François, whose aunt is one of my patients, is a *zombie?*"

"Yes," Angela and I said at the same time.

Dr. Cordier sucked in his cheeks and his shoulders began to jerk. Unable to control himself, he began with a giggle, then lapsed into a full-fledged belly laugh. His thigh-slapping guffaws began to get annoying, and I was ready to bean him one for making fun of us when, with great effort, he caught his breath, removed his glasses, and wiped away the tears streaming down his cheeks.

"Forgive me, please. It is just that…"—snigger, snigger—"I guess that…"—giggle, giggle—"…that would certainly explain everything," he finally managed to gasp.

Annoyed as I was, I still couldn't resist asking, "It would?"

"Yes, it would," he said, finally getting his cackling under control, "if it were true. Which, as a doctor of medicine I have to discount, but as a Haitian, I cannot rule out completely. I have witnessed too many things that cannot be explained by," he gave a wide sweep of his hand in the direction of the medical books lining the wall, "these."

Replacing his glasses, he quit laughing, and became somber. "I do know one thing for certain, though. You saw François receive a bite from that rabid dog, so he is in grave danger. I must leave at once for Mirebalais and try to convince the woman, even though she can be very difficult where her neph…" he saw Angela's face cloud, "uh…François, is concerned. She does not like anyone talking to or treating him. I had to force her to let me dress his hands after he received some very nasty bird bites sometime back."

Angela and I traded meaningful looks at the mention of the bird bites. She nodded and smiled. We knew we had our zombie.

Doctor Cordier rose and began packing that dreaded black bag of his.

"Uh, Doctor Cordier," I asked, "What exactly does this bird lady look like?"

He continued to concentrate on stuffing his bag, undoubtedly afraid he might forget some instrument of torture. I thought he hadn't heard me, but then he stopped packing and looked at me. "*Comment?*" he said.

"I asked, what does this so-called aunt look like?"

"Oh. Uh, she is an old, sickly woman who has lived through the harsh existence this country offers our poor; too thin, too few teeth, and in extremely ill health."

Aha! "So, is that why her eyes are white?" I said, fishing for clues.

"Yes, she is possibly...how did you know that?" The doctor asked, staring at me with a suspicious look.

"I think I may have seen her. Selling eggs in Camp."

"Oh. Yes, that would be her. She pays me in eggs from time to time."

Angela and I locked eyes. We had our woman, and we had our zombie, but Brenda Starr would want to know more.

"Doctor Cordier, you say this woman and François? They live in Mirebalais?"

"Yes, Elisabet, on the church square. In the purple house, the one decorated with a green girl fish over the door."

"Girl fish?" I asked.

"*La Sirène*. Oh, what's that word in English? For half-girl, half-fish?"

"Mermaid?"

"Yes, that is it."

That cinched it. I'd seen a mermaid painted on a rock at the *hounfort* where Doux Doux and I had first confronted François. And I hadn't made the connection until now, but I suddenly remembered that I had also seen the purple house, with *its* mermaid, on my second day in Haiti. A shiver ran down my spine, just as it had that day. Coincidences? Not likely, Miss Brenda.

Cordier snapped his bag closed, then began packing ice into a small cooler. He then nestled several vials of anti-rabies serum into the ice, took a last look around the clinic, and headed for the door. "I must attend to François," he said, "I will see you tomorrow morning at ten, *oui?*"

"Unfortunately, *oui*," I grumbled. "Hey, how about if I go with you to Mirebalais?"

He shook his head. "Absolutely not, Mademoiselle Elisabet. Even as ill as she is, the woman is difficult to deal with, and you would only be an added aggravation for her. In addition, I do not want to take the time to obtain your parents' permission. *Adieu*." He rushed out the door, jumped into the ambulance and left in a cloud of dust.

Angela gave me a smug grin. "So, little added aggravation, what we do now?"

"Ha, ha, everyone's a clown." I watched the doctor speed off and sighed. "Oh, well. I guess we should lock up? He must be pretty rattled to forget to do it himself."

"He sure be. Well child, we done what we come to do. Let us go home before you *maman* worry." She reached for my hand to pull me along, but I was rooted in place, staring at the file cabinets. I couldn't possibly pass up such an opportunity as this; Brenda would never forgive me.

Unable to budge me, Angela said, "What now, child?"

I shook off her hand, walked to the file cabinet, and gave the handle a yank. Locked. Rats. Scanning the room I spotted, hanging from the hook where the doc had taken the ambulance keys, another set. Angela followed my glance, grabbed the key chain, and, in two shakes of a lamb's tail, we were into the files. The problem was, we really didn't have any idea what we were looking for.

"We don't have any idea what we're looking for, Angela."

"That woman."

"I know *that*. But we don't even know her last name."

"Hmmm. Let Angela look."

I stood aside and watched over her shoulder. There were different colored folders, all with neatly handwritten labels, and filed by, of course, last name. It soon became obvious that the red folders were for Haitian job workers, green for village people and white, of course, for foreigners. I was sorely tempted to look into a few, but when I reached out for Doux Doux's folder, Angela slapped my hand.

"You got no busy-ness in people's busy-ness," she said as she sorted through the green folders. She hesitated over her own, then gave me a look like, "Wouldn't you like to know," and kept going.

I had already locked the front door and put the CLOSED/FERME sign on its hook outside, so we had all the time in the world. Or so we thought, until five minutes later, when someone rapped on the door, scaring the you-know-what out of us.

We froze in place for a moment, then I crouched below window level and made my way to the half-closed louvers. Through the slits I saw a pair of dark, bare feet; just a Haitian who couldn't read the sign. Soon, whoever it was shuffled off and we both breathed a sigh of relief.

Angela went back to work. We were only halfway through the green files, and were becoming discouraged. "Angela, maybe he took the witch's file with him?"

"No child. We was here and he not open this file. Just you hold tight."

I held tight, moving back to the louvers to stand watch. About three minutes later I heard Angela say, "Here it be," and we both scurried to the examining table to read the file labeled OISEAU. We looked at each other and laughed; the doctor had actually told us who she was, but we thought he meant something else: Oiseau is "bird" in French.

"Oiseau, Marie-Françoise," Angela read, squinting at the doctor's very fancy script, which looked like something penned back in the days of the American constitution signers. Momo-san, with the help of our penmanship teacher, had us learn calligraphy, but none of us had achieved this skill level.

"Wow, look at his handwriting. And another wow; the bird lady is named Françoise just like François."

"Yes, but than don' mean nothing. In Haiti almost everyone is named François or Françoise. It be like 'Joe' in America. Now let us see what we can learn about this woman who steal my baby brother."

I didn't say what I was thinking, which was that maybe Angela was hoping so much to find that lost boy from her childhood, she wasn't seeing things clearly anymore.

Angela scanned the file. "This Marie, she be…let us see…*soixante-dix ans*. Humph. She be his *grand-tante* if she be his *tante* at all, which I don' t'ink is so."

That made sense. All of my great-aunts were over sixty and this woman was seventy. I nodded and pointed to the address: Mirebalais, *maison pourpre*. "You know this house, don't you, Angela? Heck it's hard to miss when you go through Mirebalais on the way to Port-au-Prince."

"Yes. I know it, but I never see who live there," Angela said as she picked up the folder and sat down to read. I leaned over her shoulder, but she shooed me off, so I wandered around the office, reading labels on jars and checking out the books. Finally, she said, "If this be a bad woman, we don' have to worry wit' her much longer. That doctor, he say here she die soon."

"Oh," I said, not knowing whether to be glad or sad at this news. Now that I was almost certain she was the witch-egg-bird woman, I knew she wasn't very nice; she cut off chicken's heads, drank their blood, kept François as a zombie-slave and had stolen my Pee Wee. I said as much.

"Yes, child, she may be evil, but then, maybe not. Maybe she jus' be a sick ol' woman who try voodoo to make her well, who have take care of a boy who no so bright, and she just find you bird and put in cage."

"Hey, when did you get all reasonable?" I asked. I hate the voice of reason; it can make anything sound, well, reasonable. Brenda Starr, however, would keep an open mind and set out to get at the truth. So must I.

We put the file back, tidied up, and left the office, carefully locking the door behind us. Just as the lock clicked, I regretted it; I just might want back in before the doctor returned.

Angela must have had the same thought, for she smiled and shrugged. "So, now we have pass the problem to the doctor. I feel much better."

"Me, too. But you know what?"

"What, child?"

"I'd give my right arm to be there when our little doctor tries to jam that needle into François' stomach. Oh, yes, I would."

I spent the rest of Saturday perched on the edge of the bluff, over-grooming Wishes as I watched the road for the ambulance to return. Finally, at around four, Mama came outside.

"Lizbuthann, you're going to wear the hide right off that horse."

I put the curry brush down and turned around. "Yes, ma'am. He was overdue for a good bath, de-ticking and brushing. He's looking pretty fine now, huh?"

"Well, as fine as he *can* look. But," she warily lifted Wishes' tail, which I had plaited into a fancy French braid, "how's he going to swat flies away with this?"

She had a point. 'Course if he did manage to wallop one with that thick braid, it would surely never fly again. Since I was running out of excuses to watch the road, I grabbed this one. "Uh, well, you know, you're right, Mama. I'll unbraid it right now."

"Not so fast, Lizbuthann. You haven't done any of your chores for several days now. First it was the trip to Port-au-Prince, then your stomach hurt, but now, since you seem well enough to spend an entire day brushing on this horse, you're obviously ready to get back into a routine. And just because it's Saturday doesn't mean you get the day off, you know. You've been sandbagging long enough."

Rats, what I needed was a little diversion. Sympathy perhaps?

"You know, Mama, what with getting that old shot this morning, it was all I could do to take care of Wishes, but he was overdue, so I made myself do it in spite of the pain." I put on my "in pain" face, which wasn't hard because my stomach did actually ache like heck.

It worked. "Oh, well, okay, Lizbuthann. But tomorrow, *before* your shot, I want that closet of yours straightened up and Pee Wee's cage scrubbed. And on Monday, it's back to school."

"Yes, ma'am," I said, and set about, very slowly, unbraiding Wishes' tail. He made one feeble attempt to stomp my foot, but I gave him a whack on the rump. He shot me a dirty look, but settled down, even though he didn't like anyone messing with his tail and I had tried his patience by messing with it twice in one day.

Another hour went by, but no ambulance. Finally, Angela stopped by on her way home and told me Mama wanted me to take a shower before dinner. "She don' like no wet horse smell wit' her meatloaf."

"Angela, I've watched for Doctor Cordier all day, but no luck. Maybe you could stop by his office and find out how things went in Mirebalais, just in case I missed him?"

"I will do that, child. *À bientôt.*"

"*À bientôt*, Angela."

After my shower, I impatiently ate dinner with the family while Daddy told us about his day at work, and Mama recounted a little not-very-juicy Camp gossip. I was trying to think of a way to sneak away and go by the clinic when Daddy, bless his heart, said, "Lizbuthann, I need to run up to the cableway shack for a minute. Want to drive me?"

I couldn't get out of my chair fast enough, but I was in for a disappointment; when we rolled by the clinic, the ambulance wasn't there, and the CLOSED/ FERME sign hung on the doctor's door. I could have kicked myself for not leaving a clue so I'd know whether the doctor had been there and left again. Brenda Starr would never have slipped up like that.

"Uh, Daddy, can I stop in at the clinic for a minute?"

"Since when do you *want* to go to the clinic? Besides, Ann, the doctor isn't there. Can't you see the sign?"

"Well, uh, yes, but sometimes he *is* there and just leaves up the sign so no one will bother him."

"And I guess you're that no one?" Daddy teased. "Okay, pull over. I'll pick you up on my way back."

Rolling the car to a stop, I got out and then waited until Daddy drove off before running across the road to the clinic. I banged on the door, but no luck. After peering through the louvers and seeing nothing, and unable to come up with a better plan, I cocked the CLOSED/FERME sign so that it hung crookedly. Knowing Doctor Cordier's tidy habits, if he did return he would surely straighten his sign before leaving again. It was the best I could come up with on such short notice.

Five minutes later, Daddy picked me up and let me take the wheel again.

"Was he there?"

"No, sir."

"What'd you want with the doc?" he asked as I carefully steered down the main street of Camp, trying not to flatten any little kids.

"Oh, just to make sure about my appointment tomorrow."

"What time is it?"

"At ten."

"Well, I can give you a ride if you want. I'd like to drop this heap off at the mechanic's shop on my way to work. I need to get to the jobsite by nine, so if you don't mind going early, I'll let you drive."

"You bet, Daddy. I'll be ready."

After I carefully parked in the front yard, I fed Wishes and bedded him down for the night before hitting the sack myself. I made sure my louvers were wide open, just in case the doctor had missed him and François showed up in my backyard. Not that I had any idea what I'd do if he did, except maybe try to lure him down to the doctor's office. And then what?

I read a Nancy Drew novel for a few minutes, but soon my eyelids sagged and I slept soundly throughout the night, which I didn't think I'd do, what with all the things on my mind.

Up by six the next morning, I had already cleaned my closet, and had plans to tackle Pee Wee's cage before Daddy took me to the doctor's office, when Angela dropped by unexpectedly. She said she thought she'd forgotten her hat, which was pretty lame since she had hats galore. No matter what dress she wore, Angela always sported color-matched *chapeaux* made of brightly died sisal. She made a pretense of looking in a few cupboards, but I figured she was just messing around until we could talk.

Mama and Daddy finally wandered off with their coffee and I made a beeline for Angela. "Did you see the doctor yet?" I whispered.

"No, child, he not be there. That is why I come. You did not see him neither?"

I shook my head.

"Then we maybe go try to find him before you inject. Before other peoples be about?"

Rats. I couldn't leave until I washed out Pee Wee's cage. I was stuck. I told Angela that, as I'd promised Mama, I had to finish my chores, but she winked and followed my parents into the living room, where she got right to the point. "I was t'ink maybe Elisabet could go to the *marché* wit' me. On Sunday they sell the best fruit and vegetable. Then, if okay wit' you, I can go wit' her to that doctor."

Daddy put down his coffee cup. "In that case, I'll drop you ladies at the market and get on up to work."

Mama, looked from me to Pee Wee's cage, but then shrugged and actually looked relieved. I think she was dreading taking me for my injection; she had no idea I'd made my peace with the doctor and no longer tried to kick his teeth in when he administered my injections. But then I saw her frown and knew I had to close the deal.

"And I promise to do the rest of my chores just as soon as I get back," I quickly said.

Mama sighed. "Oh, all right, I guess I'm out-voted, as usual. But you be sure to tell Doctor Cordier that you have to get your shot early tomorrow. School day, you know."

"Don't remind me," I said with a groan and an eye roll.
Mama and Daddy chuckled. I can be *so* entertaining.

# CHAPTER 21

▼

"You seen the doc this morning?" Mr. Ritchie, the electrical superintendent, asked from his rolled-down pickup window.

Angela, Doux Doux and I all shook our heads. We'd been waiting for over an hour on the clinic's front porch; since just before ten o'clock. The CLOSED/FERME sign was still as crooked as I'd left it, and I was getting more worried as the minutes ticked by and Doctor Cordier didn't show.

Doux Doux, typically in ill humor, said she hoped the doctor *never* came back so we didn't have to have the infernal shot. I didn't even try to argue with her; if she was so dumb that she didn't want an inoculation that might save her life, she was past reasoning with. Besides, I decided she was just acting up to get attention, and I had no intention of giving it to her.

I walked over to Mr. Ritchie's pickup. "The doctor was supposed to be here for our appointments at ten, but so far, we haven't seen him."

"Word has it he's vamoosed," Mr. Ritchie drawled.

"Vamoosed?" I asked. A feeling of dread flared up in my stomach.

"Well, more like disappeared. One of the mechanics saw the ambulance parked on the square in Mirebalais last night when he went home from work, and it was still there this morning. He figured maybe the doc might have himself a galfriend in town, but when the ambulance was still there this morning, he gave it a look-see. Found it unlocked, and stuff was missing."

"Like what?"

"Well, since the shop services the ambulance, they pretty much know what's supposed to be in it. Riley says that there's a portable cooling unit, a small generator, and maybe some medical supplies missing, but I'd have to ask the doc about those. The guy found the doc's keys, too, which is another mystery. Sure ain't like Cordier to be so careless. Sets a man to worrin', if you know what I mean. When did you see the doctor last time?"

"Not since yesterday," I said, feeling guilty. If something bad had happened to Doctor Cordier, it was surely my fault. After all, I was the one who sent him off to hunt down a seven-foot zombie. I cut a look at Angela, whose eyes had widened with alarm.

Doux Doux stomped her foot and looked for all the world like a bratty deb in the movies. "Well, this is a fine kettle of fish. What the heck happens with our shots?"

"I thought you didn't want one, but if you insist, I'll give it to you, Doux Doux, dear," I said sweetly.

"Over my dead body," she said and stomped off a few feet to sulk. Cranky, cranky. I'd heard that Roger, her heartthrob she'd been puppy-dogging around Camp, wouldn't give her the time of day. Good for him, I say.

"You want a ride back to Camp, or you gonna wait a while in case the doc shows?" Mr. Ritchie asked.

Doux Doux whirled, elbowed me out of the way and climbed into the truck in front of me. "Age before beauty," I said with a bow. Angela and I started to follow her into the truck, but I stopped short and fell back into Angela. She caught me, and herself, before we both ended up on our backsides. "Uh, on second thought, Mr. Ritchie, I think Angela and I will walk." I slammed the door, and he waved as he drove off. Doux Doux didn't even look back.

Angela planted her hands on her hips and was about to give me a dressing down when I said, "I have an idea."

"What idea? Mos' time you idea get everybody in big troubles."

I pointed down the road at the mechanic's shop. Daddy's car sat in the parking lot, where he'd left it for a repair job.

Angela shook her head violently and tried to pull me toward Camp and away from Daddy's car.

Shaking off her hand, I said, "Angela, we have to go look for Doctor Cordier. We can be in Mirebalais in less than an hour. All we have to do is find the witch woman, and maybe the doc and François, then we can be back here in say, two hours. Tops."

"Elisabet, what about you *maman*?"

I shrugged. "We'll just have to hope she doesn't come looking for us until we get back, but we gotta get going right now. This may be the only chance we have. I'll bet you a gourde that real soon now *everyone* will know the doc's gone. We don't have telephones in Camp, but gossip flies faster than Superman around here, so let's get a move on before Mama comes to check on us."

"How we gonna get that car?"

"Just follow my lead. I'll think of something."

"You gon' get Angela fired," she protested.

I shook my head. "No I won't, I promise. If we get caught, I'll tell them I threatened to go alone and you only came to save me from myself. They'll believe that, for sure." I took her hand, we ran across the road and then sauntered into the mechanic shop. Several Haitian grease monkeys were beating on a D-8 dozer's treads, probably trying to dislodge dirt and dog blood, while an American superintendent watched. Mr. Riley smiled when he saw us.

"Hey, how're ya doin', Lizbuthann, Miz Angela," he said, tipping his hat. "We ain't got to your Daddy's vehicle as yet. Just got here."

"Oh, that's okay, Mr. Riley, he wasn't expecting you to. He sent us over to pick it up anyhow, because he forgot Mama needed the car for a couple of hours this morning." I hoped the chief mechanic didn't know that my mother did not drive. "We'll bring it back after awhile."

Charles Riley, a very nice and friendly man, didn't deserve my wicked ways, and I hated being a big fat liar with him, but sometimes you gotta take drastic measures. My great-aunt Elizabeth was always talking about the end justifying the means and I guess this was one of those ends. He threw the keys to Angela who looked puzzled for a moment, until I nudged her in the ribs.

"Uh, t'ank you," she stammered, then with a cocky grin, added, "I jus' love drive that big ole car. Yes I surely do."

Before she overdid her act, I jerked my head and rolled my eyes towards the car. Angela, who couldn't drive a lick, got the message, followed me to the car and gave me the keys. If Mr. Riley saw us take off with me at the wheel, he was probably left scratching his head.

Without the wooden blocks that Daddy always strapped onto the clutch and brake so I could reach them more easily, it was slow going at first, but once past the village I just didn't bother to stop or gear down. I drove a steady thirty miles an hour all the way to Mirebalais, hoping we didn't meet one of the company trucks headed in the other direction, toward the jobsite. *Everyone* knew my Daddy's car, and the last thing I needed was one of the workers asking my father what I was doing out on the road without him. We were lucky; we met no vehicles, only two or three chickens lost any important feathers, and I didn't graze a single Haitian, but it was pretty hard staying out of the ditches. Angela, by the time we arrived in Mirebalais, was white as a sheet. I didn't think a body could live without breathing for almost an hour, but I believe she did.

The ambulance was no longer parked in the square, and since we hadn't met it heading for the jobsite, I guessed someone had picked it up for a run into Port-au-Prince. Either that or the doctor had showed up and taken it himself. But where? And did he have François with him? I parked on the sleepy church square where a few folks lolled around in their Sunday-go-to-meeting garb. Angela asked around whether anyone had seen the ambulance or the doctor, and sure enough, an old lady wearing a shawl despite the heat told her that a company pickup arrived, a man got out, and drove the ambulance off in the direction of Port-au-Prince. But no, she had not seen the doctor.

While Angela questioned the woman, I took a good hard look at the purple house. Unlike many of the houses nearby that shared common walls, it stood alone, with little dirt ditches running on both sides to drain off rainwater and, most likely, sewage. The shutters, painted a familiar lime green, were closed, as was the front door.

"Angela," I said, "look at those shutters. That's the same color of paint that someone used to draw the mermaid at the *houngans*. And that drawing over the door; it's almost identical."

Angela shrugged. "That color don' mean nothin'. In Haiti, lime green be a popular shade."

She had a point. I'd seen more lime green in the last three years than ever before, except maybe back at a local drug store in San Antonio, whose specialty was a bright green lime-flavored ice-cream soda, so the store front was painted to match.

"Yeah, well, what now?" I asked.

"What you mean, 'what now'? This be you smart girl plan."

"Uh, well, I just didn't plan past getting us here." What would Brenda Starr do? "Okay, let's go knock on the door." Angela rolled her eyes, mumbled something about "smart girl," but followed me across the street.

I knocked.

Nothing happened.

I knocked harder.

Nothing.

I beat on the door and yelled.

Now, something happened; people started coming out of their houses to see what was going on. Angela nudged me. "I don' t'ink nobody home." Then she winked.

I got it. Very loudly, I said, in French, "I don't think anyone is home. Let us go." We got into the car and as we drove away, Angela reported that the curious were going back into their houses.

I drove to the end of town, took a sharp left and parked behind a derelict hut. From there, we circled around by foot until we were behind the purple house. The village was deathly quiet, with only bird chirps and the drone of a generator in the distance. The house had a back door and one window, both shut. I tapped, lightly, on the door and, to our shock, it swung inward on rusty, creaking hinges. I figured the whole town could hear the squeal, but no one showed up to ask embarrassing questions, like, "What are you two doing breaking into this house?" So far, so good.

"François," I whispered, "are you in there?"

A sound pulled me through the door, but Angela grabbed my arm and shoved me behind her. "You don' be getting' hurt on Angela's time," she said, and boldly strode into the one-room house with me right on her heels.

It was dark inside, especially after the brilliant glare outdoors. Again, I thought I heard a noise. "François? Is that—eeek!"

Angela let out a little scream of her own, then said, "What?"

"Something touched my leg."

"I don' see not'ing."

"Me neither. Maybe I just imag—" I shrieked again and kicked out, this time connecting with something soft, furry and, evidently, in a bad mood. The cat spit, hissed, and yowled. When we could breathe again, we laughed. Well, the cat didn't laugh; as our eyes adjusted to the low light we saw it glaring at us from under a chair.

We could see better by now, but there wasn't much to look at. Typical of a Haitian hut, cooking and entertaining was done outside, so the inside was mainly for sleeping. Two bunks, one heaped high with blankets, stood along a wall, a bare light bulb hung from the ceiling, and a water spigot jutted out of the wall over a galvanized tub. I jerked on the light cord, but I wasn't surprised when nothing happened; the village only ran their big generator for three hours a night. There was no evidence that anyone huge and dead lived in the house. I was half right.

"I guess we'd best go," I said, "before Daddy finds out his car is missing. I don't know what else we can do."

Angela nodded, but as we turned to leave, I caught a movement on one of the cots. "Angela! Something's under there," I whispered, pointing to the pile of blankets.

Neither of us really wanted to know what was under the pile, but we had to investigate. It was Angela who took two steps to the cot and pulled off the blankets. We both cried out, then began to giggle, as another cat bounded for the door. But then we took a closer look and our laughter dried up.

"Uh-oh, Angela," I croaked. "Ding dong, the witch is dead."

We couldn't get out of Mirebalais and back to the mechanic's shop fast enough. Batting both sides of the ditches all the way, I took the car up to sixty; double what I'd ever driven before. As we sped down the road, all that ran through my mind was that ditty from *The Wizard of Oz*: "*Ding Dong! The Witch is Dead! Which old Witch? The Wicked Witch! Ding Dong! The Wicked Witch is dead.*"

Had the doctor and François gone off somewhere and left a dead woman in her house? And if so, why? I'd thought by going to Mirebalais we'd get some answers, but we just raised more questions. And there was that little matter of discovering a dead person. My stomach was doing flip-flops, but I held onto that steering wheel for dear life, concentrating on keeping *us* alive.

Angela, after the first few minutes on the road, shut her eyes and prayed, or at least I think that's what she was doing, since her lips were moving. Whatever, it must have helped, because I had Daddy's car safely parked in the mechanic's yard in record time. Mr. Riley took the keys from Angela with a polite, "Thank you, ma'am," so we knew we hadn't been found out. Yet.

We went back to the clinic and sat down on the front porch steps again, trying to figure out what to do next. The doctor and François were missing, and the witch was dead, that much was fact. But, what to do about it was another thing altogether.

"Angela, should we call the cops?"

"You be crazy? These policemans t'row us in jail, then ask question. Well, they t'row *me* in jail, anyway."

"Okay, no cops. But what should we do? I mean, witch or not, I hate to leave that old lady dead without telling someone. It doesn't seem…Christian."

Angela nodded and we fell silent for a few minutes, then her face brightened. "I have idea."

"What?"

"I will tell priest. He can no do not'ing to me and he can no tell police."

"Great! I feel better, now if we can only…uh-oh."

Doux Doux, with both our mothers in tow, came walking up the road. My mama, joining us on the shaded porch, fanned herself with her hand. "Hot. Wish this weather would make up its mind. First soppy, now sultry."

"Kinda like Doux Doux these days," I mumbled under my breath.

Doux Doux stuck her tongue out at me.

"Lizbuthann," my mother said, ignoring our antics, "Dorcas tells me that Dr. Cordier wasn't here this morning to give you your injection."

"No, ma'am," I said, "he sure wasn't." I crossed my fingers inside my pockets and added, "Angela and I, we've been sitting here all this time and he still hasn't showed up." I could practically feel Angela holding her breath, waiting for my bald-faced lie to bring my mother's wrath down on our heads.

"Well," she said. Then again, "Well." She looked around as if the doctor would materialize, then shrugged and joined us on the porch steps. We'd been sitting there a few more minutes, Mother and Clota discussing the mystery of the disappearing doctor, when up drives my father, followed by Mr. Boudreaux and several others. By now my mother was visibly upset; her eyebrows twitched wildly.

"Bud, what are we going to do about the doctor?" she demanded as soon as Daddy stepped from his truck.

Daddy held up and jingled a set of keys. "Guess we'd best see if he's inside, sick or something. Riley's guy got the doc's keys when he went to refuel the ambulance for a run into Port-au-Prince."

"Refuel?" I almost messed up and asked why the doctor would leave for Mirebalais with empty tanks, but, of course, I wasn't supposed to know where he went. Life gets sooo complicated when you lie at lot.

"Yep. Along with all the pilfering, looks like someone took a joy ride. Not only was all the gas siphoned out, damned wagon was covered with red mud. Riley's a mite teed off…those tanks in the ambulance hold almost forty gallons, and they'd just topped 'em off."

Mama was so distressed that her eyebrows looked like caterpillars trying to crawl off her face. "Bud, what are we going to do about Lizbuthann's shot?"

"Yeah, Daddy," I said, "I need that shot."

Daddy stared at me, then burst out laughing. "What have you done with my daughter? You can't be her."

Some kids never get a break.

# CHAPTER 22

▼

Okay, so I never, ever, thought I'd hear those words, "I need that shot," fall out of my mouth either, so it's no wonder Daddy cracked up.

The clinic had serum and needles, but no doctor to do the dirty deed. Mama said she'd do it if she really, really had to, but that she'd probably faint, right after I did. Daddy said, "Nuh-uh, no thanks," as did Angela, but she said it in a string of Papiamento that left no doubt as to her meaning.

What a bunch of sissies. Hey, I was the one getting the needle in her gut, and I danged sure wasn't going to do it myself. Doux Doux, of course, volunteered, but she had a mean glint in her eye, so I turned her down cold.

Deciding it wouldn't be the end of the world to wait a few more hours, just in case Doctor Cordier showed, we all went home. Mama, however, then went from house to house until she found Mrs. Dahlke, a lady who'd had nurse's training. The woman, who was quite aware of my reputation, eyed me as if I were a rattler, but reluctantly agreed to give the injections if she had to.

Lucky for us all, my natural nosiness finally paid off. I had pestered Doctor Cordier with tons of questions about which muscle he had to hit and all that stuff, so I was able to educate Mrs. Dahlke before she stuck me in the wrong place. It was, after all, in my best interest to get this injection done correctly, and she must have done so, for soon Doux Doux and I both had another stomach knot to show off.

So, we were safe for the moment, but what about poor François? And where, oh, where was Doctor Cordier? And just how long would it take the jungle tele-graph to get word back to my mother that a red-haired white girl and a *café au lait* woman dressed in huge watermelon slices had recently been seen banging on the door of a now-dead old woman in Mirebalais? Oh, and after arriving in a big black car being driven by that same mop-haired kid? Sloppy work, I suspected Brenda Starr would say.

One thing for sure though, even if I didn't get nailed for the Mirebalais caper, I was still headed for trouble, because when the doctor disappeared, he took several doses of serum with him. That day, when Mrs. Dahlke gave us our injections, I volunteered to get the serum from the clinic refrigerator so I could take a quick count: twelve left.

So, Doux Doux and I had exactly six days each of serum left, which meant the doc took ten vials and we were five days short. Unless, of course, it turned out that Ti-chien was not rabid. Why, did the doctor take so much with him? I surely didn't know. Maybe he figured someone as big as François needed a much larger dose?

It didn't take a mathematical or medical genius to figure out that someone, somehow, was going to have to come up with more medicine for Doux Doux and me. Not to mention several gallons for François, if the doctor showed up with him, that is. And speaking of the zombie; if he didn't get his injections started like right *now*, they would not do him any good at all. All this math was giving me a giant headache to go with my already-sore stomach.

I had not yet mentioned this lack of serum to anyone, and Angela evidently didn't realize we had a shortage, because she never mentioned it. So, you might ask, why didn't I just tell my parents we were short? Because if I did, I'd have to think up some more lies to work around questions like, "Why did the doctor take serum and how did you know he took it?" and I was plumb weary of lying. Besides, I was also convinced that Doctor Cordier would return soon, so why complicate things?

I just hadn't counted on guerillas.

Daddy was kidding when he said I'd danged near started a revolution with firecrackers a couple of years back, but there's nothing too funny about a real one. Just ask Marie Antoinette.

I was all ears when Uncle Lloyd came to dinner and started talking about troubles in Port-au-Prince, as well as in the mountains surrounding the city. Especially since those mountains were between us and the capitol.

"Been some street fights in the city and skirmishes along the main road. This damned country has been a political cesspool since Columbus found it," he said. "One damned revolution after another until 1915, when we took over."

"We?" I asked.

"Yep, the United damned States of America. We sent in the army, ousted the troublemakers and peace reigned for years." He winked and added, "Until you got here."

"Very, very funny."

Uncle Lloyd buttered a yeast roll. "Nothin' but a damned dictator runnin' the show, that's the trouble."

"But Uncle Lloyd, wasn't President Magloire elected?" I remembered seeing faded election posters in Port-au-Prince.

"Oh, yeah. By the people, for the people and all that crap. The problem is, the people want him to leave office at the end of his term, and he doesn't want to. Won't even go to the trouble of staging an election, which is pretty damned stupid if you ask me. Another dictator, another revolution, same song, different year."

The next day I brought the subject up with Momo-san, who had drummed into us the importance of being aware of politics and of exercising our right to vote when we got old enough.

"Dictator? Look it up," she said, a little shortly. She was still slightly annoyed with me for that Bromo-Seltzer prank. Right after being bitten by Ti-chien, I'd put my head down on the study table one day and started moaning and growling. I'd slipped some Bromo-Seltzer powder under my tongue and when I raised my head, my foaming mouth and gnashing teeth cleared the classroom in two seconds flat.

Anyhow, she'd told me to look up "dictator," so I did.

"'**Dic'ta-tor,** *noun,* one who dictates; an absolute ruler or tyrant,'" I read to the class. Doux Doux grumbled, "Sounds like Lizbuthann to me." Sooo very clever, that girl.

Momo-san tried not to smile at Doux Doux's wit—dim, if you ask me—but didn't do a great job of it. Okay, so I'm a little bossy at times, but *someone* has to make the decisions. Even if they are wrong.

"Thank you, Elizabeth. Now, class, why do you think a dictator is considered a bad ruler by many?"

"Because if there is a dictatorship, there is no democracy," I piped up, hogging the limelight. I was really good in Civics and could name all past presidents, vice-presidents and had memorized the preamble to the Constitution.

"And?" Momo-san asked.

"And what?" I asked, sounding like a moron. Sometimes the limelight ain't so hot.

"And why is democracy important? Instead of, say, a monarchy."

She had me there, since I'd always wished to be a princess or a queen. Queen Elizabeth had a nice ring to it, but someone beat me to it.

"Look it up."

So I did. Instead of reading what was written in the dictionary, I summarized: "A democracy is where the people rule, or elect someone to rule for them."

"Correct. But in the case of Haiti, it seems Mr. Magloire will not allow further elections, making him, in effect, a dictator."

"Can Ike do that?"

"No, President Eisenhower cannot. We fought the British to become free, not to live under a dictatorship or a monarchy."

It was all so confusing. First we fought against the British to dump the king, then we threw in with the Brits against the Germans so the English could *keep* their king. History had a way of discombobulating kids; just about the time we figure out who the bad guys are, they change. For instance, in war movies, things were crystal clear: Germans were the villains.

Then I met Hans.

Hans was a big, jovial engineer who gave us cookies, patted us fondly on the head, and didn't even own a huge, slobbery, pointy-eared dog or say "Heil Hitler," but he was German. I liked him, even if Uncle Lloyd said he was a damned Nazi.

"Daddy," I asked one evening while were sitting on the river bank trying to catch old Trashrack, "is being German a bad thing?"

"I hope not. I'm one."

"You are?"

"Sure am. Texas German. We came to Texas a long time ago, but we're still German in a lot of ways. Your granddaddy didn't even speak English until he went into the first grade."

"But some Germans are bad. Like Hitler."

"Hitler was nuts and he got a lot of people to go along with him"

"Was he a dictator?"

"I guess so."

My goodness gracious.

Momo-san breathed a long sigh the next day in class when I told her, with great authority, that the president of Haiti was not only a dictator, he was a Nazi.

"Where do you come *up* with these ideas?" she asked, then, not waiting for my answer, continued talking. "President Magloire is not a Nazi. He's what some people call a benevolent dictator."

"Benevolent?" I asked. Even before Momo-san could say anything I grabbed the dictionary. After reading all the meanings I said, "So he's good and generous to the poor?"

"Some say so. Others don't."

"Those others wouldn't be guerillas, would they?"

The class got all excited, thinking the subject was turning from politics to jungle animals, but Momo-san straightened that out real fast.

"Guerillas," she said as she wrote it on the board, "not gorillas."

The class sighed their disappointment in unison, and pulled out Mr. Webster.

"As you can see, guerillas are irregulars, volunteers if you will, who fight with sabotage and harassment."

"You mean like Sam Houston."

For the first time ever, I saw Momo-san falter. She hadn't studied Texas history for as many years as I had, so I filled her in. "Santa Anna was a Mexican tyrant and Sam Houston and his army of volunteers, who were mostly farmers, whomped him and sent him home to Mexico. But not before old Sam yelled, 'Remember the Alamo.'"

The class, one-hundred percent Texans, gave a rousing cheer; we'd all been brought up hearing of the glories of the Texas Revolution and The Republic of Texas.

Momo-san was not so easily derailed. "Did you ever think, class, that just maybe the Mexicans had a right to defend their country against those who wanted to take it away from them?"

Heresy! We stared, open-mouthed, at Momo-san as if she had changed, before our very eyes, into the devil incarnate.

History surely can addlepate a body.

While we were all still in shock, Momo-san wrote another word on the board: cogitate

"Look it up. And then do it," she said. "Class dismissed."

Where, oh where, was Grandmother Hetta when I needed her? Back in Texas, doing me no good at all, that's where. I dug out one of my Texas history books, but nowhere could I find a hint that Santa Anna might have been anything but a bad guy. Then I remembered Daddy's moth-eaten books about Texas. I'd never read them, because the old-fashioned writing was too hard to read. But I did know that some of my ancestors were in them—ancestors who actually lived in Texas before and after the Texas Revolution.

Daddy had underlined their names in the books, and someone had drawn a chart showing the march of generations, but these little boxes with names meant very little to me. With revolution in the air in Haiti, and Momo-san's shocking statements still bouncing around in my brain, I thumbed through the books with new interest, and found, to my surprise, that my ancestors were Mexicans! I suppose that explained my fondness for tortillas and refried beans.

Not only were we Mexicans, we supported that rat Santa Anna! This was truly something to cogitate. I cornered Daddy as soon as he got home from work, since it was his side of the family that had me so confused.

"Daddy, are we Mexicans?"

"No, honey, we're Americans."

"But we *were* Mexicans?"

"I guess we were. All Texans were for a period of time."

My mother walked by just then, saw my face light up and quickly dashed my hopes. "No, Lizbuthann," she said, "this does *not* mean you can get your ears pierced."

Rats. I got back on the subject. "But this book," I waved it at him, "says we were evil because we were in the Mexican government."

"Confusin', ain't it? I guess after we fought with the Mexicans to toss out Spain we were given jobs as officials and such by the boys down in Mexico City. Matter of fact, your great-great-great-great-great-great—I think that's enough greats—Grandpappy Stockman even named one of his kids after Santa Anna. But then, when Santa Anna started being such a pig-head, we changed sides. Ann, why are you so interested all of sudden in Texas history?"

"Because we're going to be in another revolution."

"We sure as hell are not! The first time trouble starts, we're on a plane out of here, so don't you worry one little bit."

That, however, was just exactly what I *was* worried about. "Can we take Angela with us? And won't I have to have a special cage built for Pee Wee?"

"Uh…ask your mother." He took off, mumbling about having something to do, but I could tell he was avoiding my question. And before I could ask Mama, it was Angela herself who set me to worrying when I caught her crying in the kitchen.

"What's wrong?" I asked, trying to think what I'd been up to lately that would bring Angela grief. Well, other than messing with the wrong dog, losing the camp doctor, stealing Daddy's car, and finding a dead witch. Other than that, I'd been uncommonly good since the leech and bird-poopy incident.

Angela wiped her eyes and shook her head. "Not'ing for little white girls to worry wit', child."

"Maybe I can help? I'm real good at solving problems," I said.

"You be really good at *making* problems, but you have good heart. You do not have evil bones."

"Well, sometimes I have evil thoughts. Does that count?"

"We all do, Elisabet, we all do."

No amount of coaxing would convince her to tell me what was wrong. I figured she was just sad about François, even though she wasn't even sure he was her long lost brother. I suppose she just wanted to believe he was, even if we never found him again. Which brought to mind my other problem.

"Angela, I think I'm going to have to tell Daddy about François and the doctor."

She looked alarmed. "Why, child?"

"The serum. There isn't enough left for Doux Doux and me. The doctor took some for François, and I counted what was still in the refrigerator."

"How much?"

"Only ten. That's five days worth for each of us, and five days short. I can wait a couple of days before spilling the beans, but not much longer, because we'll have to go to Port-au-Prince for more. Unless, of course, we get word from the hospital where Dr. Cordier took the dog's head that Ti-chien didn't have rabies after all."

"And when we receive this word?"

"Well, Dr. Cordier figured ten days, which would make it just right, but I'm not sure we can take that chance, since I'm almost certain Ti-chien was rabid. Not that I'm crazy about those shots, but I don't want to come down with rabies, either."

Angela nodded, but tears welled in her eyes again. She shooed me out of the kitchen and went back to making potato salad.

I went to my room to cogitate.

Angela had dark circles under her eyes the next morning, so I thought I'd try to cheer her up.

"Hey, Angela, after school today I think I'll go to the village. Want to come? We can look for some neat material for your dresses."

"*Non bèbè*, we better not. It's baking day."

"Oh, goody. Can you make raisin bread?"

"*Oui*, sure, you want help?"

"Well, no, we need fruit, so I think I'll just ride on down to the village by myself."

"No!" Angela screeched.

Angela doesn't screech, so her outburst brought Mama on the run. "What's wrong? Lizbuthann, what have you done to Angela?"

"Not'ing. She don't do not'ing. But she want go to the village today and I say *non*."

"Well, why on earth not? She goes all the time," Mother said, looking puzzled.

"Yeah. Why not?" I parroted.

Angela wrung her hands. "Because it not safe this day. Bad peoples be there."

"What kind of bad peoples?"

"Poli-ti-cians," she said with disgust, carefully pronouncing each syllable.

Mother and I both giggled; Angela sounded just like Uncle Lloyd, except he'd say, "*Damned* politicians."

"You mean they're having a political rally? People making speeches and things?" Mother asked.

"Well, yes. But bad words." She reached into her skirt pocket and pulled out a piece of tattered paper. It was a mimeographed flyer, the purple ink slightly smudged. The border was decorated with voodoo signs I recognized from my "horse" book, and I could read the message, although the script was that fancy stuff Haitians were so fond of. Well, the ten percent who could even read and write. The written words, however, weren't necessary for the other ninety-percent to get the message; crude drawings made it crystal clear.

Mother, when she looked over my shoulder, gasped. You'd have to be blind not to see that the people hanging by their necks from trees were white. I thought one of them bore me a strong resemblance, but I was probably just being paranoid.

"What does it say, Lizbuthann?" my mother asked, a hint of hysteria creeping into her voice.

"Uh, well, it says, 'Death to President Magloire and his white puppet masters in their mansions on the hill.'" Mansions?

Mother turned white around the mouth. "Lizbuthann, saddle up Wishes and go fetch your father."

I felt like Paul Revere.

# CHAPTER 23

▼

It seemed we were all going to hang.

Well, those of us who happened to be pale-ish, anyway. According to the frightful flyer, light-skinned folk, who, it said, held all the money and power, were going to be thrown out-and-over so the other, darker, ninety-nine percent could run the country. Never mind that ninety-percent of the ninety-nine percent couldn't read or write, much less run anything. Angela, with her *café au lait* complexion, was borderline. Angela's husband, and our yard boy, Guilliame— traitors because they worked for us foreigners—would be safe if, and only if, they joined the rebels. I knew we could trust Angela's hubby, but I wasn't so sure about Guilliame; he was still a little huffy over me getting his lawn dug up.

As I galloped Wishes toward the jobsite to fetch Daddy for my very upset mother, I streaked by Doctor Cordier's office and it occurred to me that the doctor was very dark-ish, and a thought blacker than his skin popped into my head. Could it be that Doctor Cordier had joined up with his fellow dark-complected countrymen in revolt? And, through some diabolically evil scheme, disappeared with the serum so that at least two little white kids would die off? Boy, talk about being paranoid! I tried telling myself I was being silly, but who knew what evil lurked in the hearts of men? The Shadow, maybe, but not Lizbuthann.

As long as I was having ugly notions, I reminded myself that, on top of everything else, I was due for an injection in a few minutes. Hanged or shot or rabid; pretty big worries for such a little kid as myself. I urged my noble steed to a faster gallop.

"Daddy!" I shouted, banging open the cableway shack door. My father, who had been concentrating on lowering a full load of grout to a worker about mid-dam, came close to braining the poor man.

"*Jeezuzcrislizbuthann,*" Daddy yelped, "you scared the bejesus out of me! What is it?"

"Mama wants you home, right now."

"Is anyone hurt? Your sister? What?"

"Mama's scared because it looks like we're gonna get hanged."

"Oh well," Daddy said in an exasperated voice, "in that case, I'd best high-tail it on home. Do I bring my own damned rope?"

Uncle Lloyd came through the door about then. "Who we gonna hang? And Bud, you scared the crap out of that poor s.o.b. down at the pour. What happened?"

"Hand slipped. And I don't know who's hangin' who, but my wife sent Ann up here to get me, so she must be real upset about something. I'd better get to the house. We'll need someone up here for the next pour."

"I'll do it," I volunteered, but they ignored me. Heck.

"Ann, go on back and tell your mother I'll be there in a few minutes."

"Oh, okay," I said, reluctantly. My timing was off here. It would take me fifteen minutes to ride home, then almost fifteen back to the doctor's office, which meant I wouldn't get to hear what Mama and Daddy planned to do about the flyer. Unless, of course, Mrs. Dahlke was early and I could get my shot on the way back to Camp, which meant I could hear what my parents said before I had to leave for school.

I pushed Wishes to his limit for the short run to Doctor Cordier's office. Luck was with me: Mrs. Dahlke had just arrived. Minutes later, I jumped back on Wishes, ignoring the deep pain in my stomach muscles where the serum still stung. I beat Daddy home. Whew!

"Lizbuthann, did you find your father?" Mama yelled as Wishes and I, both pretty lathered up, rode into the yard.

"Yes ma'am, he's coming."

"You better get on down for your shot if you're gonna get to school on time."

"Already got it."

She eyed me with a doubtful look, but I raised my shirt and showed her the tiny bandage Mrs. Dahlke had stuck over the hole she'd just punched in me.

"Uh, Mama, Mrs. Dahlke said she'd like to talk to you sometime today."

"What did you do this time, Lizbuthann?"

"Nothing, honest. She didn't say what it was about." She hadn't *said* so, but I suspected Mrs. Dahlke'd finally gotten around to counting the serum vials, done her math, and wondered why Cordier had either not gotten enough in the first place, or took some with him when he disappeared.

I'd run my own numbers, as well. If the doctor had found François the day he disappeared, he, too, would be running low on serum. So, if he was able, he'd have to show up in Port-au-Prince to get more. I didn't want to ponder the possibility that he *wasn't* able, and instead, I was trying to come up with a way to worm a trip to Port-au-Prince, where I hoped to find the doc. Providing, of course, that the poor man wasn't an oooh-gah-oooh himself by now. And, even if I couldn't find him, I'd talk to the folks at the hospital in town and get more serum.

But first we had this hangin' thing to deal with.

When Daddy's truck slid to a dusty halt, Mama was waiting for him and Uncle Lloyd at our front door. She shoved the flyer into my father's hands. "Tell him what it says, Lizbuthann."

"She doesn't have to," Daddy said, twirling on that forelock. "Two minutes after Ann left, one of the foreman ran up and told us there's some kind of disturbance down in the village, and that guerillas have blocked off the road to Port-au-Prince just on the other side of Mirebalais. All the soldiers, except the six we asked to stay and guard Camp, just took off to see what's up."

"What are we going to do?" Mama asked calmly; much more calmly that I would have expected, what with us about to be in the middle of a revolution.

"Cancel school?" I suggested.

Mama rolled her eyes. "Lizbuth—"

Daddy spoke up before she could let me have it. "Good idea. Ann, go tell Momo to send the kids home, toot sweet. I'm going to ring the bell for a Camp meeting."

"But Daddy, can't I come to the meeting?"

"I think you best come back and stay here with your sister and Angela. Okay, let's go."

Dang, I wanted to hear what was going on, but once again, Wishes and I took off. Just call me Paul-a Revere.

Momo-san was calling role when I barged through the door yelling, "Everybody has to go home."

She opened her mouth to give me heck, but the Camp alarm bell started clanging. "What is it, Elizabeth?" she asked.

"Daddy's called a Camp meeting because we're all going to get—" I saw one of the first graders getting scared and screwing up her face to cry, "Uh, well, they want the kids to go home."

Momo-san shook her head. "Actually, Elizabeth, I prefer you take *all* the students with you to your house. I will go to the meeting, tell their parents where their children are and, afterwards, they can collect them."

Doux Doux, who was still bent over from her morning visit with Mrs. Dahlke, perked up. I could see her counting heads and calculating what we could make in babysitting fees.

Momo-san looked at Doux Doux and added, "You will, of course, watch them at no charge."

Doux Doux's face fell, but she helped me round up the class and herd the whole bunch back to my house, where Angela waited to comfort us with limeade and cookies.

"Say, Angela, maybe I should take some of these cookies up to the meeting?" I suggested, as soon as we had everyone settled down.

"You *maman* say you stay here, and you stay here."

"But Angela, I—"

"I, not'ing. You stay."

Rats.


Stranded again.

The soldiers had retreated back to Camp after an unsuccessful attempt to get through the rebel roadblock. The brief skirmish left no one injured, but a lot of ammo was wasted. Uncle Lloyd said they should have taken me along, as I could probably out-shoot the lot. 'Course, all I'd ever blasted was a slew of beer cans, but I have to admit, I am a pretty fair shot.

The soldiers had piled a line of sandbags across the main road, just the other side of the village, and then another at the Camp gate, which was closed for the first time ever. The Camp manager issued rationing notices, every available container was filled with fresh water, and tarps were set up to catch more in case we got surrounded and couldn't get diesel to keep our generator and pumps going. And even though black ominous clouds had been looming in that direction for days, there was talk of sending riders over the back mountain trails to the American Embassy in the Dominican Republic. I immediately volunteered and, of course, was just as immediately turned down. I was having a hard time getting my foot into the front door of this revolution.

Daddy figured if someone at the American Embassy in Port-au-Prince didn't know there was a problem at Péligre by now, they would; just as soon as some wild-eyed guerrillas attacked or turned back a camion or truck headed our way. I actually hadn't seen one of these rebels yet, but in my mind they were definitely wild-eyed.

We were, in fact, in no immediate danger. Well, most of us; Doux Doux and I were in a bit of a sticky wicket, as one of the Britishers on the job was fond of saying. We probably wouldn't get hanged, but we very well might begin frothing at the mouth in a few days. I also had to own up to the fact that if we did, it would be mostly my fault. Had I reported the missing serum sooner, maybe we could have gotten into Port-au-Prince for more in time to not interrupt the series.

I was thinking about this when someone knocked on the door, Pee Wee said, "Come on in," and Mrs. Dahlke entered, expecting to see my mother. When the nurse looked around in confusion, Pee Wee seemed very satisfied with himself.

"Oh, hello again, Elizabeth. Uh, where's your mother?" She gave my parrot a dirty look; evidently Mrs. Dahlke had heard of his reputation. Fooey, I was hoping she'd try talking to him.

"Mama!" I hollered, "you got company."

Mother came in from the backyard, gave me a head tilt and lip pucker that said I was in for a "manners" lesson later on, then smiled a welcome to Mrs. Dahlke. By the time the woman got through talking, however, my mother was no longer smiling. "Let me see if I have this straight," Mama said. "In *two* days, we run out of serum? How could this happen?"

Mrs. Dahlke shrugged. Angela, who had edged into the room, also shrugged.

"Or," I suggested, "Doux Doux could run out now and I'll run out in four days."

All three women glared at me. "Just kidding," I said.

"There is nothing at all funny about this situation, Lizbuthann," my mother declared, her eyebrows a-twitch. "Go get Clota Boudreaux, right now." She didn't say "Please," but I figured I'd best not mention this breach of etiquette.

Jeez, with all the running around I'd been doing, I could have *been* in the Dominican Republic by now.

One day 'til the foaming began, and this time it wouldn't have anything to do with Bromo-Seltzer.

Actually, we didn't have any idea what the results of stopping our shots at ten days, instead of fifteen, would be. Or how long it would take us to go mad.

Daddy, in an effort to lighten the situation, speculated that, in my case, it would be hard to tell, but Mama was not even slightly amused.

Without any communication with the outside world, we couldn't even find out if the test results on Ti-chien were positive or negative. If they were negative, our problem was solved, but my money was on "positive."

Daddy and Uncle Lloyd cooked up a brainstorm to pull an end run around the rebels; saddling up Wishes and Smokey and taking back trails around the roadblock to Port-au-Prince. Mama shot that down. There was no way in hell, she said, she was going to be stuck in the mountains with a rabid child and no way to get help for her. I suggested that, instead of Daddy and Uncle Lloyd, Doux Doux and I make a run for it, but my mother definitely nixed that.

Another plan was to take one of the work barges and float down the Artibon-ite River, hoping the rebels weren't guarding the bridge over the old ford. This was after Uncle Lloyd suggested blowing up that same bridge so the rebels couldn't get to Camp. The head soldier suggested that we shoot our way through, which I thought was a grand idea until Daddy said there was no way I was going to get to participate. Everyone had ideas, none of them too hot.

One thing was certain, though, something had to be done, or Doux Doux and I were in big trouble. We had one possibility, however, that kept my mother from having a nervous breakdown: Doux Doux and I had not actually been bit-ten by Ti-chien and it could be that we were not infected at all. That possibility didn't keep people from giving me sideways looks when I went to the clubhouse, though. I considered pulling my little Bromo-Selzer act again, but what with ten-sions being so high, and folks bristling with firepower, perhaps that wasn't such a great idea.

The day before our last injection it was decided that, as a last resort, supervi-sors, workers and soldiers would, using D-8 dozers as their front line, take out the roadblock. Fathers, husbands and sons, some I didn't even know, were willing to risk their lives for two little girls who might or might not need help. I'd never felt so rotten in my whole life; if someone got killed, it would be my fault. I racked my brain for a bright idea, something I could do to avoid a tragedy, but could come up with nothing. Brenda Starr would be ashamed of me. *I* sure was.

Doux Doux and I had but one hope: Doctor Cordier. If he was still out there, and had not joined the rebels, he would know our situation was grim, and he would be trying to get to us with more serum. But who knew if he was even alive? And what about poor François? What had happened to those two?

I pondered these questions as I sipped an orange drink at the clubhouse bar, and a picture, like a cartoon, popped up and began running through my mind.

The scene, one that would not amuse my mother, brought a smirk to my lips: François, Doux Doux and I, raging through the jungle, frothing and madly snapping the air. For practice, I clicked my teeth at an imaginary fly and snarl-laughed. Several people left the clubhouse.

# CHAPTER 24

▼

I heard the first shots just after midnight.

Anyone who's lived through a Texas Hill Country hunting season couldn't help but recognize the sound of gunfire, but this rapid popping was unlike any I'd heard before. I rushed out the back door, looked over the bluff toward Mirebalais, and saw flashes like distant fireflies lighting up the sultry night air as round after round exploded.

I wasn't the only one awake. So many lights came on all over Camp, and the village below, that there was a momentary brown-out when the generator plant hit overload.

"Lizbuthann," I heard my mother shout from the kitchen door. Rats, the electrical dip must have bogged down that noisy fan of hers and waked her up. "You come back in here until we find out what's going on."

"But Mama, I have to see to Wishes. He's scared."

"Bring him 'round to the front yard, then. Right now, young lady."

"Yes ma'am."

Wishes was not a happy horse. Each volley of gunfire sent his eyes to rolling and his neck muscles rippling. I slipped a rope halter over his fear-flattened ears, then tried gently coaxing him from his corral, but he balked, yanked on the rope and nearly unhinged my shoulder. Losing patience, I replaced the halter with a bitted bridle so he'd know I meant business, and after a couple of serious talking-to's, he finally followed.

As we rounded the corner of the house, the gun pops became muffled enough that he settled down, but I left his bridle on; that horse could be a handful when he got his back up, and who knew what was going to happen next. I tied him securely to a low-hanging tree limb in the front yard, scratched his ears, sweet-talked him for a minute, gave him a sugar cube, and reluctantly minded my mother by returning to the house.

Back in the living room, Pee Wee was letting go with a hysterical stream of off-color language so, in order to shut him up, I let him out of his cage and tucked him inside my pajama top. He settled down, content to chew on my collar and hair.

Mother, looking slightly bewildered, sat on the settee, holding my sleepy sister in her lap. I joined her just as Daddy, shotgun in one hand and tucking his shirt into his khakis with the other, came out of the bedroom. He gave us both a shoulder pat and began calmly giving us instructions that would have sounded like orders if he'd raised his voice, but he didn't.

"I'm going on up to the clubhouse," he said to my mother, "and as soon as I know what the hell's happening, I'll be back." Turning to me, he added, in a voice as normal as if he were talking about the weather, but with an unmistakable warning tone, "And Ann, do not leave this house, you hear me?"

My father knows me all too well. "Yes, sir," I said, and for once in my life, I really meant it. Who would want to go out now?

He gave me a second, doubtful look, then went on. "Lock the doors, close the louvers, and turn off all the lights, okay?"

Mama and I nodded, and she asked, "How long do you think you'll be gone?"

Daddy shrugged. "Not sure, but I'll be back as soon as I can. I'm leaving the gun, so if anyone you don't know tries to come through either door, let 'em have it with both barrels. *Through* the door, got that?"

That last command, although aimed at my mother, I took to really be for me; Mama didn't know one end of a gun from the other, and had never been too keen on having them around the house. Daddy propped the shotgun by the door, said, "Safety's on," gave us both a kiss, and left. I was getting ready to lock up behind him when he yanked the door back open, almost pulling me outside.

"Ann," he said, "I don't want you touching the gun." Dang, the man's a mind reader.

Out he went again, and I watched through the dining room screen as he roared away to the clubhouse, where the emergency bell clanged away.

Mother and I set about securing our house. Once the sisal mat was lowered over the dining room screens, I went from room to room cranking shut aluminum louvers and locking them in place. Even with the house tightly shut, enough aggregate plant light filtered through louver slits to paint us with a gloomy glow. Without any outside air, it became stuffy almost immediately, but we didn't dare turn on the fan for fear of not being able to hear outside noises. Soon becoming accustomed to the muffled gunfire, Sister, who had been whimpering, went back to sleep, and my mother was able to shift her onto the settee.

"Well, my goodness, Lizbuthann," Mama said. I waited for her to say more, but I guess she figured she'd just about summed up our situation. She stood, smoothed her nightgown over her hips and walked into the kitchen. When she came back, she had a beer in her hand so I knew she was pretty upset because I had never seen my mother drink alcohol unless Daddy was around, except maybe with a lady friend while they waited for the men to come home from work. She caught me looking at her and smiled. "Want one?"

"No thank you, ma'am, I'd rather have a rum and cola."

Mama giggled and got me a limeade. We sat, sipping our drinks, both lost in thought. I was wondering how I was going to both mind my father and still knock off anyone trying to come through the door, but Mama was two steps ahead of me.

"Lizbuthann, your Daddy isn't always...uh, well, right. Especially when he feels threatened. Like right now? He wants to be two places at once, but can't. Neither can I. So, if someone did try to come through that door, I'd feel like I had to hold on to your sister. You do what you have to, hear?"

I nodded and glanced at the gun. Unlike my many cousins, I had never shot at a living thing. I had murdered hundreds of rocks, beer bottles and jars, but when it came to hunting critters, I never liked the idea of bopping Bambi. My grandpa's house in Texas was chock full of glassy-eyed dead things hanging all over the walls, and photos of burly relatives with their guns, standing or kneeling next to everything from deer to mountain lions that they'd dispatched to animal heaven. When at the ranch, I slept on a screened-in porch at the front of the house and, mounted on the wall just above the bed, hung a ferocious looking javelina hog's head with four-inch tusks jutting from both sides of his snout. I always slipped a pillowcase over him before I turned out the lights.

Thinking of that javelina brought back the memory of human heads poked onto posts at the Port-au-Prince airport. Heads of the People. And now it seemed, the People were trying to get *our* heads. Heck, and here I thought we *were* the People, because we dang sure weren't the rich folk.

"What was that?" Mother said, jumping to her feet. Startled, I grabbed the gun (sorry, Daddy) and slipped off the safety. Mother heard the click. "Put that back on before you shoot yourself in the foot."

"Yes ma'am," I said, re-latching the safety, but keeping my trigger finger handy, just in case. She was right, of course, to play it safe; that gun was mighty heavy and it *was* aimed at my tootsies. "What'd you hear, Mama?"

"Don't know. Something, I thought. Be still."

We both sat down and strained our ears, but all I heard was the faint grinding of the aggregate plant, and the occasional pop of gunfire. The shooting had slowed considerably, and I hoped it was a sign that our soldiers had stopped the wild-eyed rebels that I pictured storming toward Camp. 'Course, there was always the possibility that the soldiers had been overrun and bloodthirsty guerrillas were on their way. Maybe they'd take us hostage, and I, without benefit of the life-saving serum, would turn rabid on them and, in a furious (but noble) rage, I'd dispatch them all with my bare teeth, and save the day before losing my valiant battle with rabies. There would, of course, be a state funeral...

"Lizbuthann, you hear anything at all? I swear I did."

Jerked from visions of heroism, I cocked my head. No unusual sounds that I could hear, unless you counted gunfire, which was becoming pretty ordinary by now. I was just glad it didn't seem to be getting any closer.

"No, Mama. But I gotta go to the bathroom."

"Right now?"

'Yes ma'am."

"Oh, all right, but you get right back here, okay Lizbuthann?"

I carefully propped the shotgun by the front door, walked into the bathroom and had barely perched on the toilet seat when I heard it: a scratching noise. I held my breath and listened. It seemed to be coming from my...oh, no!...bedroom louvers.

Yanking up my pajama bottoms, I tiptoed to my bed, unlocked the louvers, cracked them slightly, and found myself, as I feared, staring into François' middle. For crying out loud, what was he *doing* here now? What with feelings running so high, I had to get that dimwit out of my backyard before someone shot him. I scurried back into the living room.

"Uh, Mama, I have something to tell you."

Mother, who was sipping her third beer, giggled. "Don't tell me, you're getting married."

I chuckled politely, hoping the sound would drown out François' increasingly louder pawing. "Nope," I said, "that's not it. What if I were to tell you that I have a secret friend who is really nice, but maybe some people wouldn't like him too much."

"Oh, pish," my mother said, waving her hand at me, "that's normal. Especially since Dorcas is angry with you. I had me one of those friends when I was a girl. We spent hours playing together, but she was invisible to everyone else in the family."

"Mama, this one's not so little. And he's not invisible, either. As a matter of fact, he's outside right now and I really, really have to talk with him. Well, *to* him. He never has a lot to say."

"Now Lizbuthann, your father said to stay inside and keep the doors locked."

"Yes ma'am, I know he did, but maybe I could just speak with my friend through the louvers?"

Mother gave me a patient smile, reached over and patted my hand. "Sure, honey. What's your friend's name?"

"François." I inched toward the gun as I talked, hoping to nab it on my way to the bedroom just in case François had turned less than friendly.

"Well, you go on ahead and have your talk, and be sure to tell François howdy for me. Oh, and leave that weapon, please."

Dang. Back in my room, I cranked the louvers completely open. François stopped in mid-scratch, revealed a lot of teeth, grabbed a louver and ripped it from its frame. Stunned, I jumped back just as he seized another louver and jerked it out as easy as pie.

"Lizbuthann, what's all the racket in there? Y'all quiet down," Mama called from the living room, a little laugh in her tone, "or I'll make your little friend go home."

Fat chance on that. François was not acting at all like his old sweet self and, as he ripped out a third louver, my blood ran cold. Did we have a seven-foot, rabid zombie on our hands? I watched another louver fly into the yard. Even through my growing panic I was thinking that some things never change. Mad or not, it never occurred to the big numskull to simply crash through the front door, but it was only a matter of minutes before he did come through the window. I whirled and ran into the living room.

"Mama," I yelled, "run!"

"What?"

"Take Sister and run. Out the front door. I'm right behind you."

"Wha—?" There was a loud crash in my bedroom, and my mother didn't hesitate any longer. She scooped up Sister with one arm, grabbed my free hand with the other, and headed for the front door about the same time that I heard my window screen being wrenched from its moorings. Almost at the same time there was an OOOFFF, a thud, and the screech of my metal bed legs scraping across the cement floor.

As soon as we cleared the door, I jerked my hand from Mama's, ran back for the gun, turned, and began walking backwards. When François' huge frame filled the doorway, I took aim. He would be very, very, hard to miss.

"Keep going, Mama, I've got him in my sights. Don't worry though, François is really, really slow. Even walking, we can beat him to the clubhouse."

Mother stopped, turned and gasped, "Oh my Lord, Lizbuthann. What *is* that?"

"Just François, Mama. And normally he's very nice, but right now he seems a mite perturbed. He won't hurt me, I just know that, but, to tell the truth, I'm not too sure about anyone else."

"Lizbuthann, we are going to have a serious talk about your choice of little friends when this is over."

"Yes ma'am. Let's just keep walking backwards. I think he stopped."

It was about two more blocks to the clubhouse. Lights blazed from the windows and when I glanced over my shoulder, I could just make out people milling around inside. Pickups were parked every which way in front, and there were at least two soldiers posted by the door. Seeing them, I became frightened for François. What if they saw him? Even if François really wasn't rabid, it wouldn't matter to those guys; they'd shoot him on sight.

"I'll be right back," I shouted to Mama as I took off running back to the house.

"Lizbuthann, you come right back here, you hear me? Or I swear you'll be on restriction for the rest of your life. I mean it, now," Mama warned. She sounded ready to cry.

I pretended not to hear. I had to get a good look at François and, if he was all right, I needed to get him headed down the bluff. I wasn't however, taking any chances. Slipping the safety off, I carried the shotgun at arms length in front of me, just like Daddy had taught me, ready to drop to one knee and aim. At close range, even a seven-foot zombie would be no match for that gun. *If*, that is, my arms didn't go dead from the effort of holding its weight, and *if* I had the nerve to shoot.

François had finally unstuck himself from the front doorframe. He looked around as if trying to get his bearings, then headed straight for Wishes! I picked up speed, hoping Mother would give up on me and run for help. I could see François' dark hulk moving closer to my horse, but knew I couldn't get there in time to—do what?

I stopped, dropped to one knee and took careful aim at the zombie's head. My arms and knees were shaky and my stomach was quaking, but I managed, just like I'd been taught, to track my prey. 'Course, my prey was usually a Lone Star beer bottle tossed high into the Texas sky by my father, and I'd had hours on end of practice back at the ranch, but not in Haiti. Guns were illegal here—even though everybody seemed to have one—and so I hadn't had one in my hands for three years. Once thing was for sure though, that big guy was not going to get his rabid mitts on my horse.

I had to make a decision soon though, because, with a shotgun, if I let him get too close to Wishes, I'd hit my horse as well. About four feet from Wishes, François stopped, put his arm out and the horse, straining against his lead, snuffled his hand. Wishes, a great judge of character, had put his nose of approval on François and, with a flood of relief, I lowered the gun and ran to them.

"François, what in the heck do you think you're doing? Mama's gonna come back here with a posse in about three minutes flat! Get out of here. *Allez! Vite!*"

He shook his head.

"What do you mean, no?" Then I said it in Creole.

Again, he shook his head.

Frustrated, I grabbed his arm and tried pulling him towards the bluff at the back of the house, but he stood his ground. I was getting desperate. I knew for sure that by now Mama had guys who were bristling with firepower headed our way and they'd take a real dim view of a seven-foot giant who had just broken his way into our house.

I was on the verge of tears, trying to think of what to do, when François reached up and removed what looked like a cigar box hanging from a piece of twine around his neck. He slipped it over my head, then, miracle of miracles, turned and headed for the bluff with more speed than I'd ever seen him muster. Just in the nick of time, too, for I heard noises behind me and saw three soldiers making a beeline for us. Behind them was a wall of people. All they needed were pitchforks and torches. I sped to meet them, hoping to buy François a little time.

The soldiers, evidently not clued in as to what was happening, saw me running towards them with a gun in my hand, slid to a stop, and took aim at me. Daddy swept past them like a football player, knocking one on his rump and scattering the other two. In the confusion, one of them shot his gun into the air and everything came to a screeching halt. No one moved for at least ten seconds, until someone screamed, "Oh, my god! Look at that monster!"

Whirling around, I saw François disappearing over the bluff, and all heck broke loose.

The crowd divided. Half swept past me, heading for the zombie, the other half turned tail and ran back for the clubhouse. I was left sitting in the road, cradling my shotgun and praying that François had the sense to duck under the ledge instead of trying to make it all the way down to the road. I left the gun, took off like a rabbit after the big knucklehead, and reached the bluff just behind the mob. They were milling around, peering over the edge, but thankfully, couldn't spot him. I knew where he was, though.

"He's gone," I said loudly. "I think I see him headed down the road. Towards Mirebalais. See him, he's way down the road there." Then I repeated it in Creole, supposedly for the soldiers, but really for François.

"Looks like it," one of the men said, and people started leaving just as Uncle Lloyd and Mama joined me and my father.

"What was that?" my uncle asked.

Daddy shook his head, but mother said, "I believe that was Lizbuthann's imaginary friend."

"Well, she's got one hell of an imagination," he grumbled.

"Thank you," I said, drawing a look.

Mama took Sister back into the house, while Daddy posted a soldier in our backyard. He also sent several armed guards to the base of the bluff, on the road just below our house. François was trapped, but, for the moment, safe. *If* he stayed put. There was nothing more I could do for now, so bit the bullet and trudged back into the house, where my mother, I knew, was waiting for explanation. Gee, I wish I had one.

Once inside, poor little Pee Wee, who had ridden out all the excitement inside my pajama top, climbed on my shoulder and began whistling "Home on the Range."

"Pee Wee, you pipe down," my mother ordered. Pee Wee, miraculously, did. Mama looked at me with those twitching brows. "Well?"

"It is a very long story, Mama."

"I have all ni—hey, what's that around your neck?"

I looked down. In the excitement, I'd forgotten that François had remove something from his neck and put it around mine. The box hung almost to my waist. I carefully removed the string from my neck and laid the box on a table. While I was naturally curious what it contained, I was also a little worried. After all, François was a zombie, and he had lived with a voodoo witch. Heck, I *had* read about Pandora's box.

"Well?" Mama said again. "You gonna open it?"

Ever so slowly, I unwrapped a banana leaf held with sisal string to find a green metal box labeled: **U.S. Army**. Heavy steel latches held it tightly closed.

I tugged on one of the latch-downs and realized it was cold to the touch. Not just cool, like metal, but cold, like ice. When I released the second one, it popped open to reveal a bed of sisal matting surrounded by ice cubes, and in the center lay twelve small vials exactly like the ones that had been a source of my daily torture for nine days.

Mother looked perplexed, then her face lit up. "Oh, thank God."

"Well, yeah, Him, too."

Somehow, God, with a great deal of help from Doctor Cordier—and François—had come through. François, big and slow as he was, somehow managed to get through both the guerilla and army roadblocks to deliver a box of life-saving serum to me, and now, for this act of kindness, he was being hunted down like an animal by frightened young soldiers.

Only one good thing about this whole mess: I knew where François lurked, and the soldiers didn't. The problem was how to get him out of that cave under the bluff, and on his way back to where I hoped Doctor Cordier waited. Without, I might add, getting the big zombie drilled full of holes.

# CHAPTER 25

▼

Brenda Starr would, no doubt, come up with a very clever plan to save François, but she was a grownup, and she had this mystery man to help her out. I was just a kid with a very serious problem: François, who, after saving my life (once again!) by delivering the serum, was now stuck in a cave, surrounded by guys hell-bent on target practice. I had to save him.

I was racking my brain for an idea as my mother and I sat in the living room, waiting for Daddy to come back from the clubhouse. My little zombie incident had temporarily derailed the first meeting, so they were still trying to figure out what to do about the roadblock.

"Lizbuthann, you're fidgeting like water on a hot griddle. What's your problem? The gunfire has stopped and your friend, whatever he is, is long gone, thank the Lord."

I should be so lucky. One thing for sure, though, I had to at least figure out a way to see if François was all right in that cave, and I couldn't do it sitting around with my mother and sister. "Uh, I guess I'm just real tired, Mama, what with all the excitement. Maybe we should try to get some sleep? I mean, no telling what time Daddy'll show up."

"You could be right. I've been trying to figure out what on earth we're going to tell your father about that friend of yours, and I can't come up with a thing. After all, that boy, or whatever he is, *did* deliver your serum, so that means he was sent by Doctor Cordier. But he's so…big, and scary looking. And he did break into our house. Heck, he *broke* our house. Tore out an entire window with his bare hands. I have to say, grateful as I am for the serum, I'm glad he's gone. Now I have to tell your father *something* about him, and although I know he will be as relieved as I am to have the serum, don't you think he'll be just a mite worried about you hanging out with a…a…. Lizbuthann, just what *is* he, exactly?"

Good question. Now I needed a good answer. I tucked my hands under my legs, crossing my fingers as I did so. "Oh, he's just a big old slow-in-the head boy who doesn't know his own strength. He's only a little over twenty."

"How do you know that? He tell you?"

Oops. "Uh, not exactly. I just sorta…guessed." I crossed my fingers harder; I couldn't rat on Angela.

Mama gave me a doubtful look, then let out one of her "I'm too tired to get into this right now" shrugs. "Well," she said, "I, for one, am just really glad he's gone."

I wished he *were* gone, but I was almost positive François was crammed into that little cave right under the noses of the soldiers posted behind our house. I also wished I had more faith in grownups in general, especially when dealing with someone like François. In his case, I truly felt I could trust only Angela and Doctor Cordier to defend him, because my parents, while good people, were partial to me and Sister when it came to protection. François, being dead and all, wouldn't rate much mollycoddling.

I yawned, stretched and put Pee Wee into his cage. He didn't even protest; it had been a long, tiring night.

"Goodnight, Mama. Sleep tight," I said, giving her a peck on the cheek before going to my room. Someone had leaned a piece of plywood over the hole in the wall where the louvered window had been before François had so rudely removed it. I lay down on my bed and, in a minute or two, saw Mama, carrying Sister, go into her room. Covers rustled, then her light went off. I waited a full five minutes before stuffing pillows under my sheet so anyone checking on me would, hopefully, think they were looking at a sleeping kid. As further insurance, I eased my bedroom door shut.

The plywood sheet covering François' little remodel job was heavy, but not nailed down, so scooting it a couple of feet was easy enough. After scrambling through the convenient hole in the wall, I eased the board back in place as best I could.

As I dropped to the ground, I could only hope I wasn't spotted. I dared a look towards the bluff. The armed guards, silhouetted by the aggregate plant lights, stood with their backs to me. They were just inches above where I was sure poor François hid. Cigarette smoke drifted my way as the soldiers chatted and blew rings into the night air.

First light would dawn in a few hours and, with its arrival, François' chances for escape would go downhill. As I lay there, trying not to think of tarantulas, centipedes and other dirt critters that might be aching for a bite of a little red-haired Texan, it occurred to me that maybe François wouldn't have to escape. After all, if I told Daddy what François had done, surely I could convince him that the big guy was harmless. Right?

Wrong. My father could not be counted on to be reasonable when he thought his family might be in danger. He was raised in Texas, where they shoot first and then ask questions. I had to solve this myself.

Grandmother Hetta always said that big problems are really just a lot of little problems that, if solved one by one, take care of the whole thing. So, what exactly was my main problem? Lights.

As long as those aggregate plant lights shining on the bluff blazed, it would be danged difficult for a seven-foot zombie to leave his cave, and get down to the road without getting himself spotted. And shot. So, the lights had to go.

Without the handiness of being able to go down the bluff like I usually did to reach the aggregate plant, I would have to: a) make my way up the main street of Camp, b) sneak past the clubhouse, c) sneak past the guard shack with its closed gate and armed guards, d) make my way down a busy road to the aggregate plant. Okay, so now I had a plan. A bad one, but still a plan.

I stood and inched along the back wall. My eyes were riveted on the soldiers who, thank goodness, had their backs to me. Taking baby steps sideways, I hoped Guilliame hadn't left some booby trap, like a rake or something, in my way. I cleared the corner of the house, stepped back into the shadows and let out the breath I'd been holding. I relaxed just a little, turned to head for the main road, and ran smack dab into someone. I just about fainted.

"What little white girl do out this time of night?"

"Angela! What are you doing here?" As frightened as I was, I felt a flood of relief. The cavalry had arrived.

"I ask you first, child."

I heard voices, glanced back over my shoulder and saw that the soldiers were glaring in our direction.

"Get in the kitchen, quick," I said, pushing Angela towards the door. It was locked, but she had a key, so we were both inside, with the lights on, by the time the first soldier arrived. He fixed us with a suspicious squint at us, but Angela gave him a sweet smile, patted me on the head, and told him she was our maid.

The soldier grumbled, "Doesn't anyone ever sleep around here?" then rejoined his fellow guard at the bluff.

"Angela," I whispered, "François is here. He's hiding under the bluff, in a little cave there. I'm sure of it. He brought serum for Doux Doux and me, but then people started chasing him and—"

"Slow down, child. First, where you *maman*?"

"Bedroom. And Daddy, he's—"

"He be wit' my husband at the meetin'."

"Oh."

"Now, what this be 'bout our François?" she asked, keeping her voice low.

"He showed up here with more serum, and he's so danged dumb he tore out my bedroom window to deliver it. Everyone saw him. The soldiers chased him over the bluff and they probably think he's long gone, but they don't know about the hidey hole right under their feet. Daddy doesn't know about the serum yet and I can't figure out what to tell him, exactly, when it comes to François. All my father knows is that a big man tried to get to his family by ripping out a window, and he asked the guards to stay here in case François tries to come back. We have to get rid of those soldiers, and then the lights down below, so François can escape back to Port-au-Prince—or wherever Doctor Cordier is." I finally took a deep breath, hoping I had made *some* sense.

Angela shook her head. "I don' t'ink it is possible. We now be surrounded by soldiers. Hundreds of them. And they be young, stupid and scared. More dangerous, by me, than any *guerillas*. They been tol' to shoot anyone who look like trouble. White or black."

"Then what are we going to do? Can you hide François at your house?"

"No, I can no return to the village, or my house. Soldiers not let us. All peoples must stay where they be. No one can move."

"Not even Daddy? Or Uncle Lloyd?"

"Well, I t'ink they let trucks, company trucks, move between here and the dam. They know these truck be only for big bosses."

I had to t'ink. Think.

"Angela, I think I could make it to the aggregate plant if I can just get by those guys." I nodded towards the guards in our backyard. They were still watching us suspiciously.

"They need some sleep, I t'ink," Angela said with a mischievous smile.

"Huh?"

"And I t'ink they need cookies and Doctor Cordier's special orange juice."

"Angela, you are a genius," I said, giving her a hug.

Angela started dishing up cookies while I crept into the bathroom. On a back shelf under the sink, I found what was left of the magic pills Doctor Cordier had given me, dissolved in juice, when I had malaria. I replaced them with aspirin, and took all ten pills to Angela, who cheerfully mixed them with orange juice and a lot of sugar.

I delivered the goodies, then we waited and planned. We didn't have to wait long.

I slipped by the two snoring soldiers and peered over the side. There were two more guards sitting on a rock below, right next to the main road. Their backs were to me. Careful not to send rocks skittering down the bluff, I took a couple of steps, leaned forward, and whispered, "François?"

His shiny bald head popped from behind the rock, and a set of huge teeth sparkled whitely in what passed for a zombie smile. He stood, banged his head on the top of the cave, dislodging a small rock, which hit another, starting what, to me, sounded like an avalanche. I jumped into the cave—or as much of the cave as was left with François in it—and crouched down.

Below us, one of the soldiers cursed, laughed and called out, "Hey, Pierre, you idiot, stop clowning around. You almost got us that time."

Boys, even ones with guns, will be boys.

I threw another small rock and laughed what I hoped was a deep laugh. Another curse followed, then I heard the two below go back to their small talk.

"François," I whispered, "where is Doctor Cordier?"

He raised his hand and pointed vaguely in the direction of Port-au-Prince, so at least I knew he could understand my Creole, and respond.

"Oookey-dokey," I said in English. François cocked his head, looking for all the world like a puzzled puppy. I switched back to Creole. I told him I was going to leave and, that when he saw the lights go out below, he was to move down the bluff, fast. Once he reached the road, he was to go on to the river; meet me where we'd found Pee Wee the night of the storm. I knew this was a tall order for him to grasp, but when I made a false start to see if he would try to follow, François stayed put. So far, so good. Either that, or he didn't understand a word I'd said and had no plans to move, ever. Oh, well.

Thank goodness the rest of the path was soft dirt. I went into my mountain goat imitation, picking my way ever so slow and careful so I could get down without alerting the soldiers. But what then? The brush on both sides of the path to the road was so thick I'd never be able to bypass them. Of course, that brush was also the reason they didn't realize there *was* a path.

Inch by inch I moved down the narrow trail, stopping and listening after each step. I was grateful for the growling aggregate plant; the roar of stones being separated, then dumped into piles by size. When I reached the road level and was about six feet from the yakking soldiers, one of them stood, stretched, took a couple of steps in my direction, set down his gun and unzipped his shorts. I threw my hands over my head and hunkered down under a large bush, fully expecting to get peed on. Thankfully the guy had a short range.

He was happily splashing a rock three feet from me when headlights suddenly lit the road, a large army truck screeched to a halt, and someone called for him and the other soldier to get in. The zipper zipped, and in just seconds I was alone, within a hundred yards of the huge pyramids of rock and sand surrounding the plant.

Ducking into a crouch, I sprinted across the road, hoping anyone who might see me would think I was a stray dog. Once on the other side of the road, I rolled into a ditch, then peeked up to plan my route. Bushes scattered here and there would make it easy for me to move across the flats leading to the plant, but then a large mishmash of bulldozed roads surrounded the plant and sand piles.

Normally, I knew, dump trucks would be coming and going, taking loads of rock and sand to the dam site, but tonight, for the moment, the roads were deserted. A couple of large pieces of machinery sat idle, and I didn't see any workers at all. Creeping closer, I spotted one lone Haitian man sitting in the glassed, brightly lit, office. He appeared to be asleep.

One thing about being—as the family liked to joke—my father's only son and chief gofer, is that I learned things that most girls don't. For instance, I knew about control panels, junction boxes, and fuses. Somewhere, probably in a small maintenance shack, was a panel that controlled the entire aggregate plant's electricity. The secret was to figure out which building, and then which fuses or breakers controlled what. If I accidentally shut down the entire plant, instead of just the lights I wanted, the guy in the office would surely wake up and be on me in seconds. I wanted to kill only those lights shining on the bluff, and only long enough for François to get down the path, to the river.

After making sure the Haitian guy was really asleep, I moved around the corner from the office. There were outbuildings, one of which I quickly identified as a tool shed because, hanging next to a closed Dutch door, was a peg board with hooks where workers had to exchange their brasses for tools. Each employee was issued a "brass," which was a small disk, engraved with his own number. Without that brass, they could not check out tools, or even collect their paychecks. Brasses were guarded by their owners like gold, so the empty peg board told me that the tool shed was closed. No tools, no workers. Brenda would be proud.

It was in a small building next to the tool shed that I found what I was looking for. On the door was a warning, in English and French:

**DANGER!**
**HIGH VOLTAGE!**
**AUTHORIZED PERSONNEL ONLY!**
**EXCEPT FOR LIZBUTHANN**

I'm kidding about that last line.

Two minutes later I stood in front of a huge electrical control panel with breakers galore to choose from. Unfortunately, they were labeled with numbers only. Rats. I stared at them, trying to make sense of what they controlled. Lucky for me, I do pay attention on occasion, and Daddy had a similar panel in his cableway shack. The big breakers, I knew, controlled big stuff, and the little ones, little stuff. Like lights. Now the trick was to figure out which breaker would cut off which lights, because the last thing I wanted to do was turn off the lights in the office and bring the Haitian on the run. I had four breakers to choose from, and even though I was in a hurry, I wanted to get it right the first time. Slipping back outside, I counted the huge light poles surrounding the plant: four.

Aha! I said to myself and Brenda. Using my keen powers of deduction, I decided that the pole nearest the entrance road would be number one, leaving the backside, the bluff side, to be number three. Right? I pulled down number three. About three seconds later, I heard a door slam loudly, then the growl of footsteps on gravel. I pushed the breaker back on, hid under a desk, and was rewarded with another door slam. Going back outside, I peeked around the corner to see the Haitian settling back down into his chair, evidently satisfied that there had been a momentary power failure that had righted itself.

Okay, assuming the plant was divided into quarters, power-wise, and number three was the office side, then number one *should* be the bluff side. Holding my breath, I pulled down the breaker switch handle. *Voila!* The lights illuminating the bluff, and our backyard, went dark.

Checking on the man, I saw he was once again sawing logs. Great!

I could only hope that François was on the move, because I had to get those lights back on before someone spotted the problem and came to check. After all, the aggregate plant was visible from Camp, and someone was sure to notice the absence of lights. I decided to give François five minutes.

I had no idea whether the zombie was making *his* way *my* way, but I had to start the count. One-one-thousand, two-one-thousand, three...and so on until I heard, less than three minutes later, a truck coming. Unable to wait any longer, I flipped on the breaker and tore off for the river. Just as I cleared the last parked dump truck, headlights swept the area. From behind the truck's fender, I watched as a pickup, which had been speeding in my direction way, skidded to a halt. I caught my breath as I saw, standing like a big goofy statue in the glare of the truck's high beams, guess who?

"What in the hell?" I heard the driver, an American supervisor, yelled as he first jumped from his vehicle, then reached back in. Probably for a gun. His holler waked the Haitian in the office, and spurred François into action. He took off in a loopy lope towards the river. The supervisor and the Haitian worker took off after him, intent on nailing the man who fit the description—I mean, how many of them could there be?—of the monster who tore out my bedroom window. Concentrating on François, they whizzed right by me, even though I was barely hidden.

I let them go by, counting on François' long gait, and his knowledge of where he was going, to buy us time. Circling back to the front of the plant, I reentered the shack, pulled down all the breakers as fast as I could and, for the first time in three years, silence and darkness flooded the entire area.

The abrupt loss of sound and light from the aggregate plant probably woke up the entire Camp.

# CHAPTER   26

▼

The world went dark, except for the pickup's headlights, and Camp lights up on the plateau.

The two men who had been hot on François' huge heels dug in their own, slid to a halt, whirled, and stared dumbly at the suddenly pitch black and silent aggregate plant.

I took this opportunity to scoot around behind them and head for the river, knowing that, if they turned around, they would see me in the headlights. Surely, I thought, they wouldn't shoot at a little girl, but, just in case I was wrong, I picked up speed toward my rendezvous with François. Granted, not a lot of folks would rush to meet up with a dead guy in the dead of night, but as you may have figured out by now, I have a tendency to misjudge a situation here and there.

I ran like the wind, spurred by success and that little thrill of fear that comes with adventure. Brenda Starr couldn't have done better herself. Yessiree, I was really feeling my oats.

Right up to the time I reached the river.

Which was in full flood.

All along I had, in the back of my mind, figured the best escape route for François was from the other side of the river. In this brilliant, if loose, plan of mine, I would send him on his way to Doctor Cordier by leading him across the river. I knew the perfect place, too, with shallow—at least for him—water that wouldn't frighten the big zombie. Assuming, of course, he wasn't hydrophobic. Sorry, my little joke.

I knew that, from soldiers' conversations I'd overheard, that there were two roadblocks; both on our side of the river. Once I had François to the other side, he would have no problem getting to Port-au-Prince, or wherever the doctor was. I had often wondered how the big zombie managed to move around so well without causing alarm, but I figured he traveled via the hundreds of jungle footpaths not visible from the main road. He would know his way.

Many moons before, when the Artibonite was running especially low, Doux Doux and I had strung a piece of cable to the far riverbank. We'd clipped the center to a submerged tire rim weighted with rocks, then anchored both ends around exposed boulders. We'd spent many a hot afternoon cooling off in the river, holding onto the cable to keep from being washed downstream. We also had a clever way of rafting across to the other side. When fastened with a carabiner and rope to the cable, our homemade raft could be propelled across the river by the swift current. And if we got the angle just right, we'd fly across at considerable speed. Don't ask where we got the cable, carabiner, truck tire rim, or wood for the raft.

Although I had some doubts about François' weight on our handmade raft, I'd had it in my mind to use our river ferry system to get him across. Simple, yes? Except that the rainstorms in the mountains to the north had riled the river, it was flooding over its banks, and our raft was no where in sight. But then again, neither was François.

"François?" I hissed. "Are you here?"

Wide eyes and white tooth loomed out of the gloom. A small shiver reminded me that I was alone, at night, with a zombie. Good grief. "Are you all right, François?" I asked, mainly to hear my own voice.

He nodded.

I had to think. We might still manage to get across the river without the raft, but only if we could hold onto that cable against the forceful current, which, from its roar, was really raging. I didn't think I had the strength. François, on the other hand, was plenty strong, but was he savvy enough to get across without me? And then there were those boulders anchoring the ends. Just how well would they hold against the zombie's weight?

"Come on," I said, reaching for François' hand. It was so huge that I settled for a finger. He obediently followed me upstream while I tried, in the pitch black night, to locate a big white rock Doux Doux and I had marked with a red **X** when we'd anchored the cable to it.

I was concentrating so hard on finding the rock, the cable, or the raft, that I jumped about four feet when the lights of the aggregate plant sprang to life. We both hit the mud, even though we were outside the circle of light, and it was from the ground that I finally spotted my marked rock: ten feet from shore and barely visible above the swirling chocolate water. My heart sank, as we surely would if we tried to cross the river now.

I did, however, spot the raft bobbing at the water's edge where it was still tethered to a tree. A tree that had been high and dry. I toyed with the idea of simply loading François onto the raft, sending him downstream, past the rebels. He was awfully big, and the raft was awfully small and rickety, though, and I had no idea whether François could even swim, in case the raft tipped over. I nixed that brainstorm and led him further upstream.

We moved away from the lights, up along the riverbank, and toward the dam site. I knew we couldn't follow the bank for long without having to get onto the jobsite road, because mountains began their rise on both sides of the river, creating a wide, steep canyon. The canyon grew narrower upstream, and it was this very geography that made it an ideal place for a dam. The road, blasted and carved into the mountainside, eventually ran a hundred feet above the river.

When we reached the road, I nervously led François along the edge; if we saw lights coming our way, we could hide. That far from the dam, there were still places where a body could crouch behind bushes, but further up, a sheer drop-off into a raging river waited if we took even one step in the wrong direction. I thanked my lucky stars that we could reach the clinic before the roadway *really* narrowed and began to climb. So, I figured we had a good chance of getting to the clinic unspotted, but what then? I didn't even dare to hope that, through some miracle, Doctor Cordier would be there.

As we trudged north on the ever-rising road, I kept glancing back over my shoulder, praying that no one had yet discovered that I was absent from my bed, and set the hounds on us. Okay, so we didn't have any hounds, but several dozen trigger-happy soldiers and construction workers were just as bad.

It occurred to me—a little late, as usual—that anyone seeing us might think that François had doubled back and taken me prisoner or something. You could bet the ranch that Angela hadn't stuck around and waited for the soldiers to wake up, so there would be no one to set the posse straight. Would I never learn to look before I leaped? Leapt. Whatever.

Lights loomed up in front of us. We crouched behind a tree, and watched as a dump truck rumbled slowly by, headed down toward the aggregate plant. Had work on the dam started again? If so, maybe the roadblock was gone, and I could smuggle François to Mirebalais in Daddy's car, which was still at the mechanic's shop. I wasn't sure what they were doing to it, but I'd borrowed it once, so why not again? Thrilled that I had a great idea, I picked up the pace.

When we made it to the repair shop, I stashed François behind a parked truck and set about finding us transportation. Two minutes later I spotted it: Daddy's car sat behind an easily-scaled chain link fence. I had just dropped into the fenced yard when I heard, then saw, a group of soldiers walking up the road. They were chatting and laughing and passed within three feet of where I crouched behind a bulldozer blade. As they went by, I picked up from their conversation that they were on the lookout for enemy *saboteurs*, probably a whole army of them, who had attempted to take over the aggregate plant, but were fended off by the night watchman. It was all I could do not to laugh.

The soldiers had also said that the roadblocks still existed. Rats. Okay, if we couldn't go one way, we'd just have to go the other. I'd get François as far as the dam site, then he would have to make his way—possibly by making a big wide circle through the mountains—back to the doctor. Or Port-au-Prince. I had no idea *how* or *where*, but one thing was for sure, I had to get him out of the immediate danger posed by those soldiers.

I stood up and looked across the road, hoping to see a light in the clinic, but no luck. If the doctor would just return, all our troubles would be over. I was feeling sorry for myself and overwhelmed with responsibility, when I had a sickening thought: François had made his way to Camp, spent almost a whole night in a cave, and would probably not be able to get back to Cordier any sooner than two days. He had to have an injection *before* he left.

But first things first.

I was much relieved to find Daddy's car door not only unlocked but, hallelujah!, keys dangled from the ignition switch. If I hadn't been so overjoyed, I would have been indignant that they were being so careless with our car. I soon found out why, though, because when I turned the key, nothing happened. I mean nothing. No click, whir, stutter. I eased up the hood and guess what? No engine.

Disappointed almost into tears, I leaned back against the fender to think and spotted, across the road in front of the clinic, the ambulance.

I scaled the fence again, took François in tow, and we ran—well, one of us sort of Quasimodo-loped—to the clinic. There was no time for politeness; I had François rip out the doorlock.

It was dark inside the doctor's office, but I found the refrigerator easily enough and, when I opened it, the dim light inside helped me locate the last two vials of serum. I left the door open a crack, giving us enough light to see. I had watched Doctor Cordier closely enough—dreading each step—to know where he kept his horse needles. In no time I was ready for François. Or was I?

The big zombie was watching me with more than a little interest, especially when I came at him with that two-inch needle. I could only hope that Doctor Cordier had broken him in, not hurt him too much, so he'd know what was about to happen.

"Look," I said, "I don't like this anymore than you do. And it *is* going to hurt, but I have to do it anyhow. Do you understand me?"

He nodded.

"Lift your shirt."

Nothing.

I put down the needle and lifted my shirt to show him the little bandages I had on my stomach.

He lifted his shirt.

I picked up the needle.

He pulled his shirt back down.

Using my sternest voice, I said, "François, I don't have time to monkey around with you. If I have to, I'll jam this needle right through your shirt. I mean it, now."

He raised his shirt, I took aim, jammed the needle halfway in like I'd seen the doctor do, pushed the plunger down hard, and emptied the contents. He gave out an "Ooomph," but didn't move. I yanked on the syringe to remove it, but it wouldn't come out. Confused, I tried again, but nothing happened. The whole thing was stuck firmly in his muscle.

"François, I think you have to relax. You've trapped the danged thang."

He looked dumbly at the syringe hanging from his belly. He didn't seem too upset about it, but I sure was. Frustrated beyond belief, the long night was beginning to catch up with me; all the emotional ups and downs had left me exhausted. My arms felt like they weighed a ton, and my legs were going numb. I melted onto a stool. Maybe, I thought, the best thing would be to just stay here in the clinic, wait for dawn, and someone who might help us. I was having a sinking spell, loosing all my strength, when I heard footsteps outside.

Fear pumped a rush of energy through my body. I jumped up, shut the refrigerator door, and grabbed one of Doctor Cordier's heavy medical books. I waited by the door, hoping whoever it was wouldn't notice the smashed lock. Fat chance. As the door began squeaking open, I hoisted the book high, prepared to bean whoever entered.

I was just about on the down-swing when I heard, "Lizbuthann, are you in here?"

The book, when I let it go, dropped behind me with a loud crash.

"Doux Doux Boudreaux, you just about scared the pee out of me. What are you doing up here?" Jeez, don't *any* parents know where their kids are all night?

"I just knew I'd find you here, Lizbuthann, I just knew it!" Doux Doux breathed. "I heard about François, and the serum, when they came looking for you at my house. I figured you were up to your usual no good. You've got him in here, don't you? I can't see squat."

I pulled her in, slammed the door and opened the refrigerator door again. She looked around, and when she spotted François, the needle hanging from his gut, she gulped. "Oh my! What on earth?"

"I can't get the needle out. I've tried. Help me."

"You *are* joking."

"Nope. Come on, let's do it."

Doux Doux reluctantly followed me over to François. "What do you want me to do?" she asked. Even in the dim light I could see she'd gone a little green.

"We need him to relax. Got any ideas?"

"Rum?"

"Good idea, but don't have any. Wait a minute."

I went to the locked glass-front cabinet and squinted at the bottle labels; it was going to be a busy night for Doctor Cordier's little magic pills. I broke the glass, poured four pills into my hand, and handed them to François, who was used to me giving him cookies. He popped them into his mouth, ground them with his big teeth, grimaced—I guess—and swallowed.

"Guess we don't have to bother with that water chaser," Doux Doux said sarcastically.

"Doux Doux, don't even think about getting all teenagery on me tonight. I am much too tired."

Doux Doux just gave me a sour look, but she shut up.

From my own experience, I knew those pills hit a body fast, and François was no exception. Within five minutes, we had the needle out, but we also had a loopy zombie on our hands. We guided him outside, hung the CLOSED/FERME sign over the broken lock, and I climbed into the ambulance. After fumbling around in the dark cab, I found what I was looking for. The panel-wagon roared to life on the first hit of the START button; no keys necessary. How very convenient for thieves and saboteurs like us.

"You guys get in," I told them above the ambulance motor's rumble.

Doux Doux ran to passenger side and jumped in, but François didn't budge. I climbed back out and raised my voice a tad. "François?" I know it sounds funny, but I was getting where I could read the zombie pretty well and, even in the dark,

I could tell he was scared about something. I grabbed his arm and pulled him toward the ambulance, but he balked. Just for a brief moment I wondered if I could rig a bridle.

François definitely did not want to get into that wagon. Was it possible he'd never ridden in a vehicle? I coaxed him forward, trying not to lose patience. Where were the cookies when I needed them?

I got the rear doors open, thinking maybe he's be less afraid of entering through a larger opening, but he just stood there. Climbing in myself, so he could see he wasn't about to be eaten by an iron monster, I tried pulling him with me. Nope. I got out and pushed him. He shook his head and pushed back, causing me to fall on my heinie. That did it. I had had about all I could take from him in one evening. I planted my hands on my hips and yelled, in English, "Listen to me, you big lug, you get in that ambulance, and you get in there now! I have to get you to Doctor Cordier!"

His face brightened when I said the doctor's name. Well, as bright as the dim-wit's mug could get. Anyhow, it did the trick. He climbed in, I slammed and locked the door from the outside in case he changed his pea-sized mind, and off we went.

The ambulance didn't have a siren or the lights that Daddy called a bubble gum machine, which is a good thing because, if we had 'em, I'd have been sorely tempted to turn both on. As it was, though, I didn't even dare to use the head-lights. I had no idea what lay ahead, but I did know I had no intention of stopping for anyone or anything until I ran out of road, and sent François on his way to safety. Then I'd have to face the music and would probably never see the light of day until I graduated from college or reached fifty, whichever came first.

"Uh, don't you think you'd better turn on the lights?" Doux Doux said as we sideswiped a tree that was the only thing between us and a hundred-foot drop into the river.

"I'm afraid to."

"Mais cheré, seems to me someone would be a mite less suspicious of a vehicle with lights on than one without them."

Despite the rotten situation we were in, my heart melted at the words, "Mais cheré," and I realized how much I'd missed my friend. I felt my eyes water, which was the last thing I needed while driving a huge panel truck on a dark, snaking road. I flipped on the lights.

"Uh, Lizbuthann, there are soldiers up ahead."

"I see 'em. Doesn't look like they're blocking the road, though."

"Mais cheré, what if they try to stop us?"

"Maybe they won't. Maybe they'll think we're supervisors. I mean, we *are* white," I said, thinking I sounded reasonable.

"We are white *kids*, you dodo. Stop." I pulled to the side of the road and turned off the lights while she scrambled past François, who was sitting placidly on the ambulance floor. She rummaged around and came back with white coats, hats that looked like we should be selling hotdogs on a street corner, and paper masks with little strings on them. "Put these on."

A great paw reached forward and Doux Doux slapped it back. "Not you François. You play dead." We couldn't help it, we broke into giggles.

François, after some coaxing, lay flat out. Doux Doux covered him with a sheet while I started the ambulance again and flipped on the lights. We had definitely gotten the soldiers' attention; they were walking towards us. I picked up speed as we met, hoping to drive right on by, but no luck. Three of them formed a line across the road, and I had to brake sharply to stop in time.

"Let me do the talking," I said, as one of them motioned for me to roll down the window.

"Where are you going?" the young man asked. He had his rifle close to his chest and a sullen look on his face.

"We are with the American Red Cross. We heard of a serious problem up here. Death Fever," I said.

"Death Fever?" he asked. "What's that?"

Another soldier had joined him. "Death Fever?" he echoed.

I nodded. "It is a new kind. Deadly, and carried by mosquitoes. We think a batch of infected mosquitoes were released by the saboteurs who tried to take over the aggregate plant."

Both soldiers swatted the air around their heads. "Here," I said, handing them a can I'd spotted on the dashboard. "Use this, and get inside. Now, let us go before it is too late."

They moved back quickly and, as we drove by, began wildly sloshing themselves with the can's contents.

"Saboteurs?" Doux Doux said.

"It's a long story, but we be them, as Angela would say."

"Oh, just great. Why is it, that every time I get around you I get in deep you-know-what? And just what was that stuff you gave those soldiers to ward off mosquitoes?"

"Mercurochrome, but two-to-one they can't read."

Doux Doux giggled the rest of the way to the jobsite and, from the back of the van, I swear I heard a weird chuckle.

# CHAPTER 27

▼

No more soldiers tried blocking us as we raced to the jobsite. We passed a few who were lollygagging alongside the road, but they just waved us on by. We waved back.

François, judging from the hellacious snores rocking the ambulance, had fallen asleep or, more likely, passed out. I wondered whether giving him those pills was a mistake. I mean, we still had to get rid of him and we certainly couldn't *carry* him.

Doux Doux was thinking the same thing. "Uh, Lizbuthann, do you think we can wake him up when we get there? And by the way, where are we going?"

"I'm danged if I know. I just figured if we could get him past the jobsite, he could go up into the mountains and then circle back. He probably knows these trails like the back of his hand. Once he's safe, he can work his way back to wherever he left Doctor Cordier."

"Mais cheré, how do you figure that? What makes you think the big old lunkhead won't just take off for Camp?"

She had a point. What *was* to stop him from simply following the ambulance once we shoved him out? Nothing, that's what.

The jobsite was lit up, as always, like downtown Houston, but the usual hustle and bustle of the nightshift was not happening. Revolutions have a way of stopping work in progress.

"They must have called off the shift," Doux Doux said.

"Looks like it. That's good for us."

"Mais cheré, why?"

"Because, I have an idea."

She groaned.

When I skidded the ambulance to a halt in front of the cableway shack, Doux Doux looked puzzled. "Are you going to give me a clue as to what this plan of yours is? On second thought, I probably don't want to know."

"I'm gonna get him across the river, which is what I wanted to do in the first place. He'll be safe over there."

Doux Doux's mouth fell open. "Mais, how? You said the river was too dangerous to cross."

"It is. In the water. I'm gonna send him across in that," I said, pointing to where a big metal concrete bucket sat next to the ice plant.

"You're nuts."

"Probably, but we gotta do *something*." There wasn't a soul in sight when we jumped from the ambulance and ran to the cableway shack. It was, of course, locked. I, of course, knew where Daddy hid a spare key. In two minutes we were inside and had the electrical panel open. Three breakers later, we were ready to pour a zombie out on the other side of the river. And I do mean pour; when we got back to the ambulance, it soon became very clear that François, even after I slapped him around a bit, was not to be roused.

"Mais cheré, now what?"

"I'll think of something. Come on."

Doux Doux tailed me as I rushed back into the shack and plopped down into my operator's chair. Using a lever that I knew controlled the UP and DOWN movements of the concrete bucket, I eased the gears out of neutral, and ever-so-gently lifted the bucket a foot off the ground.

"Wow, Lizbuthann, when did you learn to do that?" Doux Doux breathed. All traces of her bratty behavior had evaporated, and it was wonderful to have my friend back to her old self.

"While you were out chasing boys. Daddy taught me, which will be, if I get caught, the last thing he ever teaches me. Pay attention, Doux Doux, because you I'll need your help."

"Why?"

"Just watch. It's as easy as driving a car.

"Lizbuthann, I can't drive and you know it."

"Okay, then, it's kinda like steering a bicycle…you use your hands to guide it. Watch this." I eased the bucket down to the ground, then pushed the lever in a slow side motion just enough so that the bucket tipped over sideways. I was just about to brag on myself when the bucket's own weight carried it over before I could recover. A tremendous crash echoed off the mountains and down the river.

"Gee, that went well, Lizbuthann. You're gonna wake the dead!" Doux Doux complained. Then she realized what she'd said, and we both fell into giggles.

"Wake the dead. That's a good one, Doux Doux. One can only wish. Okay, back to work. Let's see make that old bucket sing. I'll guide you through the steps."

"Why, oh, why didn't I just stay in bed?" she moaned, but took my place in the chair. After twenty minutes of practice, Doux Doux had learned the basic maneuvers of cableway operation. She, too, had crashed the bucket several more times, but, as we found when we raced back to the ambulance, the dead did not wake. *Zut!*

We were quickly running out of time; dawn couldn't be far off and neither could a whole passel of construction workers. I backed the panel wagon so the back doors faced the open end of the bucket and, with a great deal of heaving, shoving and grunting, we managed to dump Sleeping Ugly into the big container. He fell in like a sack of potatoes, and landed just as gracefully.

"Stay here, Doux Doux. I'll go right the bucket, then we'll better get it to the other side before daylight."

"I'm scared."

"That makes two of us. Just remember what I showed you. Lever one, push forward until we're about five feet off the ground, then push lever two forward, until we reach the other side, then pull lever one back until we touch down. And do it all gently, okay?"

"Wait just a minute, here, Lizbuthann, who is 'we'?"

"Huh?"

"You said 'we're': you said, 'until *we're* about five feet up.' And then you said 'until *we* touch down.'"

"Well, yes, I did. So what?"

"Mais cheré, you mean that you are going across *with* the bucket?"

"Of course I am, Doux Doux. Why do you think I've been teaching you how to maneuver it? There's no one to operate the air ram that opens the bucket's bottom like there is when they make a pour, so I've got to be with him to make sure François gets out." I grabbed her hand and started pulling her toward the shack.

She followed, reluctant and protesting. "Mais cheré, why can't you do it? Once the bucket's across, you could just dump it on its side again, and then wait for François to wake up and crawl out."

I talked as we walked. "Won't work. First off, we don't have that much time. Who knows when the pills will wear off? We can't afford to dump him and wait. And on top of that, it's gonna be light soon, and there's no way we can get away with this caper when the day shift starts showing up. They'd see the bucket on the other side and bring it right back." A mind-picture sprang into my mind and I grinned. "Oh, boy, can you imagine what would happen when they got that bucket back over here and found a zombie in it?"

Doux Doux laughed. "Lizbuthann, you have a really weird sense of humor."

"So they say. Just remember to let the bucket down real slow. Once we hit the ground, I can jump off before the bucket tips, then I can get François out. I hope."

"This is the most lame-brained idea you have ever come up with. I like it," Doux Doux said with a grin. "I just hope I don't dump both of you into the gorge."

"If you do, I'll die a happy girl. I've dreamed for years of riding that bucket like Major Madden does, and now I get to. Let's do it."

Back in the shack, I righted the bucket as gently as I could, but probably managed to give François a lump on his head. I raised the bucket about a foot off the ground, went through Doux Doux's instructions once more, gave her a hug, reminded her to watch for my hand signals, and ran to take the ride of my life.

I checked on François. He was still out, but was starting to stir. Hopefully he wouldn't stir too much!

Climbing onto the cross-bracing on the sides of the bucket, I climbed up to the **T** bar across the top opening, planted my feet firmly, held tight with one hand, and gave Doux Doux a thumb's up. At first nothing happened, and I was afraid Doux Doux had lost her courage. Then, with a loud whirr, a pulley on the main cable tightened the lift line, and we were dizzily reeled ten feet straight up. It was all I could do to hang on as the bucket stopped with a bone-jolting jerk, then began bucking on the cable like a yo-yo on a string.

With each heart-stopping dive, I could hear poor old François being banged around against the metal sides of the container. I hoped we didn't kill him trying to save him.

The wild motion finally slowed to a gentle sway, which would have been kinda fun if I had more confidence in the operator. And if I hadn't suddenly remembered that Major Madden, when he rode the cableway, always wore a safety line and harness. Oh, well. I gave Doux Doux the AHEAD sign.

This time Doux Doux, no doubt scared pee-less by that last fiasco, pushed the lever forward in tiny moves that jerked us ahead a foot at a time. I kept a death grip on the cross brace to keep from tumbling into the bucket with François. If that happened, I wasn't sure either one of us could get out when, and if, we ever got to the other side. We'd be trapped until one of the workers, or worse, soldiers, got to us.

I looped my left arm around the brace, and used my other hand to make a FASTER signal by circling my finger. Doux Doux got the message, and we took off like a bat out of Hades. She checked our speed and we crept on, bound for the other side of the river, a quarter mile—and a lifetime—away.

I got a bone-deep chill, and this time it wasn't fear. The wind funneling down the gorge caused cool updrafts that made for a cold and bumpy ride. I was beginning to think this was *the* dumbest thing I'd ever done when, finally, Doux Doux figured out we were going too slow. She overcorrected again, at first sending whizzing through the air at breakneck speed, then putting the skids to us so quickly that my stomach jumped up into my throat.

When the bucket stopped its sickening bounce, we were left dangling mid-dam. I chanced a look down, way down. With a start, I realized that it was almost finished—not the ride; the dam. I didn't have time to think what that meant to my life in Haiti, because Doux Doux hit a lever, and off we went again.

Determined to enjoy the last minutes of what I just knew would be the end of my freedom *for*-ever, once Mama got her hands on me, I looked around at the lit up job site. I could just make out Doux Doux, sitting at the cableway controls. There were a few soldiers near the ice plant, which gave me a little scare, but then I realized they were just watching my wild ride. They probably had no idea that Doux Doux and I, both decked out in hardhats, were doing anything other than business as usual. At least that's what I hoped.

Then I spotted real trouble. A string of bouncing lights; a line of vehicles, snaking up the main road toward the jobsite. They were moving fast, and we were not. Doux Doux, after several false starts and scares, had us creeping along at a snail's pace. It was beginning to look as though the procession of trucks would get to her before she got us to the other side. I had no way to warn her, but maybe she could still see my hand signals.

Letting go with one hand, I signaled with a large circular motion or my arm for her to pick up speed. Almost immediately, with a tummy-turning lurch, we took off again. Now we'd reach the other side, all right, but could Doux Doux stop us before we crashed into the tail tower emergency stops?

We were *really* moving, much faster than I'd ever seen Daddy operate the cableway.

I knew, from my own experience when I was allowed to do pours, that we couldn't stop on a dime. Or even a quarter. It must have dawned on Doux Doux that she had to slow us down, for she began cutting back our speed, but not enough. We were still hurtling dead-on toward the huge tail tower, and disaster.

Those safety stops had been installed so that, in the case of a runaway bucket, the big metal container would not pile into, and damage, the tail tower. Unfortunately, Daddy had told me, if a bucket *did* hit those stops with any speed at all, the bucket—an eight cubic yard job that had been used on Hoover Dam—would be a goner. If we crashed into those stops, I'd either be thrown off into the gorge or, if not, smushed into kid jelly. My best bet, I figured, was to jump into the bucket on top of François, and take my chances inside the protection of its thick steel walls.

I took one last look around, saw that the headlight brigade had reached the cableway shack, said a little prayer, and threw myself into the bucket. Bouncing off François' shoulders, I slid, headlong, in between the big guy and the concrete-encrusted bucket. I lost a little skin, but other than that, the landing wasn't all that bad. The problem was, I couldn't move. I had no idea what would happen to us when we hit the emergency stops, but there was absolutely nothing to do but wait. And maybe pray. Once again, I wondered about that age limit in Heaven thing. I was banking on a hope that anyone under thirteen should get ushered in by virtue of not *being* a teenager.

Just when I didn't think things could get worse, they did. François woke up.

First I heard a groan, then a yawn, then he tried to move. He, too, was jammed against the wall, but at least he was right-side-up. As it was, the top of my head was resting on the zombie's bare feet, and believe you me, they were *not* clean. I'm sure mine weren't either, what with all the slogging around in mud, dust and grime all evening, but at least I had shoes on. I just hoped he didn't try to kick his way out.

"François," I yelled, hoping he could hear me up there. "Do *not* move."

So, of course, he moved. Not his feet, thank goodness, just his arms. I felt his big hands grab my ankles and lift me, like a newborn baby, by both legs. I lost a little more skin on the way up, but he soon had me raised high enough so that I could, using him like a ladder, at least turn upright. Then the pills must have kicked in again; his eyes rolled and he went out like a light, sliding down until he was seated in the bottom of the bucket. With some fancy footwork, I ended up standing on his bent knees so that we were almost face to face. Here I was, rushing toward an early death, and all I could think to say was, "You know, François, you might want to consider laying off the garlic."

I had just said, "garlic," when the bucket suddenly stopped traveling down the cable and we went back into that sickening yo-yoing again. This time, though, it was a life-saver. And, as soon as we settled down, the bucket began to move slowly, and smoothly. We glided to a stop, were set softly onto the ground, then the bucket began to gently tip over. I braced for the worst, because the direction we were tipping, François, still out cold, would end up on top of me. Talk about your dead weight! I'd be squished like a bug.

"François," I yelled, practically in his ear. "Wake up!"

Which he did. He abruptly stood and my foothold on his knees disappeared. I dropped like a rock into the bottom of the bucket. His weight shift, however, changed the direction of the tilt, and when the bucket hit on its side, we were both thrown on our backs. I had the wind knocked out of me, but François, as though nothing had happened, pulled himself out easily, then reached back for me.

We were clear of the bucket, and I was gasping for air, when I realized it was broad daylight. We were sitting ducks. There was only one thing to do, and I did it; I threw my back against François with my arms spread wide, making myself a shield and hoping against hope the soldiers across the river wouldn't dare shoot. 'Course, if I'd thought about it, they still had a clear head shot since François was at least three feet taller than me, but it's the thought that counts.

We stood this way for a few seconds, frozen in the brilliance of a rising sun, until the big zombie must have figured out what I was doing. He put his hand on my head and pushed me behind him.

He made one big target; one that even the untrained Haitian soldiers would have a hard time missing.

# CHAPTER 28

▼

But they did miss, thank goodness.

Only one bullet even came close, ricocheting off a rock ten feet away. Haitian sharpshooter, no doubt. We dove behind the bucket just as a lot of yelling broke out across the river. No more shots were fired, and after a few minutes I dared a peek over the metal edge. Standing by the cableway shack, Doux Doux, Daddy and Uncle Lloyd, were all yelling and waving their arms. I couldn't hear what they were saying, but boy, was I glad to see them.

I stepped out into the sunlight and turned to tell François to hightail it into the trees, but he was already gone. Mission accomplished.

I knew better than to hope I'd get to ride back across on the bucket, and I was right. I stepped clear as the bucket rose and was returned to the other side of the river, then, in a few minutes, returned with Uncle Lloyd on the T bar.

"Well, Ann," my uncle said, "you've really outdone yourself this time. Your dad will be lucky if they don't think about firing him for your little adventure."

I hadn't thought of that. I was so wrapped up in my own schemes that I didn't consider that what I was doing might affect my father's job.

"Is he really mad at me?" I asked, as I clipped on and tightened the safety harness my uncle had brought with him.

"Naw, not *really*. He was worried about you, but your little friend has been telling him what you've been up to, and don't tell him I told you, but I think he's secretly pretty proud of what a brave little cuss you are."

"He won't be so proud if he gets canned."

"I imagine that would rile him a mite. I doubt they'll pull his brass, though, what with the dam this close to completion. Especially after you've made an apology to the entire Camp."

Rats! I hate public speaking. I get my mords wixed up. My tang tonguled.

"Uh, Uncle Lloyd, is the roadblock still up?" I asked, still worried about François' chances of finding the doctor.

"Ours is. The rebels have been disbanded by the army. Most of 'em took to the hills, but enough of them got caught so the government knows who the troublemakers are."

"Who are they?"

"Most of them are just poor folks who are tired of being poor. The head guy, some doctor who wants to be president, is rumored to be getting money from outside the country to pay and train his boys with. He wants to take over the country using guerillas and, of all things, voodoo."

My mind reeled. Doctor? Voodoo? Was I the only person making a connection?

"You okay, Lizbuthann?" Uncle Lloyd said, looking closely at me. "You're not scared, are you?"

"Oh, no. I was just thinking about something."

"All right, then. You get into the bucket; we're going back across."

"Can't I ride outside with you, Uncle Lloyd? I mean, I've already done it once, and believe you me, the ride was a rough one. With Daddy at the controls, the trip will be a breeze."

"Oh, why the hell not. Your mother will probably kill me. Okay, let's move."

Good old Uncle Lloyd. I just wished someone had a camera to photograph my *very* last adventure. Honest.

As we traveled slowly and smoothly across the gorge, I looked back into the jungle and saw François, grinning and waving. I waved farewell and wondered, now that his aunt was dead, where he would live. And who would take care of him.

"That friend of yours ain't the purtiest thing I've ever seen," Uncle Lloyd said with a grin.

"No, but he's got a good heart."

"Your friend, Dorcas, she says he's a zombie."

"Doux Doux has a vivid imagination. Of course he's not a zombie."

Uncle Lloyd just grinned again. "If you say so, Ann. You ready to face the music?"

I turned and looked in the direction he'd nodded. Waiting by the ice plant was my mother. And she looked mighty mad.

G-R-O-U-N-D-E-D. Grounded.

Doux Doux found that word out of a *Seventeen* magazine she'd gotten for Christmas, and I guess it was a pretty good description for what happened to me.

No horseback riding, no nothing. I was allowed to go straight to school, then straight home. No movies at the clubhouse, either. I was so bored that I rewrote a Nancy Drew book, changing the character's names and the location. The heroine was, of course, me.

It was hard to believe that it had only been a week since Doctor Cordier had disappeared. Still no word from or about him. It was like he dropped off the face of the earth. I guess the "no news is good news" thing was true in the case of François, though; I knew for sure that if something had happened to a seven-foot oooh-gah-oooh we'd surely hear about it. With every day that passed, my hopes that he'd reached safety rose.

I was sitting at the dining room table, writing the last chapter of the Lizbuthann Drew mystery, when Daddy came home from work, threw his keys on the table and looked over my shoulder.

"Wha'cha doin', Ann?"

"Writing a novel."

"Oh, is that all?" He laughed.

"I got lots of time on my hands," I complained.

"Hey, don't gripe to me, I'm not the one who grounded you."

"I know, Daddy. I also know I deserve it, but it sure is boring." I picked up his keys and began jingling them. "Did they get our car fixed?"

"Yep. It's parked out front. Too bad you can't take her for a spin," he teased. The man has a mean streak.

I stared at his keys. Something about them was setting off jangles in my brain, but what? Daddy had wandered into the kitchen for a beer and I sat with the keys in my hand, racking my brain for...what? Daddy came back and saw me practically hypnotized by his keys. "Boy, you are bored," he said with a laugh.

I threw the keys down. "Daddy, still no word on Doc Cordier?"

"Nope. I imagine, though, that when he gets back he's gonna hear about you stealing his ambulance."

"I didn't exactly steal it, I just sort of borrowed it for a little..." I stopped in the middle of the sentence and my mouth fell open. "Daddy! Doctor Cordier left his keys in the ambulance when he disappeared!"

"Well, yes, he did."

"But why?"

"So whoever found the ambulance could start it, I guess."

"But Daddy, it doesn't need keys to start. The wagon has that button thingy, like the one on your pickup."

My father shrugged, "You know, you're right." He went outside to visit with a neighbor.

My head spun. Could it be that Doctor Cordier had, by leaving his keys, tried to send us a message? I had to find out. Thank goodness, I had one last shot coming.

I hardly slept that night for thinking about what, if anything, could a key ring mean. I was already dressed when Mama came to wake me.

"Well, look who's so bright-eyed and bushy-tailed this morning," she said. "What's the occasion?"

"My very last injection."

"I see. I guess when a body's grounded, any little thing can be a celebration."

"Yes, ma'am, it surely can. Uh, you haven't thought about how long I'll be grounded, have you?"

"Nope. But long enough for you to think about the error of your ways."

I sighed, and went to look for someone more sympathetic.

"*Bonjour*, Angela," I said loudly, then lowered my voice. "Any word on you-know-who?"

Angela cut her eyes toward the living room and shook her head. "You want crepes this morning?" she asked. She couldn't do enough for me these days, since I hadn't ratted her out. I even told the parents that it was I, not Angela, who doctored the soldiers' orange juice. I mean, I was already in a world of trouble, so why drag someone else in with me?

"Oh, yes. How about the ones with little pieces of mango in 'em?"

"*Les crêpes Elisabet*, comin' up."

I giggled and glanced at the clock. Only one more hour until I could leave for the clinic. Somehow, I just *knew* that the key to Doctor Cordier's disappearance rested with his keys. And those keys would be at the clinic.

Doux Doux and I were waiting for Mrs. Dahlke when she showed up at the clinic. I had vowed to keep others out of my capers from now on, so I didn't tell her my suspicions. Heck, I didn't even know what my suspicions *were*, only that I had them.

"Good morning, girls. I guess we're going to have to stop meeting this way after today."

"Thank God," Doux Doux said with an eye roll.

I was watching Mrs. Dahlke's right hand, the one fishing the doctor's keys from her pocket. Like a cat watching a bird, I tracked the keys from her pocket to the door. She turned the lock, it clicked, and she pushed the door open. I held my breath, waiting for her to put the keys back in her pocket, but, miracle of miracles, she left them hanging in the door.

I pushed Doux Doux inside. "Age before beauty. You can go first today."

"Gee thanks, Lizbuthann," she said sarcastically, but then she grinned and followed Mrs. Dahlke into the examining room.

I nabbed the keys.

Within ten minutes, our series of painful injections finally came to an end. So much had happened in the past two weeks that it was almost a let down. At least, with my trip to the clinic each day, I saw a little daylight. From now on, probably for the entire rest of my life, I'd have to settle for the short trip to school and back each day. Prison life is hard on a body.

I talked constantly to Mrs. Dahlke, distracting her as she tided up the office, then walked out to the porch. She reached back inside, turned the lock, and shut the door, not even noticing that the keys were gone. I held my breath the whole time. Feeling slightly rotten, but not enough to say something like, "Oh, Mrs. Dahlke, your keys fell on the floor and here they are." Not on your life.

I couldn't wait to get home so I could get a good look at those keys.

I rushed to my room, supposedly to get dressed for school, but really to inspect the keys for clues. Sitting at my desk, I dug the ring from my pocket, trying not to make a jingling noise. Pee Wee, seeing something new and shiny, crawled down my arm and began chewing on the keys as I sorted through them. There were two keys that I recognized as belonging to the clinic door, and the medicine cabinet. Too bad I hadn't had them long ago; the carpenters wouldn't have had to replace the medicine cabinet glass I was forced to break—and pay for out of my allowance. The third key on the ring was very large, and old.

Made of heavy, tarnished brass, the key looked handmade. Ornate curly cues and etching decorated the whole thing, but it was so dirty that they were hard to see. I took it into the bathroom and gave it a good scrubbing. I could now see a pattern of decorative grooves. Back at my desk, I used a pencil eraser to polish away even more grime.

Starting at the base, I worked as fast as I could. I was concentrating so hard that I almost jumped out of my skin when my mother said, from my bedroom door, "Lizbuthann, you have a visitor." Her voice sounded funny.

I stuffed the keys into my desk drawer and went into the living room. Angela was there, sending me funny looks that I interpreted as, "play dumb," which comes naturally to me. Mother, looking puzzled, stood next to a tall, dark priest.

"Lizbuthann, this is Father Vermette from Mirebalais. He has invitations for you and Angela."

"Uh, that's nice," I said.

"To a funeral."

"Oh."

The priest handed me a black envelope. I opened it, and sure enough, I was invited to attend the funeral services of Mme Françoise Oiseau. I didn't know what to say, so I mumbled, "*Merci.*"

Angela, who had an identical envelope in her hand, looked at my mother and gave an innocent little shrug, so Mama zeroed in on me.

"Lizbuthann," my mother said, "do you know who this woman is. Was?"

Think fast, dummy, I was saying to myself. "Uh, yes ma'am, I believe I do."

My mother wasn't buying my stall. "Well, would you care to tell *me*?" Her eyebrows were on the move.

"Uh, well, uh…"

"She be the egg woman," Angela said.

"Oh. Well, thank you for the…uh, thought," Mother said, turning to the priest, "but I'm not sure Lizbuthann is old enough to attend funerals. Especially for someone she hardly knows."

"But Mama," I said, "it would be…educational. And Angela will be with me."

"Ask your father when he gets home."

Yippee, I was going to a funeral.

Okay, so most folks wouldn't be so overjoyed to attend a funeral service, but I would have gone anywhere, just to get out of the house.

As soon as the priest left, I had to go to school, so the key polishing had to be put on hold for a few hours. Oh, well, at least I'd have something to do after school. When Angela handed me my mid-morning school snack in a bag, she whispered, "I wonder if François be at this lady funeral." Poor Angela, she still hadn't laid eyes on the man she hoped was her long lost brother, and it was looking like she never would.

"I dunno. I don't even know why we got invited."

Angela pointed to herself and said, "I t'ink I do it. When I sent message to that priest, Father Vermette, I write I had stop by my 'friend' house, and she no answer door, and I be worry. He go look at house, find that lady dead. I guess he invite all friends."

"Yeah, but how did *I* get fingered?"

"You 'member that ole lady in square by church when we go to Mirebalais that day?"

"Sure. She had on a shawl, and it was about a thousand degrees out."

Angela nodded. "She al-ways be there. She see everyt'ing, and she tell everyt'ing. Little red-hair white girl knocking on dead lady door be big news."

"Just great. You know, Angela, I've been meaning to ask you something. Where did the witch lady get her eggs? There weren't any chickens at her house—except us, when we took off like bats out of Hades after finding her body."

Angela shrugged. "Maybe she buy eggs somewhere."

"Yeah, probably. Well, see you later."

"Study well, Elisabet. I will find you funeral clothes and get ready for tomorrow."

"Funeral clothes? Like what?"

"Anyt'ing black."

I looked like a five-year-old playing dress up.

Since I didn't own anything in black, Angela and Mama spent the day cutting down an old suit of my mother's. And I do mean old. It had padded shoulders, for crying out loud. Lucky for me, I had a pair of old black ballet slippers that still—barely—fit, so at least I didn't have to wear someone's high heels. To top off my chic ensemble, Angela fashioned a hat out of netting and black silk flowers. I just hoped no one saw me before we made it out of Camp; I resembled a miniature, red-haired, Joan Crawford.

While my fashion designers cut and sewed, I continued to polish that big key of Doctor Cordier's. I didn't have any idea what I was looking for, I just had this niggling feeling that the doc had left a clue, and the key was all I had. With a little thrill, I saw that my cleaning was revealing something on the key's fat round shank. I was so busy trying to read it that I didn't hear my mother come up behind me.

"Lizbuthann," she said, just about stopping my heart, "where'd you get that old skeleton key?"

"Uh, found it."

"Sure is interesting looking."

"Mama, why did you call it a skeleton key? Is it for dead people or something?" Hey, this was really getting interesting.

"No, silly. I think it's because it looks like a skeleton."

"Oh."

"Now, stand up and try this on. We've almost got it finished."

"Oh, great," I said, trying to sound enthusiastic. I didn't want to hurt her feelings, especially since she and Angela had worked on my outfit all day, but let's face it, black ain't my color.

She pinned a few tucks and left. I scrambled around in my drawer for a magnifying glass, then remembered that Mama took it away from me when I set the curtains on fire. Rats!

Thar's more 'n' one way to skin a cat, I always say. Holding a piece of tracing paper tightly against the key, I rubbed it with a soft pencil lead so the engraved lines showed white against the lead smudging. I still couldn't quite make it out, so I held the paper up to the light.

It wasn't writing; it was the drawing of a mermaid! I flipped the key over and, after another rubbing, made out the word, "ERZULI." Pulling *Tell My Horse* from its hiding place under my desk, I found Erzuli in a flash. She was, as I remembered, the voodoo goddess of love.

And she was, also as I remembered, a mermaid.

# CHAPTER 29

▼

The next morning I woke up with a pounding headache. With my medical history and luck, I figured the rabies shots hadn't worked.

It was also the day of the egg lady's funeral, so I wasn't about to let anyone know I felt punky. Rummaging through a drawer my mother stocked with Mercurochrome, bandages, and calamine lotion, I spotted one of Doctor Cordier's prescription bottles; the one I'd filled with aspirin after dumping the real drugs into the soldiers' orange juice Mickey Finn. I was pouring a couple of pills into my hand when I heard my mother calling me.

"Lizbuthann," she said, "Angela's here. You ready to go?"

"Yes, ma'am," I yelled back. I stuck the pill bottle into my pocket.

Angela's husband drove us to the funeral in Daddy's car. I think he was commandeered by my parents to act as my parole officer. Angela, much to her husband's annoyance, insisted that she and I sit in the backseat. Heaven knows where she found it, but she came up with a peaked cap that Mr. Calixte, drawing the line, flatly refused to wear. She did, however, have him decked out in a black suit coat and white shirt. "Pierre, you be chauffeur man today. It don' hurt to impress the *pauvres*," Angela told him with a mischievous smile.

"We *are* the poor," her husband countered, but he knew he was beat. As we got into the back seat, though, he whacked Angela on the rear. She gave him a haughty look. "Don'," she said, "get fresh with *grande dame*."

"Yes madame," he said, taking a sweeping bow. Angela giggled. This was gonna be one fun funeral.

I'd gulped down two aspirins and was feeling much better by the time we neared Mirebalais. "Angela," I whispered, "have you figured out how we're gonna sneak around to check out the key?"

"No, *bébé*, but Angela will. You just trust she will."

"Okay. Say, we won't have to look at her…uh…the body, will we?"

"No, child, she already in tomb. This be a memory service."

"Memorial. Thank goodness. I don't think my heart could take seeing her laid out twice."

Angela just chuckled, then caught her husband looking at us in the rearview mirror. "Driver," she teased, "mind the road."

Mr. Calixte groaned and shook his head. "You fine ladies don't mind if I just leave you at the church do you? I'll come back after the service. I don't like dead people."

"I t'ink you be goin' to find a domino game and a rum drink, that what I t'ink, Monsieur Calixte," Angela said, but she smiled.

"Sounds good to me," I said, and we laughed, but quieted down as we pulled up in front of the church. Playing his role, Mr. Calixte got out and opened our doors.

As he handed Angela out, she whispered, "Don' you come back drunk."

"No, Madame Calixte. Of course not, Madame Calixte," he said with a wink and a bow. Then he drove away. Several people in the square, including the old woman in her shawl, stared at us. Father Vermette, standing on the church steps, seemed to be waiting for us. After a brief greeting, he ushered us through the heavy wooden doors.

I had never been inside a Catholic church before, and didn't know what to expect. If great-aunt Elizabeth were to be believed, it would be filled with child-eating devils. The plain whitewashed walls outside hadn't prepared me for the incredible beauty indoors. Stained glass windows high in the arched ceiling lit the gleaming crosses, frescoes and glittering candles with a, well, heavenly glow. I had never seen anything like it, except maybe a movie theatre in San Antonio that had angels and clouds on the ceiling. I was spellbound, thinking to myself that, if I could get past Aunt Tody and her cloud, this is what Heaven must look like.

I had been so busy gawking that I didn't notice who else was in the church. Angela elbowed me to stop my rubbernecking, and it was then that I realized the entire congregation was staring at me. Blushing, I gave a little nod and followed Angela's lead, crossing myself, dipping, and then scooting into a pew at the back of the church.

Father Vermette talked for-*ever*, his voice a monotonous drone that threatened to put me to sleep. My knees, after the first ten minutes of kneeling, grew numb. The oppressive heat didn't help, either. There were ceiling fans, but they sat idle as the congregation sweated. Just when I thought I was going to pass out and embarrass Angela to death, everyone stood up, and sang something they all knew by heart. I tried to hum along. As people began filing out, I recognized a couple of vendors and maids, but no François, and no Doctor Cordier.

"Elisabet, go talk to Father Vermette."

"Why me?"

"Because I say so, child, that why. I am goin' to see if you key work in that bird lady door."

"Oh, okay. What am I going to talk about?"

"Weather. I don' know. Somet'ing."

Angela hustled out of the church, leaving me to t'ink of somet'ing.

I hung back and short-stopped the priest as he followed his congregation down the center aisle. "Nice service, Father," I said.

He looked a little unnerved to be stuck alone in the church with me. He looked over my head at the open doors, "Uh, *Merci*. Where did your friend go?"

"Uh, ladies room." I doubted there was a ladies room in the entire village, but what the heck.

Oddly enough, the priest seemed to think my answer was just fine. Either that, or he wasn't about to get into a bathroom discussion with some little white girl. He nodded and said, "Ah."

"So, nice weather today, don't you think?"

"Oh, yes, but rather warm."

"Well, you could turn on those fans," I suggested, pointing to the big, ornate jobs hanging from the ceiling. Gee, what a fascinating conversation.

"Yes, but we won't have electricity during the day until the dam is finished. If you like, we can wait for your friend outside, where it is a little cooler."

I didn't want him out there yet; not until Angela got a chance to try the key in the egg woman's door. "Uh, sure, but first, could you tell me about all these paintings?"

He went on for-eee-ver again, falling into that drone of his. On about the fifth saint, I started swaying slightly, and my ears began to buzz. In the nick of time, Angela returned. She gave me a small shake of her head. Rats, the key didn't work.

We all walked outside and, although a breeze did make the air cooler, the faint hum in my head, instead of getting better, got worse. Then I realized it might not *be* in my head. "Father Vermette, what's that noise?" I asked.

"I believe it is a generator."

"But, if the generator is running, why didn't you turn on the ceiling fans in the church?"

"Oh, it is not the town generator, Mademoiselle, it is that of the plantation. A new owner has evidently taken up residence, for a generator has been running day and night for over a week. They must have," he said with a smile, "much more fuel than our poor town can afford." Wondering whether he was taking a swipe at the spoiled inhabitants at Péligre, I felt the need to defend our honor.

"I'm sure we wouldn't have twenty-four hour power at Péligre either, Father Vermette, if they didn't have to run the jobsite lights, ice plant and rock sorters."

"Oh, I didn't mean to imply…" he seemed flustered, and Angela shot me a dirty look. I felt about two feet tall, but the priest recovered and smiled. "I am certain," he said, "that Plantation Erzuli also has many systems that require power. I shall have to pay the new people a visit soon. It has been many years since anyone lived there." He gave a nod and went back into his church, leaving Angela and me standing, in shock, on the steps.

"*Non.* Absolutely not. Angela and I will both lose our jobs if I take you to that old plantation. Right, Angela?" Mr. Calixte asked his wife.

Angela shrugged a little shrug and her husband blew out an exasperated breath. "Angela, surely you do not think we should take this child anywhere except straight to her home. Her parents gave strict orders not to deviate from our route. Besides, I hear the place is haunted."

"Well, husband, who will know if we just drive by?"

I bobbed my head. The poor man looked back and forth at the two of us, sighed, and said, "You are both mad."

"Then you'll do it, Mr. Calixte?" I asked, trying to look adorable. Which isn't easy when one is dressed like Joan Crawford.

"Maybe. But only if you," he gave his wife a glare, "tell me why you would even consider this madness."

He had Angela on the spot. She had never told him her suspicion that the monster who had been terrorizing Camp might be her long-lost brother, the zombie. Actually, I was kind of enjoying this; I wanted to hear what she'd have to say.

"Because…because…we t'ink Doctor Cordier be there. Maybe he be sick or somet'ing."

"And why would you think he is in an old abandoned plantation?"

"Not abandoned," I said. "The priest told us a generator has been running out there for days—maybe the generator that's missing from our ambulance. Listen, you can hear it for yourself. Please, Mr. Calixte, it'll just take a few minutes."

"Please, Pierre," Angela said.

Mr. Calixte cocked his head, evidently heard the generator, and sighed. "Oh, all right. What can it hurt?" He looked at his watch. "We must be back on the road to Péligre in less than an hour, is that understood?"

What must once have been a grand entrance was now just plain spooky. The rutted, muddy road leading to the plantation caused us to bog down twice, but Mr. Calixte and I got us through; he pushed and I drove. He was covered in sticky red mud—and was getting in a worse and worse mood—by the time we pulled up to a set of rusty, vine-covered, iron gates. They were closed and, when he pushed on them, locked.

"This is as far as we can go. Now, you have seen this place, and we must return to Camp," he said.

I could hear a generator droning along, but still could not see a house, or a single living thing inside the dilapidated iron fence and gate.

"But what if the doctor is there and needs help?" I asked.

"The gate is locked," Mr. Calixte said. "I will not trespass."

"What if we have an invitation?" I asked.

"What do you mean? Invitation?"

Angela waggled the big brass key and beamed. "This be it, I t'ink."

The key turned smoothly in the lock, and the gate creaked open when the three of us put our combined weights behind it. Mr. Calixte, who had, up until Angela produced the key, been very reluctant to join in our snoopery, had a sudden change of heart. Especially after I told him that Doctor Cordier had given us the key. Well, the doc sort of did, didn't he?

We drove the quarter mile of overgrown track to the main house. The only evidence that anyone had come this way in years was one set of tire tracks, mostly washed away. Whoever was here, running that generator, had been there a while, or had walked in, unless there was a back entrance.

The house, two stories high and built of moldy stone, was covered in creepy vines, and had the look of a place kids dared other kids to enter. I was having second thoughts.

"Now what?" Angela asked as we stood in front of the huge, rotting, front door.

"Ring the bell?" I teased. Angela gave me a dirty look.

"Okay, then," I said, stepping forward and giving the door a sharp rap with my knuckles. Several lizards darted in every direction from under the vines, causing all of us to jump back, but then nothing happened. I knocked again and called out. Nothing.

"Come on," I said, more to myself than to the others. I turned around to see if Mr. Calixte and Angela had any bright ideas when, behind me, I heard the door creaking open.

From the looks of fright on my friends' faces, I really, really dreaded turning around, but I did. And there stood François. I knew him well enough to know two things: he wasn't himself, and he wasn't happy to see us. He also was not alone.

"So, Angela, is he your brother?" I whispered. Angela, who had been staring at François ever since we entered the house, started to open her mouth, but the heavily armed man sitting in a dilapidated chair across from us barked, "*Ferme la bouche.*" How rude. But, as ordered, she shut her mouth. She did, however, give me a little shrug and head shake. Oh great, after all this, she still didn't know if the big zombie was her not-quite-as-dead-as-the-last-time-she'd-seen-him brother?

Mr. Calixte, who was tied to Angela, gave the rude guerilla a dirty look for barking at his wife, but also kept his mouth closed. He shot me an unmistakable warning to do likewise. I went back to sulking, and trying to work the rags that held my hands tied. Brenda Starr had gotten herself in this situation lots of times, and *she* always got out of it. With the help of her mystery man. *Zut!* I didn't have one. Except, of course, for François.

We had been in the house for only a short time when I heard a commotion from another room, and Doctor Cordier was pushed roughly through the door. François, who had been standing in a far corner looking more like a zombie than I'd ever seen him, made a move toward the doctor, but Cordier yelled, "No. Stay," and François went back to resembling a wooden Indian.

"Doctor Cordier!" I yelled, so glad to see him that I forgot to stay quiet. One of the guards took a threatening step my way, and once again François seemed to come out of his stupor, this time taking a step in my direction. The rebel raised his gun and, once again, Cordier told François to stay put. He did.

A man dressed in some kind of uniform swaggered into the room, took a look around, and shook his head. "*Quelle dommage,*" he said, to no one in particular. Then to Doctor Cordier, "I assume these are friends of yours, Jean-Claude?"

Doctor Cordier didn't say anything, just shook his head. I noticed he had a big bump on his forehead, one eye was swollen shut, and a lens on his thick glasses was cracked.

"Liar. Not that it matters much. Whether they die now, tomorrow, or the next day, is of little importance. The Doctor's cause is just, and we are only players in a grander plan."

"Just? Killing children and innocent people is *just,* Colonel Duffaut?" the doctor spat. He made "Colonel," sound like a dirty word. "I would expect it from the likes of you, but Doctor Duvallier is a man of medicine. He is a discredit to my profession, and to my country." Duffaut drew back his arm as if to hit Cordier, but this time François moved so fast that he took the colonel and his men by surprise. He had the man by his scrawny neck and was shaking him like a dog with a toy, when one of the soldiers stuck a pistol to Angela's temple. "Let go of the colonel, or I will shoot this woman," he growled.

François let go of the rattled rebel and I actually breathed. Poor Angela, white as a sheet, nevertheless managed to seem calm and even a little haughty. Her husband, on the other hand, looked murderous.

Colonel Duffaut brushed himself off, and growled, "Doctor, I suggest, if you value your life, get your…whatever he is, under control again. I would prefer to stick with my plan for him, but it I have to, I will kill him right now. Do you understand?"

"I am out of the medicine that controls him," Cordier said. "I must get to the clinic at Péligre for more."

"Out of the question. In that case…" he motioned to one of the men, who took out a pistol and started across the floor towards François.

"I have pills!" I yelled.

Everyone looked at me.

"Don't hurt François. Give him the pills. They're in my pocket."

The colonel looked perplexed by my outburst, but he motioned one of his men in my direction. As the man advanced, Doctor Cordier warned, "Be very careful with the girl. She is François' special friend."

Colonel Duffaut ordered his man to a halt, then he said, "Under other circumstances I would love to hear how an oooh-gah-oooh and a small white girl became special friends, but I do not have the time. Little girl, what is your name?"

"Doux Doux Boudreaux," I said. I ignored Angela's eye roll.

"Well, Mademoiselle Boudreaux, stand up and walk over to Doctor Cordier, who will release your bonds. You look harmless enough." I could see a slight smirk on Angela's lips and could almost hear her say, "*Well, he don' know you.*"

I struggled to my feet, no easy feat—you should pardon the pun—with my hands tied. Once the doctor freed my wrists, I reached into my pocket, and handed over the bottle of pills to the colonel. He inspected it, gave the bottle to the doctor, and said, "So," he sneered, "this girl, who you say you do not know, seems to indeed have a bottle of your magic pills, Doctor Cordier. How would you explain that?"

The doctor looked defeated, but took the bottle, poured two pills into his hand, cut me a surprised look, and gave the tablets to François. "Looks like you win, Duffaut," he said.

While all this was going on, I got a look into the next room, which turned out to be the kitchen. On one end, by a large sink, was what looked like a crude chemistry laboratory, a two burner stove, and the ambulance's missing cooling unit. Next to the door leading outside stood a stack of open wooden crates. They were stamped, in English:

## DANGER
## EXPLOSIVES
## PROPERTY OF BROWN AND ROOT, INC.

Uncle Lloyd's dynamite, my guess. I really, really needed to have a little chat with Doctor Cordier.

# CHAPTER 30

▼

I finally got that chat with Doctor Cordier. Of course, we had to talk over a lot of clucking and squawking, since we were locked in a chicken coop with about a hundred of its residents, but at least we weren't tied up.

"So, what do you figure they'll do with us?" I asked, not really wanting to hear the answer.

"I do not think our chances of survival are very good. We must escape."

"What I don't understand is, why are they keeping us locked up? I mean, if they're gonna do us in anyhow, why wait?"

"Mademoiselle Elisabet, I would not suggest this to them if I were you."

Despite the situation, I giggled at his little joke. I shooed a rooster from a bench, took a seat, and looked around. "Well, at least we won't starve to death; plenty of eggs, if you like 'em raw."

"Madame Oiseau has raised chickens here for years, although she moved to town when her health began to fail."

"So, this is where she got her eggs. She lived here?"

"Oh, yes. First with her parents, then with her husband. But she simply could not afford to keep the big house in repair. It has been for sale for twenty years."

"I suppose that explains why the priest thought there were new owners. Where did she come by François?"

"I do not know. All she would say is that this place was to be his when she was gone. The paperwork is still in her house at Mirebalais, no doubt."

"I just came from her funeral, you know."

"No, I did not. I *did* know she died—she was dead when I returned from Port-au-Prince with your serum. I had planned to leave François here at the plantation, then go back and make burial arrangements for her, but it was not to be. We were attacked and taken prisoner when we entered the grounds. I had no idea that rebels were using this place as their headquarters. I do not think Madame Oiseau knew, either."

"More like a chemistry lab."

"That, as well," the doctor said with a sigh. "After they siphoned off most of the gasoline, and then took the generator and refrigeration unit, they took the ambulance back to Mirebalais, hoping, I suppose, that whoever found it on the square would think *I* had stolen the goods and disappeared."

"And it almost worked, too. But Angela and I knew where you'd gone and we came looking for you. 'Course, all we found was Madame Oiseau. It took a while, but I finally made the connection with the keys you left in the ambulance. But Doctor Cordier, if the rebels had you as prisoners, how did François get away from here to bring me the serum?"

"It was a test."

"A test?"

"Yes. I convinced the colonel to let François take the serum to you. François was watched, so they knew he was able to get into Camp. I was hoping he would not return, but unfortunately you managed to get him across the river and come back he did. These pigs have been training him well, I am afraid. His—and our—fate is sealed."

"I don't understand, Doctor Cordier."

"He will take another package to Péligre, this time to the dam site. And this time he will not return."

"I still don't get it."

"The rebels have been removing nitroglycerine from the dynamite. They have created a deadly package for our François to carry to the dam. He knows how to activate the timing device, and I believe that he will do what he is told, because they have threatened to kill me if he does not. I do not think François realizes that, after he trips the switch, if he does not run away, he will blow the dam, and himself, into tiny pieces. Colonel Duffaut first plans to take out the dam, then, when the dust settles and their guard is down, attack and kill every American in the area."

My mouth fell open. Blow up the dam? Kill everyone? My mother, father, sister, and Uncle Lloyd? This information was so scary that I really wasn't able to think. Little sparkles lit the edges of my eyes, and I gasped for breath.

Doctor Cordier, seeing that I was about to conk out on him, rushed to my side. Several chickens squawked and flapped out of the way. "Are you all right,

Elisabet? I'm sorry to frighten you so, but you had to know. You have to understand why it is imperative that we escape. At least one of us."

I took a few deep breaths, and my head cleared a little. "No problem convincing me, Doc. Let's go."

He grinned and looked around the gloomy coop. It was built of solid stone, with high walls, a tin roof, and had but one, heavy iron door. "Would you like to suggest how, Elisabet?"

"I'll think of something."

"I suggest you do it soon. I have run out of ideas, and time. The plan is for me to send François tonight. Taking the back trails, he will arrive just as the jobsite shift is changing tomorrow morning, so the explosion will have the maximum effect."

"You mean kill the most people," I said glumly.

"Exactly."

We both fell silent, each thinking our own dark thoughts.

"Doctor Cordier, what do you think about this place," I asked after a while.

"*Ça fait un peu boui-boui, mais il y a de la jolie moisissure.*"

"Huh?"

He grinned. "I said, 'It's a bit of a dive, but it has some nice mold.'"

"Very funny. I meant about getting out of here."

"*Here*, this building? Or *here*, this plantation?"

"Both."

He sighed. "I think you and I could escape, but that is why they have Madame and Monsieur Calixte, and François, in a separate building from us—so we will not try."

"That colonel is counting on our loyalty to our friends to keep us in line."

"Exactly."

I had to think about that. Grandmother Hetta told me that there was no honor and loyalty amongst thieves, and when I asked her what that meant, she said people without honor can be counted on to rat each other out. Well, she didn't exactly say it that way, but I got the drift. She also said that meant that people without honor or remorse can be counted on to underestimate it in others. A wise woman, my grandmother.

"Do you think the colonel really believes that we would not sell out our friends to save our own hides?"

"Strangely, I believe he does. Colonel Duffaut himself is loyal to Doctor Duvallier, but only for his own selfish reasons. He knows that if the evil doctor gains control of the country, he will be promoted to *General* Duffaut. Why do you ask, Elisabet?"

"Just wondering where we stood. How smart is this character?"

The doctor shrugged. "Smart enough, I guess."

"What does he know about me? He didn't seem to know I gave him a wrong name."

Cordier grinned. "I noticed that. I think the man who followed François as far as the edge of Camp only reported that François had delivered the package, but not to whom. In fact, it was François who told me of his wild ride across the river. Oh, and of the death fever."

I giggled. "It was quite a night. François talked that much?"

"We have had many long hours together. After we tried an escape, they locked us in an inner room and put a guard on the door. I have kept François alive by giving him drugs so he is docile enough not to pose a threat to the rebels, but, as you know, I have run out. I am very worried about him right now…especially after only giving him aspirin."

"Sorry. I was afraid they were going to shoot him right then and there."

"You did the right thing at the moment. I just don't know how long he will contain his anger. Right now, I am sure they have him back in that room, but once they discover he is not under control, I don't know what they'll do to him. And us. We are alive because they do not wish to make him angry. They need him, he needs us; therefore, they need us. It is that simple."

"Some simple. What time is it?"

"Three."

"Mama and Daddy will start to miss us in another hour, and will come looking. I hope they bring the entire Haitian army."

"Shhhh, someone is coming."

We listened as footfalls approached the coop, then the door swung open. Colonel Duffaut stood bathed in bright light. "Cordier, come out here. It is time we sent François on his way."

Doctor Cordier walked to the open door and peered outside. When the doctor stepped out, I shadowed him, but was roughly shoved back inside. *Zut!*

"Hey," I yelled, "why can't I come?"

I got no answer, but the door slammed shut with a bang.

Okay, so I was stuck. But I was also free to do what I wanted to do in the first place: escape. A chicken coop, even one with stone walls, is no place to hold the likes of Lizbuthann Starr. I was outside within minutes, having already spotted a rusted-out spot in the tin roof that was just big enough for me to snake through.

My shoulder pads were badly shredded by jagged metal edges, but I never liked the Joan Crawford look anyhow. A tree, conveniently growing alongside the chicken coop, gave me easy access to the ground. I peered around a corner of the coop: no guards between me and the main building. So far, so good.

I was creeping along the path to the main house, trying to come up with some kind of plan, when I heard loud voices from the kitchen area. Sprinting behind a tree, I climbed up a couple of branches and got a bird's-eye view through the window.

Doctor Cordier and Colonel Duffaut stood in the center of the room, obviously arguing about something. I couldn't hear what they were saying, but François loomed into sight and my heart skipped a beat. I was afraid he was attacking the colonel again, but then I realized he had been pushed into the room by three of Duffaut's goons.

While I watched, Doctor Cordier talked with François, then the big zombie stood quietly as the doctor strapped what looked like an army backpack onto him. With growing horror, I realized they were actually loading up a human bomb. I also knew that, as soon as François left on his mission of murder, Angela, her husband, Doctor Cordier, and I were finished. Kaput! *Fini.*

Shinnying down the tree, I skirted the building, taking care to stop and listen for guards along the way. I was in luck; they were all gathered around my father's car, talking and smoking. Somehow, I had to get rid of them, get François into the car, and…what? Oh, well, I'd think of something.

I had a good hiding place behind thick bushes on the side of the house. Dressed in black, with my hat veil pulled low over my face, I blended into the shadows quite nicely. As long as no one checked the coop and found me missing, I was free to do as I wished. My first thought was to run for it, somehow get to the jobsite and warn the soldiers and my family. But I'd be condemning my fellow prisoners to certain death as soon as the rebels realized I had vamoosed.

Rats! I wished I'd come up with a plan before Doctor Cordier was taken from the coop, but now I had no way of getting a message to him. My brief spurt of joy at flying the coop began to disappear. Once again I had leaped before I looked. I was tired, hungry, thirsty, that headache was back, and I was out of aspirin. I would have cried if I'd had the energy.

The front door banged open, startling me, and I made myself as small as possible, hugging my knees, and hoping some critter didn't crawl out from under the porch and up my skirt. A skirt, I might add, that would never see another funeral or any other occasion. I had managed to rip both seams almost to my waist, and if I hadn't been so determined to get us out of this mess, modesty would keep me hidden behind those bushes forever.

"I'm telling you, Duffaut," the doctor said, "the boy will do as I say, but not if you hold the others here. He will not leave without them."

"Then we will kill you all now, and deliver the explosives ourselves."

"You are not thinking clearly, colonel. Look, you have an American's car, his driver, his maid and, more importantly, his daughter. You can hold me as insurance. They can, if you let them leave soon, arrive at the perfect time for today's shift change."

"An interesting possibility, Cordier, but what makes you think they will blow up the dam? Why would they not simply sacrifice you for the greater cause? No, I think I would need two hostages to guarantee success: you *and* the girl. Or better yet, I will keep the girl, and send you to make sure François does his job."

Yes! Please, please, let it be so. I closed my eyes and said a little prayer.

Cordier argued a little more, but in the end, Colonel Duffaut called out to his men, they slid off Daddy's car, and followed the colonel and Doctor Cordier into the house. As soon as they went inside, I dashed for the front gate. It was, thank goodness, open.

From another tree just outside the gate, I could just barely see the house through the thick leaves. The prisoners were shoved onto the front porch, then marched to the car, with Angela crying and struggling all the way. Assuming that I was still held hostage, she didn't want to leave. While I was touched by her loyalty, I mentally willed her to calm down before she messed things up. As if my thoughts had somehow gotten through to her, she froze in place and looked in my direction. My heart gave a thump before I realized she, and therefore the rebel, couldn't possibly see me. She be, like she says, one witchy woman.

After some last minute instructions to François, who kept looking back into the house and had to be pushed into the car, Daddy's car inched my way with all my friends inside. Sliding down the tree, I took off, running like the wind towards Mirebalais, wanting to get some distance between me and the front gate. I certainly didn't want to mess up everything by having the rebels spot the car stopping for me to get in.

I was winded, hiding behind a large bush, when I heard the car's motor working overtime. They were having just as much trouble getting back out over the muddy road as we had getting in. Good, this time it worked to my advantage. I began to carefully backtrack.

"Put your back into it," I heard Pierre yell. The tires were making that high WHIRRY-WHINEY noise they do when trying to gain traction in mud. I picked

Tires smoked and mud flew as Daddy's Ford leaped about six feet forward, fishtailed against the bushes, and headed straight down the road. The men coming towards us, who had slowed when they'd heard all the noise, now stopped, turned, and fled. It was time for me to scram, as well. Knowing full well that I should be fleeing for my life in the direction of Mirebalais, I couldn't do it. Curiosity killed the kid, you know; I trotted after the car to see what happened next.

Following its own deep ruts in the mud, the big black Ford, like some oversized and very angry beetle, perfectly threaded the open gates, charged up the front steps, and slammed into the double doors of the old plantation house. Colonel Duffaut, from the look on his face, was shocked silly by the attacking vehicle, but he still managed to dive sideways at the last minute to avoid being crushed by the car's huge bumper.

Fascinated, I watched as the car demolished the old wooden front doors, plowed into the house, and disappeared. In a split second, men began leaping from windows, and some were still in mid-air when, with a deafening blast, *everything* exploded. Even as far away as I was, the first KA-BOOM flattened me into the mud and I stayed there, covering my ears, as explosion after explosion rocked the air. Pieces of car, house, chickens, and heaven-knows-what else, rained down around me. When things finally went deadly silent, I dared a look backward and was surprised to see not only the Calixtes, François and Doctor Cordier, but also my mother, father, Uncle Lloyd, Father Vermette, and—Lord love her little busybody soul—the old lady in the shawl. Everyone seemed as stunned by what had happened as I was.

François, what with "dazed" being his natural state, was the first to move. Lurching a few steps down the road, he leaned over and picked up a twisted piece of chrome bumper. Out loud, he said what I was thinking: "This not good."

▼

# CHAPTER 31

# Weclom to Port-au-Prince

They *still* couldn't spell it.

No scary, stinky heads on posts this time, but the airport fences were lined with jumpy, armed soldiers.

I wore no Mary Janes, no gloves, and my hair was in its natural frizz. I suppose to anyone just arriving, we looked a little like the missionaries who visited Camp wearing much-washed homemade clothes, and shoes that didn't quite fit and had been re-soled over and over. Even my mother, normally cool and crisp, no matter what, was a little wilted. She wore dark glasses, even in the darkened building. Almost everyone in the terminal building looked the same, however: bewildered and bedraggled. Attempted coups have a way of making folks that way.

The airport was more chaotic than ever; seemed everyone wanted to leave Haiti at once. I stared out the grimy windows, watched two tanks rumble by.

"Wish you were going with us," Doux Doux said. "Just think, Dr. Pepper, moonpies and Fritos. And boys."

"Just don't get in circumstances. I'll miss you," I told her, "but I'm glad Mama and Daddy decided to stick it out here. Uncle Lloyd says that that Doctor Duvallier doesn't stand a chance in the elections after he messed up his coup. I hope they put him in jail."

"Mais cheré, you're lucky *you're* not in jail."

"I know. I'm just glad it's all over so we can stay here."

"Even if you're grounded for the rest of your life?"

"Daddy forgave me about the car. And I've promised to stay close to home, what with the troubles and all."

"That'll be the day. Check on Smokey for me once in a while, will you?"

"He'll be fine with François. He's a plantation owner now, you know."

"I know. Who'd'a thunk an egg woman would own a plantation. Mais cheré, it's too bad you blew it up."

"Only the house. Doctor Cordier is building a new one, and he's hiring men to replant the banana trees."

"So what do you think? Is François really Angela's brother?"

"She treats him like one. And now that he's living with Doctor Cordier, he's downright social. For a zombie, that is."

We giggled, then Clota called, "We've got to board now."

I took my friend's hand. "I'll go out with you, Doux Doux."

We left the shade of the building, walking onto the runway. The DC-3 waited with a uniformed stewardess standing by the metal steps, greeting passengers as they boarded. Gooey tarmac oozed around my sandals and damp heat rose to dampen my bougainvillea print sundress. I loved it.

I gave my friend a last hug, and she started for the plane. "Hey, Doux Doux," I shouted as she neared the stewardess, "Be sure to ask for one of their snow cones."

# From Me To You

Thank you for being a reader.

Even if no one ever read my work, I would still write books. It gives me great pleasure to write, but my special reward for all the hard work it takes to turn out a novel, is the knowledge that my words are being shared.

I would like to hear from you. Go to my website at

**http://embark.to/schwartzbooks**

and send me an email if you have questions or input. Please do not send attachments, as I never, ever, open them. I also do not wish to be on anyone's mailing list for jokes, etc.

If you have the extreme intelligence and foresight to want to buy film, television, dramatic or audio rights to any of my books, e-me.

If you would like for me to do a book signing at your local bookstore, especially any B. Dalton, please contact the store.

If you would like to attend a book signing, please check my website for a list of events.

I know that most books have mistakes, omissions, and typos. For this reason, I am loathe to read one of my own works after it goes to press for fear of finding one of these dastardly varmints. However, if you find one, let me know and I will try not to weep.

Also, don't forget that you can write a review of my books by going to Barnes & Noble.com. Just click on any one of my books on my website, and you will soar through ether right to the site. Put in your two cents worth; I can take it.

All that said, I would love to hear from you.

Elizabeth (Jinx) Maul Schwartz
**eschwartz@theriver.com**

0-595-29065-5